FIC

D1049334

I promised mys[...] size eight and h[...] had months of endless dieting time, weeks to discover a passion for running and a love of salads. I'd sworn that chocolate would never again pass my lips and vegging out in front of the telly would be just a memory. I'd start tomorrow, wouldn't I?

Except that *tomorrow* never actually came and now it's *today*, the day I've had circled on the calendar for months. The sunny August day I'm to be shoehorned into lacey underwear, poured into ivory silk and expected to look like a supermodel. If it weren't so desperate it would actually be funny. Even Harry Potter couldn't achieve that kind of transformation.

I close my eyes and experience for the millionth time a plunging elevator sensation. All we've done for months, the love of my life and I, is plan this wedding. We hardly ever see each other without the wedding planner in tow and I can barely remember the last time we had mad, passionate sex. Or any kind of sex, actually, now I come to think of it . . .

If I could turn back time, would I still be doing this?

ENFIELD PUBLIC LIBRARY
23 Main St. P.O. Box 1030
Enfield, NH 03748

Ruth Saberton was born in London in 1972. A chance meeting with a stranger while holidaying in Cornwall resulted in Ruth marrying a fisherman and moving to beautiful Polperro, near Plymouth. In between writing novels and short stories, Ruth also teaches Media Studies and English at a secondary school in Cornwall.

By Ruth Saberton

Katy Carter Wants a Hero
Ellie Andrews Has Second Thoughts

ELLIE ANDREWS HAS SECOND THOUGHTS

Ruth Saberton

An Orion paperback

First published in Great Britain in 2011
by Orion
Orion House, 5 Upper St Martin's Lane,
London WC2H 9EA

An Hachette UK company

3 5 7 9 10 8 6 4

Copyright © Ruth Saberton 2011

The right of Ruth Saberton to be identified as the author
of this work has been asserted by her in accordance with
the Copyright, Designs and Patents Act 1988.

All rights reserved. No part of this publication may be
reproduced, stored in a retrieval system, or transmitted,
in any form or by any means, electronic, mechanical,
photocopying, recording or otherwise, without the prior
permission of the copyright owner.

All the characters in this book are fictitious,
and any resemblance to actual persons, living
or dead, is purely coincidental.

A CIP catalogue record for this book is available
from the British Library.

ISBN 978-1-4091-3549-4

Typeset at the Spartan Press Ltd,
Lymington, Hants

Printed and bound in Great Britain by CPI Group (UK)
Ltd, Croydon, CRO 4YY

The Orion Publishing Group's policy is to use papers that
are natural, renewable and recyclable products and
made from wood grown in sustainable forests. The logging
and manufacturing processes are expected to conform to
the environmental regulations of the country of origin.

www.orionbooks.co.uk

To everyone in Polperro.
Thank you so much for all your friendship,
encouragement and support.
This book is for you.

Acknowledgements

My deep gratitude and appreciation to:

My wonderful parents, Brian and Mary Saberton, my sister Lizzy (who has had to read and re-read this novel), and my brother John, who knows how to keep my feet on the ground.

My colleagues at Bodmin College, who put up with me on a daily basis and have been nothing but supportive and encouraging – thank you all for buying my books and keeping me calm as deadlines approach!

My students – you constantly challenge me to be the best and certainly keep me on my toes. Tristan and Isolde in this book are dedicated to you all.

My dearest friends, Lizzie, Sheila and Kim, who are always there as guinea pig readers/moppers up of tears/ buyers of pink wine!

Caroline, Steve, Rob and Becky at The Blue Peter Inn for supplying the pink wine!

My fabulous readers for all your lovely emails and encouragement and my writer pals, Miranda Dickinson and Victoria Connelly, for keeping me (almost) sane. Thank you!

Eve White, my fantastic agent who is always there for me, believes in me, and has made every step of my writing journey so far an absolute delight.

Natalie Braine and Sara O'Keeffe, whose editing and insight make every page of my novels the best they could ever be. I couldn't do it without you.

And last, but by no means least, the amazing team at Orion for all your hard work on behalf of this book.

20 *August* 2011

I'm having a fat day.

Not the type when I pig out on the sofa eating my way through all the crumbs furring the bottom of the biscuit tin (because everyone knows the bits don't add up). I'm not even having the kind of fat day when I catch a glimpse of my thighs in the glare of changing room lights and desperately tear off to buy some Spanx.

No, it's worse than that because this is a *seriously* fat day, and although it's not even half past six in the morning, I've already scoffed enough to double as a sumo wrestler. In fact, I'm sure I can feel my stomach growing with each passing minute, swelling and straining like a scene from *Alien*.

Well, it's too late to worry now. I might as well carry on eating seeing as I've started. Besides, I'm going to need my strength today. So instead of following a workout DVD for a sweaty hour, I exercise my biceps by yanking open the freezer and lifting out some Häagen-Dazs. Walking to the drawer to fetch a spoon has to burn some calories too, right? You see, I really have thought long and hard about losing weight for today.

Honestly, since the small diamond solitaire was slipped on to my finger, I haven't thought about much else.

At least I've tried not to . . .

In a frenzy of despair I polish off some left-over pizza and then make a round of toast and Marmite.

I promised myself faithfully that by today I'd be a svelte size eight and have better abs than Gavin Henson. I've had months of endless dieting time, weeks to discover a passion for running and a love of salads. I'd sworn that chocolate would never again pass my lips and vegging out in front of the telly would be just a memory. I'd start tomorrow, wouldn't I?

Except that *tomorrow* never actually came, and now it's *today*, the day I've had circled on the calendar for months. The sunny August day when I'm to be shoehorned into lacy underwear, poured into ivory silk and expected to look like a supermodel. If it weren't so desperate it would actually be funny. Even Harry Potter couldn't achieve that kind of transformation.

I close my eyes and experience for the millionth time a plunging elevator sensation. All we've done for months, the love of my life and I, is plan this wedding. We hardly ever see each other without the wedding planner in tow and I can barely remember the last time we had mad, passionate sex.

Or any kind of sex, actually, now I come to think of it . . .

If I could turn back time, would I still be doing this?

6.28 a.m.

'Morning, Ellie,' chirrups my housemate and best friend Samantha, bustling into the kitchen like a dreadlocked sunbeam and whacking four thick slices of Mother's Pride in the toaster. 'You're up early! Excited, huh?'

'Mmm,' I reply. That's one way of describing this piranhas-chewing-on-my-intestines sensation.

'I was going to bring you breakfast in bed,' she continues, attacking the Nutella with a spoon. 'How does smoked salmon with scrambled eggs sound? And maybe a very small glass of champagne? Not too much though, babes, nobody wants to see a pissed bride.'

'I'm fine for breakfast, thanks.' I slap a virtuous expression on to my face. 'I want to fit into my dress.'

'You're not still dieting?' Sam wrinkles her nose. 'Honestly, Ellie, I don't know why you bother.'

'Err, because I need to squeeze my size twelve self into a size eight wedding dress?'

She rolls her eyes. 'You're such a muppet. Why didn't you just buy a bigger size? Dieting is pointless.'

Right. Like Sam Delamere knows anything about dieting. She makes Victoria Beckham look hefty.

'Anyway,' continues Sam, whacking chocolate spread an inch thick on to her toast, 'you're not fat. I was thinking you look really slim this morning.'

'There's an explanation for that.' I peel down my pyjama bottoms to reveal a gargantuan pair of control pants. 'Ta-da!'

'Bloody hell!' Sam sprays toast and Nutella across the kitchen. 'What are those? They're hideous! Tell me you're not wearing them under your wedding dress? Your circulation will be cut off. Actually, never mind your circulation. You don't seriously think you'll get it tonight wearing those? He'll need a crowbar to get into them!'

The pants are practically melded to my skin, a marvel indeed of modern underwear engineering. And yes, they bloody kill, but I wore them all night and I must surely have dropped a dress size by now.

3

'This is the latest in slimming technology,' I say proudly. 'Bum bra and thinning pants combined.'

Sam shakes her head. 'Ellie Andrews, you're mental. You're about to get married to a man who adores every inch of you. Don't you think he knows what's under the wedding dress by now?'

That's thin people for you. They just don't get it.

'I want today to be about me,' I say. 'I want people to look at me and think I look beautiful, or at least as good as my sisters.'

Sam rolls her eyes again, because she's heard this lament a few thousand times before. We met as first years at St Hilda's School for Girls, hiding beneath the coats in the cloakroom in a desperate attempt to skive PE. A mutual love of Robbie Williams and loathing of lacrosse sealed a sacred bond and now, years on, we share a house in Taply-on-Thames and argue over who is actually going to marry George Clooney.

And just in case you're wondering, George isn't the lucky man.

'Not this again,' groans Sam. 'Those sisters of yours are more plastic than Barbie! Don't beat yourself up about not looking like them.'

I pull a face, because this is easy for Sam to say. If *she'd* grown up with four sisters who make Lily Cole look fat and ugly, Sam might have the McCain factory's worth of chips on her shoulder too. Tall and leggy, with long manes of blonde hair, hourglass figures and creamy skin, my elder sisters have the ability to command attention wherever they go, and have earned themselves the nick-name 'the Amazing Andrews'. Being short and curvy, with curly brown hair and freckles, I've given up trying to compete with them. I like to think I make an interesting contrast.

'Not another word about your sisters,' scolds Sam, adding her plate to the mound of dishes in the sink. 'You've got a million times more personality than any of them. You're funny, you're clever and you are *not* fat. You're sexy and curvy. Men adore women like you!'

I catch a glimpse of my reflection in the glass conservatory doors, but I can't say I recognise the person Sam's describing. The girl who stares dubiously back has wild corkscrew hair and hides her body under a billowing dressing gown. I don't want to be funny and clever and have a good personality. That's just compensation for not being beautiful and thin. After all, no one tells Kate Moss how clever she is, do they?

Sam shakes her head. 'You'll never believe me, no matter how many times I try to tell you. Talk about being screwed up by your family! Well, bugger them. This is *your* day and you're bloody well going to enjoy every minute of it. You're about to get married to a lovely man who totally worships you.'

Just why my fiancé loves me is one of life's great mysteries. Of course I'm delighted he does and I was over the moon when he proposed, but recently I've been starting to wonder if we're doing the right thing. After all, there's more to a marriage than frilly frocks and a finger buffet.

'I really hope I'm doing the right thing,' I say nervously, as the stomach piranhas return for another munch.

'Ellie! Get a grip! Of course you are. Will you please go upstairs and start getting ready?' Sam places her hand in the small of my back and gives me a shove. 'We've got loads to do before the hair and beauty girls arrive and Poppy turns up with the flowers. Why don't you go and run yourself a relaxing bubble bath and leave everything to me? I'll even crack open some champagne so we can celebrate your last morning as a single girl.'

My last morning as a single girl. Oh. My. God.

In seven and a half hours I'll be following in my sisters' footsteps down the aisle of St Jude's, Taply-on-Thames. An hour later and I'll be married.

I'll never be able to eat toast in bed again or snog another man.

Not that I want to snog another man. But eating toast in bed's a different thing entirely . . .

'Don't look so worried, it's not as though you haven't had enough practice at weddings,' Sam points out, misreading the terror on my face. 'You've been a bridesmaid four times, remember?'

As if anyone who's been forced to wear sickly pastel satin four times could *ever* forget it.

'Have a swig of this,' she orders, shoving a foaming champagne flute into my hand. Unfortunately, the manicurist has Super-Glued talons on to my own bitten stumps and, like a cat that's lost its whiskers, my poor fingers haven't a clue where they begin. Acrylic scrapes against the icy glass and my hand closes around thin air.

The champagne flute hits the slate floor, showering my French-manicured toes with glass and icy liquid.

I stare down, aghast. The pair of champagne flutes was an early wedding present and now only one remains intact. Is this an omen?

'Of course it bloody isn't.' Sam is scathing when I voice this thought. 'Get a grip, Ellie! Everything's going to be fine. I solemnly swear as your chief bridesmaid that I've got everything under control, so just relax.'

I'd be more relaxed walking on hot coals. My experience of weddings hasn't exactly been positive. The fact that I'm getting married at all is a triumph of hope over experience.

'Give me that,' I say, taking the champagne bottle with slightly too much force. 'I need a drink.'

Sam laughs, but her green eyes are worried.

As I climb the stairs, swigging champagne from the neck of the bottle, I reflect that in many ways if it hadn't been for Sam I might not be getting married at all. Things could have turned out very differently.

I shut my bedroom door, rest my head against the cool wood and close my eyes. The events that have led me to this point flicker through my mind like a badly edited home movie. Have I made the right choices? Have I chosen the right man? Am I doing the right thing? Or will I wake up tomorrow and regret this?

Oh God. Oh God. Oh God.

Breathe, Ellie, breathe!

The alarm clock says it's not even seven a.m. yet. Outside the day is all pearly new and the birds are singing. There's hours to go before I leave for the church.

Plenty of time if I decided to change my mind.

Not that I'm going to change my mind. That's just the nerves talking. I haven't got any more doubts about getting married today than any other bride would have. Every girl's allowed a few nerves on her wedding day. It's only natural to be a bit apprehensive, because getting married is probably the biggest and most important decision anyone ever makes. I'm choosing my life partner. The rest of my

7

life is at stake. If I *wasn't* nervous, there'd be something wrong with me.

This churning feeling *is* totally normal and there's a perfectly good cure for it. Thank goodness Sam opened the Moët. A few more mouthfuls of champagne and all my nerves will vanish . . .

6.55 a.m.

With the door of my bedroom firmly shut and the best part of a third of a bottle of Moët inside me, I start to feel slightly less panic-stricken. Perching on the bed, I try to pretend this is just an average Saturday morning. In a moment I'll meander downstairs for a bacon sarnie and watch a bit of kids' TV before trawling round the shops with Poppy and enjoying lunch in The Riverman pub. For a moment such is the power of my imagination that I'm almost looking forward to a bowl of cheese-smothered nachos and a glass of icy Chardonnay, until I catch sight of my wedding dress hanging on the outside of the wardrobe and my heart starts racing again.

Oh Lord. This really is it. I'm getting married, really and truly married. At this very moment, all our nearest and dearest are en route for Taply-on-Thames, clutching presents from the long list we made. Like someone in a dream, I'd agreed that I needed a Dyson, and of course I couldn't live without a pasta maker, when actually I was more than happy with my ancient Hoover and diet of tinned spaghetti.

A panicky sweat breaks out between my shoulder blades. What was I thinking by adding a pasta maker to my list? I've never felt the need to make pasta *before* getting married, so what's going to change afterwards?

The answer to this, of course, is everything. I've seen each of my sisters get married and transform from cocktail-swilling party-goers into goddesses so domesticated that Nigella looks slovenly in comparison. Then, after the wedding and the smart dinner parties, along come the chubby babies and endless conversations about first teeth and first steps, followed shortly by fretting about catchment areas and waiting lists.

I feel faint. I can't have a baby! I'm not old enough for all that responsibility. I wouldn't know where to begin. Besides, I'm rubbish at looking after things. I even killed the school stick insects when it was my turn to take them home for half-term. So what if I was only five and didn't realise it wasn't conducive to their health to give them a bath? I haven't changed *that* much since then. Goodness knows what damage I could do to a poor baby.

I chew my new acrylic thumbnail. Everything's got out of hand. I never really wanted a big church do and the guest list longer than Mr Tickle's arm. This wedding has taken on a life of its own, and although it's exactly what my mother wanted, I'm having panic attacks on an hourly basis. I don't need six bridesmaids, a ring bearer or a five-course reception.

I take another gulp of champagne and bubbles shoot up my nose, making me cough. Great. Now I'm too stressed even to drink.

Putting the champagne aside, I fall backwards on to my bed, yelping with pain when my head encounters something hard. Sitting up quickly, I discover I've walloped my skull on my sister's wedding album, loaned to me as a shining example of what the photographer will also do for us. This album is thicker than *War and Peace*, edged with brass and studded with a huge treasure-chest-style lock, the imprint of which is now stamped into my head.

Maybe I can postpone the wedding due to head trauma?

I pick the album up and the heavy volume falls open at one of the group photos. There, beneath the tissue paper, is a scene already seared into my memory – for all the wrong reasons. My sister Annabelle is beaming into the lens, all big blue eyes and golden curls, her slender hands clutching a bouquet of fat pink roses while the little flower girls tumble at her satin slippers. Our parents flank the happy couple, but my gaze is drawn to a red-cheeked bridesmaid in a tight peach frock who's trying desperately to disguise a Cheddar Gorge cleavage with her bouquet while she hides behind the other guests.

I shake my head in despair. Hadn't I tried to diet then too? How depressing. I flick through the album and pause at a photo of the wedding party, tracing one dear face with my finger, filled with regret. If I had my time again, would I do things the same way? Or would I make some very different choices?

I remember my sister's wedding day vividly. It may have been just over two years ago, but I'm still suffering from post-traumatic stress. Whenever I try to identify the precise point when my life began slipping out of control, I always return to Annabelle's wedding. Not that my life was exactly a bed of roses before that. If I'm honest, it was more like a bit of scrubby wasteland choked up with weeds and rusting tin cans, but at least they were *my* weeds and *my* tin cans.

I was happy in my own way. Just how did I get from there to here?

Snapping the album shut and trying hard not to look at my own beautiful wedding dress, I recall that meltingly hot

June day when, poured into peach satin and looking more porcine than Miss Piggy, I prepared to follow my sister down the aisle . . .

Bridesmaid Revisited

'I look like the Michelin Man!' I wail, pirouetting in front of the mirror and grimacing. Peach satin is *such* an unforgiving fabric. It really isn't my fault I look like a sausage splitting its skin.

My sister Annabelle wrinkles her perfect nose. 'I thought you said you were going to lose weight for today?'

I tug at the fabric straining across my chest, making me look more like an exile from the Playboy mansion than a demure maid of honour. 'Are you sure the dressmaker got the measurements right?'

'There's absolutely nothing wrong with my dressmaker,' Annabelle snaps. 'You're the problem. Luckily nobody's going to be looking at you. It's me they want to see.'

Brides only choose bridesmaids' dresses in order to make themselves look even better, it's no secret. Why else would a normally sane woman dress her adult friends and siblings in revolting pastel hues and more frills than Barbara Cartland's knickers? Annabelle's been quite blatant about this, and like all brides has stuck to the sacred commandment *thou must find a bridesmaid with a bigger arse than thine*. For good measure she's even stuck a massive bow on mine.

I'm more aware of these ugly truths than most twenty-seven-year-olds, because Annabelle's wedding is the fourth time I've been recruited for bridesmaid duty. This is the price I've had to pay for having four older sisters, as if being picked on and tormented for my entire life wasn't enough. Seriously, family weddings are the twenty-first-century equivalent of the press gang. One moment you're trundling along in your own sweet way, going to work, having disastrous love affairs and getting horribly plastered at the weekends; the next you're whisked away to dress fittings, make-up sessions and church rehearsals. Then, after hours of being used as a human pincushion, you end up wearing something even Jordan wouldn't be seen dead in.

Weddings are hell in lace, especially when you're put in charge of three headstrong bridesmaids and a pageboy who's intent on excavating the contents of his nose.

'Cut it out, you little monster!' I yank my nephew's finger from his nostril. Then, with the practised skill of one four times a bridesmaid, recently promoted to maid of honour, I simultaneously pull Imogen's peach skirts down from over her head and remove the roses from Laura's mouth. Tear-filled infant eyes regard me resentfully, bottom lips wobbling, but my heart is hardened by hours of wedding rehearsals, so I just fix them with my most chilling stare. Inside, though, I'm also longing to throw myself on the floor and have a good old-fashioned tantrum.

'For goodness' sake, Ellie,' snaps Annabelle. 'Keep those brats under control!'

She glares at me from beneath her foaming veil. This is her big day and my sister isn't going to let any of us forget it. On this perfect summer Saturday, Annabelle Andrews is about to fulfil her greatest dream. After years of make-believe weddings, cutting off my Barbie's hair and forcing it to be the groom, months of trying on practically every wedding dress in London, and driving the entire family to the brink of a nervous breakdown, my big sister is finally getting married.

So much for feminism. As I listen to Annabelle yapping on about the joys of wedding lists and taking Mark's name, I realise that for her the sexual revolution really is something that happened to everybody else. The sooner she's married, quits her job in the art gallery and takes her new husband's wallet for a spin in Harvey Nicks, the happier she'll be.

And the sooner this wedding's over, the happier I'll be. I'll be able to eat a sausage roll or maybe even a Big Mac without looking over my shoulder.

Once at the church, Annabelle goes into full diva mode. 'Is my veil straight?' She tilts her chin a little while I tweak and fuss obligingly, feeling like Mammy attending Scarlett O'Hara. 'Is Mark here yet?'

'We're the ones who are late,' I mutter through clenched teeth. Annabelle's instructed the chauffeur to drive around the block three times just to make sure the journalists from the *Daily Mail* have had time to arrive. The fourth Amazing Andrews wedding is guaranteed to make the social pages, and my sister wants every column inch that her manicured hands can grab.

'God, Ellie, you really should have dieted.' Annabelle eyes me critically. 'Make sure you're standing behind the children in the photos.'

As the rich tones of the organ ring out with 'Ave Maria', only the fact that I'm twenty-seven and not seven stops me socking her in the mouth. Annabelle always knows exactly how to get to me, like the time she joined match.com on my behalf ('It's the only way you'll ever find a man') and tried hard to persuade me to go on a date with Steve from Slough who enjoyed trainspotting and birdwatching.

Biting my tongue and promising myself that in just over two hours' time I'll be getting sloshed on all the free booze, I psych myself up to follow Annabelle's rose-trimmed backside down the aisle, trying hard not to think about my own Lopez-esque derrière. Like my sister says, nobody's looking at me anyway. Pretty much the story of my life.

'Ready?' asks the vicar.

Annabelle nods slowly, not wanting to dislodge her headdress.

'Marvellous!' He turns to me. 'Now, my dear, when you're happy with that train, give the bride a sign.'

'Any sign I want?' I ask hopefully. Flipping Annabelle the bird would make me feel so much better.

The vicar winks at me over his bifocals. After enduring two strenuous wedding rehearsals, having to repaint the porch to match Annabelle's colour scheme and nearly breaking his neck on her endless train, he's got the measure of my sister and is probably gagging to flick a few V-signs himself.

'As long as it's polite,' he replies, to my great disappointment.

Might as well get this over with, I decide, tugging half-heartedly at the enormous train. There. It looks fine, or at least as fine as something that would be better suited to sitting on top of a loo roll ever will. Giving my sister the thumbs-up and the baby bridesmaids a shove, it's all systems go and we're walking with excruciating slowness down the aisle, Annabelle smiling mistily at the congregation and undergoing a miraculous transformation from Attila the Hun to Wedding Dreams Barbie.

St Jude's is absolutely packed; wedding guests in large

hats and starchy suits spew from each row of pews, craning their necks to get a good look at the bride. The two front rows on the left-hand side are reserved for my family, who by now are very used to such occasions. It's actually no wonder that what remains of my father's hair is grey. The cost of four big weddings could probably have sorted out the national debt. Even the swathes of pink and white roses would go a long way towards decreasing my overdraft.

Unfortunately for my father, Mum outdid herself last year with Emily's wedding. Everybody agreed that it could have given the royal family a run for their money; my father muttered darkly that he needed the royals' income to bloody well pay for it all and that he wished he'd done a Henry the Eighth and cut my mother's head off when she produced daughter number one. How we all laughed, except for my poor father. Still, it was way too late now; the pattern was set. Each sister's wedding had to equal, if not outdo, the one before it.

Well, Dad can relax after this bun-fight, because there's absolutely no way I'm going to be following in Annabelle's silk-slippered footsteps. No, I have enough stress in my life without adding some man's dirty laundry and washing-up to my lengthy list of things to do. I've absolutely no desire *whatsoever* to meet Mr Right, float down the aisle and stagnate into coupled-up life. I'm happy being single.

At least, I will be happy once I *am* single. But that's another story.

We pigeon-step down the aisle, and when the gaggle of bridesmaids and pageboys finally collide at the altar, a respectful hush falls over the congregation. This is the point in the proceedings where Mum dabs at the corner of her eyes, taking care not to smudge the make-up applied at such cost by the beautician, and where my nephew attempts to pull the girls' dresses up. I glare furiously in his direction and draw my finger across my throat. Now is *not* the time for a game of doctors and nurses.

'Ellie!' hisses Annabelle, shoving her vast bouquet in my direction and almost suffocating me with pollen. 'My train!'

Hastily I gather up acres of lace and silk into some sort of order and shoo the children into a pew. I can feel the underarms of my dress beginning to get damp with a most unladylike sweat.

Placing the bouquet down beside Imogen, I heave a sigh of relief. Another duty ticked off the trusty mental list. Soon I'll be stuffing my face with canapés and swigging all the free booze. Andrews family weddings do have some advantages. All I have to do until then is keep the ankle-biters from killing each other and sing a few hymns. I'll just perch on this pew, take the weight off my poor tortured feet and sit it out for a bit. Easy-peasy.

As I sit, I catch the eye of the best man, Rupert Moore-Critchen, who smiles at me with a soppy look in his melting Malteser eyes. I twist around and check out the pew behind to see which of my divine sisters might be the cause of his mushy expression, but there's only Great-Auntie Ethel, her false teeth sitting jauntily on her tongue.

I feel a niggle of alarm. That soppy look's aimed at me. Uh-oh. Not good, not good at all.

It's fair enough that Rupert's looking at me; he is my boyfriend. Well, my boyfriend in that light-hearted sense of the word that means occasional trips to the cinema, plus the odd candlelit dinner and snogging session. At least that's the way I see it; we're not serious in a *let's play at choosing our children's names* kind of way. The trouble is, though, recently I've started to get the uncomfortable feeling that Rupert doesn't view our liaison in quite the same casual light. You don't need to be psychic to work out what romantic cards and bouquets of flowers mean. I'm now on first-name terms with the man from the florist's.

Standing at the altar, Rupert certainly looks handsome in a nervous and bespectacled Hugh Grant type of way; at any moment I almost expect Andie MacDowell to waltz past in a huge hat and sweep him off his well-shod feet. I'd definitely feel a whole lot better if she did, because not only is Rupert my boyfriend, he's also my boss. Not a happy combination if I'm going to finish with him. Filing and typing in a solicitor's office is hardly mind-blowing stuff, but at least it pays the rent.

Poor Rupert. He hasn't actually done anything wrong. He's perfect in every way. He has a top career as a barrister, owns a dinky little mews house in Marlow, and my mother adores him. She's a bit stumped as to what he sees in me, of course, but is a fully paid-up member of the school of thought that I ought to grab a suitable and available man while I can. If I'm brutally honest, I'm a little bit guilty of stringing poor Rupert along just because it keeps Mum off my back. Besides, in some ways she's right. Rupert is perfect. Perfect in every way except one.

I just don't fancy him any more. Isn't life a sod?

As I rise to join in 'All Things Bright and Beautiful', my mind's battling this problem like Darth Vader and Luke Skywalker at the end of *Star Wars*. The trouble is, I'm an emotional coward, too soft for my own good and for anyone else's, and such sentimentality is definitely not a bonus when it comes to dumping boyfriends. I have a terrible track record of dragging things on for ages, until they're driven to end it for me. But right now, looking at

Rupert's dewy-eyed gaze, I don't see him minding much about the state of things between us, as long as there are still things to be in a state about.

I can't put it off any longer. I'll have to tell him tonight. It's only fair. I'll say something along the lines of us being better off as friends; that it's not him, it's me, etc., etc. And live in even more hope he doesn't sack me on the spot.

After making this decision, the wedding ceremony passes in a blur of agonised self-reproach. God only knows how I manage to smile for the photos while my innards are marinated with guilt. Why is it always so complicated for me? How come everybody else seems to meet *the one* with sickening ease? Maybe God's calling me to be a nun. It'd certainly be easier, and those baggy habits would hide a multitude of sins. As I clamber into the wedding car, I'm almost convinced this is the ideal solution.

'Poo!' shrieks Imogen happily. 'Poo!'

Trying to ignore a four-year-old isn't easy, especially when they combine all the most persistent family traits.

'Poo!' shrills Imogen again. Now a noxious odour is filling the wedding car. 'Auntie Ellie! You've stood in poo!'

Bollocks. She's right.

Horrified, I kick off my slippers, wind down the window and in a most un-bridesmaid-like way, lob them out of the car. Unfortunately at this point we're on the main Henley to Taply road, passing The Riverman pub, which is doing a roaring trade on such a lovely summer's day. People are sprawled across the expanse of sun-parched lawn clutching wine glasses, enjoying the sunshine and generally minding their own business.

And it's here that life decides to flick a V at me.

At the precise moment I throw my shoes, the Rolls brakes sharply to avoid a cute little family of ducklings wandering across the road en route for a leisurely swim down the Thames. My shoes sail in a delicate arc to land, with a precision and accuracy that evaded me all of my sporting life, in the lap of some hapless drinker. For a moment he's frozen with surprise, looking up at the sky in total shock, before he glances in my direction as the realisation of what's happened suddenly dawns.

I feel the blood gallop into my face.

'Go! Go! Go!' I screech to the chauffeur while my victim mouths wordlessly. I can imagine exactly what he's saying, and I feel rather queasy. Please God, don't let that be a designer suit he's wearing!

Actually, what makes me feel *really* sick is the fact that this unfortunate stranger is absolutely gorgeous, the type of man I'd normally do anything to be introduced to. But not today, when I'm all dressed up like a fancy loo roll holder and merrily throwing my smelly shoes about.

Mills & Boon it ain't.

The chauffeur obligingly puts his foot down, probably imagining himself in a glamorous *Crimewatch* reconstruction, and roars away with a screech of tyres, while my young charges whoop with glee at the sudden surge of speed and a wet patch spreads from beneath Imogen's skirt.

Indecent Proposal

Annabelle's wedding reception is being held at my parents' house, which is fortunate for me because I'll be able to dash to my old bedroom and search for an ancient pair of Doc Marten boots to wear under this peach monstrosity.

The Rolls, now smelling of wee rather than lilac air freshener, crunches up the perfect arc of gravel drive to the front of the house, where the guests are already arriving in their droves. My parents live in a sprawling mock-Tudor affair that backs on to the Thames and has acres of velvet-smooth lawns tumbling down to the glittering water. Today a huge marquee has covered the grass and the fruit trees are festooned with white fairy lights and peach ribbons. Waitresses circulate amongst the guests handing out glasses of champagne. By a rose-covered archway, Annabelle and Mark head a large queue and shake endless hands while the strains of Vivaldi drift in the warm breeze. It's the perfect setting for my sister's perfect day.

Note to self: do not get legless and wreck it.

'Granny! Auntie Ellie threw her shoes at a man,' hollers Imogen, exploding out of the car.

Mum holds Imogen at arm's length. Urine and Floris mingle in a most unpleasant way.

'Ellie did what?' she asks.

'Kids!' I laugh, while shooting a look at my niece that

says no ice creams/Christmas presents/bedtime stories ever again if she so much as squeaks to Granny. 'Such vivid imaginations!'

But my mother's gaze travels from her granddaughter to the hem of my dress, where sure enough my bare toes are peeping out. She sighs wearily.

'Eleanor, I don't know what's been going on, and quite frankly I don't think I want to. Please go inside and freshen up and find some shoes. We'll be having more photos in a moment and I want a nice one of you and Rupert. Oh look, Rupert's over there and he's waving! Why don't you go and join him?'

Mum at a tangent is a trial at the best of times, but once she gets on to the topic of Rupert she's virtually unstoppable. Now is probably not the best time to tell her it's over. She's practically reading our banns. Lately, she's become totally obsessed with marrying me off. She was just the same with Annabelle, and lovely though Mark is, I'm really not convinced it's a match made in heaven. They don't have anything in common. Not that this bothers my mother. I overheard her telling Dad that at least Annabelle is one less thing for her to worry about.

Luckily I'm saved from any further lectures about St Rupert by the wedding planner's announcement that the wedding breakfast is about to begin. Accepting a glass of champagne I make my escape, knowing that my mother will be totally distracted by her mother-of-the-bride role for at least the next five hours, which leaves me free to get plastered. Helping myself to a miniature Yorkshire pudding, I feel much more cheerful. Things are starting to look up. Free alcohol and food. What more could any girl ask for?

'Bloody hell, Ellie! What do you look like?' A slender

figure appears beside me, trying to balance a tray of canapés as well as two glasses of champagne in each hand. 'You're right, you do look like a sausage.'

Sam's wearing her usual collection of tasselled and bell-covered clothes. Her tiny hands are crammed to the knuckles with silver rings and she's sporting a diamond nose stud and two hoops through her lip as well as a festering chin piercing. I'm amazed she's actually here, because as well as running Blue Moon, her New Age shop in Taply, she's also flat out orchestrating a major campaign to stop a bypass being put though local woodland.

'I thought you'd be far too busy at the site to make the wedding,' I say, as we chink glasses. 'What if someone puts a digger through while you're here drinking Moët with the capitalistic pigs?'

'Mud's in charge,' Sam says airily, which doesn't exactly answer my question. When it comes to Mud, her dread-locked, grungy boyfriend, the words *piss-up* and *brewery* spring to mind. All any contractor needs to do is skin up and Mud will probably unchain himself from the gate and happily smoke his way into oblivion while the diggers tear up a thousand years of ancient trees. Still, I don't say any of this to Sam. Love is blind and all that.

Although I have to say that in her case it also has no sense of smell.

Sam grimaces. 'Much as I adore your charming sister, I have an ulterior motive for being here. Lots of your Tory bastard guests are just the types who'd happily sacrifice ancient woodland to reduce their commute to London. I thought I could spread the word and prick a few social consciences.'

Now I notice her recyclable shoulder bag stuffed with leaflets that scream *Save Ethy Woods* in bright-green letters.

23

My parents will have a fit if she uses Annabelle's wedding as part of her protest. Besides, my father can't wait to have ten minutes shaved off his commute to the city, and frequently mutters that he'll chop the bloody trees down himself and force those hippy layabouts to get jobs. He's even written to our local MP to complain, but now probably isn't the time to share this knowledge with Sam.

'I need all the help I can get,' Sam continues, mounting her high horse before my very eyes. 'People are so ignorant. Don't they understand that trees are the lungs of the planet? Can you believe that some tosser property developer has bought the pastures either side of the woods and is trying to prosecute us for trespassing on his land? When I find out who he is, I'm going to give him a real piece of my mind. It'll take more than that to stop us!'

Her face turns crimson with rage. Experience tells me that if aversion tactics aren't applied with immediate effect, she'll be off on a full-scale rant, probably yelling at my mother for not serving line-caught tuna steaks or organic wine before lecturing my father about squandering electricity with all these fairy lights and patio heaters.

I love my best friend to bits, but sometimes all this hard-core eco stuff is very tiring.

'Have another drink,' I say, swiftly relieving a passing waiter of two more glasses. 'I'm on my second now, and things are starting to look up.'

'Just as long as you don't get blotto and lose the plot,' she warns. 'Like at the Year Eleven prom.'

'That was a long time ago,' I say hastily. *Why* do my friends always remember my least gracious accomplishments? OK, so getting plastered on cheap cider and falling face first into the prom cake probably wasn't the proudest moment of my life, but in fairness I had a very good reason.

'Yes, it was a long time ago,' agrees Sam, 'yet you're still holding a grudge against my brother. It's been eleven years, El. You need to let it go.'

That's easier said than done. I'd defy any girl who's been publicly stood up and humiliated at her high-school prom to be able to *let it go*. Even all these years on I still feel a hot flush of shame when I remember how stupid I must have looked.

When I was fifteen, I decided I was going to marry Sam's elder brother Jay. Forget Mr Taylor the PE teacher, forget Robbie Williams, forget every member of Blue; this was a *serious* crush, if not true love. For months I'd written *Jason Delamere loves Eleanor Andrews* all over my exercise books and frantically tried to fiddle sums to reach a respectable love percentage, or had signed my name *Ellie Delamere*, just to see. I'd even taken to following the Taply under-eighteen rugby team in the vain hope that Jay might notice me waving by the touchline. But it was not to be. Jay dated a string of gorgeous sixth-formers who were tall, braceless and certainly not mousy and freckly, while I played the *Titanic* theme over and over again and cried myself to sleep. In fairness to Jay, my stalking must have driven him demented, but even so there was no excuse for what he did to get rid of me.

'He didn't realise you'd taken him seriously,' Sam points out, for what must be the millionth time. 'He thought you were kidding when you asked him to go to the prom with you. He was joking when he agreed.'

'Yeah, right,' I mutter. Of course he'd known I wasn't joking. He'd gone along with it for weeks, even agreeing to match his bow tie to my blue dress, all part of an elaborate ploy to get shot of me for good. His horrible friends were in on it too; they'd even taken limo hire money from me –

a detail I'd always been too ashamed to share with Sam. I felt stupid enough being fooled by her brother, never mind that the rest of his cronies had duped me too.

'I did try to warn you he didn't mean it. His mates would have ripped it out of him for ever if he'd gone with you.'

'I wasn't that bad!' I protest.

'Of course you weren't, but teenage boys are crap. They only care what their mates think. Consign being stood up by my rubbish brother to the dustbin of life,' Sam advises. 'It's not good karma to be angry for so long.'

Bugger karma, I think as I gulp my champagne. If Sam had been left waiting in her sparkly dress on the most important night of a teenage girl's life, for a date that never showed, I bet she'd still be fuming too. Logically, I know it's pathetic to be angry after all this time, but I don't think I'll ever get over the mortification of waiting for Jay to collect me until it became painfully clear he wasn't coming. Finally my father drove me to Taply Manor, where I had to suffer the humiliation of walking in without a date and with all my so-called friends laughing at me. *Where's your hot date?* they sniggered, which I probably deserved seeing as I'd bragged about going with Jay for weeks. But the final straw was seeing him draped all over Arabella Elliot, a skinny, blonde sixth-former.

'That's her?' Arabella sneered when I tried to ask what was going on. Jay and his friends laughed too, and I fled. Tearfully I turned to my smuggled cider. Before long I was legless, and somehow ended up dancing on the buffet table and declaring my undying love for Jay before passing out face first in the prom cake.

How had I, Ellie Unamazing Andrews, ever thought I

stood a chance? Twelve years on and dressed like a pork sausage, I don't feel as though much has changed.

In the years since, Jay has always gone out of his way to be nice to me, which is somehow even more humiliating. Last time he came home, he even asked me out for dinner, which was kind but about a decade too late. Obviously I turned him down; after all, no girl wants to be taken out on the dating equivalent of a mercy shag, and I was relieved last year when he decided to take a permanent yacht designer job in the States. Surely several thousand miles is a large enough distance to enable me to forget the entire excruciating episode?

Or forget it as well as I can when I have friends like Sam to remind me.

She fans the air about my face. 'Don't tell me you're still embarrassed!' She lowers her voice and dips her head in Rupert's direction. 'Besides, you've got a real admirer over there. Looks like I'm going to have to advertise for a new lodger.'

I'm just about to tell her how things really stand with Rupert when the wedding planner starts herding us all into the marquee to take our seats. I'll tell Sam later, I decide, plonking myself down at the top table and cursing the person who invented the tradition that the maid of honour and the best man sit together. Rupert will be trying to hold my hand under the tablecloth or feed me little morsels from his own plate as I'm mentally ringing the death knell for our relationship. I consider moving down a gap to sit with Imogen, but the sight of her avidly blowing spit bubbles is too much even for an experienced aunt like myself. The only way to survive the next few hours is to get very drunk.

Soon everyone is seated, a hush falling over the wedding

guests as Rupert taps his knife against a wine glass. Then he clears his throat and pushes a lock of floppy blonde fringe out of his eyes. Every gaze was on him. Mum's looking at me in a very peculiar way, and even Sam's giving me a sentimental smile. I must be more pissed than I realized, because now I'm at that paranoid stage where it seems everyone's in on something I don't have a clue about. Whatever happened to loud and lairy followed by maudlin? If I don't eat soon, I'll be progressing to spinny-room stage.

'Ladies, gentlemen, children,' Rupert begins, looking very nervous. 'I apologise for delaying the meal; I can see you're all dying to taste the marvellous wedding breakfast that Mr and Mrs Andrews have supplied, and as a barrister I know you're well within your rights.'

There's a polite ripple of laughter at the joke. I stifle a yawn. The alcohol's making me sleepy and I hope he won't take long. I need to line my stomach if I'm going to last through to the speeches.

'I'm full of respect and awe for Mark and Annabelle making this commitment today,' Rupert carries on, 'and being best man has prompted me to do some serious thinking about a commitment that *I* want to make.'

He pauses dramatically, and a little ripple of interest spreads across the guests. *Get on with it*, I think impatiently, looking up from my drink and meeting his brown-eyed gaze. It's a rerun of the church scenario, only ten times more sentimental and Bambi-eyed. What has got into him?

Then I notice my mother's gloating smile, my father's deepening worry lines and Sam's wide grin, and I start to feel light-headed.

'Ellie and I have been seeing each other for a while

now,' Rupert continues, beaming in my direction. 'And it will come as no surprise to anybody that today, when two other people have promised their lives to each other, I think it's appropriate that I take the opportunity to say something to Ellie that I've been longing to say for ages.'

Every Saturday I sit glued to the lottery, desperately trying to predict the big-money balls, and now, in a stuffy marquee on a summer's afternoon, I have a sudden flash of psychic genius that would give Derek Acorah a run for his money. I know even before Rupert moves from the table and falls to one knee exactly what he's going to say, and judging from the rapt expressions on the faces of the spectators, so do they.

Delving into his waistcoat pocket, Rupert plucks out a small box and opens it slowly. Sitting on a bed of smooth velvet is a large diamond ring, the solitaire glinting at me like an eye.

Suddenly I'm not hungry any more. In fact, I feel very, very sick.

'Ellie,' says Rupert, reaching for my cold and now sweaty hand, 'will you marry me?'

Perfect Stranger

The social highlight of the weekend was the wedding of Annabelle Andrews to the Hon. Mark Roxworth. Mark, the son of Lord Roxworth, works for City bank Millward Saville, while Annabelle is yet another of the Amazing Andrews sisters, granddaughters of Sir Henry Andrews, Bt. However, the focus of this wedding was not the nuptials, but the very dramatic proposal of eligible barrister Rupert Moore-Critchen to Eleanor Andrews, and her extremely public refusal. The wedding proceeded minus best man and chief bridesmaid. The youngest Andrews sister is quite a character. I await her next move!

I groan and chuck the *Daily Mail* across the room. Annabelle's going to kill me; there's no way she'll suffer a slight like this and not want Ellie-flavoured blood. This is far, far worse than the time I borrowed her white Alice Temperley dress and tipped a bottle of red wine down it. Not only have I ruined her wedding breakfast, but I've also taken up all the word space in the social columns.

'It's a good write-up, isn't it?' Sam says from her corner of the sofa. She can't look at me because she's trying to plait her hair into hundreds of small braids, a process that takes hours and usually involves me patiently holding beads and elastic bands until I'm so bored I can see the house plants photosynthesising.

'It's all right for you.' Injured by her lack of sympathy, I decide not to help with the braid she's waving at me. '*You* were treated to free entertainment, booze and food. But me,' I pause dramatically, 'I've lost my job, my family aren't speaking to me and when Annabelle reads the *Mail,* I'm doomed.'

'Probably,' agrees Sam. 'Though I can't believe you really had no idea Rupert was going to pop the question. We could all see it a mile off. I nearly advertised for a new lodger.'

I ignore her, knowing full well that there are very few people in Taply-on-Thames with the inclination to rent a house that reeks of patchouli oil and has various Shivas and Brahmas dangling off the ceilings. Besides, only a true friend could tolerate Mud popping in between various stints up trees or digging tunnels.

'I was going to finish it with Rupert!' I protest indignantly. 'It was just a case of choosing the right moment. I didn't want to hurt him.'

'Well, you've screwed up there, haven't you? Not only has Rupert been hurt, but now he looks like a prize berk *and* gets it written about in the national press. You being a coward made everything worse for him, not better.'

'I know.' I hang my head. I've never felt so miserable or guilty in my entire life. I haven't even touched the monster-sized Dairy Milk Sam's bought to cheer me up. It's languishing in the fridge, which is most unusual.

The rest of Annabelle's wedding was a complete nightmare, worse in fact because there wasn't the faintest hope of waking up. Time seemed to stand still as Rupert knelt there at my bare feet, smiling up at me. The ring twinkled merrily in its velvet nest and for a moment I was overwhelmed. I literally had all my mother's dreams at my fingertips. A chance to jump down from the shelf, dust off the cobwebs and follow my sisters up St Jude's aisle in a froth of lace. Visions of elegant country houses, shopping in Harvey Nicks, Range Rovers and children dressed in Laura Ashley flashed before my eyes. It was all there. Apart from one thing. The man offering me his life wasn't the man I wanted. Rupert wasn't *my* dream man. He was my mother's.

'I can't,' I whispered, my eyes filling when I saw the stricken look on his face. 'I meant to say something earlier; I should have done, I know, but it never seemed like the right moment. I'm sorry, Rupert, but I can't marry you. I'm not in love with you. I like you a lot but I don't love you. I'm so sorry.'

A gasp of shock/outrage/callous enjoyment swept through the guests. Rupert's brown eyes were suspiciously bright as he slowly stood up and snapped the ring case shut. He looked so pale that for one awful moment I thought he was about to faint. Then, in a most un-Rupert-like manner, he swept his arm across the top table, sending flower arrangements, plates and champagne flutes crashing to the floor. Annabelle screamed, and another gasp flew around the marquee.

'*You're* sorry, Ellie?' he shouted, and I shrivelled under his anger, knowing that I deserved it. 'Not half as sorry as me!'

Rupert hurled the top tier of the wedding cake at me before storming out, closely followed by Mark. My mother burst into hysterical sobs, Annabelle turned paler than her dress, and all was in uproar. I had five hundred pounds' worth of wedding cake oozing down my chest and the eyes of every guest trained on me. I had never before understood the true sentiment of wanting the earth to swallow you up; at that exact moment I did.

Reliving this hideous scene makes my intestines do macramé, and I chew nervously on the skin around my thumbnail.

'Stop chewing,' Sam scolds. 'Snap out of this self-pity and sort yourself out. You're supposed to be meeting your mum soon. Hadn't you better get your butt in gear?'

I burrow deeper into the sofa and begin to develop an all-encompassing interest in *Homes Under the Hammer*. I can't go out now. I'll never know whether or not that dilapidated bungalow in Kent makes the reckless buyers a profit.

'Ring her, Sam, tell her I'm ill. I'll wash up for a week. I'll even clean the grill pan. I'll do anything, but please just ring her for me!'

The thought of facing my mother makes me feel faint. In the two days since the wedding we've only spoken through our mobile answerphones and I'm more than happy to keep it that way.

'You're doing it again,' Sam says sternly. 'Putting things off. It's time to grow up and face the music, El. You need to see your mum.' She fixes me with a stare. Her stares have never failed over the past fifteen years. They've gained her access to my homework, new clothes and have even wormed Mud into the house.

'OK, you win.' Grudgingly I heave myself off the sofa, one eye still on the telly, and reach for my boots. 'I'll take all the abuse she can throw at me. And then I'm coming home, shutting my bedroom door and staying put until Taply-on-Thames forgets this whole bloody mess ever happened.'

Sam drops her braid and studies the scuffed toes of her Doc Martens. Am I imagining it, or does she look a bit shifty, the way she does when she's helped herself to my cereal without asking?

'Oh dear,' she says. 'There might be a little problem with that, El.'

'Such as?' I'm busy tugging on my platforms. At three inches high they cripple me, but the height advantage is well worth the agony.

'I may have let your room.'

'What!' I cry, jumping to my feet so fast that I over-balance and topple back on to the sofa, narrowly missing an ashtray and a half-eaten tuna roll. 'You've done what?'

'I've let your room.' Sam's expression is defensive. 'I was convinced you were about to bugger off and move in with Rupert.'

'Who told you I was moving in with Rupert?'

'Where do I start? Annabelle told me, your mum told me, even poor bloody Rupert told me.'

'But *I* didn't tell you!'

'I thought that was another of your famous putting-off tricks,' Sam explains, obviously feeling that in the light of recent events she has a valid point. 'I didn't want to be left to pay the rent on my own, so I let your room.'

'Well un-let it.'

'I can't.'

'Who's so important that you'd throw your best friend out in the street?' So much for all the years of sharing everything from cider to menstrual cycles.

'You won't like it, Ellie.' Sam looks ashamed. 'I've let your room to Jay.'

I gawp at her. Jay, my teenage crush? Jay, who stood me up at the prom? Back here? In my house? In my bloody bedroom? When I was fifteen, this thought would have filled me with joy. Now I just feel sick.

'He's back from America for a while and he needs a place to stay. Dad's too busy with his string of bimbos to bother with us, so I told Jay he could crash here. He's quit his job and has had a really crap break-up, so he needs a bit of time out. He's going to help with the protest too. I didn't think you'd still be here!' Abandoning her plaits, Sam puts her arms around me. 'Don't panic. We'll think of something.'

I shrug her off.

'I'm sure he'll be delighted to kip on the sofa bed while he mends his broken heart,' says Sam hastily. 'Don't worry, I won't throw you out.'

'I should hope not!'

'But how will you feel about having him here after, well, you know . . . ?'

'I wasn't the one in the wrong,' I say coolly. 'Make up the sofa, park his rucksack and throw a party if you must, but don't expect me to like him being here.'

Once outside, I let myself into Esther, my ancient and not always trusty Fiesta.

Driving across Taply is very lazy and would shock the likes of Rosemary Conley. It also explains why I have cellulite like bubble wrap and she doesn't. Mud and Sam deplore my lack of green feeling, although they're never too proud to clamber into my vile pollution machine when it tips down with rain. But there isn't time for me to walk. Never mind save the planet, it'll be save Ellie if I'm late and wind my mother up any more this week.

Waiting to turn left down Taply High Street, I find my thoughts wandering towards Jay with the kind of fascinated dread usually reserved for smear tests. In fact, an embarrassing position and a cold piece of metal seem like a positively cheery alternative to being stuck with him for the foreseeable future. I comfort myself by thinking that all those months in the States will have changed him. He'll be wrinkly from the ozone exposure and have a massive gut from living on fast food. Besides, there's nothing in life left to dread now, because what can ever be worse than Saturday's traumas? Sharing a house with the once love of my life will be nothing in comparison, and anyway, I'm an adult now with a degree and an overdraft, not a spotty schoolgirl.

Mind you, it wouldn't hurt to get a haircut and a leg wax before I go home.

I'm so intent on examining the state of my split ends that I don't realise how close I am to the car parked directly in front of the tea shop. The first I know about our fatal attraction to a sexy BMW convertible is a horrible crunching sound as two bumpers meet in a passionate embrace.

'Shit!'

I stamp on the brake but my platform boot slides on to the accelerator, and with a jolt Esther leaves a massive dent in the shiny red car.

'Damn!'

Parking more carefully the second time, I switch off the engine and take a deep breath. I pull open the glove box, sweeping magazines, chocolate wrappers and Tampax on to the floor, and unearth my emergency cigarette supply. Lighting one, I inhale gratefully. Then I tear up the packet and, retrieving an eyebrow pencil from the assorted clutter on the dashboard, write out my name and phone number, telling myself proudly that a lesser (but richer) person would have just driven away. I'll get to heaven yet.

I tuck the note under the BMW's windscreen wiper and pray that the owner doesn't roll on by. Call me a chicken, but I'd rather be a safe distance away when they discover what I've done to their beautiful car. Then I finish my cigarette and head towards the tea shop.

The Bun in the Oven is Taply's premier tea room, highly favoured by the moneyed set, and has a stunning view across the Thames to the sumptuous houses where the likes of ex-Beatles and film stars live. Here you can sit at a frilly table, be served by a frilly waitress and eat frilly cakes to your heart's content. Just going through the door into the cinnamon-scented air puts about three inches on my hips. Although I prefer the parsnip soup in Blue Moon's café, nothing short of a violent personality change would ever persuade my mother to eat shoulder to shoulder with people in thick ethnic jumpers and army boots.

I push open the door and instantly spot Mum sitting by the window, sipping her Earl Grey tea and gazing across the river. The rigid line of her shoulders is enough to set my heart plummeting into my platforms. She might look like your average ash-blonde Home Counties housewife, but my mother has an inner core of razor blades.

I'm definitely in for it.

'You've been smoking,' she says accusingly as I kiss her. 'Darling, why? You know how bad it is for you.'

'It's my last one. I'm giving up,' I reply, crossing my fingers behind my back and plonking myself down on the chair opposite.

Mum looks at me as though she's sucking a particularly acidy part of an acid drop, and stirs her tea so violently that waves of Earl Grey slop into the saucer.

I brace myself for a lecture. Over the years I've had them all. The 'you must revise for your A levels' lecture, the 'why don't you get a proper job in Daddy's company?' lecture, and best of all, the 'how lovely Rupert is' lecture. Which will it be today? While she's making up her mind, I reach for a Bath bun.

'Don't eat that!' she gasps. 'You're not like the others; you need to watch your weight.'

Dropping the bun faster than a hot brick, I groan inwardly. So it's that old classic, the 'you're nothing like your sisters' lecture. As Mum launches into her opening speech with the kind of gusto more usually reserved for Shakespearean soliloquies, I tune out and fix my gaze on two mallard ducks drifting merrily beneath Taply Bridge. I remember standing on that very bridge in my St Hilda's uniform, cheering for Jay as he rowed beneath. Will I ever escape feeling like that gawky lumpen schoolgirl? I haven't been her for years now, but she never seems very far away. I have a feeling that even if I dieted myself into Kate Moss-like proportions (highly unlikely but a nice thought) I'd still feel exactly the same.

'You're nothing like your sisters,' sighs my mother for what must be the millionth time. 'I've never had any trouble from them.'

If only Mum knew the half of it! The truth is that the others are just much better at hiding things from Mum, or *mushrooming her*, as Emily once put it, keeping her in the dark and feeding her crap. I'm far too truthful, that's the problem.

'So, what have you got to say for yourself? Do you realise how embarrassing this is? The wedding was an absolute fiasco after you turned Rupert down. Annabelle's devastated and I've never been so humiliated in all my life. And as for poor Mrs Moore-Critchen, she's absolutely distraught. She'd already bought you a complete set of Louis Vuitton luggage as an engagement present and planned a party. How do you think she feels?'

'How about me? What about how I feel?' I cry. Several tea drinkers' heads swivel in my direction. I lower my voice a few decibels. 'I don't love Rupert, Mum! There was never anything serious between us as far as I was concerned. He got completely carried away. I had every intention of calling it off.'

My mother frowns. 'But you didn't call it off, Ellie. This is just typical of you. You assume everybody can read your mind as you plunge from one disaster to the next, always running away from the consequences. One day, my girl, the results of your actions will catch up with you. Are you listening to me?'

'Of course!' I fib. Then, deciding that attack is my best form of defence, I add, 'Anyway, Mum, haven't you got your priorities ever so slightly wrong? You're *my* mother and you're supposed to want the best for *me*. How can you possibly be angry because I've refused to marry a man I don't love? You ought to be comforting me and mopping up my tears, not having a go. That wedding wasn't exactly a barrel of laughs for me either.'

My mum has never understood me. The fact that I've chosen to do things differently from my sisters confuses and horrifies her in equal measure. I could explain until I'm blue in the face that I want to be my own person, but she'll never get it, will never understand that by being independent I stand out from my sisters in a positive way. Mum was mortified when I rented a room in Sam's house rather than taking the family flat, and was even more perplexed when I turned down a job with Dad's company to find my own employment. She simply doesn't understand that I want the space to be *me* rather than just the girl who is nothing like her sisters.

To my horror, Mum pulls out a delicate hanky and dabs

her brimming eyes. 'I do want the best for you, darling. All I want is to see you settled and happy. I want you to be secure and taken care of like your sisters, not living in a tatty student house and drifting from one useless job to the next, always worrying and always alone. Rupert could've given you so much. He's going to be made a partner in the firm, you know. He has excellent prospects.'

What is this? A Jane Austen novel? She'll be wheeling in Mr Collins next and suggesting I marry him.

'But I don't love Rupert,' I point out. 'It all just got out of hand. He never even asked me about getting engaged! Until Saturday, I had absolutely no idea he was planning to propose so publicly. I couldn't just say yes to save face for the family, could I?'

Mum's expression says that actually, yes I could.

'At least the wedding got a massive piece in the *Mail*,' I add, trying to put a positive spin on things. Alastair Campbell would be proud of me. 'Besides, maybe I like being a single girl about town.'

'It's all very well gadding about, but you're not getting any younger, Ellie, you know. Unless you invest in some decent moisturiser, you'll soon have a serious problem with lines.'

I sneak a glimpse at my reflection in the highly polished teaspoons. Sure enough some frown lines are creasing my freckly brow, but to be honest, I think I'm getting off lightly with those after the last forty-eight hours.

'You'll never find a decent man if you're not looking your best,' concludes my mother with all her usual tact. 'A woman has to work at her looks when she reaches her thirties, Ellie. You need to make the most of yourself to find another man who wants to marry you. You need to take things more seriously.'

I pull a face. 'What's the urgency? I've got years yet!'

My mother reaches out and takes my hand.

'*You* might have years,' she whispers, and her voice is so soft that I have to lean across the table to hear. My boobs narrowly miss a cream cake. 'But I don't know if *I* do.'

Time suddenly stands still and every detail of the café becomes sharp and very clear. The steam running on the windows, the whistle of the kettle, the chink of bone china as the waitress replaces it in the dresser. I have a horrible sensation that the floor's shifting beneath me.

Last year my mother found a breast lump and underwent surgery and treatment. Seeing her reduced to a shadow of her former self shocked my sisters and me beyond belief. The words *radiotherapy* and *chemo* still strike cold terror into my heart.

'It hasn't . . .'

She nods, her eyes swimming with unshed tears. Mine fill too.

'I didn't want to tell anyone until after the wedding, but the cancer's come back and this time it's more aggressive. The oncologists say I need a double mastectomy and more chemotherapy.'

'Oh, Mum, no!'

'Darling, don't panic. If I have this operation then I've got an excellent chance of beating it for good this time,' she says firmly. 'I should have had it done before, of course, but I wasn't brave enough. Having cancer does strange things to a mother, darling: you start to worry more, you want to make sure that everyone you love is safe and taken care of, just in case . . .'

Her voice tails off and she takes a deep gulp of tea. The cup rattles noisily against the saucer.

'That's why I need to see you all settled and taken care

of. I don't want to worry about you being alone. I want to know that you're safe and that I can put my mind at rest knowing all my girls are happy and secure. I lie awake at night worrying about my family, but most of all I worry about you, Ellie.'

I feel a sharp stab of guilt. How selfish I am, worrying about trivia like cellulite and calories when Mum has serious stuff to fret about. In spite of her brave words, I can see the fear in her eyes.

'I love you, Ellie,' my mother says, touching my cheek. 'But I worry about you so much. You seem to lurch from one disaster to another. I can't bear the thought of these disasters still going on when or if I'm not here to watch out for you. I have to know you're safe. If you were married to a wonderful man, then I would relax. And how much fun would it be to arrange one more wedding? That would really have given me something to take my mind off all the other stuff. That's why I'm so disappointed about Rupert. One last wedding was all I'd hoped for . . .'

'When's the operation?' I ask once I've managed to swallow the football that's appeared in my throat.

She shrugs, and is it me or do her shoulders suddenly seem frailer? 'We're not sure. The consultant says I'm not strong enough yet. I've got to sort out my iron levels first, then have a lumpectomy. The mastectomy is a final precaution. Hopefully it'll do the trick.'

What a terrible secret to have kept. How awful to have had to pretend to be happy in the run-up to Annabelle's wedding when she had such a burden to bear. I don't know if I could ever be so unselfish. A tear rolls down my cheek and splashes on to the tablecloth.

'Enough of all that. It's too depressing for words. Besides, I'll be just fine. Now, what are you going to do about work?' Mum asks, firmly changing the subject. 'I can't imagine you're employed by Rupert any more?'

I think this is even less likely than bin Laden going to work for the FBI, but now's probably not the best time to tell my mother that Sam's offered me a job in Blue Moon. It's doubtful that Mum will see making parsnip soup as a sound career move, even if I think it sounds like fun. Blinking back my tears, I plump for a spot of mushrooming.

'Rupert said he never wants to see me again. Don't worry, though, I'll find something.'

'It's such a waste of your degree. You could do anything, Ellie! Daddy knows lots of people in the City. Let him find you something suitable. It's high time you got a proper job. Then you could move out of that horrible house.'

The mere thought of being condemned to spend the next forty years of my life crammed into the underground, wedged in strangers' armpits and developing Tube rage when they pinch my seat, is enough to send me cold. Doesn't she get it? I don't want to have a so-called proper job. I enjoy working in Taply, where I know everyone, and there's a lot to be said for having a job I don't stress about when I go home at night. Besides, I like living in number 43. OK, so it might be a little messy, and on the rare occasions that my mother visits we have to practically fumigate the place and send Mud to the pub, but it's a relaxed and fun place to be, which isn't something I could ever say about my parents' house. I spent my formative years trying not to tread dirt into the carpets and being told off for leaving sticky fingerprints on the windows.

'I'm sure Emily could find you something at the bank,' my mum continues confidently, as though my sister works as a cashier in NatWest rather than a high-powered bond trader at Goldman Sachs.

I pull a face. Trust Em to get brains *and* beauty. She truly is the girl who got the lot. Even when we were kids, she was charging me to borrow her Sindys, in between the child modelling assignments, of course.

'Just because Emily's a merchant banker doesn't mean I can be one. I failed my maths GCSE, remember?'

'Oh tush,' says Mum, as though this is just a minor issue that won't stand in the way of my glittering career in high finance. 'Well then, how about Lucy? She could find you a job on a magazine.'

Lucy, my second eldest sister, used to be a model and regularly graced the pages of *Marie Claire* and *Elle* before she married Henry-no-chin and gave it all up to float around Henley having beauty treatments and hanging out with the other yummy mummies. The only magazine likely to feature me is probably *The Big Issue*.

'I don't think so,' I say. 'I'm too short to be a model.'

My mother nods. 'True. Oh, what a shame Charlotte and Annabelle don't work. I'm sure they'd have helped.'

I nearly choke into my teacup. Does she really know her daughters so little? Charlotte only cares for anything that has four hooves and a mane, and Annabelle would rather poke her eyes out with lolly sticks than help me after the wedding fiasco.

'We'll think of something,' Mum says, patting my hand. 'You won't be the odd one out for ever.'

When you have four big sisters who all look like Botticelli angels but you look more like one of those plump, curly-headed cherubs from a cartoon Christmas card, the only real option *is* to be the odd one out. I've worked very hard not to be anything like my sisters because I've always known there's absolutely no point competing. Living in a shared house, dating men who do – shock, horror – manual jobs, and not having a glittering career is my own small rebellion. But now I have a nasty feeling that my time is up.

As my mother departs in a cloud of Floris, I head for Esther, thanking God that the BMW's gone. I can't stand any more emotional trauma. Standing at the kerb, puffing furiously on the last of my fags, I swear on Esther's Ford badge that if it's the last thing I do, I'll bag a suitable man and make my mother proud. If I focus on project *find a suitable man* it might just keep me from collapsing in a sobbing heap. I don't know an enormous amount about cancer, but I do know that unless I keep myself busy, I'll be in bits.

So, finding a decent man, settling down and making my mother happy will be the top three things on my to-do list. And, unlike my usual lists, which usually brim with excellent ideas such as *pay off overdraft* and *join a gym*, I'll actually do these things.

I'm having trouble convincing myself, though. Suited lawyer types are really not my thing, and when Rupert used to drag me along to corporate dos, I was so bored I could practically see my nails growing. But this isn't just about me any more. It's about making Mum happy, and after all the grief I've caused lately, it's the very least I can do.

I finish my cigarette. That is the last. I examine my reflection in the windscreen, squinting at my newly emerging wrinkles and pushing tangled hair out of my eyes. Throwing all financial caution to the wind, yet again, I decide to go and get my hair done and buy some new smart clothes for the new smart me who's going to bag the perfect man and make her poorly mother happy.

I reckon I deserve some retail therapy.

'Look at you!' exclaims Poppy, Sam's right-hand woman, when I enter Blue Moon several hours later. 'Give us a twirl!'

I prance obligingly in front of the cash desk, narrowly missing a rack of incense sticks, and toss my newly cut hair in my best supermodel impression. It's a jaunty shoulder length and dyed glossy mahogany to complement my newly tinted eyebrows and eyelashes. My legs are so damn hairless they practically squeak, and as for my bikini line, if that's a landing strip no wonder pilots need twenty-twenty vision!

'Blimey,' says Poppy. 'Who is he?'

'Nobody.' I'm most disappointed by her lack of feminist sympathy. Somebody who works in a New Age shop and wears vegetarian Doc Martens ought to be more in touch with her inner woman.

'Well, I approve,' decides Poppy, pushing her long black hair behind her ears. 'Change of image after Saturday, eh? I love that ginger colour. What a clever disguise so that Rupert's friends and rellies can't recognise you.'

'It's not ginger, it's deep auburn,' I protest.

'It suits you,' Poppy says, delving under the counter. 'Tell you what, how about I do you a tarot reading? We'll see if things get any better.'

She slides the red silk from a dog-eared tarot pack and orders me to shuffle the deck. While Poppy spreads the cards out, I chew my thumbnail and worry about my mother.

'Wow, look at this, El,' Poppy breathes, poring over the spread, her slim fingers pushing and probing the faded pictures. 'These cards represent your present and the over-all picture shows chaos, disaster and change.'

'What a surprise,' I say drily. 'Is there any good news, or shall I drown myself in the parsnip soup now?'

'You're such a drama queen,' admonishes Poppy. 'Give me a moment to look at the rest of your spread. I'm sure the future will be just peachy.'

She turns the rest of the cards over, looks at me and then looks back at the spread, a frown crinkling her brow. 'This is weird. I've never seen anything like it.'

'Why? What's weird?'

'Your future shows nothing but men! They're everywhere, you slapper!' Poppy starts to giggle. 'According to the cards, your future's full of guys.'

I goggle at her. Bearing in mind my very recent oath to find Mr Perfect and make my mother proud of me, this is spooky stuff indeed.

'Seriously?'

'Seriously! You have three major arcana here, which represent significant men in your life. One you must beware of because he has the power to hurt you, one will be a lovely friend whom you can trust, and the other . . .' She pauses and frowns. 'Actually, I can't make him out. He's a bit hazy.'

Typical! Why do psychics always stop at the good bits?

'Don't talk in riddles! Come on, who are they?' I demand. 'Is one of them Rupert?'

'I can't see that, can I? It's all symbolic. Don't be so impatient.'

'Symbollocks, you mean,' I mutter. I can't believe I've almost been sucked in.

'It's starting to make sense.' Poppy looks up from the spread. 'This last card is The Lovers, and it represents marriage. There's definitely a marriage. It looks like the union of a lifetime. Blimey, Ellie! That's who the third man is! He's your soulmate!'

'Really? Who is he?' I cry, cynicism instantly forgotten. If she can tell me, it'll really speed up this whole getting married business! Mum will be over the moon. I only hope it isn't Rupert. I don't need tarot cards to predict what he might say if I ask for a second chance. On the other hand, if he really loves me as much as he claims, he might take me back with open arms. If Rupert *is* the love of my life, of course . . .

But Poppy's looking at me as though I'm stupid.

'I can't *literally* see who he is, can I? Tarot reading isn't an exact science. I can't even tell what order you'll meet them in. You might already know the love of your life, or he could be just around the corner. It's dead exciting, though, isn't it? I wonder who he could be?'

We stare at each other, both so intrigued that we ignore the man who's abandoned his rucksack by the tie-dye flares and is waiting patiently for some service. *Could* the cards be right? Is fate about to change my life?

I really hope so.

'I hate to interrupt you,' says a deep, sexy voice, hitting me somewhere about the knicker region. 'I'm looking for Samantha Delamere. Is she here?'

The cadence of those words and the voice that utters them make my heart drum so fast I'm afraid it's going to explode.

Turning round very slowly, I meet a familiar smile and feel myself lose twelve years faster than you can say 'Oil of Olay'.

'Hello, Ellie,' says Jay.

'I can't believe you're still sitting there in your dressing gown!' scolds Sam, kicking open my door and plonking a tray on my bedside table. 'You should be wallowing in a bubble bath by now and enjoying a glass of champagne.'

Then her eyebrows shoot up into her fringe when she sees just how much I've already knocked back, and she swipes the bottle back. Sam takes her chief bridesmaid responsibilities very seriously and is running this wedding with all the military precision she usually applies to her eco protests and demonstrations. There's no way I'll fail to make it up the aisle on her watch.

'Hey!' I protest. 'Give that back! I need a drink!'

'I think you've had quite enough already,' Sam says firmly, tipping the remainder into a wizened spider plant. 'Nobody wants to see the bride staggering down the aisle.'

'I don't think I can do this sober,' I say. 'What if I'm making a mistake? What if I'm doing the wrong thing?'

But Sam isn't prepared to listen to any of my last-minute worries. Instead, she places her small hands on her hips and gives me a hard stare.

'Not another word! You know he's perfect for you. We all do.'

I glance down at the photograph album, flicking through it so fast that the tissue paper sighs and the images blur. Since that sunny day and those moments forever captured in time, so much has changed. Some of the people have moved on, some have passed on and some have even split up. Nothing's worked out the way we thought. What if this wedding turns out to be the same?

'Don't be so wet,' Sam says when I repeat this maudlin

train of thought. 'Life doesn't come with any guarantees. That's what makes it so much fun.'

And there you have it, the major difference between us. Sam thrives on risk and change, whereas I cling to the past like a short, plump limpet and procrastinate so much I make Hamlet look decisive. That I ever decided to get married at all is a miracle.

I guess that's being in love for you. Or at least I hope it is. Whatever 'in love' means, as good old Prince Charles once said.

'Have some toast to soak up all that champers,' Sam orders, perching on the bed and waving a slice at me. 'I've made loads.'

She isn't joking. NASA could probably use this stack of toast and Marmite to get men to Mars. Just how many loaves has she used?

'Eat up,' she urges as I take a slice. 'It's just what you need.'

But as I raise the toast to my lips, a very weird thing happens. Something that I've waited most of my adult life for, have dreamed of, and was starting to fear would never happen.

My appetite vanishes. I could no more eat this toast and Marmite than I could chomp through my bedside table. I don't feel at all hungry. I just feel sick.

Brilliant timing, appetite. Why couldn't you have done this six months ago when I was frantically trying to diet into this wedding dress? For weeks on end I went to Chub Club, sticking religiously to red days and green days and eating so much Laughing Cow extra-light cheese that I was in danger of going moo. I practically mainlined slim-line soup and munched so much celery I got lockjaw. And still I only lost a pound – although to be fair, I don't think you're supposed to eat the entire multipack of cream cheese triangles in one sitting. Still, I pressed on because I really didn't want to walk down the aisle looking like Jabba the Hutt. I finally accepted that I wasn't cut out for slimming clubs after one memorable meeting where we were all clapping one poor deluded soul who'd delightedly informed us she'd had a great day because she'd visited McDonald's and only had a Diet Coke. My jaw was nearly in my diet hot chocolate. That wasn't a great day. That was a terrible day!

And so it came to pass that I fell off my diet wagon with an enormous crash, tearing to McDonald's and chomping my way through supersized fries, a Big Mac and a Rolo McFlurry. Nothing had ever tasted so good. Then I'd gone home and spent an amazing evening with my favourite men, Ben & Jerry and Mr Kipling. Heaven for my taste buds. Hell for my waistband.

But now, just when I really need some carbs to soak up the excess champagne, I can't even force down a crumb. I'm so sick with terror I can't eat a thing.

This is much worse than I thought. If I can't eat, then it must be bad.

Sam checks her watch. 'Right, I'm going to call Poppy and find out what's going on. The other bridesmaids will be here any minute and then the make-up girl's arriving. I think the hairdresser is here at ten, so we need to get moving.'

Get moving? I'm rooted to my bed. In fact I want to burrow under it and vanish. I wasn't even this terrified when Sam forced me to go on Oblivion at Alton Towers.

'You eat something and then hop in the bath. I won't be long,' says Sam merrily. 'I just need to check I've got your passport packed in the going-away bag so that you can leave straight for your honeymoon. It's in your new name and everything! Just think, after today you won't be Ellie Andrews any more. Isn't that a thought?'

And off she goes in a jangle of silver bangles, leaving me fighting the panic that's surging through me like the Severn Bore. If I'm not Ellie Andrews, then who on earth will I be? A wife? Mrs somebody? Mrs? That sounds ancient! I'm not old enough to be a Mrs. I still buy funky pink stuff and like Groovy Chick pencil cases!

And talking of Groovy Chick, there's my old diary, stuffed into the bookshelf and spewing half its contents while the pink glittery cover hangs off. That's the diary I was keeping back when . . .

Nerves and toast forgotten, I spring up from the bed – or rather I creak up from the bed, because it's not easy to spring anywhere in a bum bra – and pull the diary from the shelf. Pages fall out like word-covered snow, and with them a postcard of a stately home, dog-eared and worn. On the back, written in faded ink, are the once cherished words, *I think I'm falling in love.*

I clutch the card in my shaking hands and close my eyes. Once upon a time, I'd thought so too . . .

Crushed

'Hello, Jay,' I say, trying desperately for a deep sexy drawl but instead sounding horribly like Minnie Mouse. Frantically searching him for signs of decay USA-style, I'm bitterly disappointed. Where's the bald patch and beer gut? And what about the violent-migraine-patterned Hawaiian shirts and socks 'n' sneakers combo? How dare Jay come back looking every bit as gorgeous as when he left. Nobody deserves to be so tanned and toned.

Why haven't I bothered to be the new improved me until today?

'Where's Sammy?' asks Jay, biceps rippling as he leans companionably on the counter. Against his golden skin his T-shirt is shockingly white, unlike my distinctly grubby hoodie. I feel like bashing my head on the till in despair. Even washing machines love him, whereas when they see me coming they gobble socks and invariably turn everything pink.

'Sam's at home,' I manage to say eventually. Breathe, Ellie, breathe. You're twenty-seven, not fifteen. Get a grip. Don't gawp at him like he's Brad Pitt and Johnny Depp all rolled into one sexy package, and *do not* stare at his sharp cheekbones or the glint of an earring somewhere amidst the dark curls.

'You've had your ear pierced,' I blurt. Damn! I'll be asking him to the prom next.

Jay looks a bit surprised at my scrutiny.

'I had it done a few years ago, during my surf phase. Do you like it?'

I study the scuffed toes of my platform boots, which have suddenly become the most interesting things I've *ever* seen.

'It's OK,' I mutter.

Great, Ellie, just great. What scintillating conversational skills you've acquired over the past twelve years. Bet he's dead impressed.

While I fight to gain control of my brain and vocal cords, both of which have suddenly gone AWOL, Poppy is visibly weighing up this newcomer's infinite attractions and giving Jay the benefit of her flirty smile. I watch with mingled despair and interest; better men have fallen victim to her charms. Poppy collects guys with the same single-mindedness with which big-game hunters pursue tigers. But Jay, I notice with a sense of relief, seems oblivious to her magic and just smiles before turning back to me.

'You're looking well, Ellie,' he says kindly. 'Sam tells me that you used to share a house with her? I'm amazed you've survived! Last time I stayed with Sam, she was going through her mushroom phase. Mushroom omelette, mushroom risotto, mushroom soup, you name it, we ate it. I nearly died when I realised she was growing all the bloody mushrooms in human waste!'

I remember this episode well and shudder. Heaven knows I'm all for recycling, but the thought of eating anything grown in what Sam and Mud are only too delighted to recycle . . . well, let's just say that I have my limits.

'We're just about to close, actually,' Poppy tells Jay as she darts around the shop, blowing out candles and turning off lava lamps. 'You're lucky to catch us.'

'I'd hoped to catch Sam.' Jay yawns widely, revealing rows of neat, dazzling white teeth. Hang on, they never used to be that perfect. What a cheat! He's only gone and got himself a set of American teeth. I instantly shut my own mouth. I'm no Austin Powers when it comes to my gnashers, but I can't possibly compete with such perfection.

Jay passes a hand across a chin dusted with dark stubble, yawns again and smiles apologetically. 'Sorry, guys, I don't mean to be rude, but I'm shattered. I've flown straight from Boston, no sleep, no wash, nothing. I know it's a cheek, but would one of you give me a lift to Sam's place? I seem to remember it's a bit of a hike from the station.'

I stand in awe of anyone who can endure a long-haul flight, no sleep and still look this good without even the help of make-up. He could've stepped straight from a Calvin Klein ad. The past twelve years have, if anything, improved Jay. How am I going to be able to bear sharing a house with him? Maybe it's time to start looking for alternative accommodation. I could always take Mum and Dad up on that flat . . .

'I don't drive,' Poppy is telling Jay proudly. 'My feet and public transport are good enough for me. I don't want to kill Mother Earth.'

This is ironic in the supreme. I've spent hours chauffeuring Poppy about the Home Counties. The truth is she's never actually learned to drive. Why bother when there are enough other suckers to give her a lift?

'Ellie will drive you to Sam's,' continues Poppy airily,

happy to send me on my way in my vile pollution machine. 'You're going that way anyhow, aren't you, El?'

I'm already convinced that today's not a good day for Esther and me. The mere thought of attempting to drive home with Jay's denim-clad bum perched on the various piles of sweet wrappers and magazines is enough to make me sweat. My powers of concentration aren't good at the best of times. I'll probably kill us both.

Jay, blissfully oblivious to the danger he's in, swings his rucksack on to his shoulders and picks up two huge suitcases as easily as if they were filled with feathers. It's impossible not to notice the way his biceps swell under the T-shirt.

The sooner I get home and under a cold shower, the better.

Esther's a tip, more like the inside of a dustbin than a car. Leaning forwards, I sweep coverless magazines and sandwich wrappers off the passenger seat and into the footwell.

'So, what's going on with you these days?' Jay asks innocently as we pootle down the high street. I know he's making conversation, but what an opener. How exactly I reply to this is a challenge. *Well, Jay, I created carnage at Taply's Wedding of the Year on Saturday?*

'This and that,' I say airily, crunching the gears as we follow the road around the market square. 'Nothing very exciting.'

'That's not what Sam said,' Jay grins. 'Dumping men in the national press doesn't sound like nothing to me.'

Bloody Sam!

'You always were one for drama!' he chortles.

I shoot him a black look, but unfortunately for me, his arms are stretched above his head, and the T-shirt lifts to reveal the beginnings of what looks suspiciously like a six-pack stomach, and whorls of curling dark hair that lead to . . .

Good God! I need to calm down. Keep your eyes on the traffic, woman! Watch out for those Japanese tourists taking pictures of Taply Bridge and don't forget that your own stomach resembles uncooked dough.

I fix my gaze on the road. There's no way I'm going to discuss Rupert, the latest in a long line of my dating disasters, with Jay, my biggest dating disaster of all time.

I'm just on the brink of coming out with a witty and sophisticated reply when a gentle rumble interrupts me. Glancing across, I realise that Jay has fallen asleep, his chin resting on his chest and his eyes tightly shut.

I park my car and kill the engine. My hands tingle from gripping the steering wheel so tightly. That ten-minute journey has to be the most stressful of my life. How on earth could anyone have slept through it? The bit where the old granny launched herself on to the zebra crossing and nearly sat on Esther's bonnet will surely be responsible for my first grey hair.

But against all the odds, Jay really is sound asleep. Very carefully and very quietly, I turn my head like a bird-watcher who's just sighted the lesser-spotted hunk variety. I'll just have a peek at him. What harm could a little nostalgia trip do?

Now, I'm a girl who knows her men. I've drooled over George Clooney, once grabbed a Jack Sparrow lookalike at Disneyland (the less said about that the better) and even screamed at the Chippendales on Annabelle's hen night, but hand on heart, Jay beats the lot. With that thick, inky hair, square jaw, laughing green eyes, and a body to die for, he really has got it all. At least I had good taste when I was fifteen. Much better to still admire Jay rather than learn that the god of my adolescent fantasy is actually a rather nerdy type who wears polyester. Respect to my fifteen-year-old self!

'Sorry, I must have nodded off.' Jay smiles up at me from beneath half-opened eyelids, and I look away guiltily.

'We're here,' I say quickly, fiddling with my seat belt to cover my embarrassment at being caught gawping. 'I've got lots to do and I'm sure you're dying to see Sam.'

'OK.' Jay grins at me, but I'm having none of his green-eyed charm. Henceforth he will have as much effect on me as Peter Stringfellow would naked.

Leaving him to hump his suitcases up the garden path, I race into the house, push open the kitchen door and nearly die of fright.

'Oh my God!' I scream, dropping my car keys and bag in terror.

In the corner of the kitchen stands a headless man, and I'm transfixed with terror.

'Mmmph arright ssme,' moans the apparition, clearly suffering some fiendish torment. Then a head appears. 'It's all right, it's only me, man,' the creature repeats, and through a dense tangle of dreadlocks I recognise the beaky face and stoned eyes of Sam's boyfriend, Mud.

I should have identified him from his stale smell and the pungent odour of cannabis in the kitchen.

'Sam knitted me this jumper from recycled wool,' Mud explains helpfully, 'but the head hole is too tight. It's taken me fifteen minutes to get into it, man. Does it suit me?'

'You looked better before,' I reply sourly.

Mud squints at me suspiciously. He can't quite work me out.

'Chill out,' he says.

Ignoring him, I open the fridge and pull out what remains of my Dairy Milk, about two squares with what look suspiciously like teeth marks in them. I'm possessed by a murderous impulse towards whoever has dared attack it. God help Mud if it's him. Bad enough having him entrenched in the house, but eating my chocolate is punishable only by death.

'Hiya, Ellie. Thanks for giving Jay a lift.' Plaits flying, Sam bursts into the kitchen and launches herself into Mud's arms. A very scruffy greyhound follows her, trailing a piece of string and pausing now and again to scratch itself. I back away hastily, my appetite vanishing. I wouldn't put it past them to have fed my chocolate to the dog.

'My pleasure,' I say darkly, but Sam's too busy snogging Mud to notice. Such a hygiene risk is hideous to contemplate, so I retreat back into the hallway and head for my bedroom. The narrow hallway is always crammed with Mud's camping gear and festering boots, and now Jay's suitcases have joined the scrum. Even Victoria Beckham would need to lose weight in order to squeeze through.

It doesn't help either that Jay's blocking the way.

'Excuse me,' I mutter.

'There's nowhere for me to go,' points out Jay reasonably. 'I've been here for five minutes trying to figure out what to move first. It's like playing chess! How about I breathe in so that you can get past?'

Breathe in? Is he saying I'm fat? I suck in my stomach, but squeezing past without brushing against his honed torso is easier said than done.

'Last time I came home to visit, you weren't around much,' Jay says conversationally. His arms are either side of me, braced against the wall as he tries not to lose his balance while edging past Mud's bike.

'I'm a busy woman,' I fib. Actually there are more holes in my diary than in a Swiss cheese. The truth is that I spent Jay's last visit hiding at my sister Charlotte's, and since her evil twins make hanging out with Chucky look like a safer alternative, you've got a good idea just how much I wanted to avoid him.

'I'm sure you are.' Jay nods. 'You were even too busy to come out for dinner with us all the night I left, which was a real shame. Sam says your social life is one big whirl.'

Since the only whirling I do is watching my washing go round in the machine, I send a silent thank-you in the direction of the kitchen. Sometimes it seems that water is thicker than blood after all.

'That's me,' I agree.

'So how about grabbing some dinner tonight?' Jay suggests. 'I don't know about you, but I think Sam's chickpea and carrot curry is best left for her and Mud to excavate.'

He's right. Sam's curries glow brighter than Rudolph's nose. It doesn't bear thinking about what they do to your insides. And as for the fallout the day after . . .

For a moment I teeter on the brink. Jay is undoubtedly attractive. He used to have a good job before he dropped out; my mother approves of his family connections . . .

Could project *find a suitable man* be ready for lift-off?

For a moment I'm seriously tempted.

'We could go to Taply Manor.' Jay raises an eyebrow and shoots me that sexy lopsided grin. 'And I promise I'll turn up this time!' he adds.

My face starts to burn at the memory. 'Thanks for bringing that up again.'

'Hey, I'm trying to make it up to you. I'm only teasing.'

There's a massive lump in my throat. Why do I still feel so humiliated all these years on? Squashed here in the hall, I feel fifteen again, and ringing in my ears is the mocking laughter of everybody at the prom.

'What can I say? I was just a kid.' Jay's digging himself deeper with every word. 'I meant it about having a meal. It'll be great to catch up.'

'I'm not hungry,' I say, and my stomach chooses that very second to do a Vesuvius of a rumble.

'Obviously not,' he observes. 'Look, El, that was all years ago. I know I was an idiot, and believe me, I'm not proud of what I did back then, but I was just a stupid teenager. Come on, let's bury the hatchet. It's going to be hell sharing a house for the next few months otherwise.'

Months? Who said anything about months?

'I'm going to pay my way, I promise,' continues Jay. 'And I'll sleep on the sofa bed. I had no idea you hadn't moved out, and of course you can keep your room.'

I feel a twinge of guilt. If I'd told Sam the truth about my feelings for Rupert, then I wouldn't be in this situation. Still, I'm not quite ready to forgive Jay for reminding me about the humiliating prom incident. It might well be years ago as far as he's concerned, but I'm just as mortified as though it were yesterday. Well, I'm going to at least *sound* mature about this, even if I still feel fifteen inside.

'Look, Jay, it's been a long day. My mum's poorly and I'm still trying to recover from Annabelle's wedding. I'm not really in the mood to be sociable, so don't take it personally. If you'd just let me get by?' I'm still trapped between his arms and squashed up against his chest.

In spite of all my best intentions, my nipples harden. Traitors!

Jay's brow crinkles into a frown and I can't help thinking that he even looks cute with wrinkles.

'I don't know what I can do or say to make up for what I did back then. It was stupid, cruel even, but you know what teenage boys are like. They'll do anything not to lose face in front of their mates. I'm not proud of myself for being such a dick, but I was only eighteen.'

'Forget it,' I say wearily. 'Like you said, it was years ago. Now, if I could just get past?'

Jay's arms drop from the wall but his eyes are on my boobs. I wish I hadn't worn my white T- shirt. He raises his eyes to mine and then lowers them.

'Fine.' He shrugs. 'I tried.'

Jay retreats into the sitting room, and I'm just on the brink of fleeing to my bedroom when Sam hollers from the kitchen that there are two answerphone messages for me.

'One's from your sister Lucy,' she adds. 'It sounds like she wants you to call her back asap!'

With a groan I return to the kitchen, arming myself with a large mug of Pinot Grigio and a handful of Hob-Nobs. When my sister Lucy calls, it's because she wants something. Usually a free babysitter. She was just the same when we were kids; only then I was cleaning out her rabbits in return for being allowed to borrow her GHDs. The bunnies ponged a bit, but scrubbing their hutch was a better option than paying the exorbitant rent Emily would have charged for using her straighteners.

'You have two messages,' drones the answerphone in its usual bored manner, while I chomp contentedly on a biscuit and promise I'll go to aerobics tomorrow. 'Hello, Ellie? It's Lucy. Just checking that you're still available to babysit tonight? Well, you'd better be, it's Consuela's night off and Henry is taking me to a very expensive restaurant and I'm not missing it. Seven o'clock sharp, please, and remember to take your shoes off when you come in; it took us weeks to get the dirt off the carpet last time.' Lucy pauses and adds as an afterthought, 'Oh, hope you're all right after Saturday. You certainly caused a scene. See you at seven.'

This is all I need, a night with beastly Imogen and equally vile George, wiping noses and worse parts of their anatomy. I cheer myself up by thinking about raiding their Waitrose-stocked fridge and trying out Lucy's impressive range of beauty products.

And it's a night away from Jay.

'Message received at four thirty-seven p.m.,' continues the answerphone while I fetch the entire packet of Hob-Nobs.

'Hello, Ellie Andrews?' I pause mid-munch, biscuit frozen between mouth and hand. The recorded voice is loaded with so much testosterone I feel weak just listening to it. 'I'm Marcus Lacey. You hit my car this afternoon in Taply, I believe? We need to talk at some stage to finalise the claim. You can contact me on my mobile . . .'

I daren't believe it! This is my mother's dream son-in-law; well-spoken, with a public-school name and a nice car. A bit unfortunate I've just wrecked it, but at least he didn't sound too angry. He obviously appreciates just how honest I've been. I'll call him later from Lucy's. A few glasses of her expensive wine and I'll brim with the confidence to deal with him; I'll assume my sister's poise and self-assurance through osmosis.

Or I'll get pissed.

'Does my bum look big in this?' I ask, craning my neck to get a clearer view in Lucy's antique mirror. Trying to look for cellulite or fat gets me into positions that my ex-boyfriends have taken years to persuade me to sample. I pass my hands over the soft leather of Lucy's Versace jeans and suck in my stomach, thinking how bloody unfair it is that Lucy has given birth twice but still remains a neat size ten. People who are married and settled shouldn't be allowed to be thinner than their very single and plumper sisters.

Imogen regards me from a nest of cushions on Lucy's vast four-poster.

'Well?' I repeat. 'Does my bum look big?'

My niece sucks a chocolate lolly thoughtfully, her mouth a small red circle in a sticky brown face. 'No.'

What a loyal child! All the years of babysitting have finally paid off.

'It looks *huge*, Auntie Ellie, it looks all big and squishy like a nellyphant's bum!'

Imogen bursts into squeaks of laughter and buries her face in the pillows. I'm not sure what horrifies me the most: being compared to an elephant by a four-year-old or the thought of trying to explain to Lucy why there are smears of chocolate all over her white bedspread. Imogen ought to have been in bed hours ago, and God only knows where her brother's gone. He's probably out mugging old ladies.

One hour later I collapse on to a sofa with the remote control to the mega plasma screen in one hand and a large glass of Chianti in the other. Next to me is an Everest-sized pile of glossy magazines, the type that I'd need a part-time job in order to afford. I flick through them, which depresses me further when I see Annabelle in *OK!* smiling next to Laura Bailey at some glam party as usual. I help myself to a slice of gateau from the fridge to cheer me up, but unusually, even this doesn't work, even though I am the girl who once ate an entire frozen Sara Lee cake just because Jay laughed at her braces. For a moment I fantasise about grinding the gateau into his face, but when this thought is rapidly followed by my imagining licking the sticky cake off his gorgeous body, I have to bring myself up short.

To take my mind off these disturbing images, I decide to call Marcus Lacey. I pick up the phone from the coffee table and, reading the back of my hand, punch in the number.

'Marcus Lacey.'

I didn't imagine it. How can anyone have a voice so sexy? Thank the Lord he's on the other end of a telephone. My hormones are clearly throwing a hissy fit today.

'Hello. This is Ellie Andrews. I'm afraid I hit your car today in Taply.'

'Hit it?' Marcus Lacey sounds amused. 'It looks as though you were auditioning for *Scrap Heap Challenge*.'

'I'm so sorry,' I say. 'I'm perfectly prepared to pay for the damage.'

Marcus Lacey laughs. 'Have you any idea how much that will cost, Miss Andrews? I think it would be better all round if we went through our insurance companies.' He lowers his voice. 'The BMW is actually a company car. I'm pretty certain I can claim on its insurance and save you the trouble. I just wanted you to know I appreciated your honesty. Most people would have hit and run. I guess we ought to meet to sort out details.' I hear the flipping of pages as he trawls through his diary. 'When would you be free?

'Any time!' I squeak, and could instantly have ripped my tongue out. Now he'll think I'm a social misfit with no friends and nothing written down in *my* diary. 'Any time this week,' I correct hastily, flipping noisily through *Marie Claire* for good effect.

'How about lunch, tomorrow?'

I wait, wanting to give the impression that I have to think about fitting him into my hectic social life. 'That seems to be free,' I concede eventually.

'I'll pick you up from your address at midday. We'll lunch at Cliveden, if that suits you?'

Did it ever! I can hardly contain my excitement. He's only just offered to feed me at one of the most exclusive hotels in the country.

'That sounds lovely,' I tell him graciously. 'I'll see you tomorrow.'

I press the red button, count to five and then shriek with excitement. If I were Imogen I'd wet myself, but being twenty-something I do the adult equivalent and pour another glass of wine.

Blind Date

'Are you mad?' Sam asks when I tell her about meeting the mysterious Marcus Lacey. 'You don't even know the guy!'

I shrug. 'Plenty of people go internet dating. What's the difference?'

'If you wanted dates you should've just said. Me and Mud have got loads of friends who'd love to date you.'

Since most of Sam and Mud's friends have multiple piercings and an aversion to washing, I feel I can be forgiven for not jumping at this offer.

'You're the one who said I need to get back out there after the whole Rupert debacle,' I remind her. 'Besides, how can I give my mum the wedding she's longing for if the only man I hang out with is Mr Kipling?'

While Sam works out her next argument for my calling off the date, I turn my attention back to the huge pile of clothes covering my bed. There are tight designer numbers stolen from Lucy, a few of my own more generously sized outfits, a DKNY dress I borrowed from my sister Emily and never returned, and even some of Sam's tie-dyed skirts. In a fit of desperation I've raided every wardrobe I can find. I *have* to look the part for meeting Marcus. The success of today's lunch and my mother's happiness might rest upon what I choose to wear. But after trying on nearly twenty outfits, I'm in despair.

I've managed to squeeze myself into Lucy's green Prada shift dress, and as I twirl in front of the mirror, I marvel at what Spanx and Wonderbras can do for a girl's figure. OK, so I feel like I'm being sawn in half, and my cleavage is more *Sunday Sport* than *Tatler*, but the satisfaction of actually fitting into something of Lucy's is enormous. I suck in my stomach hard and crick my neck to scrutinise my backside. Imogen's remark is still a bruised spot on my ego.

'Does my bum look big in this?'

Sam's mouth is pursed up like a cat's bottom.

'Earth to Planet Ellie! Are you receiving? You don't even know this person, yet you're prepared to meet him alone? You can't possibly go through with it.'

'It's no worse than going on a blind date,' I protest, smoothing the green linen over my bottom and wondering whether I have a severe case of VPL or not. 'Besides, you were pretty keen to set me up on a few blind dates yourself before Rupert. What's the difference?'

Sam has the grace to look a bit ashamed. Like most coupled-up people, she has the zeal of a religious fanatic when it comes to trying to set up her friends. I'd finally had to resort to going to B&Q, buying a shelf and pointedly sitting on it in the lounge until she got the hint and left me alone.

'I'm only taking your advice,' I say sanctimoniously. 'Giving the universe a chance to deliver, like in that stuff you read me from *The Secret*.'

'You thought all that was bollocks! You don't fool me. You're only going because it's Cliveden.'

'At least I'll be murdered on a full stomach and in complete and utter luxury,' I point out. 'Stop worrying.

You can write down his registration number and I'll call you on my mobile the minute we arrive. I'll be fine.'

'You can't go. You've got a shift in Blue Moon this afternoon, remember?' says Sam, playing her trump card.

'Blue Moon or expensive lunch?' I use my hands to imitate scales. 'Oh! The expensive lunch wins! Besides, you owe me one for springing you know bloody who on me.'

'Who? Mud? Or Jay?'

'Exactly!' Triumphant, I move in for the kill. 'Count yourself lucky I'm not demanding paid leave.'

'Don't push it,' Sam warns, throwing herself on to my bed and resting her chin in her hands. I haven't seen her this narked since I broke my vegetarian phase by eating what I mistakenly thought to be a top-secret bacon sandwich ('Pigs *died* to make that bacon, Ellie.')

'Come on,' I say. 'Just one little afternoon off? And I'll never, ever moan again about Mud leaving the loo seat up?'

'That sounds like a deal, although Mud only uses the composting toilet in the garden shed now,' she reminds me. 'I guess Poppy won't mind the extra money. Just remember, Ellie, there's no such thing as a free lunch. What does he want in return?'

'Sex, hopefully!' I decide to stick with the green dress.

Sam sighs gustily. 'I think you're nuts,' she says as we crash down the stairs and into the kitchen. 'You don't need to go on blind dates. You had Rupert, he was absolutely loaded and nice. If I wasn't taken, I'd quite fancy him myself.'

Glancing in at the pit that doubles as our lounge, I spot Mud with his army boots up on the coffee table surrounded by the debris of a strenuous few hours in front of *This Morning*. Even buried beneath empty cans of Fosters and a pizza box he's still remarkably unattractive; with his nose and eyes peeping through his dreadlocks, he's a dead ringer for Dougal. In fact, he looks as though he's just stepped off the Magic Roundabout and is having a particularly confusing trip. No wonder Sam fancies Rupert. Shuddering, I follow her into the kitchen.

'Anyway,' Sam continues thoughtfully, as she fishes a grubby mug from beneath our mountain of washing-up, 'it's not as if you need to panic. You're the last of the Amazing Andrews sisters. I bet there are loads of chinless wonders just longing for an introduction.'

'But that's the worst of it!' I wail. 'The others are so gorgeous that any poor sod who gets landed with me at family parties always looks as if he's dropped a pound and picked up a penny!

But Sam isn't listening any more; she's too busy inspecting the coat of the scruffy greyhound that Mud found wandering the streets of Manchester when he was on yet another eco protest. Now I love dogs, but this has to be the only one I've ever met with absolutely no redeeming features whatsoever. It scrounges, it steals and it farts constantly.

'I think Serendipity's got fleas,' Sam observes, crunching something between her fingernails.

'Serendipity?'

The dog looks at me in a resigned way.

'Doesn't it suit the darling?' Sam kisses it on the nose and the dog looks even more fed up, probably wishing it had been left to roam the streets of Manchester in dignified peace.

'What are you doing, Sam?' Jay bursts into the kitchen, his arms full of Marks & Spencer carrier bags. 'Given up hoping Mud will turn into a prince? And isn't a frog the usual creature of choice?'

Just as Sam opens her mouth to reply, a big black Jag pulls up outside and hoots throatily.

'That's Marcus!' I shriek at Sam. 'Are you sure my bum's all right?'

She gives me a swift hug. 'You look lovely. Doesn't she, Jay?'

From the doorway Jay smiles at me, a slow, appreciative smile, which would have made me blush if he hadn't been my housemate and I didn't fancy him at all.

'She looks great,' he replies, looking straight at me. 'You're not going out, are you, Ellie? I was planning to make us all lunch.'

Normally nothing short of death would part me from anything that might have originated from the Marks & Spencer food hall, but not today.

'Ellie's going on a blind date,' explains Sam, filling him in on the details as I tear around like the Tasmanian Devil in a frantic hunt for my bag. The car hoots once more and I dash for the hall but in my haste cannon into Jay, sending the shopping and myself flying.

'Sorry!' I gasp, retrieving a wedge of Brie.

Jay puts his hands on my shoulders. He's so close I can smell the sharp, spicy scent of Aramis. In his thickly lashed eyes I glimpse a mini reflection of myself, revealing far too much untoned leg.

'Els, tell me you're not going to get into a car with a complete stranger?'

Great. He's only been here five minutes and he's trying to lay down the law.

'Of course I'm going,' I say with dignity, or at least as much dignity as a girl crouched on the lino showing half her knickers can. 'I'm looking forward to it.'

71

Jay shakes his head. 'That really doesn't sound safe to me, especially if you've never met this guy.'

The Jag hoots again.

'Maybe one of us should come with you,' he suggests, looking worried.

Horror at the very thought must show on my face.

'Not on the actual date,' Jay says hastily. 'I could sit in the bar or something? Just to be on the safe side? I don't think it's a good idea to go alone.'

'I'll be fine,' I tell him. 'Sam has my mobile and she'll jot down Marcus's registration number. Besides, I'm going to Cliveden in broad daylight. I think I'll be pretty safe.'

He shrugs. 'Well, if you're sure. I still don't think it's a very bright idea, but then what do I know about dating?'

And with this enigmatic parting comment he wanders back into the hall to collect the rest of his shopping.

'What's that supposed to mean?' I ask Sam. 'Is it some sarky reference to the school prom?'

She pulls a face. 'Will you stop being so bloody paranoid? Not everything is about you, Ellie! He's just sore because his girlfriend's dumped him. You go and have fun and leave me to deal with him. And don't forget to text, OK?'

I nod and scoop up my bag. Then Sam opens the door and suddenly I'm in the open air with the warm sun on my face and the roar of the main road in my ears. Breathing deeply and sucking in my stomach, I pull the handle of the passenger door and swing myself carefully into the beautiful car.

'Hello, Ellie.' The driver turns to face me, holding out a beautifully manicured hand. For a moment I'm mesmerised by the perfect half-moons and smooth skin. My nails resemble a schoolgirl's, with their chewed skin and bright polish. Perhaps painting them lime green to match my dress was a mistake? Too late to worry now, though, seeing as we're shaking hands.

'I'm Marcus,' he says.

I'd like to reply with something witty and amusing, but instead I'm doing my stupid cod impression, because Marcus Lacey is absolutely gorgeous. I've never seen anything like him in real life, only in magazines or on the big screen where I can scoff popcorn to my heart's content and promise myself I'll diet tomorrow. He has cropped dark hair, cheekbones my sisters could ski off, skin as rich and smooth as toffee, and when he removes his Ray-Bans, thickly lashed slate-grey eyes twinkle at me.

Oh my flipping goodness. Somebody's put Johnny Depp in a suit and given him a Jag! I really should crash my car more often if this is the end result.

'I'm glad that you could make it,' Marcus says. 'I wasn't sure whether you would.'

'I don't normally jump into cars with total strangers,' I reply, once my vocal cords have recovered sufficiently to work. 'And my best friend did try to talk me out of it.'

One neat eyebrow is raised in a way I've only seen Mr Spock or Roger Moore do before. Impressed, I make a mental note to practise it myself.

'But it's not as if I'm a total stranger, is it?' Marcus says with a grin.

He does look very familiar, and I trawl the murky depths of my brain in a frantic attempt to place him. Perhaps he's a friend of Rupert's, or maybe I've seen him in *Tatler*, the last time my mother pointed out suitable young men? Try as I might, though, I just can't figure out where I've seen him before.

While Marcus replaces his shades, I settle back into

the cream leather seat and hope desperately that my legs don't make fart noises. Looking at the contrast between the leather and my thighs makes me exceedingly glad I stole Lucy's Fake Bake. I had no choice but to turn to crime, because the only way to achieve toned-looking legs in less than a week without being humiliated in the gym is to get a tan. I sneak a peek at my palms. Not too orange, I'm glad to see, apart from the telltale tidemarks around the wrists. Hastily I tuck my hands under my bag.

'I expect you're finding this all rather odd,' Marcus says conversationally as he swings his car on to the Maidenhead Road. 'You crash into my car and I invite you out for lunch.'

'I didn't crash,' I point out quickly. 'I scraped it. I expect I need driving glasses.'

Marcus laughs, a low, husky roar that makes me shiver. I can't help noticing the clean line of his throat as he tips his head back. There's none of that dark stubble that Jay has. Not that I'm thinking about Jay, of course.

'Sorry. I meant to say you *accidentally* scrape my car and I invite you out for lunch. It doesn't exactly make sense.'

He changes gear and I try to pull my eyes away from his wrists, tanned and strong beneath Persil-white cuffs. Get a grip, Ellie. You're sounding like a second-rate bodice-ripper!

'I'm afraid I have a confession to make,' he continues, not sounding the slightest bit abashed, and flinging me a smouldering glance, which makes my heart thud in my ears.

'Really? What's that, then?' Nerves make me sound like a strangled chicken. Against the leather seat my legs begin to sweat.

'I knew exactly who you were,' Marcus tells me with a

perfect smile. 'I met you last year at the Henley Regatta. You were with the Moore-Critchen party, weren't you?'

I rack my brains but, not surprisingly, recall very little. To be honest, all I can remember of that day is cramming myself into a dress of Annabelle's and feeling a total prat in a little straw boater that made me look like a truant from St Trinian's. I vaguely remember hiding from Rupert in the refreshment tent, guzzling vodka and champagne for several hours and dancing enthusiastically to a string quartet. Then I passed out face first into a rowing boat.

Oh crap. I really hope I didn't meet Marcus that night.

'You don't remember? I'm not surprised.' He sounds amused and I feel very hot under the collar, or in this case Wonderbra. He *did* see me then. I look out of the car window and wonder what sort of damage I'll incur if I jump out. Such behaviour never seemed to do the Dukes of Hazzard any harm, and Daisy was far skinnier than me. I'm bound to bounce.

'I've seen you even more recently, though,' continues Marcus. 'Why don't you open the glove box? There's a clue in there.'

'The glove box?' I swallow nervously. I've seen this film. There'll be a severed head inside and then he'll drive me to his secret lair where he'll chop me up and make a coat out of my fake-baked skin.

'Don't look so worried! Here, let me.' Keeping one hand on the wheel, he leans across me to open it up. The side of his arm brushes against my breast and I feel a stab of good old-fashioned lust. What a relief! It isn't a renewed crush on Jay that's turning me into a quivering jelly; I'm just suffering from an extreme lack of sex. Things weren't particularly active with Rupert in that department.

'Do these jog your memory?' Marcus drops two objects

into my lap and I can practically hear his grin as I stare down in disbelief.

On my lap sit my bridesmaid's slippers. Thankfully for Lucy's dress, some kind soul has cleaned them up since Saturday. These are the very same shoes last seen sailing through the air into the lap of a very surprised and very sexy stranger.

Bollocks.

'I'm sorry!' Marcus is wiping his eyes behind his shades and not looking in the least contrite. 'That wasn't fair, but I just couldn't resist.'

'I suppose I deserve it,' I admit. 'Although I was rather hoping that peach taffeta and a headdress was some kind of disguise.'

'No chance. But anyway, let me spoil you with lunch to make up for such a rotten trick.'

As we drive the fifteen miles to Cliveden, it becomes clear that Marcus Lacey is far from the axe-wielding psychopath Sam anticipated. By the time we arrive at the beautiful gates of the mansion, we're chatting away like old friends. Before long, I feel at ease enough to stop holding in my stomach and to laugh at the dreaded shoe episode. Of course Marcus's Johnny Depp looks also help to relax me, and I can't help but notice that when his leg moves from the accelerator to the brake, his thigh muscles are taut against his cream linen trousers.

OK, I admit it. All in all it takes about five seconds for me to fall head over heels in lust with him.

I'm also a hopeless romantic, with the emphasis firmly on the *hopeless* part, and as the car sweeps up the long gravel drive, past obese purple rhododendrons and secret-looking temples, to the elegant stately home, I'm lost. It's like a fairy tale, and sitting in the lovely car in my (borrowed) designer frock, I feel like a princess. This isn't the usual activity of Ellie *nothing like her sisters* Andrews. Looking like film stars enables the others to demand film-star treatment and The Ivy. But me, well, I've always been happy to get a table at Pizza Hut.

The car pulls up outside the entrance of the hotel, and liveried footmen appear from nowhere to park for us, show us inside, take our coats and seat us. I almost expect to be taken to the toilet. Marcus tucks my hand into the crook of his cream linen arm and I cringe at the brightness of my lime-green nails. If he notices them, he is too polite to comment, steering me gently into the cool entrance hall and chatting away. I'm impressed by how reverently everyone treats him, the maître d' even calling him by name. I scrutinise him carefully as we're ushered into the sumptuous dining room but am still stumped. Poppy and I know every gorgeous male that Hollywood spits out but I'm pretty sure Marcus doesn't hail from Tinseltown. It's all very puzzling.

Once seated and looking at a menu, which may as well be in Chinese for all the sense that I can make of it, I sneak a look at my luxurious surroundings. It doesn't take a genius to work out that we're sitting at the most expensive table in the place, as it's situated just far enough away from the nosy onlookers who stroll across the terrace and try to peep in, but near enough to have a breathtaking view over the lawns down to the Thames. While I admire the view, Marcus pours two glasses of exquisite red wine; as he sits swirling his thoughtfully, I gulp mine. Looking up from my drink I meet Marcus's sea-grey eyes and blush furiously, because my fingers are stroking the delicate stem of my wine glass in a manner that would have given Freud a field day.

'Ellie?' Marcus sounds alarmed. 'You're spilling wine down your dress.'

'Oh no!' In horror I grab the nearest napkin and prepare for emergency surgery on my dress. Unfortunately I've snatched the tablecloth, and as I tug it I send the beautiful table arrangement flying. Flowers sail merrily past into the lap of a nearby diner, plates smash at a hundred decibels and the bottle of 1983 claret gives the unfortunate Marcus an impromptu shower. The silence in the restaurant is colder than Frosty the Snowman's gonads.

Luckily for me, the deep-seated reserve of the English saves the day. As Marcus and I sit dripping claret and flower water, the other diners continue to talk politely and chink their cutlery against their bone-china plates.

'Marcus, I'm so sorry,' I begin, but stop in mid-grovel because Marcus is doubled up in fits of laughter. Tears run down his face and he clutches his sides as if in agony.

'Ellie Andrews!' he gasps. 'What is it with you? Do you destroy absolutely everything that you come in contact with? Are you some sort of weapon of mass destruction?'

In spite of my mortification I start to laugh.

'I think we'd better freshen up,' Marcus says to the footman at his shoulder. 'We shouldn't be long.'

The footman nods to Marcus but gives me the sort of look you'd give a slug that's taken up residence in your Marks & Spencer's bagel. Trying to be as dignified as one whose boobs are covered in red wine can, I follow Marcus from the restaurant and into the cool of the hallway.

'Don't look so worried.' Marcus takes my hand and turns it over to trace my palm with his smooth forefinger. 'It's not the end of the world. We can freshen up.'

And then I'm back in the world of Mills & Boon, because he keeps hold of my hand and leads me up the sweeping staircase. I take the stairs two at a time partly to keep up with his long legs and partly because I've heard it's good for the bum.

Marcus pauses by an ornate door and gently pushes me into a room decorated in a manner that probably cost thousands of pounds to create and which screams luxury. Champagne cools in an ice bucket by the bed, flowers are strewn across the counterpane and filmy lace curtains flutter in the warm breeze.

'Wow,' I say. Some room. The likes of me would probably be more likely to clean it than use it in real life, but for a minute it's fun to pretend.

'Do you like it?' Marcus asks. 'I usually book it when I stay here because it's more private to dine up here. You understand how it can be for me.'

I still don't have a clue who he is. If I ask now, he'll think I'm an idiot, or even worse, he'll be really insulted. I'll just have to wing it.

'Make yourself at home.' He smiles. 'Lunch will soon be served.'

I kick off my shoes, pad across the thick carpet and lean on the broad window ledge. The view's absolutely stunning; from my vantage point I can see over the formal gardens where fountains sparkle and visitors stroll right down to the pewter ribbon of the Thames a sheer drop away beyond the topiary. This has to be one of the premier suites and must cost a fortune.

Just who *is* Marcus Lacey? Actor? Minor royal? This is going to drive me mad.

'I've another confession,' says Marcus as he uncorks the champagne. He pours a brimming glass and hands it to me. 'I saw you putting your little note under the wiper of my car. I'd only popped into the off-licence and I saw the whole thing happen.'

I feel my confidence pop away like champagne bubbles. So now he knows I wear platform heels as well as being crap at parallel parking.

'You were so sweet, Ellie. I knew then that I had to meet you properly. I've thought about nothing but you all week.'

Really? I gulp. 'Marcus, I don't know what to say, I—'

'Don't say anything.' Marcus is gazing into my eyes with the burning intensity of Edward Cullen faced with fresh blood. 'Just let me look at you. My God, you must be the most amazing girl I've ever met.'

Well, who could resist a line like that?

'May I kiss you?' Marcus asks softly, his slate-grey eyes burning down at me.

May he kiss me? Most of the blokes I've been with don't ask, they just lunge in for a sink-plunger kiss and then look pleased with themselves while I fight the urge to wipe my mouth.

'OK then,' I agree, not daring to move a muscle just in case a bit of my flab wobbles and turns him off. It's not easy trying to look sexy and suck in your stomach at the same time. 'If you like.'

'I do like,' Marcus says firmly. 'I like very much.' Then he kisses me, a soft kiss that makes my insides flip like Shrove Tuesday.

We kiss for what feels like ages. It's like being a teenager again, only way better, because this time a) I don't have braces and b) nobody tries to put their hand down my bra. Somehow Marcus scoops me up without a crane or putting his back out and carries me to the bed, and when his lips stray to my throat and neck I think I've died and gone to heaven. Or maybe that's just the *trompe l'oeil* cherubs on the ceiling confusing me.

He pushes my curls back from my face and smiles down at me. 'I must remember to take you out for lunch again.'

'You haven't taken me out for lunch yet,' I point out. 'We never got past the wine stage.' As if in agreement, my stomach rumbles.

Marcus checks his watch. 'My God, it's nearly three! I can't possibly stop for lunch now, I'm way off schedule.' He drops a kiss on the top of my head. 'We'll have to take a rain check, I'm afraid. I've got an important meeting in Westminster and I simply cannot miss it. I'll call you, OK?'

'OK,' I reply, thinking death by mobile it is then.

'You're fantastic,' Marcus whispers, flicking his tongue against mine just long enough to turn my legs to jelly and holding me tightly. 'I'll see you soon.'

'Really?' I can't quite believe it. I've doused him in red wine and made him miss his lunch, haven't shagged him and he still wants to see me again?

'Listen,' he says huskily, his fingers twining with mine, 'if I say I'll call you, then I will, OK? Don't believe everything you hear about me or read in the papers. It's mostly bullshit, I promise.'

I'm intrigued. Time, I think, to fess up that I haven't a clue who he is.

'Marcus, I—'

But he silences me with a kiss so toe-curlingly sexy I stop asking questions. To be honest, I nearly forget to breathe.

'I can't ignore the whip, Ellie Andrews, not even for you,' he tells me finally. 'The vote's at six, so I really do have to shoot.' Straightening his tie as he goes, Marcus pauses in the doorway. 'Charge a cab home on my account and feel free to order anything you want to eat. I'll call you.'

And then he's gone. Gone to vote for something, or someone. I'm not the most politically switched-on person, but even I know the next general election isn't due for at least a couple of years. And what's that about whipping?

This has to be one of the oddest dates of my life. I can't wait to tell Sam all about it. The adventures of today are certainly a lot more tasteful than the tale of how she got together with Mud in his sleeping bag at Glastonbury.

As I dial her mobile, I feel a little guilty because I promised to call the minute I arrived. Hopefully she'll understand why I was so distracted.

'At last,' says Sam after about half a ring. 'Don't say a word. He shagged you senseless, right?'

My mouth swings open. Is this really what my friend thinks of me?

'Right?' Sam persists.

'Wrong. We just snogged, actually. And he was lovely. You might sound a little bit excited for me.'

Sam says nothing, but her disapproval crackles down the phone like static.

'Why say a thing like that?' I add huffily. 'I've only just met the guy.'

'Because of who he is!' Sam pauses. 'You *do* know who he is, don't you?'

I remain silent, and Sam sighs.

'For pity's sake! Ellie, you're so politically unaware, you probably think Gordon Brown's a type of gin! Your Marcus Lacey is only the Tory MP for Taply-on-Thames!'

The penny drops. Of course! No wonder Marcus seems so familiar. During last month's by-election, his handsome face smiled down on me from posters the length and breadth of Taply. I'd have voted for him on looks alone if Sam hadn't gone off on a rant and forced me to vote for her friend who was the Green Party rep.

But hang on a minute. Doesn't Marcus Lacey have the kind of reputation that makes Casanova look like a monk?

'He's the MP with the worst reputation in Westminster!' Sam is shrieking. 'Wake up, you dozy cow! *Marcus Lacey!* He was caught with the Minister for Education's daughter! He makes Wayne Rooney look like a model partner!'

Sitting on the giant bed, I feel cold all over. No wonder he seemed so familiar. I've spent many a lazy Sunday reading about Marcus's sexual exploits. According to the gutter press, he has the master key to everyone's chastity belts, and has sown more wild oats than the Quaker porridge factory.

And these are the *nice* things people have said about him.

Flower Power

I feel like such a muppet you could paint me green and call me Kermit.

I leave the room pretty swiftly, after checking carefully that my lipstick isn't all over my face and my hair messed up. Obviously everyone at Cliveden thinks I've been up to no good, but I don't need to advertise the fact. Actually, I'm not sure if I'm relieved or annoyed that nothing actually happened. Is it a compliment or an insult to spend time alone with Marcus Lacey and not have my honour compromised? Maybe I'm not up to his usual standards? After all, he did once date Sienna Miller.

Collecting my bag from reception, I order a cab. As it crawls past The Bun in the Oven, I'm reminded of my mother's illness and her longing to have all her daughters settled, and feel another stab of guilt over failing to grant what, God forbid, might be her dying wish.

I must try harder. It's the story of my life.

When I walk into the hall, I'm struck by the silence of the house. The air is stale with cigarette smoke, and in the kitchen the sink and every other conceivable surface is piled with plates. Mud and Sam have probably gone to some save-the-world meeting and Jay will be working out his amazing body somewhere.

I make a coffee and plod into the hall. On the telephone

table the red eye of the answerphone winks suggestively. Answerphones and 1471 always crush the fragile little hope that you've missed his call. Thanks to modern technology, Millennium Woman is never left to wonder. She always knows for certain that he simply can't be bothered.

There's no way now I can just carry on upstairs and slob out in blissful ignorance. How can I concentrate on *The One Show* if I'm being tortured by not knowing whether Marcus has called? I need to know what he's playing at. Before I can stop myself, I'm pressing that evil little button.

'Hi, Ellie, it's Marcus. I must apologise for leaving you so abruptly this afternoon. It was unforgivably rude but I had to race away to the House because we're voting tonight. I won't bore you with the details, but even I can't argue with the PM. Anyway, listen, I'll be in touch, because it was amazing getting to know you. We'll have dinner soon, if you'd like to? Oh,' he added, almost as an afterthought. 'Look in your bag. I left something there for you.'

I'm stunned. Marcus Lacey has actually bothered to call, and only an hour or so after we've parted? In my shock I slop coffee all over myself, and the blistering heat brings me to my senses. I tip my bag upside down, scattering lipsticks and leaky biros all over the floor until I find a glossy postcard of Cliveden. He left me a postcard?

I flip it over, and there, scrawled in loopy black ink, is a message that makes my blood pressure skyrocket.

I think I'm falling in love.

For a second, I'm stunned. Then I have to find Sam's Rescue Remedy and glug most of it and apply some of the steady breathing techniques she's shown me until my pulse rate stops auditioning for *Casualty*.

Marcus Lacey thinks he's falling in love with me?

After one afternoon?

This is crazy! Flattering, but crazy. And am I falling in love with him?

Err, no, although if I try very hard I might be able to give it a whirl.

As I puzzle over the postcard and my rather muted reaction to it, and mop the green dress with the nearest item of fabric, which just happens to be the curtains, I notice a large van pull up outside. Dark green and with Harrods of Knightsbridge emblazoned across the flank, it's clearly nothing to do with us. Sam and Mud would deplore such blatant capitalism, I'm too stony broke to go to Primark, never mind Harrods, and Jay's more of a Marks & Sparks kind of guy. Feeling like the particularly nosy, net-curtain-twitching type of neighbour, I watch with interest as the driver gets out and opens up the van. What's going to come out? I wonder as I scrub at Lucy's frock. If anything the stain seems to be getting worse. When was the last time we bothered to wash the curtains?

Mid-scrub there's a sharp knock on the door. Harrods man, lost in the wilderness of Taply-on-Thames, is trying to deliver exquisite goodies to a house full of hippies and hangers-on, as Annabelle so nicely puts it. Grabbing a cushion to cover up my wet patch, I answer the door.

'You must have got the wrong address,' I tell the delivery man on my doorstep. Unfortunately, because his arms are full of the most exquisite flowers imaginable. Roses in delicate shades of pink, cream and peach, swathes of ivy and ferns and tumbling honeysuckle fill the doorway.

He consults the address card. 'Delivery for Ellie Andrews, 43 Shakespeare Avenue? This is definitely the place.'

I do a goldfish impression. For me?

'I'm Ellie Andrews,' I say excitedly. 'So I guess I'd better take them.'

There's no message attached to the flowers, only a simple card that reads: 'Sorry.' Still, it doesn't exactly require Einstein brains to work it out. Who's already apologised to me today? Who thinks he's falling in love with me? And who can conveniently pop into Harrods on his way to Westminster? This entire extravagant gesture has Marcus Lacey stamped all over it. What a shame the tabloids never let on that he's so sweet and generous. This has to be the most romantic gesture of my entire life!

I can't wait to tell Sam, or Jay for that matter. Yes, I think smugly as I head to the kitchen, there's certainly a big fat *I told you so* coming in his direction. But as usual when something exciting happens to me, there's absolutely nobody to tell. Even Serendipity has gone AWOL.

I root under the sink in a fruitless search for vases, finding instead crusty tins of shoe polish, a broken wok and three packets of chocolate HobNobs. At last! After many bored/frantic/desperate afternoons of searching, I've discovered where Sam stashes the chocolate she selfishly hides from me. Triumphantly stuffing a biccy into my mouth, I turn my attention to flower arranging.

Twenty minutes later, the kitchen contains enough botanical beauty to reduce Kew Gardens to shame. Leaning against the Welsh dresser, I survey my work with pride. Improvising with jugs, beer glasses, saucepans and even a pair of riding boots, I've managed to find a place for every beautiful bloom.

'Who robbed the florist's?' exclaims Poppy, waltzing in through the back door without so much as a knock. Helping herself to a biscuit from Sam's rapidly diminishing secret supply, she perches on the work top. 'Leftovers from the wedding?'

'They're mine, actually,' I say proudly. 'My lunch date sent them as a thank-you.'

'Well, I won't ask what he's thanking you for, but it must have been bloody good!' grins Poppy, waggling her eyebrows suggestively. 'Are my predictions coming true, then? Men everywhere and all that?'

'Not quite. And it was only lunch, so don't go spreading rumours or we'll have my mother over here clutching the Harvey Nicks wedding list and towing a vicar.'

Poppy shudders. 'I've never met anyone so obsessed with marriage. She ought to work for Relate.'

'She won't be happy until I've been frogmarched up the aisle,' I say, tweaking a sprig of ivy into place. 'If I got married it would make her feel better. And she's really worried about her next operation . . .' The sentence hangs unfinished between us.

'You can't get married just to make your mother happy,' Poppy says gently, her dark hair swinging forward as she touches my arm. 'You already know that, otherwise you'd have said yes to Rupert. Wasn't he Mr Suitable as far as your mum was concerned? Marriage has got to be taken more seriously than just a nice dress and a holiday in the Caribbean.'

'I know, I know, but I always feel like I'm letting her down.' I sigh. 'The others are so sorted. I spoil the set because I've chosen to do things my way. Sam once told me that stress can cause cancer, and that's all I am to Mum these days. Stress. What if it's my fault she's sick? What if worrying about me makes her worse?'

'That's bollocks,' snorts Poppy. 'You have not given your mum cancer! You need to listen to yourself sometimes. Cancer is a genetic mutation, not something the universe has delivered. Stop stressing about stuff you can't control, and have a drink.'

Comforted by her sound advice, I open a large bottle of plonk brought back from Cherbourg on a drunken booze cruise. It's extremely rough and normally reserved for cooking, but after several mugfuls we're used to the furry sensation on our teeth and I'm telling Poppy all about my most peculiar afternoon.

'Careful,' she warns. 'Remember, one of the men I saw really wasn't to be trusted.'

Maybe I'll just bide my time and see what happens. But how much time my mother has is a pretty uncertain thing, and if I'm going to make her happy, I can't afford to drag my heels.

Mud's arrival, some time later, is heralded by the noxious smell of Serendipity, who stands by the kitchen table looking longingly at the biscuits. The subsequent babble of the TV indicates that Mud has planted himself into the sofa for the night.

'What have you guys been up to?' Poppy asks Sam, who's in the doorway tugging off her boots. The boots are caked in clay and Sam's army surplus trousers are splattered with so much dirt that even the camouflage is camouflaged.

'Digging tunnels,' says Sam. 'I'm so tired, Ellie, I'm not even going to ask about your fantastic afternoon with Mr Marvellous. Nor am I going to have orgasms over the flowers. I'm not doing anything until I've had a slug of whisky. Besides, I find it ecologically deplorable to cut flowers just so that we can look at them.'

'Spoilsport,' I mutter. She deserves to have her Hob-Nobs nicked.

'I'll make you a cup of herbal tea,' says Poppy sooth-ingly, jingling across the kitchen, her long skirts swishing dangerously close to my makeshift vases. 'Just sit there and think calming thoughts. Do your yoga breathing.'

'I haven't even got the breath to hum.' Sam lays her head on the table and closes her eyes. 'We're eating dinner and then we're going straight back to the woods. There's not a lot of time left, so we need to make the most of every minute we've got before those bastards bring their diggers in. I can't imagine how they found out we were moving in this week. We've been really careful who we've spoken to.'

'I thought there was going to be a public meeting about all this?' I ask.

'There is, but Taply Construction have pre-empted us.' Sam starts to twist her plaits around her fingers, a well-established nervous habit and a good indicator of Sam stress. Things must be really bad. 'Mud's got a contact who works for the company, and the word is they're moving on to the site this week, which gives us hardly any time to finish the tunnels and get the tree networks up and run-ning. Somehow they got wind of our preparing the site. Thanks.' She accepts Poppy's tea gratefully. 'So it looks as if we'll have to move in soon in order to get there before they do. You guys will have to take care of Blue Moon and bring supplies up to the woods. I'm not sure when I'll be back. This could be a tough one, because that land's worth an absolute fortune and I don't see them giving up with-out a fight. If only we knew who was really behind that company, we might be able to find a way of stopping them.'

This is the point where I ought to have the courage of my convictions and join their protest. Sam once called me a champagne socialist, which I found most unkind. It isn't my fault that I need my home comforts, and can't bear heights, small enclosed spaces, or spiders and all the other creepy-crawlies that generally hang out with Sam and her crowd. That's just the way I am. Delivering supplies and running Blue Moon, though, I can handle.

'Leave the food to me. It's all in hand,' I assure her.

Sam doesn't look convinced. She hasn't quite forgiven me for the time I delivered food to her last protest. To be fair, the construction workers did look really hungry and the foreman was absolutely gorgeous. What else could a girl do but give him a sandwich?

'I promise to get it right this time,' I say.

Sam gives me a look that says I'd better not stuff up again or I'll find myself homeless. Then the doorbell shrills and she groans. 'That'll be Jay. He's lost his key again.'

'Why can't he climb over the wall and use the back door like the rest of us?' I grumble as I sweep biscuit crumbs from my chest and chin and go to open the door.

'Thanks, Ellie,' says Jay, his tall frame filling the hall. 'Glad to see you're back in one piece. I take it the date was a success?'

I beam at him. 'It was great!'

'Good,' Jay says, but he doesn't look desperately pleased. Did he want me to come home in a body bag just so that he could say 'I told you so'?

'I'm not stupid,' I say, and then, because I fancy making a point, 'I'm a lot more choosy who I go on dates with these days.'

'You're never going to forgive me, are you?' he asks quietly. 'Well, it's none of my business what you do.'

'No, it isn't.' I mean to sound angry but somehow I can't quite manage it, not when those green eyes are looking so sad, and that curling dark hair is all wet and shiny from the shower where . . .

I give myself a mental shake. What's wrong with me today? Am I turning into some kind of nympho?

'It's just I can't bear to see you making yourself vulnerable,' Jay is saying, his voice low and husky. 'I didn't want him . . . I didn't want him to hurt you, Ellie. You're far too lovely to be used.'

I gulp.

'Ellie,' Jay whispers, and his hand is cupping my cheek. His face is so close to mine our eyelashes are practically touching. Then the room starts to dip and roll. The cooking wine must be stronger than I thought, because for a split second I think he's going to kiss me.

'Hiya, Jay!' The cheerful voice of Poppy interrupts this odd moment as she waltzes into the hall. 'What do you think of all the flowers Marcus sent Ellie? He must really like her!'

Abruptly Jay's head snaps back into its usual position and away from mine. The speed of this movement sends me zooming back to reality and I open my eyes just in time to catch a split second of hurt register across his face before the indifference returns.

'I hate to tarnish Mr Lacey's already grubby reputation,' he says, 'but those flowers aren't from him – they're from me. I wanted to apologise.'

I don't know what to say. *Now* he wants to apologise?

Jay smiles ruefully. 'Judging by the look on your face, I'm too late, aren't I?'

I nod sadly.

Twelve years and one amazing afternoon in Cliveden too late.

OK. Don't panic. Everything's going to be just fine. Just because Poppy's not answering her phone and the make-up girl's sat nav has taken her fifty miles out of her way does *not* mean this marriage is doomed. They are *not* signs that you're about to make the biggest mistake of your life. You've spent too long working in a New Age shop, that's all.

All I have to do is lie back in this bubble bath and relax.

But although I've tipped in a gallon of relaxing aroma-therapy oils, lit a joss stick and whacked some angel music on, I'm so wound up I'll start chiming in a minute. Putting all this effort into reaching a state of blessed-out nirvana seems to defeat the object a bit. I'm so busy concentrating on not being stressed that I'm feeling worse by the minute.

'Ellie! Are you all right in there?' hollers Sam, hammering on the door.

'I'm fine!' I call back, just in case she's starting to panic that I've drowned myself – though the thought has crossed my mind. 'Just relaxing!'

'Great! How's the music helping?'

'Wonderful, I feel much better now,' I fib. I'm in a state of mild panic. My stomach has that hideous see-sawing sensation it normally experiences when I open my bank statements, and my heart is doing some weird kind of Bollywood dance routine. I don't feel better at all, I feel mildly hysterical, but there's no point telling Sam this. For a chilled-out hippy, she can get remarkably uptight.

Besides, Sam's never done the whole big white wedding thing, has she? So what would she know about how I'm feeling? The sensation of rats gnawing my intestines is probably totally normal for a bride.

'Mud's on the phone,' Sam shouts. 'The boys are getting ready and the groom sends his love. He can't wait to see you! Do you want a word?'

My stomach lurches. I do, of course I do! But what can I say?

'He says he bets you look pulchritudinous!'

I laugh in spite of my nerves. I'm sure I do, whatever it means. Typical of him to pick a word I'll have to look up. That's one of the things I love about my fiancé. He keeps me on my toes, or at least he did before all this wedding stuff got in the way. Now we seldom discuss anything unless it's wedding related. When something hard prodding my thigh woke me up the other night, I thought my luck was in until I realised I'd fallen asleep on the order of service he'd been reading to me earlier.

With my body I thee worship, I'd read gloomily. In my dreams. The nearest I've got to sex lately is walking past Ann Summers.

I would have been happy with a small wedding but that was never going to happen. Not with my mother's wish list to consider. My fiancé and I have spent so much time with the vicar, I'm surprised he's not coming on honeymoon with us. In fact, I'm wishing he could, because what the heck will we talk about once the wedding's over? Maybe that's why people have kids. It's a great conversation filler.

'Ellie?' Sam raps on the door. 'He wants a word!'

Normally I chat so much you could wire my gob to the national grid and power Buckinghamshire for a week, but suddenly I'm speechless. I know if I speak to my future husband he'll instantly know I'm not happy, and before I can help myself all my worst fears and doubts will come zooming out of the marital Pandora's Box. And then the wedding will be off for sure.

And I'll have let my mother down, again. How can I live with myself if I do that?

'No, it's unlucky!' I shout, and then I duck my head under the bubbles so I can't hear any more. By the time I resurface, Sam has gone. Excited voices drifting through angelic chimes suggest that the doorbell is shrilling and my bridesmaids have arrived. Even my mobile joins in now, buzzing like a wasp from its perilous perch on the edge of the bath as a text message comes through.

Just remember that I love you.

I pull the plug and watch the water swirl away. Let's hope my doubts and fears drain away too or I really am in trouble, because there's no kidding myself now.

Project *get married* is go.

The Lady Doth Protest

'What's the matter, Ellie?' Marcus asks solicitously, leaning forward to cover my hand with his own beautifully manicured one. 'Don't you like the sea bass? Would you rather try my bream?'

I look up from my plate, where I've been intent on making patterns in the lemon butter sauce. Since we're dining in a very new and very exclusive fish restaurant in Henley, it doesn't really seem the time or the place to admit that the only way I can stomach fish is smothered in a million calories of batter and accompanied by lovely greasy chips. This thing on my plate looks more like a scene from *Jaws* than dinner. And more to the point, where's the ketchup?

'I guess I'm just not particularly hungry,' I say lamely.

'Never mind.' Marcus continues to tuck into his own meal, skilfully removing bones and tissue like something out of *Holby City*. 'Save yourself for the dessert. Apparently the crème brulée's legendary.'

I surrender my cutlery with relief and wipe the lemon sauce from my mouth with a heavy blue napkin. I wished Marcus could have embraced his inner chav and gone to Dave's Chippy at the end of the road, then strolled with me by the Thames eating our dinner out of newspaper. Although we've been seeing each other for several months and he's been nothing but attentive and adoring, I'm feeling more than a little out of my depth. In fact, I'm drowning. The opera, the ballet, the theatre, you name it, he's taken me there. Expensive restaurants, friends' yachts and even over to Dave and Sam's for supper, where I was introduced as his girlfriend, much to the Camerons' joint shock. They covered their surprise beautifully but, like the rest of Britain, they weren't used to Marcus Lacey seeing the same girl for more than a day, let alone having a relationship.

But it seems a relationship is exactly what we're having, and Marcus has applied himself to the task of being the model boyfriend with all the zeal he's previously dedicated to collecting conquests. My mum's over the moon with joy; Sam Delamere has had to eat her words, and even Jay has grudgingly apologised for being negative at first. We're not really talking, which doesn't exactly make for a comfortable house share, and the weird moment in the hall hasn't been alluded to again, so life's pretty much back to normal.

Well, my version of normal, anyway.

'What do you think of the restaurant?' Marcus asks, taking my hand and raising it to his lips. 'The decor's really something, isn't it?'

It certainly is. The small restaurant, exclusive to the point of only being able to seat a dozen couples at a push, has been designed to look like the interior of a boat. Only not your usual nets and brass type of look, but more like the first-class accommodation on the *Titanic*. I'm starting to feel more than a little seasick.

'It's great,' I agree feebly.

'I'm glad you think so, because a great friend of mine owns this place: Richard Leigh Hewlett. We were at Eton together; both rowed and all that.' He leans forward and tops up my wine generously. 'You'll have to meet him soon. In fact, I want you to meet all my friends. And my family. Would you like that?'

Call me paranoid, but is Marcus rushing things just a little? What's happened to the Lothario the tabloids loved? It's all a bit surreal.

Can it be that the Right Honourable Member for Taply-upon-Thames is actually serious about me? It's certainly looking that way, and I ought to be jumping for joy. Marcus is sex on a stick, with his thick chocolate hair, sculpted body and golden skin; any woman would want to be with him.

I smile at him and remind myself that I fancy him like mad and that I'm the luckiest girl in the room. But inside a little voice is whispering that Marcus is like caramel and praline Häagen-Dazs: desirable, delicious, decadent, but not really something you can exist on long term.

Ignoring it, I turn my attention back to what Marcus is telling me about his plans for the next election. I haven't a clue, but by nodding furiously and saying *mmm* in all the right places, I think I get away with it. While he waffles on about foundation schools and academies, my thoughts drift back to my mother.

Mum almost passed out with excitement when she heard just who it was I'd dined with at Cliveden. Luckily she doesn't read the *News of the World* and has taken great delight in telling all and sundry that her little Ellie is courting 'that nice young MP'. Last time I went home, the latest copy of *Brides* magazine had pride of place on Mum's coffee table, and all she could talk about was how wonderful it would be to have a spring wedding. Although I'm pleased that Mum's happy, I'm starting to feel as if somebody's placed me in a box and is slowly shutting the lid. Still, she must feel a lot worse. Her operation's booked for next week, even though, in true British style, we're all busily trying to pretend it isn't.

Marcus and Rupert are both perfect husband material, so the fault must lie with me. Maybe I should take Sam up on that past-life regression thing. Apparently I've been reincarnated fifteen times, which does kind of raise the question of why am I still messing up.

After settling the bill (thank God Marcus insists on paying; the meal costs more than I get paid in a month), it's fairly late, so he drives me home in his beautiful Jag.

'Thanks for a lovely night.' He parks up, and then kisses me gently on the lips. The car's flooded with a sickly orange light from the street lamp. 'I had a wonderful time. I always do with you.'

'Me too. Do you want to come in for a . . .' oh heck, it sounds so corny, 'a coffee?'

'I'd rather shag your brains out all night.' He flashes me a wicked grin, and my pulse at last, thank heavens, begins to race. Then a hideous thought occurs. My bedroom looks like the aftermath of the Next sale. I can't let him in there!

Luckily for me, Marcus is shaking his head. 'Much as I'd love a *coffee*, I've got to be in the House early tomorrow, so I'm planning to stay at the flat.'

I paste a disappointed expression on to my face, but inside I'm turning cartwheels with relief. I really don't want beautiful Marcus to enter my world of knickers draped over radiators, gone-off milk and no loo roll. A girl has to keep some mystery.

'I'll see you soon then,' I say, kissing him back. 'My sister's threatening to throw a dinner party, and she'd love to have you there as guest of honour.'

'I'll do my best. What about your housemate?' Marcus asks, in between tracing a string of kisses across my collarbone. 'Isn't Sam invited with her partner?'

'No,' I laugh, 'they're definitely not invited. Annabelle and Sam can't stand each other. Anyway, Sam and Mud won't be around for the next few weeks.'

'Why not?' Marcus's hands are straying lower now. I close my eyes and sigh. He certainly knows how to press all the right buttons. 'Why not?' he repeats, his breath warm against my skin. 'Where are they going? On holiday?'

It's really sweet that Marcus is so interested in Sam, even though he's only met her once and been frozen out for the sexist, capitalist pig she believes him to be. If I hadn't read all about Marcus's preference for leggy blondes, and lately curly-headed brunettes, I'd swear he's developing a taste for dreadlocked eco warriors. I'm impressed he's showing an interest in green issues too. I must be a good influence.

'They've gone on a road protest. You remember, the one at Ethy Woods, not far from my house,' I tell him as he presses his lips against my neck. 'They're moving into the trees this week.'

I visited the woods earlier and was impressed by the intricate web of tree houses and rope ladders and the network of tunnels that Mud and various others were still constructing. Somebody was playing a flute, there was singing and chatting, and a campfire had been prepared for the evening. It was all very Famous Five and I was quite inclined to stay and crack open the sardines and ginger beer until Sam reminded me there weren't any toilets.

'They're in the trees? Already?' Marcus's lips leave my neck abruptly and he looks shocked. 'But that's impossible.'

'Well, not really, all they do is rig up some rope walk-ways and Bob's your uncle,' I explain helpfully. 'It doesn't take long. They were supposed to go in weeks ago but there was a hold-up and Taply Construction couldn't get on to the land. Sam said it was an ownership problem.'

'That's all sorted now,' Marcus says. 'Or so I've heard, anyway.'

'Sam says somebody must have been involved in back-handers, because the council bought the woods originally as a nature reserve. Ethy Woods is a site of unique eco-logical interest,' I tell him. See, Sam, I do listen!

For a second a frown clouds Marcus's face. Then he smiles and ruffles my hair absently.

'I'd better be going. It's past twelve already and I've several meetings tomorrow, plus a television interview with BBC *Breakfast*. I'd better get some beauty sleep.' He leans forward and kisses me, and before I can even draw breath I'm out of the car and standing on the pavement, listening to the roar of the engine as he speeds off towards London.

I let myself in and try to calm my galloping pulse. I check to see whether Jay's boots and jacket are in their customary position on the floor by the stairs before locking up the house. Then I make my lonely way up to bed.

The next morning I'm up bright and early to open Blue Moon, so it comes as something of a surprise to find Poppy sitting outside in the sunshine texting furiously on her mobile.

'You've got to go over to Ethy Woods and drop off supplies,' she tells me, firing another text off into the ether. 'Sam just called in a real state. Apparently news of the protest has leaked out and the contractors are planning on moving in today. Sam reckons there's a mole in the group reporting everything, because the contractors seem to know her every movement.'

I'm surprised. 'That seems rather unlikely. Don't they know everybody really well?' Even the uninitiated like me know how close and committed the protesters are. It's inconceivable that any one of them could be a traitor.

'That's the mystery.' Poppy's dark brows draw into a frown. 'Sam knows everybody there so well that she can hardly believe it's the case. But somehow Taply Construction always seems to be two steps ahead. Sam reckons that the cherry pickers and the diggers are due any minute, so she needs as many supplies as you can take. I'm sorry to leave all this to you, but I can't drive and one of us has to man Blue Moon.'

An hour and a half later, after a mad trolley dash round Waitrose, I head to Ethy Woods. Esther's boot is groaning with carrier bags full of food. The shopping trip has been a challenge, because I'm not quite sure what to buy for people on an eco protest. Do they eat meat? Are they vegan? Will they refuse to eat anything non-organic? And how on earth are they going to cook up trees and underground anyway? In the end I plumped for loaves of bread, great wedges of cheese, chocolate biscuits, crisps and fruit. In a sudden flash of genius I also bought bottled water, because I wouldn't put it past the contractors to cut off any water supply. Yes, I decide smugly as I pull up next to the gate leading into the woods, I've managed to think of everything.

However, one thing I haven't factored in is how I'm going to lug twelve heavy carrier bags over a gate, down a muddy path and up a steep incline. At first I try to carry six in each hand, staggering about drunkenly and cutting off the circulation in my fingers before I collapse on to the ground, surrounded by groceries.

'Bugger, damn and blast,' I say crossly. The damp earth is soaking through the seat of my velvet flares and there's no way I can carry the shopping to base camp by myself. I'll just have to go and find some big, strong eco warriors to help me.

Abandoning the groceries, I clamber over the fence and slither down the bank, clutching wildly at ferns and weedy-looking saplings in order to remain upright. Already I'm regretting wearing my platform boots.

Slithering inelegantly to the bottom of the slope and clambering up the other side is the most strenuous exercise I've had for ages, and I'm gasping for breath by the time I arrive at the camp. There's no pipe music or sitting around fires today. Instead people are winching themselves up into the trees by a complicated network of ropes and pulleys while a chain of mud-smeared men carry supplies across to the gaping mouth of a tunnel.

'Hey! Ellie!' cries a voice from above. Cricking my neck, I see the slim figure of Sam silhouetted against the sky, dizzyingly high up. 'Wait there, I'm coming down!'

Within moments she's whizzing to earth in a makeshift rope lift that her body weight pulls along.

'Cool, huh?' she says, gesturing to the tree network.

'Very cool,' I reply while my stomach lurches. Surely she won't ask me to carry the shopping up? I want to help out, but I'd thought in a feet-firmly-on-the-earth kind of way.

Sam smiles, but beneath the smears of dirt she's pale and tired. 'We've worked all night to finish this lot. Hopefully it'll give those gits at Taply Construction a run for their money. Our tunnels go for miles. They won't dare start digging because they'd kill somebody and that wouldn't enhance their image.'

'What about the people in the trees?' I ask. 'Won't they just pull them out?'

'Eventually. We're there to create more hassle. It will set them back a day, two at most, to get us all out. That buys Mud and Animal more time in the tunnels. Hopefully it ought to make the local news. If we're lucky, maybe the national news teams will run a piece too. Eco protests aren't common occurrences these days.'

She isn't wrong. There aren't many road protests in green and leafy Bucks either. The inhabitants of the land of sports cars, tea on the lawn and polo tend to be more concerned with buying up large chunks of the environment rather than saving it.

Suddenly, two of Sam's friends come tearing into the camp, shouting loudly and waving their arms. Their faces are white, and as they near the tunnels, the protesters go crazy, scattering like a disturbed nest of ants.

'Quickly! Into the trees, hurry! The contractors have arrived! Go, go, go!'

Before I realise what's happening, Sam's grabbing my hand and hauling me across the leafy ground. Her feet barely seem to touch the earth and I stumble behind her like a particularly clumsy elephant. I can hardly breathe, can't see for the hair in my eyes, and am deafened by shouting and the ominous rumble of what sounds like distant thunder. Sam is tugging me in her wake through crowds of rainbow-jumpered bodies.

'It's starting!' she yells, above the din. 'How the hell did they know to come so early?'

And then I see them; at the edge of the wood, like throwbacks to some ancient primitive time, squats an army of yellow mechanical monsters. With a ruthless certainty they move forward amid a roar of caterpillar tracks and a rattle of chains. My mouth dries. It's like something out of my worst nightmares.

All around me the protesters are dispersing like the well-organised warriors that they are. Doc-Martened feet dangle above as they're winched into the tree networks, rope ladders thud discarded to the earth, and even Serendipity is pulled skywards in a makeshift sling, wearing her habitual look of resignation.

'THIS IS TAPLY CONSTRUCTION LTD!' booms a voice over a megaphone. 'THIS SITE IS TO BE CLEARED! YOU ARE TO REMOVE YOURSELVES NOW!'

'Go screw yourselves!' somebody yells. I begin to feel the first stirrings of panic.

'Grab this!' a voice shouts. A rough length of rope is pushed into my hands and entwined through my legs. Terrified, I clutch it, because the big yellow machines are creeping ever nearer.

The rope jerks and abruptly I'm tugged up and away from the soil with gut-spewing speed. I close my eyes and cling on as I am winched up into the Ethy Woods tree defence network. Heaven only knows what a ridiculous sight I must make; the only bright point on my horizon is that I'm not wearing a skirt today. Mind you, the contractors would probably run screaming at the sight of my grey knickers and cellulite.

'Grab her!' somebody cries. I feel people clutching at me and pulling me towards them but I don't dare release my hold, even though my hands are smarting. I feel dangerously light-headed and my stomach's churning.

Something tells me it's slightly too late to point out that I can't bear heights.

Strong arms lift me and prise my fingers away from the rope. Sagging against a strong, broad body, I feel rough wool on my cheek and my senses reel with the overwhelming smell of unwashed body and engine oil. Opening my eyes reluctantly, I almost pass out when I discover I'm at least twenty feet above the earth and balancing on a flimsy platform that spans the gap between the tops of two oak trees. Far below is the campsite, where builders scuttle about like hard-hatted ants streaming from bulldozers the size of Dinky toys. To the left of me, the Thames winds through the lush floodplain like a silver ribbon, while to the right is the duller grey of the main road to Taply, with miniature cars whizzing along it. Between the two is a red splat amongst acid-green foliage surrounded by patches of white: Esther and my groceries. Leaning over, I throw up my breakfast.

'Jesus!' exclaims a voice with a thick Irish accent. 'You nearly got me.'

I wipe my mouth with the back of my hand and whimper.

'Sure, and you've no head for heights I'll be thinking,' continues my observant companion cheerfully. 'It's brave of you to be here.'

'It's not brave of her, Sean, it's a bloody mistake.' Sam sounds furious but I have never been so glad to see her. Up a tree or not, Sam can get me out of this.

'Sam,' I croak. 'Please let me down.'

'I'm afraid it isn't quite that easy,' says Sam. 'You may be up here for a while.'

'Jesus, Mary and Joseph, look at the colour of her!' says Sean cheerfully. 'We'd better be sitting her down.'

Between them they manipulate me into some kind of awkward hunched position, with my back propped against a branch and my knees under my chin. With Sam on one side of me and Sean on the other, I begin to feel slightly more reassured that I'm not about to topple earthwards. If I try really hard, I can pretend I'm sitting anywhere, anywhere but up a tree with nothing but thin air beneath my feet and the rock-hard earth.

'Better now?' asks Sam.

I nod, and to my great relief the world stops spinning. 'Lower me down and I'll be fine. Don't worry about the contractors, I'll just tell them it was all a horrible mistake. I don't look like an eco warrior. They'll understand.'

At this thought I begin to feel a lot brighter. There's no way I can possibly be arrested. It's far more likely that a hunky bulldozer driver will brew me a cup of hot, sweet tea in sympathy for my ordeal at the hands of the eco terrorists.

'I'm ready to go down now,' I say bravely. 'Don't worry about what they'll do to me. Just focus on your protest.'

Sean's eyes are bright with amusement. 'Like Sam says, there's a wee problem with that.' He jerks his head earthwards, and in spite of myself I follow his gaze. What I see makes my heart sink. Curled like sleeping snakes on the ground are ropes. Lots and lots of ropes.

Oh bugger. There's no doubt about it. I'm stranded.

'We threw the ropes down to make it more difficult for the contractors to get to us,' explains Sam. 'Our job is to stay up here, not get down again. You'll just have to make the best of it and look on the bright side.'

'Look on the bright side!' I screech, causing several men in yellow hats to look up. 'I'm up a tree, I have vertigo, I am scared to death and I don't want to be here! Where's the bright side in that?'

'Why not look on it as a chance to escape from your daily routine, to relax, listen to the universe and think,' Sean says kindly.

I stare dumbly at him. I like my daily routine. I like my sofa, my job in Blue Moon and wallowing in bubble baths.

Talking of bubble baths . . .

'Where's the bathroom?' I ask slowly. 'Where's the loo?'

Sam gestures to a bucket hanging jauntily from a branch.

'Get me down!' I shriek.

'You're here now, Ellie, so you may as well take part in our protest. You never know, you might even raise the profile, given that you're dating the local MP,' says Sam, ever pragmatic.

'You know that this is kidnap?' I point out sulkily. 'I'm your first hostage. That could make a good story, too. You're eco terrorists, that's what you are.'

'Stop moaning,' says Sam. 'It's not as though you've got much else going on. Now for phase two!'

She locates several sets of handcuffs from one of her numerous coat pockets and flourishes them. 'I knew I hadn't forgotten these. There you go, Sean.'

'Grand!' Sean snaps one cuff around his wrist and the other to a branch. Sam does the same while somehow managing to handcuff me to her other wrist.

'We shall not be moved!' she crows.

'But I want to be moved!' I wail. 'So what happens now?'

'We sit and we wait for the cherry pickers,' Sean replies, jerking his head earthwards.

I follow his gaze towards the gateway. It hasn't taken

the construction workers long to get through the chains and padlocks that the protesters spent ages looping around the ancient five-barred gate. Somebody in a hard hat and a smart suit is waving bolt croppers in the air. Behind him looms an army of machines, of a type I usually watch on the news from the comfort of my armchair. I begin to feel more than a little worried about being handcuffed to an eco warrior who's chained herself to a tree. How will they remove me? I look at the angry men below, and decide I'd rather not know the answer to that question.

Then, as if things weren't bad enough, I feel a horrible tickling sensation crawling across my arm. Pulling my right hand up, I try to scratch, which is no mean feat when you're handcuffed to a tree, and for a minute the itch subsides. Then it resumes, only this time it's higher up and crawling towards my shoulder. Yanking the hand that's shackled to Sam, I'm about to make a sarcastic comment about Serendipity's fleas when I spot it: an enormous spider with hairy legs and blue speckles. And fangs.

Well, maybe not, but I can't be sure and I scream my head off.

'Jesus!' Sean jumps, his backside almost leaving the rickety platform. 'What the feck is up with you?'

'A . . . a . . . a spider!' I gibber, pointing in horror to the tarantula-like object crawling towards my neck. I have horrible visions of it lunging suddenly for my jugular and me dying a most agonising death simply because I'm stranded up in a tree miles from the antidote. That always happens in those old black-and-white Tarzan movies.

'Calm down, it's only an itsy-bitsy little spider.' Sam tries to twist her body around so that she can reach the offending insect. Unfortunately the handcuffs leave her fingers several millimetres short.

'Flick it off!' I yell, and from below, the construction workers look up in surprise, no doubt thinking this is some elaborate war cry.

'I'm trying!' Again her fingers miss, and to my total horror I feel the spider stroll across my collarbone and shimmy on down my more than ample cleavage into my bra. I feel quite faint. There's hardly room for me in there, let alone a spider.

'I came to deliver your supplies, not to audition for *I'm a Celebrity*,' I wail. 'Get that spider off me! Now!'

'I love you, Ellie, but I'm not putting my hand down your bra,' says Sam primly.

'To be sure, I don't mind if you do put your hand down her top,' chips in Sean, with a glint in his eye. 'Two chicks getting it on in handcuffs with me watching. Up a tree! Bejaysus!'

'I'm sure it's gone, El.' Sam's clearly not going to help me out here. For somebody who can almost braid her armpit hair and doesn't believe in deodorant, she's ridiculously squeamish about women's bodies.

'Are you positive?' I wiggle a bit and feel no spider.

'Hold on a moment.' Suddenly Sam is leaning forward, dangerously so, and peering intently down at the ground, my close encounter with the eight-legged monster totally forgotten. 'Pass us the field glasses, will you, Sean?'

Sean delves into a grubby rucksack and, after pulling out Rizla papers and a copy of *Ulysses*, produces the binoculars.

'Shit,' breathes Sam, squinting furiously. 'Now it all makes sense.'

'What's wrong?' I ask.

'Who's that man, the one in the suit, at the front?' she demands. Her small hands twiddle frantically at the binoculars as she struggles to focus on her target.

'I'm thinking to myself that he's very familiar.' Sean scratches his head and narrows his eyes. 'But I don't think I've seen him here before.'

'He's got his back to me.' Sam shifts her position a little in order to get a better look. 'He's being joined by two others, who look important. Here,' she passes the binoculars over, 'have a gander and tell me what you think.'

Sean looks. 'I recognise those two right enough. That's James Ryan on the left and the other fellow is Bernie Jones; they're both major shareholders in Taply Construction. They're a right pair of eejits; neither of them gives a feck about anything but money. What does it matter to them if centuries' worth of trees are destroyed as long as they can both get to London five minutes quicker and make more cash?'

'Give me back the glasses!' Sam trains the binoculars on the third figure again, while I close my eyes wearily.

'I am going to throttle you, Ellie Andrews,' she says slowly.

'Why?' I'm offended. If anyone has the right to feel pissed off, it certainly isn't her.

'Have a good look through these and then tell me exactly what you have to say for yourself,' Sam says, thrusting the binoculars at me.

'You don't have to be so rude,' I grumble as I fiddle with the binoculars, which one-handed takes some doing, and eventually focus on the activities below. I find one particularly hunky builder and use his neat denim-clad backside to adjust my lenses. Maybe it's not so bad up here.

'Stop messing around,' snaps Sam. 'Focus on the men in suits and tell me what you see.'

It's normally wise to obey Sam when she gets into one of her bossy moods. And since I'm twenty feet up, I won't start arguing now. I train the binoculars on the business-men, and what I see nearly causes me to fall off my perch.

Far down below, in a beautiful Paul Smith suit and a rather unbecoming hard hat, is none other than Marcus. There's no mistaking that muscular body, the honey-hued tan and the chiselled profile. And there's certainly no mistaking the camera crew hanging off his every word and gesture.

The Right Honourable Member of Parliament for Taply-on-Thames, the man who's pursued me with a persistence normally reserved for bloodhounds, my current boyfriend and potential mother-pleasing fiancé, is right here at Ethy Woods.

'Sam! You'll never guess what,' I cry excitedly, handcuffs rattling. 'Marcus is down there. I think he's come to get me!'

And all at once I have this lovely romantic vision of Marcus cherry-picking me from the tree, sweeping me into his arms and driving me away in a JCB. I send up a quick prayer that if he does, I will marry him out of sheer gratitude and be the perfect settled daughter that my mother longs for.

'Ellie!' Sam snaps. 'Marcus isn't here because of you. Well, actually he is, but not quite in the way you want him to be. Shit!' She slaps her hand against her head. 'And to think that we just couldn't work out how Taply Con-struction were always one jump ahead of us! It's all so bloody obvious.'

I stare at her, confused, and Sam shakes her head sadly.

'Ellie, don't you get it? The interest in our protest? The sudden conversion from serial shagger to boyfriend of the year? Marcus has played us all for a bunch of idiots! He's the one who sold that protected land on to the construction company, and greased a few Westminster palms so that nobody kicks up about green-belt issues. No wonder I couldn't figure out who the mole was. It never occurred to me that it would be you!'

The Laws of Attraction

As I stare down at Marcus, the nasty truth begins to dawn.

Suddenly everything starts to make perfect sense. Marcus's mysterious business meetings, the pressing phone calls that so often required him to cancel dates and shoot away early, his interest in the activities of my housemates and burning desire to discuss green issues; it's all so horribly clear. I feel sick when I recall all the seemingly innocent little chats we've had about the protest, about the whereabouts of my housemates and their plans for the week ahead. This wasn't the polite interest of a boyfriend, but instead a cynical trawling for information. How could I have been so stupid? How could I ever have believed that Marcus Lacey had been genuinely interested in somebody like me?

Tears sting my eyes. How dare he! No wonder he'd recalled seeing me at the Henley Regatta and various other local events; he'd probably been waiting for the perfect moment to pounce. He must have nearly wet himself with joy when I crashed into his car that ill-fated day. Why hadn't I listened to Poppy's warnings?

'I'm going to kill him,' I seethe. 'Just wait until I'm out of this bloody tree. If he thinks I wrecked his BMW, he hasn't seen anything yet.' And I begin to pursue a lovely fantasy in which I take Esther to the Jag, the scissors to his designer wardrobe and a very sharp carving knife to a tender and most beloved part of the MP himself. How dare he use me like this?

'Calm down!' says Sam hastily as I try to pace up and down the narrow platform.

'After the way I've been used? I don't think so!' I begin rattling the handcuffs furiously. 'Take these off, Sam! Now! I mean it! I don't care about a peaceful protest. I'm getting out of this tree, jumping in the nearest JCB and giving his suit the best pressing it's ever had.'

'I can't take them off.' In spite of everything I've done, now it's Sam who's looking guilty. 'I haven't got the key.'

'Well, who has?' I roar.

'Wasn't it Mud who took the keys?' Sean recalls cheerfully. 'Didn't he plan to chain himself up in the tunnel?'

I want to weep. 'The keys are buried with Mud? Please, tell me you're kidding?'

'Wait a minute!' Sam gasps, her eyes lighting up. 'I've had a brilliant idea!'

I think I can be forgiven for failing to jump with joy. The last brilliant idea of Sam's involved sharing bath water in order to save the planet. The only brilliant thing about that particular idea was that I took to going to the gym every day for the showers and in the process almost noticed my cellulite waving the white flag.

'Marcus loves publicity, he needs to look the good guy, right?' says Sam excitedly. 'Well, now's your chance to change his image, Ellie! How totally humiliating for him to discover his girlfriend taking part in a protest against his own policies! The papers will love it, and what's even better is that he can't possibly go ahead with you here. He'll look a total bastard. It's perfect!'

The last thing I want is more publicity. On the other

hand, maybe I could do a kiss and tell with the *News of the World*. That might pay to get Esther through her MOT.

'OK,' I say warily. 'What exactly do you have in mind?'

It isn't the most devious of plans, but even I have to admit it might just work. The one thing Marcus does have going for him in a political climate where Tories are about as trendy as socks with sandals is the fact that he always comes across as Mr Nice Guy. The public love to read salacious reports about his sex life but always forgive him thanks to his good looks, humour and gentlemanly manner. How are they to know that he's a total bastard? If I haven't cottoned on while we've been happily swapping body fluids, then why should the inhabitants of his constituency know?

It's my public duty to shatter the illusion.

'Hey! Lacey! Up here!' Sean's Irish brogue fills with menace as he shouts down to the gathering crowds below. His hands grip my shoulders, and when he shakes me for effect, I feel just a little nervous. I'm thankful I'm still handcuffed to the tree.

Beneath his yellow hat, Marcus looks skywards. His eyes widen when he spots me chained to a tree and being manhandled by a dreadlocked eco warrior.

'Hello, darling!' I call weakly. 'Thank goodness you're here. These people have some crazy idea that you want to put a road through these lovely woods, and they say they won't let me down until you promise not to. Can you tell them it's all a silly mistake? I know how much you love the countryside. And anyway, if you *were* involved, wouldn't it be a conflict of interests? I've told them that's illegal and you'd never dream of it!'

For once, it's Marcus doing a stupid cod impression. Whatever he expected to see, it certainly wasn't his girlfriend dangling aloft like an Ewok in flares. In spite of crippling vertigo and a badly dented ego, I'm starting to enjoy myself.

'Marcus! Help!' I plead, trawling the depths of my limited acting skills. 'I can't bear heights! Tell them to let me go! Get me down! Please!'

'Call your diggers off and we'll let her go,' growls Sean. 'Otherwise she's staying here with us. And who knows what will happen to her?'

The *Bucks Today* team is beside themselves with excitement. They don't know what to film first. A huge fluffy grey microphone hovers like a crazy bird of prey above Marcus's head and cameras point skywards. He's saying something now to the suited man beside him, which involves a lot of head shaking and discussion.

'Well?' shouts Sean. 'What's it to be?'

'Darling, please! I feel so dizzy. Please get me down! I love you!' Goodness, it's amazing how GCSE drama comes flooding back. Any minute now I'll be spouting that scene I learned from *A Midsummer Night's Dream* at the audience below.

Beneath his hard hat, Marcus is scowling, and even from my lofty perch I can see the fury in his expression. How come I never noticed before how cold his eyes are and how tightly set his mouth is? If I weren't dangling from a tree, I'd have kicked myself.

Marcus turns to the man at his left and says something, and then blows me a kiss. He's the master of spin; after all, hasn't he spun me the perfect image of a devoted boyfriend? Even now, though I know exactly what he's been up to, I find it hard to believe that he's been playing the long game. He seemed so genuine when he told me he loved me, and that being with me was changing him for the better. To think I'd started to believe I might feel the same way! He saw me coming, that's for sure.

'Call the diggers off,' Marcus orders his foreman. 'And please get Ellie down from there.'

'Thanks, darling,' I call, put out when rather than rescuing me himself, Marcus marches back towards the construction workers with the television crew in hot pursuit.

'Bastards!' Sam shrieks.

Advancing across the forest floor like a dystopian scene from *Terminator*, a hellish host of machines crawls towards us. Inside them, beside them and behind them is a horde of construction workers and a crew of what looks alarmingly like riot police.

'Let battle commence,' Sam says bleakly. 'Sit tight, Ellie. Something tells me we're in for a rough ride.'

And then the chainsaws start to buzz.

'Hand over all your personal belongings and place them on the counter.'

The young police officer on night duty regards me stonily. He's probably irritated that a nice, quiet night has been rudely interrupted by the arrival of a bunch of hippie dropouts, and I can't really blame him. My vanload must have been at least the third to arrive. He's been through this little routine about fifty times.

I regard him more closely. Pimply skin and very smooth cheeks? God, it's scary when policemen look younger than I do. I make a mental note to pop over to Lucy's and pinch the biggest pot of anti-wrinkle cream I can find. After nearly two days stuck up a tree, two days in which I've learned to live without chocolate and to pee into a bucket, I think some pampering is definitely in order.

'Surely this isn't necessary?' I ask, widening my eyes in what I hope is a winning way and flicking my hair back from my face. Unfortunately my eyes are red and my hair is so tangled my fingers get stuck in it. How come when this kind of thing happens in the movies, the heroine always has fluffy hair and immaculate make-up? Thelma and Louise looked glam even when they drove their car over the edge of the Grand Canyon.

'I'm sorry, miss, but you need to hand over all your personal belongings,' he insists, holding out a clear plastic bag, which he rustles right under my nose.

'I'm really nothing to do with this protest, Officer,' I explain as I place a motley collection of snotty tissues, car keys and ancient lipsticks on to the counter. 'I was only there by accident.'

'I see.' Is it my imagination or do his lips twitch? I feel like howling with frustration. How on earth can I ever make anyone believe I managed to be twenty feet up a tree by accident?

'I went to deliver food.' I pass him a lighter and a purple nail varnish. 'Then I was pulled into a tree by mistake. It's been on the news. I'm Marcus Lacey's girlfriend. This is all a huge misunderstanding.'

Actually, am I still Marcus's girlfriend? Probably not, seeing as I wouldn't spit on him if he, by a huge stroke of luck, spontaneously combusted.

'Name?'

Oh no. This is it. I feel sick to my stomach. I've been glued to *The Bill* for years and I know exactly what will happen next. I'll be allowed to make one phone call and then be given a full body search by a big, butch WPC.

'Ellie Andrews,' I whisper.

After filling in a property form and pretending I'm an orphan with no family whatsoever, I find myself in a cell with two dreadlocked inmates, known respectively as Skye and Baggy. After two days trapped with Sam and Sean, I've absolutely no desire to talk any more, so I perch my backside on the very narrow bed and chew furiously at the skin around my thumbnail.

My fellow inmates are slumped on the floor and whispering excitedly about the tunnel networks. For a fleeting moment I think of Mud burrowed beneath the earth, waiting to be dug out. I think too of Sam, and wonder where they've taken her. Even though I want to thump her, I wish she were here. Sam and Mud have been arrested plenty of times; she'd be able to tell me what to do.

I lean my head against the cold brick wall.

'Ellie Andrews? Ellie Andrews!'

The shouting drifts into my dreams. Warm breath fans against my face. I know I have to get up. Only a few more minutes . . .

Wait a moment. Whose mustard breath is that? Opening my eyes, I see Baggy's head lolling contentedly against my shoulder and a uniformed WPC standing beside me. I groan.

I struggle to sit up and push Baggy aside. She murmurs but nestles down on to the narrow bed and within moments is snoring gently.

'Your friend's come to collect you,' the WPC informs me.

'I can go?' I ask incredulously.

As it turns out, none of us are to be charged; we were merely held overnight as a precaution. I suppose Marcus has arrived to rescue his poor little girlfriend, aided by his publicist, several spin doctors and a camera crew. I'm no longer white hot with rage, but I am simmering.

I sign for my plastic bag, then wearily make my way out of the reception area and into the sharp morning sunlight. But where is Marcus? Narrowing my eyes against the light, I look for the Jag, the film crew or at least his PA, but there's no sign whatsoever of the Right Dishonourable MP's entourage, and I start to seethe anew. It's a long walk back to Shakespeare Avenue in platform boots, and since I look like the wild woman of the west, I don't exactly relish the idea of a jaunt through town, where I'm very likely to meet my mother.

Clutching my plastic carrier tightly, I make my way across the car park, feeling as though I'm wearing a stripy suit and dragging a chain. I ache from head to foot and all I want to do is curl up in bed and sleep for at least a week.

'Ellie! Over here!'

'Ellie! Hey, Ellie, look this way!'

There's a sudden explosion of flashes and popping noises. Fuzzy balls of light dance before my eyelids, and for a split second I'm dazzled and stumble into a crowd of bodies. Then sense prevails and I fling my hands over my face in a desperate attempt to hide from the probing lenses.

'What do you think of the rumours about Marcus?'

'Have you been charged?'

'Are you pregnant?'

'Was he taking backhanders from Taply Construction?'

The words fly thick and fast like a hail of deadly gunfire, and I don't know what to dodge first, the cameras or the questions. I do suck my stomach in, though, because that pregnancy question stings.

No matter which way I turn, flash bulbs explode in my face and reporters shove microphones under my nose, blasting questions into my ears.

'Get away from her!'

Abruptly a strong arm is draped around my shoulders, pulling me close and shielding me from the glare of the cameras. My face is pressed against the rough oiled wool of a fisherman's sweater and I breathe in the tangy smell of Aramis mingled with the sharp lemony scent of clean male skin. Jay! All of a sudden I don't care about Marcus, or about being made to look a fool, because I'm just so overwhelmingly glad to see him. If anyone can get me out of this mess, he can.

Jay shoves our way through the gaggle of press, shielding me from the curious eyes and prying lenses. Somehow he manages to propel me towards a silver BMW and shoves me into the passenger seat before starting the engine with a roar. There's one more furious explosion of cameras and then we're away and tearing down the Henley Road.

'My God,' breathes Jay. Without taking his eyes off the road, he places one strong hand on my knee and pats it. 'That was crazy. Are you OK?'

'I'm not sure. That was surreal.'

Jay shakes his head. 'This kind of thing never happens in the States. The British press are a disgrace.'

I press the electric window control and let a rush of cold air pass across my cheeks.

Jay swings the car down a narrow leafy lane. 'It could be worse; I didn't have to stump up bail for you, not like the last time Sam was arrested.' He glances in the rear-view mirror. 'I think we've lost them for now, but it's only a matter of time before they work out who I am and where you've gone. You need an action plan.'

'I need a miracle,' I say glumly.

I sneak a look in the passenger's vanity mirror. My hair is frizzy, my skin blotchy and my eyes are bloodshot. So this is how I'll appear in the papers. Every reader in Britain will be siding with Marcus Lacey. Nobody could blame him for leaving me up a tree.

'How are you feeling?' Jay sounds concerned. I can't help noticing how muscled his arms are as he steers the car one-handed along the wiggly road, how dark the hairs are against his golden skin. While his gaze is fixed ahead, I'm free to appreciate his strong profile and thick ebony curls. Get a grip, Ellie. Right now you ought to be fretting over salacious headlines and Marcus's duplicity, not drooling over your housemate.

'Ellie?' asks Jay. 'Are you OK?'

'I think I'm in shock.'

'You were bound to attract their attention after you appeared on the local news,' Jay points out. 'It makes a great story: the ruthless MP, a road protest and his gorgeous girlfriend held hostage up a tree by eco terrorists. Just chuck in a few horses and you've got a Jilly Cooper novel.'

'I'm not his girlfriend any more. I never want to lay eyes on that double-crossing bastard again.'

Jay nods. 'Sam told me exactly how the details of the protest were leaked to Taply Construction when I collected her earlier. I'm sorry, Ellie, you didn't deserve to be treated like that. The guy's a total shit.'

I exhale slowly. 'It doesn't matter.'

And as soon as the words are spoken, I know this is

absolutely true. It really doesn't matter that Marcus has used me. After all, haven't I used him too, in my own way, as an ego boost and as an olive branch to my mother? I shake my head and laugh.

'What could possibly be funny at a time like this?' Jay asks. The wide grin he tosses in my direction makes my poor empty stomach flip over. Goodness, life is unfair sometimes. I look like a bag lady and he looks like a model in his ancient Levis, desert boots and thick sweater.

But when we turn into Shakespeare Avenue, neither of us has anything to smile about.

'Bloody hell!' Jay brakes to avoid the crowds of reporters camped six or seven deep in front of our door. 'Quick, get down!'

Before I even have a chance to think, he grabs the top of my head and pulls me across the car until my face is buried in his lap. The gear stick digs painfully into my ribs and I'm acutely aware that my face is nuzzled against a very personal part of his anatomy.

The car accelerates. I close my eyes and pray. If the paparazzi get a shot of this and my mother sees, I'll be history.

'OK, we're clear,' says Jay. His fingers skim gently across my cheek. 'You can sit up now, Ellie,' he continues, a note of amusement creeping into his voice. 'Although I'm perfectly happy for you to stay there.'

Cheeks flaming, I sit up quickly. Jay is laughing and clearly not at all embarrassed.

Ignoring him, I look out of the car window and pretend to be totally absorbed in the early-morning goings-on of Taply until my heartbeat slows. Several minutes pass, and as the scenery changes from mellow stone cottages to leafy lanes, I realise that Jay is driving away from town and deep into Oxfordshire.

'What am I going to do until the press go away?'

'You can't go home, that's for sure. I don't see that lot giving up in a hurry. We need to get you some place safe where they can't find you,' Jay says firmly. 'You'll have to sit it out.'

'So where are we going?' I ask wearily.

'I thought we'd head to Dad's place for now, grab some breakfast and freshen up. You can have a bath and I'll sort out some eggs and bacon.'

'Won't your dad mind?' I ask. Jay and Sam's father is a very wealthy and extremely attractive divorcee with a glamorous job at the BBC. In fact, so distinguished and so loaded is Jason Delamere Senior that Annabelle contemplated making a play for him before she finally plumped for the younger and far more biddable Mark. That was a tense time in the Shakespeare Avenue household, because the thought of having Annabelle as a stepmother was enough to drive even a pacifist like Sam to contemplate violence.

I have no desire whatsoever to catch my best friend's father in a compromising situation with his latest flame. On the other hand, I've always loved visiting the Delameres' Elizabethan manor house and pretending I'm a Georgette Heyer heroine swishing along the long gallery to meet her secret lover, who in my teenage fantasies always looked uncannily like Jay.

'Don't worry about Dad,' says Jay cheerfully, pulling the car up in a sweeping arc in front of Abbot's Court. 'He's shooting a documentary in Scotland, so the house is ours. Help yourself to whatever you want in the master bathroom and relax. You look like you've been in the wars.'

'I have,' I say with feeling. How many other twenty-seven-year-olds can say that they've been on an eco protest, on national TV, dumped by their celebrity boyfriend and arrested all in the same week?

In the early-morning sunlight, Abbot's Court is at its most beautiful. The grey Oxfordshire stone is warmed to a caramel hue and the leaded windows sparkle. The sun is hot on my face and Jay's hand is firm on the small of my back as he guides me towards the porch.

'Here we are,' he says, leading me up the stone steps and into the panelled hall. 'You know where everything is, so why don't you run a bath, and by the time you're through I should have breakfast ready.'

Ten minutes later I'm neck deep in bubbles. Pure, unadulterated bliss. It's only now, with freshly shaved legs, squeaky-clean hair and an exfoliated face, that I start to feel halfway to human. Just being in this bathroom is enough to raise my spirits. The huge free-standing bath with lion's claw feet is straight out of a Cadbury's Flake advert, and just wallowing in it makes me feel all sexy and beautiful. Filmy muslin curtains drift in the breeze, and above the gentle fizz of the bubble bath I hear pans clattering in the kitchen and the strains of Radio Two.

I duck my head beneath the water, then surface blinking rapidly. One thing puzzles me. Here's an entire fabulous house, empty most of the time, and available to Jay totally rent-free. Why on earth is he living at number 43, where he has to camp out on the sofa, share our disgusting kitchen, have his razor blunted when I shave my legs with it and put up with Mud and my PMT to boot? It doesn't make sense.

I wrap myself in a huge white, fluffy bathrobe and my mouth waters with the smell of bacon that's drifting up the stairs, but nothing will induce me to go down unless I can locate some make-up first. Rummaging through the bathroom cabinet, I'm relieved to discover that some obliging ex has left behind the most impressive Clarins collection, the total value of which would probably pay my rent for a year. Then I towel-dry my hair and spray myself liberally with Chanel No. 5.

When I finally wander into the kitchen in a cloud of perfume, Jay is busy at the range juggling frying pans and saucepans in an endearingly inexpert fashion.

'At last!' he says, prodding sausages and stirring beans. 'Hope you're hungry.'

'I'm starving,' I say. My mouth waters at the delicious smells. 'For cooking this, I could *almost* forgive you the prom incident.'

'Almost, huh?' smiles Jay. 'I must cook for you more often in that case. Take a seat and tuck in.'

I sit down at the battered refectory table. Jay has cut a loaf into thick wedges and I smother a slice in butter. It's been a long time since I last ate, and I munch away happily while Jay busies himself at the stove. Starting to feel pleasantly full, I reach across the table for my second slice of bread just as Jay leans across clutching two steaming mugs of tea. For a split second our arms collide, and then scalding brown liquid slops on to my very clean and very bare skin.

'Arrgh!' I cry.

Jay is mortified. 'I'm so sorry!'

He propels me towards the kitchen sink. 'Put your arm under the tap. No, don't move, just stay put for a minute or so.'

I stand at the sink and desperately try to bite back my tears, wishing I wasn't one of those people who turn into a frog whenever they cry. But my poor arm really does hurt, and after the past couple of days it's the last straw. To my shame, I start to sob noisily.

'Don't cry, Ellie!' Jay pleads. 'I'm sorry for being such a clumsy idiot.'

His right hand holds mine in a firm grip under the cold tap while his other hand reaches over my shoulder, the muscled forearm gently brushing my breast and pulling me back against his chest. I stand there, shaking and limp.

After several minutes my arm is just throbbing rather than threatening to fall off. Unfortunately it isn't the only part of me throbbing, because I'm still conscious of the pressure of Jay's arm against my breast and his body pressed closely to mine. All those years of longing finally catch up with me and I feel a pang of desire so sharp that it takes my breath away.

Bollocks. I still fancy him.

But what have I got to lose? Apart from my pride, my dignity, fifteen years of trying to get over my teenage crush . . .

'Is there anything I can do to make it better?' Jay murmurs, and I freeze; am I imagining it, or do his lips graze my temple? His hand is caressing the nape of my neck, and those fingers, icy cold from the water, send little ripples of excitement flowing over my skin.

I turn my head a fraction so that I'm looking into eyes the same clear green as a Cornish rock pool, and my stomach lurches.

'What can I do, Ellie?' he asks softly.

'You can kiss me better,' I whisper, pretty bravely I think, seeing as it's only nine-thirty in the morning and I haven't been anywhere near the vodka.

Jay couldn't look more shocked if I'd told him I wanted him to hang-glide naked across Taply.

I open my mouth to say *only kidding*, except I can't speak or think or do very much at all actually, because Jay is kissing me so deeply I feel dizzy.

'Did it work?' he whispers.

'I think it's going to take much more than one kiss to make that pain go away,' I say.

'Really?' Jay traces the line of my collarbone with his thumb. Then, before I know it, he's scooped me up into his arms and, just like in one of my teen fantasies, is carrying me across the kitchen and up the stairs. I don't have time to worry about how much I weigh or whether he's noticed my fat bits, because he's kissing me again.

He leaps up the remaining stairs with the most amazing burst of speed, kicks open the door to a light and airy room and places me down on a large four-poster bed as gently as though I'm made of china, not nine and a half solid stones of flesh and bone. Then he tenderly brushes the hair back from my face.

For ages we kiss and laugh and whisper, and I'm feeling so blissed out that for a while I don't register the jangling noise that seeps note by note into my consciousness. Once I do, though, there's no ignoring it. We are not alone.

I sit bolt upright. 'Jay! That sounds like the doorbell.'

'Ignore it, it'll just be a courtesy call,' he says, pulling me on top of him and starting to kiss me again. I surrender joyously, the bell gives up and with a happy sigh I abandon myself to the million and one delicious sensations coursing through me. After all, how often does a girl get to have her teenage fantasies fulfilled? Robbie Williams never married me, and as for George Michael . . . well, what a tragedy for the entire female population. But here I am with gorgeous, sexy Jay and the reality's a million times better than the daydreams that whittled away the hours between Year II physics and the bell.

'Ellie, I need to tell you something,' Jay is saying softly, 'And this time I want you to listen to me.'

I start to reply, but he clamps his hand over my mouth. 'I really have to tell you that I'm totally—'

My stomach turns into London Zoo's butterfly house, but whatever Jay totally is I never discover, because before he can even draw breath to tell me, the tinny strains of Mozart begin pealing from his iPhone.

Jay pulls a face. 'It's probably Sam; she promised to call if anything developed.'

He springs from the bed and pads across the thick rug to retrieve the phone from his jeans pocket. The caller can't be Sam, though, because Jay looks horrified when he answers.

'Here? Right now?' He turns away from me and peers out of the window, running his hand distractedly through his hair and leaving it sticking up. I have an insane urge to run over to him and smooth it down but I manage to restrain myself. Something in the sudden stiffening of his shoulders and the tone of his voice holds me back and changes the atmosphere between us in a subtle but very tangible way.

'Well, yes.' Jay's voice is lower now. 'Of course I understand. I always see things from your point of view, that's the trouble. Yes, of course I'm coming.'

He ends the call and turns to face me. I feel self-conscious all of a sudden and pull the robe tightly around my body, drawing my knees up against my chest.

The doorbell jangles again. And again. And again.

'I think you'd better answer that,' I say.

Jay is whiter than the bed linen. Then he tucks in his T-shirt and is thudding down the stairs. I wait a second before jumping off the bed and haring after him. If anything awful has happened to Sam or Mud, I want to know about it.

By the time I reach the galleried landing, the front door is open and a mountain of Louis Vuitton luggage is piled high on the chequered floor. Beside it, a stunning blonde is throwing her arms around Jay's neck and kissing him as though her life depends on it. When she catches sight of me, her eyes narrow dangerously.

My voice trembles. 'Jay, who's this?'

He looks stricken. 'Ellie, I—'

'Jay! You naughty boy! Haven't you been telling your friends about me?' the blonde asks, her eyes wide blue circles of surprise. Raising a perfect eyebrow, she stretches out her left hand, and it's impossible to miss the huge diamond sparkling on the third finger of her left hand. It draws my gaze like a python draws its prey.

'I'm Roxy, Jay's fiancée!'

10.02 a.m.

I knew that trying to relax was a bad idea. One minute I'm up to my neck in bubble bath; the next I'm having hideous flashbacks. I'd have been much better off with the champagne. Those are the kind of bubbles that work for me.

Back in my room, wrapped in my ancient green towelling bathrobe, I'm sitting at the dressing table while the hairdresser tongs my hair and chatters on about weddings. Not that I'm really hearing a word, because I'm far too busy flicking through my old collection of *Hello!* and *OK!*

until I get to the cover I'm looking for. It isn't hard to find. I've kept it especially to torture myself with.

'Oh! That's Roxanna Ross!' says the hairdresser, taking a break from transforming my hair from a frizzy bird's nest into glossy ringlets. 'Isn't she gorgeous? She's got to be one of my favourite models.'

'I don't see it,' I say darkly.

'Really? But she's so beautiful. I'd love long legs like hers!'

'The bridesmaids are here!' Sam bursts into my room, closely followed by Serendipity, who's wearing a big pink bow and looking even more fed up than usual.

'Is that Roxy on your magazine?' she asks. 'I still can't believe my brother ever pulled anyone that stunning, let alone got them to marry him.' Her silver-ringed hands fly to her mouth. 'Oh God! Sorry, Ellie.'

I shrug. 'Hey, don't look so worried. It was a long time ago and we've all moved on.'

'You're right,' nods Sam, braids bobbing in agreement. 'And now you're getting married yourself. I can hardly believe it.'

That makes two of us.

Sam busies herself pulling the plastic wrapping from moss-green bridesmaids' dresses. I almost inflicted pink on Annabelle, but what would be the point? She'd still look amazing. I slip my mobile from my pocket and scroll through the texts. Aha. There's Marcus's latest message. Is it bad luck to reply, or does that just refer to seeing the groom on your wedding day?

I open the text, read it and frown. Marcus still has a strange effect on me, even all this time on. Some of the things he's done in recent months are so unbelievably generous and incredible that even I struggle to get my head round them.

Then the phone buzzes, and sure enough here's another little gem just to cheer me up.

All have sinned and fallen short of the glory of God. x

Lovely. Nothing better than chatting about sin on your wedding day, although I was hoping to save that bit for tonight!

The phone buzzes again.

Meet me?

Meet him? Today of all days? I'm not big on superstition, but even I know that this isn't a good idea. I'm duty- and tradition-bound not to leave this house unless it's in the wedding Rolls and under the eagle eye of my father, otherwise I'd be straight down the pub in search of Dutch courage. Getting married feels like the most terrifying thing I've ever done. Marriage is for life, a bit like getting a puppy I suppose, except husbands aren't quite as cute, and require a lot more house training.

Besides, Marcus's religious streak freaks me out sometimes. Life was easier when he was just a conniving Tory bastard. At least we all knew where we stood.

He's not the guy he used to be; nobody knows that better than I do, but the last thing I need right now is a chat about religion or my immortal soul.

'I'm not staying a second longer if that bitch is here!'

Ah, the dulcet tones of Annabelle. Isn't it wonderful how my impending nuptials have united all my nearest and dearest? If Annabelle is screaming and yelling then it can only mean one thing: Poppy has finally arrived and World War Three is breaking out among the bridesmaids.

Maybe I should forget all the bad-luck nonsense and summon Marcus to wallop my sister over the head with his bible. Anything for some peace. What does it matter whether I see him or not? I'm getting married in less than four hours.

It's a bit late now to worry about superstitions.

Model Girlfriend

To say I feel stupid is an understatement. Here I am wearing just a fluffy bathrobe and a stubble rash and suddenly Jay's previously unmentioned fiancée has turned up.

The silence in the hall is deathly. I don't dare look at Jay because I'm shaking with a lethal cocktail of rage and shock. How could he have done this to me? And to think I'd really believed that . . .

Obviously I'd got that totally wrong as well. Although quite how I'd managed to misinterpret him kissing me from head to foot is pretty hard to explain.

'Are you OK?' Roxy asks, with all the sincere concern of Wily Coyote checking on the health of the Road Runner. 'You look kinda pale.'

Time for the Oscar-winning performance of a lifetime. There's no way I'm letting this stunning woman know that my heart has just shattered into a thousand pieces. I do have some pride left, or at least as much pride as a girl who's been wrestled from a tree in front of the national press can have.

'I'm fine!' I trill, stretching my face into a huge smile. 'I'm just a bit exhausted, that's all. I've been on a protest and I've not had any sleep. Jay brought me back here for a bath. Just a bath.'

'Don't panic, honey,' Roxy drawls, in a voice that literally drips with sickly sweetness. 'I'm not about to scratch your eyes out with my acrylics. I believe you.'

Of course she does. Just look at her, all long, slim golden limbs and tumbling blonde mane. Why would Jay look twice at me when he's engaged to her?

'Roxy? What's going on?' Finally Jay finds his voice. He looks as shocked as I feel. 'You should have called.'

'And spoil the surprise?' says Roxy, widening her eyes. She glances at me scornfully, and I realise that she knows *exactly* what sort of surprise her arrival has been, and what's worse, she finds it amusing because she knows that nobody could possibly compete with her.

It's Arabella Elliot and the prom all over again. Have I learned nothing?

'Well,' I say, forcing a light note into my voice, 'I'm sure you and Jay are dying to discuss wedding plans, or whatever it is that engaged people do.' I avoid looking at Jay. 'If you'll just call me a cab, I can get back to Taply and leave you both in peace.'

'Don't rush off,' pleads Jay. 'We need to talk.'

'She's trying to be tactful, darling,' Roxy purrs, twining her arm through his. 'She knows we want to be alone.'

'I'll just finish getting dressed and then I'll be off,' I continue, hoping desperately that the smile stretched across my face isn't about to crack. 'I've got loads to do.'

I sweep past Jay, resisting the temptation to elbow him in the groin, and tear up the stairs. Once safely back in Mr Delamere's dressing room, I bury my face in a fat pillow and scream. How could Jay have pretended I might have meant something to him? And why hadn't he told us all he was engaged?

I fly around the room, searching for the clothes I

discarded so speedily in my haste to leap into the bath. I scoop up my gypsy top and squeal when a very blue and very dead spider tumbles on to the carpet. I *knew* that spider had gone down my bra!

Shuddering, and determined not to go anywhere near my bra and top, I kick the clothes under the bed and then rifle through the wardrobe to see what the ex-girlfriends have left behind.

Unfortunately for me, all Mr Delamere's girlfriends seem to have been tiny, so in the end I have to retrieve my red velvet flares and team them with a fisherman's jumper of Jay's that is so big it keeps slipping off my shoulder. I can't face my spider-soiled bra so I'm risking going without, which will be fine if I follow the habit of a lifetime and don't run anywhere. My hair has air-dried into a mass of bubbly curls that I push behind my ears. A smudge of blusher to disguise my pale cheeks and another quick dash of mascara and I'm good to go. Or at least as good as I'll ever be. I could live in a tub of Beauty Flash and I still wouldn't look as good as Roxy.

Just as I'm lacing up my platforms there's a tentative knock at the door and Jay's head pokes round.

'Ellie,' he says softly, 'I swear to God I had absolutely no idea Roxy was going to turn up.'

'Well, you're one up on me.' I yank the ends of my laces with such violence that Jay looks nervous. 'At least you knew she existed.'

'I know I've completely messed up,' admits Jay, blithely stating the obvious. 'But this isn't how it looks. You've got to believe that.' He moves towards me, trying to take me in his arms, but I sidestep neatly and swing my bag on to my shoulder.

He is not sucking me in for a third time. I need to knock this silly crush on the head once and for all.

'It's cool,' I say breezily. 'We got carried away. It was probably the emotion of the protest. Celebrating my freedom and all that.'

'Carried away? Is that how you see it?'

'Of course,' I say brightly, marvelling at how I manage to carry on idle chit-chat while inside my heart's splintering. 'Don't worry, Jay, I won't tell her we had a snog.'

'I'm not worried that you might tell her, for God's sake!' Jay says angrily, and his eyes look dangerously bright. 'I just want to tell you that I . . .' He pauses, seemingly at a loss for words.

'Listen,' I say, 'much as I would love to stand here all day chatting, I've got places to go.' I look at my watch for emphasis, the effect slightly spoilt because I'm not wearing one. 'We'll catch up later, and you and Roxy can tell me all about the wedding plans and show me which piece of Royal Doulton you want for your dinner set. But right now I've got to shoot.'

'You don't need to.' Jay still blocks the door, his six feet of muscular height looming over me. 'I'd like you to stay.'

While his gorgeous girlfriend drapes herself all over him like a chest bandage? I'd rather brave the spiders. I try to give a light, careless laugh, but unfortunately sound more like a strangled chicken. It's difficult to play the *I don't give a damn* role when all I really want Jay to do is pull me into his arms, throw me on to the bed and kiss me until I turn blue from lack of oxygen. I have to think *very* hard about the fact that he's lied to me, humiliated me and has a fiancée downstairs. So what if he turns my insides into a pool of melting ice cream? He's not to be trusted as far as women are concerned.

138

'I think I'll pass on that,' I say.

'Ellie, this really isn't what you think—' he begins, but I'm not falling for his patter.

'You just get back to planning your big day, but hey, don't go putting me down for bridesmaid duty,' I tell him brightly. 'We all know what I do to weddings.'

'You're angry with me and I deserve it,' says Jay, as he steps aside and lets me pass. 'I should have told you everything, but it's so hard. And painful. Can we talk tomorrow? Will you be back at the house?'

'No idea,' I croak as I flee down the stairs.

'So where are you going?' Downstairs now, and hot on my heels, Jay catches hold of my arm. I shake him off quickly. The memory of those strong hands stroking my skin is far too fresh, but recalling our intimacy lends me a quick and cruel flash of inspiration.

'I'm going to Marcus's place, if you must know, and I intend to stay for a while,' I fib. I'm more inclined to fly to the moon than I am to forgive Marcus, but I'm not telling Jay this.

He stares at me. 'After everything he's done? Lying to you about his involvement in the development? Using you to stay ahead of the protesters? And not even bailing you out from the police station?'

'Once he's explained, I'm sure we can work things out,' I lie. 'He'll have had his reasons.'

Jay's hands drop away and his mouth twists into a grimace.

'You're making a big mistake if you think Marcus Lacey can make you happy.'

'And I almost made a bigger one to think that you could,' I retort. 'Now, if you don't mind, I'll wait for that cab at the gate. Say goodbye to your fiancée from me.'

And with these words I let myself out, slamming the door behind me. The cool air hits my face like a slap, but I hold my head up high as far as the end of the drive, just in case Roxy is watching. Once out of their sight, my resolve evaporates and tears spill down my cheeks. By the time the cab arrives, I'm crying so hard I can hardly make myself understood.

Where to go? I can't go back to Sam's house, as it's surrounded by press; my mother will drive me mad; Charlotte and Lucy will use me as slave labour; Emily will charge me sky-high rent; and Poppy's revolving carousel of boyfriends will make me giddy. There's only one real option and I can't say it makes me feel very happy, but don't they say that blood is thicker than water? Let's hope so, or it'll be a cardboard box for me at this rate, and the way my luck's going lately, I probably won't even find one of those.

★

'Are you out of your tiny mind? Do you really think after everything you've done I'm going to let you stay here?'

OK, so I'm wrong. I'm about as welcome at my sister's house as Mohamed Al-Fayed at a Buckingham Palace garden party. Annabelle must have iced water flowing in her veins and concrete for a heart, because absolutely nothing is going to persuade her to let me inside. As soon as she answers the door and spots me, her beautiful face turns puce and she launches into an amazing fishwife impression.

As days go, this has to be one of the worst. I'm exhausted, dumped, homeless, infamous and even my immediate family members detest me.

'I'm begging you, Annabelle,' I plead, wondering what I

can do to win her over, short of turning back time and not wrecking her wedding. 'I've got nowhere left to go.'

'And whose fault is that?' sneers Annabelle, looking at me as though I'm something very nasty on her shoe. I know that look of old. I saw it when she locked me out of her bedroom when her friends came round for tea, when she tied me to the washing line and conveniently 'forgot' to release me, and when she deliberately chose a bridesmaid's outfit that made me look like a giant frankfurter. It's tangible proof of how desperate I am that I'd consider throwing myself on Annabelle's mercy.

'Where am I supposed to go?' I ask her, feeling dangerously close to hysterical. 'My house is surrounded by the tabloid press and I can't tell Mum what's happened because she's got enough on with the operation. I'm begging you, Annabelle, please let me in.'

'Are you stupid?' shrieks Annabelle, the very set of her shoulders and the snarl of her top lip suggesting that the answer to this question is a resounding *yes*. 'You've totally humiliated me, everyone is talking about *you* as bloody usual, and they all know that it was my sister there with those spongers!'

'That's hardly fair,' I say, rather unwisely, because my sister hates being argued with and I'm supposed to be getting on her good side. If it exists, obviously. 'Nobody could possibly call Sam a sponger; she works really hard in her shop, and at least the protesters care about something worthwhile.'

'Well, you seem to have found your niche,' Annabelle replies coldly. 'So why don't you just crawl back to your tree? And do it quickly; the fewer people who know we're related, the better. I don't blame Marcus Lacey one bit for walking away when you were stuck up there. He was an idiot to get involved with you in the first place.'

With this final cutting comment she goes to close the door.

'What on earth is all this noise about? Oh! Hello, Ellie, lovely to see you.' Mark's head appears above Annabelle's sleek blonde one in the ever-decreasing aperture. 'Open the door and let her in, Annabelle; she can tell us all about her brush with the law. My sister-in-law the rebel!'

Annabelle rounds on her husband with all the viciousness of Lady Macbeth on a particularly evil day.

'Shut up!' she hisses. 'If Katherine Smythe and Lady Beatrice de Warren find out that I'm linked to this protest, they'll never have anything to do with me again. Their husbands have equity in Taply Construction! We won't be invited to the shooting party at Hillingborough House, I won't be introduced to the right people and *Tatler* certainly won't want to run that feature on me.'

'Annabelle! Stop!' Mark begs. He pushes past his wife and joins me on my lonely doorstep. There's something very comforting about his stocky presence, and also something very sad about the pain etched so clearly on his open face. I find myself wondering for the billionth time what such a nice guy ever saw in my sister. Her stunning looks, I suppose.

'Keep out of this!' Annabelle rounds on him, blonde mane flying. 'It's none of your business. If you like Ellie and her disgusting hippie friends so much, why don't you join them?'

'You might sneer at people like Sam and Mud, but at least they stand up for what they believe in!' I shoot back. 'It's really dangerous what they do, but at least they have principles.'

Annabelle slams the door so hard that a flock of ducks nestling on the lawn dive headlong into the Thames. The miserable expression on Mark's face suggests that he feels like following their example.

'I'm so sorry, Ellie,' my brother-in-law says, wrapping his arms around himself in a pitiful attempt to get warm. 'I didn't handle that too well, I'm afraid.'

'It's me who should be sorry,' I say. 'I didn't mean to drop you in it.'

'It's not your fault, you just picked a bad time to appeal to Annabelle's better nature,' he replies wearily. 'We've been arguing all morning. I've been offered a new business venture that I'd really love. It's a not a good career move for me, at least not in terms of status and money, but I'm so stressed with banking in the current climate and I'd love a change. Annabelle's furious, though, and won't hear of it. She says that if I take the job she'll leave me.'

I'm appalled. 'After only two months of marriage?'

'Afraid so,' says Mark, giving me a watery smile. 'You're the last straw since she's been watching you on the news all morning and the *Daily Mail* just called asking for a quote.'

There's a blast of wind, and goose bumps ripple beneath my sweater.

'Come into the garage,' Mark says, taking my elbow. 'I've got some brandy in there from the last time Annabelle threw me out.'

'The last time?' I parrot. 'This is a regular occurrence? Your wife regularly kicks you out and leaves you to freeze in the garden?'

'It's not all bad. The other day I strolled into Taply and had lunch with Jay. We actually had a very enlightening conversation.'

I don't want to hear about Jay, so I ignore this and allow myself to be steered in the direction of the garage. I think I need a brandy to get over the drama of today.

When Mark says garage, what he actually means is an outhouse large enough to house a lesser mortal, me for instance, quite comfortably. We could probably fit the entire footprint of number 43 inside and still have room to spare. The garage contains Mark's vintage cars, upon which he lavishes a lot of time and energy, much to Annabelle's intense annoyance. The old MG Midget is sparkling and the E-Type Jag would have done Austin Powers proud.

'Wow,' I breathe, running my hand over the bonnet. 'I don't suppose you'd have a go at Esther for me, would you?'

Mark says gently, 'I restore cars. I don't work miracles.'

He reaches up to a high shelf, pulls out a bottle of cognac and two glasses, sneakily hidden behind a row of Haynes manuals, and pours two generous measures. I knock mine back, enjoying the warmth that spreads throughout my body.

'So, what's this new job then?' I ask.

Mark looks at me with sad eyes. In spite of his sallow face and pale hair, he's an attractive guy in his own way. Not heart-stoppingly sexy like Jay, but OK all the same. Annabelle's been lucky to find him, although I suspect she's more in love with the wallet than the man.

'You'll probably think I'm mad and have total sympathy with your sister.' Mark sighs as he clambers into the Jag and fiddles a bit with the gear stick and pedals. 'This car stuff's a real passion for me. See this old girl here?' He pats the Jag's dashboard. 'Jay found her rotting in a farmyard over in Burnham. The farmer was keeping chickens in her and hadn't a clue what she was. Anyway, Jay bought her for fifty quid and had her towed over here for me to play with. He reckons car restoration could be big business if I want it to be.'

'Jay's right.' I nod.' You've done an amazing job.' Yet I'm puzzled. Jay is only living with Sam to save money. He isn't due to start his next boat design contract for a while, so how come he can afford to pay Mark to do up a Jag?

'Word gets about, and I've had several enquiries,' Mark tells me. 'Some production people from Pinewood rang up this morning and offered me a contract restoring period cars for two films, with the possibility of more work in the future from them and other television companies. It's a real start, Ellie! I could have my own business.'

'Wow!' I say warmly. 'Well done you.'

'I telephoned my old man right away,' Mark continues, 'and he was thrilled, so was the old girl. They offered me the stables at Roxworth Hall as my work space and said that Annabelle and I can live there with them for free until the business gets off the ground. It's the chance of a lifetime and it's what I really want to do, but . . .' His voice tails off and the light fades from his face. 'Annabelle won't have anything to do with it. If I decide to make this decision, then it's over between us as far as she's concerned. God!' He thumps the steering wheel. 'We've only been married a few months and we're on the rocks already.'

'Oh dear,' I say, somewhat inadequately. I am, however, surprised just how little he knows his wife. Roxworth Hall is the ancient seat of Mark's blue-blooded family, a huge and crumbling pile that looks like something straight out of *Brideshead Revisited* but with slightly more rot and mould. It's conveniently close to Glastonbury, and Sam and I popped in once on the way back from buying lots of weird and wonderful New Age things for Blue Moon. Lady Roxworth was delighted with the angel cards we gave her, and Lord Roxworth even more delighted with my see-through sari skirt, joyfully pinching my backside on several occasions. They are both completely crackers, which is probably why I loved them and is definitely why Annabelle can't bear them for longer than five minutes. Sam and I adored the ancient mansion, complete with draughts, precariously balanced suits of armour and resident ghosts, whereas Annabelle detests the cold, the lack of hot water and the assortment of dogs wandering about the place. The eccentricities of the English aristocracy are certainly not to my sister's taste. Polo, titles and social status, yes. Death duties, wacky relatives and leaking ceilings, no. I can no more see Annabelle married to a mechanic and living in the depths of Somerset than I can see myself becoming an astronaut.

Suddenly my problems don't seem quite so bad after all. At least I only have myself to contend with. If poor old Mark really loves my sister and wants to stay with her until death do them part, then he'll have to resign himself to being a merchant banker for ever and picking up the bills for her lavish lifestyle.

'Never mind, it'll all come out in the wash and all that,' says Mark, with innate English optimism, while I feel very depressed. Is there nobody in the world happy in their relationship?

'Let's go for a spin!' says Mark, with a sudden burst of energy. 'I don't know about you, but I could certainly do with a change of scenery.'

'You can drop me at Poppy's place,' I suggest. 'Then I can decide what to do next. I can't really stay in your garage for the next few weeks. You'll soon be out of brandy.'

Minutes later, wearing a bobble hat and ski glasses and with the hood defiantly down regardless of the weather, I'm the excited passenger in a gorgeous vintage Jag. The feeling of the wind in my face is totally exhilarating, and I make a firm promise to buy a convertible if I ever win the lottery. Failing that, I can always take a can opener to Esther.

We haven't even reached Poppy's front door when it swings open and she sticks her head out, looking left and right down the street in an exaggerated fashion. She's dressed very oddly in dark glasses, a deerstalker hat, red embroidered sari and, over the top of this crazy ensemble, an ancient army surplus sweater.

She hustles Mark and me inside, shielding us from view with her body, then slams the door behind us, double-locking it, shooting two bolts across and putting on the chain. I didn't know that Poppy was so safety conscious. She's obviously been watching far too much *Crimewatch*; this is genteel Taply-on-Thames, not the Bronx.

'OK,' she breathes, pink-cheeked and triumphant. 'We're safe.'

'Safe from what, exactly?' I ask.

'The police, of course! This is our safe house,' Poppy explains. 'When Mud finally gets out of that tunnel, and I'm saying when, not if, he's going to need somewhere to hide from the filth where he can carry on the cause. Because of you, number 43 is out of the question, so it's got to be my place. Sam rang earlier, in a real state. The police have cleared the protest area, but Mud and Animal are still in the tunnels and will be for as long as possible. You should have seen the headlines. This protest really is huge. The whole of Britain's talking about it! You're on every news channel.'

'Great,' I say faintly. My mother is going to freak. This will seriously raise her stress levels. My guilt levels crank up. My latest antics will not speed her recovery.

'Nobody knows how safe those tunnels are. They don't dare to dig in case they collapse,' continues Poppy. 'But when Mud comes out, you can bet your life the capitalist pigs will be after him. We'll hold this house against them.'

Mark is staring at Poppy as though she's the most amazing creature he's ever laid eyes on. Actually, she probably *is* the most amazing creature he's ever laid eyes upon. Girls with waist-length black hair, pierced noses and henna tattoos don't tend to frequent the same social circles as aristocratic merchant bankers, and as he gazes in awe, my heart plummets. Poppy eats men like Mark for dinner, then moves on to dessert before finally seeking out the cheese board. I have to distract her. Now.

'Poppy, it's been a crap few days,' I interrupt. 'I've been handcuffed to a tree, publicly humiliated, arrested, had my heart broken and been disowned by my sister. And it's only lunchtime. I'd really love a cup of tea. Can we talk about the revolution a bit later?'

I make tea in Poppy's rainbow-patterned teapot, pouring liquid the colour of treacle into three chipped mugs of dubious cleanliness. Figuring that any stray penicillin can only do us good, I carry the teapot into the lounge, helping myself to several tablespoons of sugar and a handful of rather soft cookies.

Poppy is sitting cross-legged on the floor, listening to Mark as he repeats his tale about the car restoration business. She's taken off her hat, revealing hair streaked a lurid pink, swept up on to her head and pinned in place with a

148

biro. Mark can't take his eyes off her. In the ylang-ylang-scented room, surrounded by bubbling lava lamps, the strains of New Age music and white fairy lights festooning the ceiling, Mark is as far away from the world of Henley as it's possible to be.

'So that's it really,' he finishes sadly. 'If I follow my heart, I'll lose my wife. But if I don't give this my best shot, I'll probably regret it for ever.'

The look on Poppy's face says that she doesn't think giving up Annabelle is much of a loss.

'What do you think I should do, Ellie?' Mark appeals to me. In the half-light of Poppy's lounge, he looks young and vulnerable.

'Oh, Mark,' I say wearily, sinking down on to a pile of tie-dyed cushions. 'I really don't think I'm the right person to ask about life-changing decisions, seeing as my own's a total shambles. But,' I add, taking a slug of strong, sweet tea, 'I do know that you have a talent and I think you should do whatever makes you happy.'

'Blimey,' says Poppy. 'So why don't you take some of your own advice? You're absolutely right; it *is* your call, your life, and you can do whatever you want. Both of you. Do you want me to read my crystal for you, El?'

'No thanks,' I say hastily, remembering the trouble she so accurately predicted by reading my cards. I'm terrified of what she might tell me next. 'Swing a crystal for Mark if you want, but I'm going upstairs to sort myself out. Can I borrow some of your stuff until I can get back into my house?'

'Help yourself,' she says as she rummages beneath her army sweater and pulls out a crystal on a fine gold chain. 'You know where it all is.'

I leave Poppy swinging her crystal and climb despondently upstairs to her exotic boudoir. The bed with crimson drapes and velvet cushions, the scattered tasselled throws, the billowing orange curtains, the candles and the joss sticks all create an opulent air of seduction and luxury, which is slightly at odds with the overflowing ashtrays, empty wine bottles and dirty plates. Still, Poppy's success rate with the opposite sex is pretty high, so she's clearly doing something right. Plopping myself down on the bed, I thumb through a tattered copy of *Titania's Book of Spells*, pathetically turning first to love spells, but I'm not convinced that a waxing moon, a red ribbon and a white candle would do much for anybody's love life, except maybe a kinky MP's, and I've had enough of those for one lifetime. Tossing the book aside, I turn my attention to raiding Poppy's wardrobe.

Eventually Poppy joins me, throwing herself on to the bed. 'That green skirt really suits you. Take it with you.'

'Thanks,' I say. 'I'll return everything once I know what I'm doing and where I'm going.'

'You don't have to run away,' Poppy says gently. 'I know you're embarrassed right now, but it won't last for ever. You will get over Marcus.'

Ah yes, Marcus. I'd forgotten about him.

'The press will soon get bored,' she carries on. 'Wayne Rooney's bound to do something, or Jordan will go on a bender and they'll totally forget about you.' She pats me consolingly on the arm. 'Your sister's a bitch, but at least you're not married to her. Don't run away. Stay here; I love you even if you are a walking disaster.'

I feel like I owe Poppy the truth. Besides, her kind words open the floodgates and before long I'm blubbing out the entire sorry tale. She hands me a man-size tissue (called this presumably because the people who sob into them usually have *man*-sized problems) and waits patiently while I blow my nose.

'So you see,' I finish sadly, 'I need to get away from here for a while and go somewhere where I can't possibly bump into Jay or Marcus. You were right when you read my cards. It's a disaster.'

'The Tower,' agrees Poppy, a grim expression on her face. 'I just can't believe that Jay had a fiancée all along. I always had him down as a decent bloke; a bit of an idiot at times, but that generally comes with having a willy. I can't believe he lied to us all.'

'Well, he has.' I feel my eyes well up again.

'Where are you going to go? I agree that number 43 isn't an option, and neither is your mum's.'

'Charlotte's? My grandparents' place?'

'No way, Ellie. Charlotte spends all her time hunting defenceless animals for fun. As a fellow employee of Blue Moon, I absolutely forbid you to go there. And I thought you couldn't stand your grandparents?'

'I can't, but these are desperate times,' I reply gloomily. My maternal grandfather, Grandad Stevens, is a Church of England vicar in Chudleigh-under-Bucket, or some ridiculously named Oxfordshire village. Well-meaning as he is, Grandad Stevens does have a habit of asking me where I stand with God, which is a pretty hard question to answer at the best of times, especially for a girl who doesn't even know where she stands with her calorie intake. Granny is obsessed with polishing brass and arranging flowers, and was delighted several years ago when I seemed to share this passion. What she didn't realise was that I was having secret *Thorn Birds*-type fantasies about the young curate, who looked like a younger and more approachable version of Daniel Day-Lewis. I spent many happy sermons fantasising about the body lurking beneath his cassock. Once he moved on to a trendy inner-city parish, I rapidly lost interest in polishing the lectern and attending church twice on a Sunday.

'No, that won't do,' says Poppy vehemently. 'You can't possibly go to your grandparents; your sense of guilt will totally screw you up. You need to go somewhere completely different.' She chews her bottom lip thoughtfully for a while, and then shrieks, 'I've had a brilliant idea!'

I'm a little cautious. Poppy's last brilliant idea involved her, Sam and me renting a cottage in Snowdonia for a weekend in January. This was fine until the snow set in and trapped us for nearly two weeks. Things really turned nasty when we started to squabble over the final tin of baked beans. Rupert went ballistic, because he had to pay a temp to take my place, which didn't exactly improve our relationship.

'Go on,' I say warily.

'My family have got this cottage down in Cornwall,' Poppy begins excitedly. 'It'd be the perfect place to hide away. Nobody will know that you're there. It's ideal. You can stomp on the cliffs to your heart's content and get all the angst out of your system. There's loads of pubs too, so you can always drink your way into oblivion.'

I nod slowly. This is certainly appealing. I might die of alcohol poisoning, but with all that walking I'll at least die thin. The more I think about it, the more seductive the idea of running away becomes. I picture myself striding forlornly along a deserted quay, my hair blowing artistically in the wind and wearing a sweeping cloak, like something out of a Daphne du Maurier novel. I'll go for long walks every day and eat lots of healthy fish that I'll buy straight from the arms of hunky young fishermen. What

I'll do for money is slightly less of a romantic proposition, so I push that thought aside.

'Won't your family mind?'

'God no, they'll be glad somebody has saved them the hassle of going down there and airing it.' Poppy jumps to her feet and is burrowing like a demented terrier beneath a mound of debris on her dressing table. Clutching a ripped envelope and a kohl pencil, she sits down again, scribbling furiously. 'There,' she says at last, handing me a rather smudged series of hieroglyphics. 'That's a little map of where it is, and that's the name of it, Slipway Cottage in Polperro.'

I pocket the scrap of paper cautiously, trying not to smudge it.

'Well,' continues Poppy, glancing across at her sunflower clock, 'there's no time like the present. We'd better get you to the station and send you on your way.'

Almost before I know it, I'm bundled out of the door and frogmarched towards the Jag.

'Is that yours?' cries Poppy, when she clocks the beautiful Jag. 'Can I have a ride in it?'

Mark swells visibly beneath her admiration and I groan inwardly. If Poppy now declares an undying love of rugby and crumbling Somerset mansions, Annabelle can wave farewell to her marriage. I'm rather suspicious that there may be a distinct subtext to my speedily arranged departure. Much as I loathe Annabelle right now, she's still my sister and I know darn well she's no match for Poppy in full flirt mode. As Mark stows my carrier bag in the tiny boot, I look up to heaven and try to convince God that this latest development in the Ellie Andrews chain of disasters really isn't my fault.

Somehow the three of us squash into the car. By the

time we arrive at the station, the weather matches my dismal mood and decides to tip down a torrent of icy rain. Poppy grabs my arm and pulls me after her. 'The train's in! Hurry, Ellie!'

Pushing through people and shouting hasty apologies, scattering pigeons and nearly breaking my neck when I fall headlong over a suitcase, I only just make it on to the train.

'I've bought you a first-class ticket.' Mark hugs me through the window. 'I thought you might as well enjoy the trip.'

I hug him back. 'Thanks, Mark, I owe you one.' I pause, not quite sure what to say. 'Please sort things out with Annabelle.'

He smiles sadly. 'I'll try.'

'The key's under the flowerpot by the front door,' Poppy calls as the guard blows his whistle and the train begins to move.

'Poppy! Don't tell anyone where I am. Especially Jay! If anyone asks, tell them I'm fine and just having a break!'

'OK,' she hollers, 'but you ought to know that—'

The noise of the train drowns her words and I wave until my arm begins to ache and Poppy and Mark are just two specks on the distant platform. Then the train is leaving Bucks behind and gathering speed for Exeter St David's, Plymouth and then loads of Cornish-sounding places. It feels as though I'm travelling to the end of the world.

As I snuggle down into my plush red seat and watch the fields pass by in a whirl of colour, I realise just how tired I am. I close my eyes, but all I can see playing like a movie image before my gaze is that moment when Jay kissed me so tenderly and swept me up into his arms. I blink hard, and in time with the wheels of the train I chant to myself:

'I will not cry. I will not cry. I will not cry.' Yet with each mile that I journey, I feel steadily worse. I've really let my mother down this time, I've made an idiot of myself over Jay, yet again, and I can't bear to even think about Marcus Lacey. My mobile shows three missed calls from him, which I'm going to ignore. What could he possibly have to say to me? Sorry I played you for a fool?

Pressing my forehead against the cold window and thankfully ignored by the rest of the great British public in the carriage, I begin to cry. Silently, relentlessly and all the way to the West Country.

Runaway Train

The train pulls into Liskeard station, where, according to Poppy, a taxi will be waiting for me. But thanks to signal failures, by the time I arrive I'm running two hours late and my taxi has long since given up on me.

I lug my bag along the platform, through hordes of holidaymakers and weary commuters and up a steep flight of stairs to the station café. By the time I reach it, I'm puffing harder than Dot Cotton on a Benson & Hedges. Flushed and wheezing, I order a cup of coffee, collapse on to a plastic seat and rest my head on the sticky table. It's only six p.m. but it feels like midnight.

As I sip my drink, I become aware that I'm being watched. I have that feeling where the back of your neck starts to prickle and you can practically feel somebody's gaze sweeping you. At first I try to dismiss it as intense paranoia; after all, it's highly unlikely that anyone in this café would link a quiet coffee-sipping girl with the deranged-looking madwoman on the news. My gaze drifts around the room. I see customers, a flashing fruit machine and a selection of food that looks as exhausted as I feel. And then my heart misses a beat.

Standing in the doorway, sunglasses dangling from his hand, is Jay.

Oh dear Lord, I've lost it. Now I'm hallucinating. I close my eyes, but when I open them he's still here.

I am going to kill Poppy when I next see her.

'What are you doing here?' I demand as he approaches. Part of me wants to throw my arms around him and snog his face off; another part is annoyed that my plan to bury myself and sink into a decline has been well and truly scuppered.

'I could ask you the same thing.' Jay sits down without being asked and reaches for my coffee. 'God, I need this after a five-hour drive. Why didn't you stay to listen to what I had to say?'

I stare at him. He makes it sound as though he's the innocent party here.

'Who told you where I was?' I say, ignoring his question. 'I bet it was Poppy, wasn't it?'

Jay rakes a hand through his hair until it all stands on end. He looks exhausted, and beneath his rock-pool eyes are violet shadows.

'It took a great deal of persuasion to get the information out of her, if it makes you feel any better,' he says with a smile. 'She drives a hard bargain, does Poppy.'

I'm well aware of this. Why else would I have parted with my signed photo of Robbie Williams that I queued hours in the rain to get? But times were tough, I was premenstrual and I needed that last chocolate biscuit in Poppy's tin more than I needed Robbie's autograph.

'What did you have to give her?' I ask, thinking *please not your body*. Poppy has been known . . .

'Remember that Jag that Mark restored for me?'

I nod.

'That Jag's not mine any more.'

I'm taken aback. This is steep even for Poppy. 'But Poppy can't drive!'

Jay shrugs. 'You can bet your life she'll be buying L plates today. She was pestering Mark to give her driving lessons when I left Taply.'

I'm stunned. Jay has traded that beautiful car just to find out where I am? I can't look at him.

'Never mind the car,' he says, swigging coffee and wincing as it scalds his mouth. 'I'm waiting for an explanation as to why you ran out on me this morning. And that's my sweater you've stolen.'

'I haven't stolen it. I've borrowed it. There is a difference, you know. And I'm sorry you don't like me putting your clothes on as much as you seem to enjoy taking mine off.' I start to peel the sweater off; the effect of this gesture is ever so slightly spoilt by the fact that I get my head stuck and my stream of invective is muffled for a while.

'Don't be so stupid. Keep the bloody thing,' Jay says, his emerald eyes buried in a deep scowl.

'I'm not stupid!' I protest. But I'm relieved to leave the jumper on. As I now recall, I have nothing on underneath it except a grey bra of Poppy's that doesn't remotely fit my double Ds. I look like Barbara Windsor in her *Carry On* heyday.

Jay sighs and lowers his voice.

'I'm sorry, I've never thought you were stupid. Except maybe the time when you and Sam actually tried to smoke the lawn.'

'We were thirteen. How were we supposed to know what grass was really made of?' I protest. It wasn't one of the highlights of my teenage years. As I remember, we puked our guts up all afternoon while Jay and his friends wet themselves with laughter.

'Anyway, you ought to know by now that I don't think you're stupid, or pointless, or short or fat or any of those other things you think about yourself.' Jay's voice grows softer and his scowl seems to fade away like the sun peeping out from a stormy sky. I try hard to tear my eyes away from his, but that clear, sea-green stare has me mesmerised and I find myself wanting to reach out and trace the dimple on his chin.

'Why didn't you tell me about Roxy?' I say, tucking my hands under my bum so that they can't move.

'Because it's over and it didn't seem relevant. Believe me, I was as shocked to see her as anyone. We broke up months ago.'

'If you're not engaged, why did she say you are?'

He shrugs. 'Believe me, Roxy does a lot of very odd things. I'd need a month to tell you half of them. That's one of the reasons why we split up. I couldn't work out any more what was fantasy and what was the truth. I don't think she could tell either. She's got a lot of issues, as they say in the States.'

'But the ring?'

Jay tugs my hand out and laces his fingers through mine. 'I let her keep it. Honestly, Ellie, what more do I have to do to convince you? Speed-dial her shrink?'

I stare at him. Jay has dumped somebody as gorgeous as Roxy and *she's* the one with the shrink?

'But she's so beautiful,' I say.

Jay shakes his head. 'There's more to life than looking like a model, you know. Personality and a sense of humour kind of help.'

'Ah, yes. Those good old staples in the chubby girl's box of tricks. Keep him laughing so much he doesn't notice your wobbly bits. It's the first commandment as far as I'm concerned, closely followed by my personal favourite, *don't forget to cut the size 14 labels out of your clothes.*'

Jay chuckles. 'You always make me laugh, you know that, Ellie? That's one of the things I love about you.'

The buzz of the café grows dim.

'What did you say?' I whisper.

'I said that I love you.' Jay touches my cheek gently. 'Surely you must have realised? Why else would I kip for weeks on that flea-ridden sofa when I could have moved in with my old man and lived in the lap of luxury? Would you choose to sleep somewhere where Mud's arse has been festering all day unless you had a very good reason?'

'I thought you were broke.'

Jay shakes his head. 'And there I was thinking I was making it obvious. Come on, let's go and talk in the car. It's more private there.'

Once inside his dad's BMW, Jay reaches across for his road map and studies it intently.

'I can't go back to Taply,' I tell him.

'That makes two of us,' Jay agrees. 'I can't face hitting the motorway for another five hours. I'll be seeing white lines all night as it is. Let's find Poppy's cottage. That'll give us a chance to let the media circus die down a bit and talk about things.' Glancing at me he adds, with just an edge of uncertainty, 'If you want to, I mean. I kind of presumed you wouldn't mind if I stayed too . . .'

The memory of this morning makes my heart beat faster, and I think I'm showing considerable restraint by keeping my greedy little mitts off him for this long. I'm not exactly well known for my willpower.

'Tell me about you and Roxy,' I say as Jay starts the car. 'How come you never told anyone you were engaged?'

His jaw clenches. 'It's a long story. Only Sammy knew, and when it went wrong, she was the first one to tell me to come back and sort myself out. One thing you need to know about Roxy is that she seriously messes with your head.'

Sam is good at keeping secrets. Not like me. I'd be a rubbish spy. All they'd have to do is give me a good-looking Tory MP and that'd be it.

'I was in Boston last year, working for the company,' Jay continues. 'My boss was really excited because we'd just landed a major contract. Chip Ross, the software tycoon, had placed an order for a racing catamaran worth over six million dollars, a yacht designer's dream come true. We had carte blanche with the design, an endless budget and the opportunity to work with some of the top names in the business. I drew the designs of my life and we built her. God, she was one hell of a boat! Chip threw a launch party for her, and just about everyone who was anyone turned up: actors, congressmen, billionaires; it was a huge bash. Chip's daughter Roxy was there too, but she was a shadow of herself because she'd just come out of a clinic where she'd been treated for substance abuse. We got talking, and she told me about her life. It was so bloody sad, you wouldn't believe. She had been brought up by a series of nannies, none of whom gave a toss about her, and she was bought off by her father with ponies and clothes. She started modelling at the age of thirteen; by fourteen she was anorexic and by fifteen she had a three-hundred-dollar-a-day coke habit. Her life ever since has been a constant shuttling back and forth to rehab clinics. I wanted to look after her, I guess.'

'So you got engaged.'

'She was insecure and I thought getting engaged would help her believe I was the one person who wasn't going to abandon her. But when I got to know her better, I soon came to realise that she was pretty manipulative in her own screwed-up way. She played on the addiction thing, and I used to run myself ragged making excuses for her and trying to protect her. She would have affairs with other guys to make me jealous and to keep me to heel. Pathetic of me, but for a while it worked and whatever she did I forgave her because I thought she couldn't help it.'

Roxy is starting to make Marcus look like a contender for Partner of the Year.

'Then in April she ran off with one of her father's friends without giving me so much as a backwards glance or even a Dear John letter.'

'That must have hurt,' I say.

'It hurt my pride,' admits Jay, shifting the car into fifth and heading into the Cornish countryside. 'I was used to being part of a charmed circle, used to having Roxy on my arm and her dad's millions to play with. Call me a shallow bastard, but I liked having it all: the job, the money, the trophy girlfriend.'

'You're a shallow bastard,' I tell him.

'Yeah, I am, but I'm a bloke. Anyway, after my wounded pride recovered, I found that I actually didn't miss Roxy in the slightest. We have absolutely nothing in common, we bore each other rigid and it would never have worked in a million years. I wasn't in love with her, Ellie. She's never made me feel the way that I do when I'm with you.'

'And how exactly do you feel when you're with me?' I fish.

'Exasperated, happy, angry, protective; about a million

and one emotions. I'm certainly never bored. Plus,' he grins wickedly, 'I have an overwhelming urge to shag your brains out! Can't say I ever felt like that with Roxy. She's like a work of art; beautiful, but cold and untouchable.'

Blushing, I ask, 'So why is she back if it really is over? It didn't seem to me like Roxy thinks it is.'

'The other guy's dumped her. It didn't last more than a few weeks between them. Her father doesn't want to know any more unless she cleans up her act, and her model agency's threatening to drop her unless she quits the coke for good. She needed me so she came back. I always took her back before, so I guess she thought it wouldn't be any different this time.'

'And is it?' I hold my breath.

Jay looks across at me. 'Yes,' he says slowly. 'This time it is. When we get back to Taply, I'm going to tell her it's definitely over. Because it is, Ellie, I swear on my life. That's why I came back to England. I never thought in my wildest imaginings she'd follow me.'

A silence falls between us.

'I know you don't have the best opinion of me,' he says quietly. 'And I understand that maybe you think I'm a player and not to be trusted, but I'm not that eighteen-year-old guy any more. I've tried to make up for not taking you seriously all those years ago, but you haven't given me a chance to show you I've changed.'

I think back to my fifteen-year-old self. I owe it to her not to balls this up now.

'OK,' I tell him. 'But on one condition. You never mention proms or falling into cakes again.'

'It's a deal,' says Jay with a wide grin. Turning left at a roundabout, he swings the car into a lay-by alongside a railway line and kills the engine. Then he draws me to him and kisses me and kisses me and kisses me . . .

My fifteen-year-old self would be proud.

★

The sun is setting when, an hour later, we finally make the steep descent into Polperro. My lips are still tingling from Jay's kisses and I'm pretty sure I'm sporting a very fetching case of stubble rash. Not that I care. I feel drunk with happiness, and every now and again I look across at Jay.

The BMW's headlights sweep through the dying evening until the lights of Polperro meet us. Jay slows the car, negotiates a mini roundabout and then pulls into a massive car park that could have swallowed several football pitches.

'Why are we stopping here?' I ask. 'Poppy said her family's place has a sea view.'

'You can't take cars through,' Jay explains. 'The streets are too narrow. But I bet you'd give it your best shot!'

'What exactly are you insinuating about my driving?'

'Nothing!' He throws up his hands in mock innocence. 'Only I can't see how you manage to plait your hair and paint your nails as you go along.'

'That's because you have a willy,' I say, 'and therefore will never have the skill required to achieve such a major feat of multitasking. If you let me drive back home, I'll show you how it's done.'

'Not a bloody chance.' Jay laughs as he kills the engine and stretches. This time I don't avert my maidenly gaze from the tanned six-pack that reveals itself. It's a pity the car park's busy.

We wander through the village, marvelling at the narrow streets and stopping to look in shop windows. We hold

hands, and such a simple contact sends shivers of anticipation washing over me. My guardian angel has finally got
it right! I'd been starting to think she had a sick sense of
humour with all the unsuitables I've encountered so far.
Still, ten out of ten for effort now, I decide, as Jay buys me
some fudge. A sex god with a sweet tooth. Who could ask
for more?

A pound of fudge and two pasties later, we head for the
harbourside cottage. Darkness has fallen, and all I can see
is a narrow slice of moon and the inky blackness of the sea.
Trawlers ride the swell of the tide, groaning and straining
against their moorings, and high up on the hillside the
lights of cottages twinkle like a thousand stars. It's the
most romantic spot I've ever seen. Strains of music drifting
on the evening breeze draw my gaze to a pub on the far
side of the harbour. Coloured lights ripple and fragment in
the water, and I feel like I've walked right into a postcard.
Taply, Marcus, cancer and protests feel worlds away. Moments later we're letting ourselves into the tiniest cottage
imaginable, with a low-beamed ceiling and an inglenook
fireplace.

'The kitchen must be on the next level,' says Jay, looking
around in delight. 'And the bedroom in the attic. Isn't it
amazing? It must be at least sixteenth century.'

Taking me by the hand, he ducks a lethal beam and
together we explore the tiny cottage, climbing down the
spiral stairs and wondering at the small kitchen that opens
right on to the water's edge. The second floor of the cottage consists of a narrow bathroom with an ivy-smothered
window and a surprisingly light and airy bedroom.

I peer out of the window and across the harbour, feeling
nervous suddenly at being alone with Jay. This is for real. I
can't put it down to being drunk, or even to giddy relief at

being rescued from the media frenzy. It isn't an accident or a weird coincidence any more; we are making this happen.

Jay flings himself on to the very pink bed, and the springs groan alarmingly. The thought of joining him on the four-poster terrifies me, and years of pent-up desire trickle away. Jay will see me in all my cellulite glory. There'll be no hiding my wobbly bits now, or hoping that he'll shut his eyes. I felt a bit sick knowing how I must compare to Roxy. No matter what he might say, Jay is used to a total goddess, whereas I'm most certainly flesh and bone.

'Come here, Ellie,' he says softly. In the moonlight that streams from the sash window, he's breathtakingly gorgeous. The silvery light illuminates the planes of his face and makes dusky oceans of his eyes. His skin is dark against the pillows and the arms held out to me are strong and firm, corded with muscles and sinews.

I'm rooted to the spot, my heart doing a techno beat in my chest.

'Ellie,' Jay says patiently. 'I don't bite.'

Reluctantly I cross the room and perch on the edge of the bed. This ought to be a romantic moment, but the springs make the sound of an enormous fart, and in spite of my nerves I crease up with laughter.

'That's it!' chokes Jay, pushing me away. 'You are sleeping on the couch!'

I poke him in the ribs, 'Fine! You look good in girlie pink, so stay here if you want!' and make to get up.

'Not so fast, Miss Andrews!' Jay's arms close around me and I'm pulled hard against his chest. His green eyes are black in the gloom.

'Is that your come-to-bed-look?' I quip. If in doubt, crack a joke.

'You're already on the bed,' points out Jay. 'This is my get-your-kit-off look.'

As he speaks, he slides his hands down my sides, hooking his thumbs under my sweater and brushing the skin of my midriff. I tense a little at this point, well aware that I could be a body double for the Pillsbury Dough boy, but Jay doesn't seem to care, and once he starts kissing me, neither do I.

I won't bore you with the details – there's nothing worse than loved-up people, is there? Suffice to say that *quite a while later*, we go out to catch last orders.

Inside the pub, it's dark and hot. People jostle elbow to elbow at the bar and vie impatiently with each other to attract the barmaid's attention. In the window seat tourists pore over guidebooks, while the locals, crammed into a dim corner at the far end of the bar, chat amongst themselves.

'Two pints of cider, please,' I say to the barmaid, while Jay goes to find a seat.

As she takes my money, the girl keeps looking at me.

'Excuse me,' she says finally, as she counts out my change, 'but aren't you that girl from the Taply protest? The one who's going out with that gorgeous MP?'

'No, but several people have commented on the fact that we look quite similar. Besides, I'm here with my boyfriend.' I incline my head in Jay's direction. 'Not a Tory MP in sight, honest.'

'Oh, sorry. You just look so much like her.' She smiles apologetically. 'It's awful, isn't it?'

'Absolutely.' I nod. Seriously, she has no idea just how awful life as an eco warrior really is. Only two days stuck up a tree can teach you that.

'I can't believe that some people are selfish enough to

plough up ancient woodland just to make their own lives more convenient. If there weren't protesters to do something about it, our entire planet would probably end up covered in concrete,' chips in an older lady at the bar.

The barmaid nods. 'Too right, Monica.' To me she says, 'Have you seen the latest news?'

I've been doing just about everything in my power to avoid the news. The *Sun* ran the headline *M Peed Off!* with a very unflattering shot of Marcus glowering treewards. I moved seats on the train to get away from staring at it.

'I've been busy,' I say.

The barmaid follows my gaze to the window seat, where Jay is gazing out over the restless sea. 'Don't blame you! Still, even down here we can't escape the media. I think it's shocking the way they sent the diggers in anyway. They must have known there were still people in the tunnels underneath the site. Protesters always dig themselves in.'

I go cold to my bones. 'What?'

'The diggers went on to the site this afternoon.' She's speaking over her shoulder now as she serves another customer. 'That MP claims he didn't know there were two guys chained together in a tunnel. He says he was only representing the best interests of his constituents. The tunnels have collapsed, of course. The last I heard was that they reckon the two poor sods in the tunnel have got to be dead. Nobody could survive that, could they? Apparently fire crews and medics are on site trying to rescue them. Hey!' she calls as I push my way through the crowd in my hurry to reach Jay. 'You've forgotten your drinks!'

Oh God, poor Sam. What must she be going through? I might not comprehend her feelings for Mud, but if ever a couple were devoted to each other, it's those two. Mud is as much a part of life at number 43 as the dry rot and the overgrown garden. I suddenly feel very ashamed of myself when I recall all the nasty things I've said to and thought about Mud, who's probably lying dead in a tunnel at this very moment, an unlikely martyr to a cause whose doom I helped to bring about. Marcus was aware of every detail of that protest, thanks to me, and he knew almost exactly where the tunnels were. However unintentionally, I've helped to kill my best friend's boyfriend.

'Ellie!' Jay is alarmed when I stumble towards him. Catching sight of my reflection in the mirror above the fireplace, I see how pale I've turned. If I don't get outside, I'm going to vomit all over the sticky pub floor, so I push my way out of the door, barging through the smokers on the steps, and tear down to the harbour, where I throw up into the dark oily water until my throat is raw and I'm gasping for air. Then I sag against the railings and close my eyes.

Jay crouches at my side, smoothing damp hair back from my face and cradling me in his arms. From somewhere he finds a tissue and gently wipes my mouth with it. This is more than I deserve. When he finds out what's happened to Mud, he's going to hate me every bit as much as I hate myself.

'What's up?' he asks, tenderly curling his large warm hands around my cold shaking fingers. 'Was it something you ate?'

'No,' I whisper, closing my eyes in despair. 'It was something I did.' And then I tell him every sorry detail. I don't spare my own involvement, because he deserves to know the truth about how weak I am, the truth about me being stupid and vain enough to think Marcus Lacey could actually care about me or be interested in my sad little life.

Jay whistles. 'I had Lacey down as a shit, but this is something else. You were totally conned by him, Ellie. Don't start to blame yourself. No normal person would ever suspect someone of being twisted enough to pull a low-life stunt like that. If it makes you feel better, we were all convinced he was nuts about you. He seemed genuine.'

'Has Sam called?' I ask shakily.

Jay pulls his mobile out of his jacket. 'Damn, there's no signal. She could have been calling all evening. We'd better find a phone and see if we can get hold of her.'

He takes my hand and together we walk to the call box balancing precariously on the edge of the harbour. While Jay speaks to his sister, I sit on the quayside. The soft wind dries the tears on my cheeks, while the slapping of the waves against ancient stone calms my racing heart. Jay and I are a team now. He'll know how to help Sam, and how to put this right.

'Right,' says Jay, stepping out of the call box and sitting next to me on the low wall. 'Take a deep breath and stop panicking. I've just spoken to Sam at the site. There's no news about Mud or Animal, but it's the entrance to the tunnel that's collapsed, not the tunnel itself as far as she knows. She says that the part of the tunnel where the boys are was reinforced with steel beams and props and she reckons that it should have taken the impact of the machinery's weight. There's every hope that they are still alive.'

I'm giddy with relief. 'What about oxygen? Can they breathe in there?'

'I don't know. The fire brigade are trying to dig them out as we speak.'

He puts his arms round me and holds me tightly while I sob with relief and fear.

'You've got to realise,' he murmurs into the top of my head, 'that they all knew this could happen when they agreed to go into the tunnels. People like Sam and Mud are aware of the risks involved when they fight these environmental battles. They're both prepared to die for their beliefs if it comes to it, because that's how much these causes mean to them. Sam even said that Mud would be delighted with the publicity that his being trapped has generated. Apparently all the major news agencies are at the site and Taply Construction have been forced to halt work completely. Marcus is in deep trouble with David Cameron too, apparently. So all is not lost.' He kisses my right temple.

I feel very small and ashamed. To think I had Mud and his friends pegged as hippie dropouts who got to skin up all day and wriggle out of having to go to work. I even once told Mud to go and get himself a job, when actually what could be more important than ensuring that our future children have a safe world to live in? Without the Muds and Sams and Animals of the world, so many beautiful places would be nothing more than bittersweet memories by now.

'We've got to go back,' I say.

'We will.' Jay strokes the hair back from my face. 'We'll go back to the cottage and get some sleep, and as soon as it's light I'll drive us back to Taply. Everything will be all right, I promise.'

I don't reply, but there's a small knot of unease in the pit of my still-churning stomach. Bitter experience has taught me that normally when a man promises me something, the opposite happens. So I say nothing, just hug him back and wish on the biggest, brightest star, the planet Venus according to Jay, that everything will be fine.

And then I remember with a sinking heart that the same star is also known as Lucifer.

Be My Baby

The journey home is fast, as the roads are practically empty. As Jay drives, I fiddle with the radio, desperately trying to find news bulletins that might tell us more about the Taply protest. But no such luck. Overnight, the British media has learned that a famous film star has taken a teenage bride, and this juicy snippet of trivia hijacks the airwaves, sweeping the fate of Mud and Animal into insignificance. I turn the radio off.

As the day dawns bright and clear, the miles fly by until at last we reach Reading and turn off for Taply-on-Thames. By this time it's almost ten o'clock and the traffic has begun to grow heavy.

'Do you want to go home first, or shall we go straight to the site?' asks Jay. He looks exhausted but still manages to smile reassuringly at me.

'Straight to the site,' I say without hesitation. Each moment without news is torture.

We turn off the Taply Road at the entrance to Ethy Woods, and I'm amazed by the change. Yesterday there was a gate, two police cars and the assorted diggers and cherry pickers that belonged to Taply Construction. Today we can't even park for the police cars, ambulances and film crews gathered around the entrance. Across the gap where the gate once stood is a strand of orange tape with *Police* written on it.

'Christ,' breathes Jay, as he reverses back up the lane. 'It looks like the shit has really hit the fan.'

'The shit's over there.' I spot Marcus cocooned among a gaggle of his aides and spin doctors. He looks disgustingly well-groomed and elegant for someone whose greed might be responsible for killing two people.

Tucking the BMW in behind Esther, Jay and I walk the short distance to the woods. It feels like a lifetime ago that I so blithely carried the food over to the camp. I don't even feel like the same girl any more.

'I'm sorry, you can't enter this site.' A burly policeman stops us. 'You can only enter if you've got authorisation.'

'My sister's in there,' Jay says, craning his neck to see past the crowds of police and firemen swarming about the clearing. 'Samantha Delamere? She's the girlfriend of one of the guys stuck in the tunnel.'

'I'm sorry. I still can't let you through.'

'Could you try and find her, please?' Jay suggests. 'I just want to make sure she's OK.'

The constable looks torn. He's obviously been given firm orders, but the worry written so plainly on Jay's face moves him.

'Well,' he begins, 'I don't see why not . . .'

'Ellie! My God, are you all right? What happened to you? Where did you go?' Like a whirlwind in Armani, Marcus races over and sweeps me into his arms, raining a monsoon of kisses on to my face. I'm so stunned that I just stand there like an idiot. 'Did any of those ruffians hurt you? If I find out who kidnapped you and forced you into that tree, I swear I'll kill them.'

Gobsmacked doesn't even come close to describing how I feel. Marcus actually thought I was kidnapped? Surely my acting wasn't that convincing? And *he's* upset? Hang on a minute, I think as I turn my head to dodge the lips that are trying to latch on to mine, isn't he the bad guy here?

'When you weren't at Maidenhead police station with the others, I was terrified.' Marcus's grey eyes are bright with emotion and he squeezes me hard. 'Why didn't you answer my calls? I've been worried sick about you.'

'You came looking for me?'

'You didn't think I'd abandoned you?' Marcus looks horrified. 'Ellie, this road stuff is constituency business and I have to see it through, but you're a million times more important than that. I thought you knew how I feel about you?'

'You've totally betrayed me,' I say, staggered. 'Everything I told you, you used against my friends.'

Marcus sighs. 'Only an idiot would have ignored what you were telling me. But all that became less and less important the more I got to know you. In fact, it doesn't matter at all now.'

'I bet it doesn't!' I glower at him. 'You've got what you wanted. You've totally used me!'

'Honey, that's nonsense,' Marcus pleads, then, seeing the look on my face, he admits, 'Well, maybe at first, just a little. You'd have done the same.'

'No I wouldn't,' I say. 'I'd never betray anyone I love. Which unfortunately isn't something I can say about you.'

Marcus glances at Jay and his eyes narrow. 'Are you sure about that, Ellie?'

I try and wriggle out of his arms, but Marcus has spent more time in the House of Commons gym than I've given him credit for, and I can't move. It's like being embraced by Arnie. Finally I have to resort to dirty tactics, jumping down hard on his toe – which must be pretty painful, seeing as I'm nigh on ten stone and wearing hobnailed platform boots. While Marcus howls with pain, I make my escape.

'Stay away from Ellie,' Jay tells him icily, pulling me close against him. 'She's had enough dealings with you for one lifetime.'

Marcus's lip curls. 'Now I get it. Thanks, Ellie. Nice to know where you've been hiding while I've been chasing all over Buckinghamshire frantically trying to find you. I turn my back for ten minutes and you're off with another man. Any others I ought to know about? Is your friend Sam having fun too while her boyfriend's buried?'

I don't lose my temper very often, but seconds later Marcus's nose is dripping more blood than one of Stephanie Meyer's vampires. I haven't survived living with four sisters and not learned a trick or two.

'Ellie!' In the middle of all this commotion, Sam leaps between the cowering MP and me. 'It's bad enough having Mud trapped down there without you being charged with ABH.'

Marcus is staring at me. Blood flows from his nose but he makes no attempt to wipe it away. Instead he's shaking his head and gazing into the distance with a look of horror on his chiselled face.

'What have I done?' he moans.

'Probably killed two people just to keep your smug Tory voters happy,' hisses Sam. 'How can you live with yourself? Is being in Parliament really worth that much?'

'I didn't mean this to happen! If I'd known they were there I'd have done anything to stop the workers going in!' Marcus pleads, but nobody's listening to him, least of all me.

'Won't this make a lovely story for the lunchtime news?' says Sam drily, pushing aside the police barrier and leading

176

Jay and me across to the mounds of earth where firemen are digging frantically. 'Now we won't just be loony lefties, we'll be violent as well. Bloody great.'

Jay hugs his sister. 'If ever a man deserved a smack in the face, it's him.'

'One small blow for a girl, one huge wallop for woman-kind,' I quip, but inside I'm shaking. Yesterday this was just another business transaction for Marcus, but now it's personal. If I had money rather than the black hole Nat-West optimistically call an overdraft, I'd bet it all on Marcus doing the talk shows and the sympathetic Tory press this week. He'll be the victim trying to improve transport links for the hard-working masses, and we'll be a raving lefty bunch of crazed militants. He'll suck up to the *Loose Women* and Carol will love him. Why did Richard and Judy have to leave telly? I'm sure they'd have given me a sympathetic hearing.

'I'm so sorry, Sam.' I feel terrible. 'If I hadn't got involved with Marcus, none of this would have happened.'

'Of course it would. Maybe not quite as quickly, or quite as publicly, but it would have happened eventually. Mud knew the risks and he was willing to take them. It was his decision to be in that tunnel, not yours, Ellie.' Sam gives me a steely look. 'I know you've never understood why I love Mud; you think he's grubby and a sponger, and maybe he is sometimes, but he's also the bravest person I've ever met. He has a real passion for the things that matter in life, and he's the kindest person I know. Look at how he rescued Serendipity!' Her voice shakes. 'I don't know what I'll do if anything happens to him. I can't imagine us being apart.'

I put my arms around Sam and hold her tightly. For a brief moment she sags against me, before taking a deep breath and straightening up. Our eyes meet and she gives me a watery smile.

'It's going to be all right,' I tell her.

Sam nods bravely. 'Of course it is.'

'What's the news about Mud and Animal?' asks Jay.

She shrugs. 'Same as before. The tunnel's collapsed in some areas and the boys are trapped underneath. We think there's enough air for a day or two, but after that . . . well, let's just hope that we get them out before oxygen becomes an issue. The rescue team say that the longer they dig, the less hope there is. The problem is that we don't know whereabouts in the tunnels they went.'

'There's more than one tunnel?' Jay is aghast.

Sam nods. 'We dug about six, all interlinked, to make it really hard for them to get us out. The boys could be trapped anywhere in this area.'

'And what happens once they're rescued?' I want to know. 'Are the woods safe from the developers?'

'I doubt it. We've cost Taply Construction a fortune, but there's no reason once we're removed that they shouldn't press on with the road-building project. The land has been sold and it's legit, even if Marcus has sailed rather close to the wind morally. The only thing that can stop this road going ahead now is if we somehow find it to be an area where a unique or rare species lives. Like the snails at Newbury, remember? But I can't see that happening here. You know what, though, as long as Mud gets out alive, I'm not sure that I care too much any more. There's no way that people like us stand a chance. Not against governments and big money.'

We stand in despondent silence watching the digging men. There's an eerie stillness about the place, almost as though the trees sense their own demise. No birdsong trembles from the leafy canopies, and even the rescuers are quiet as they work. In spite of the warmth of the sun, I shiver.

'Can we do anything?' Jay asks eventually. 'Do you want us to take you home for a shower?'

'I'm not leaving here without Mud. But you could go back and feed the dog. She's been in the house since last night. Roxy's there too, waiting for you, Jay, but she doesn't strike me as the kind of girl to look after animals. More the kind to wear them.'

He grimaces. 'Great.'

'Besides,' continues Sam, giving us a weak smile, 'haven't you two got some news to break to her? Thank God you've finally got it together at long bloody last. It's been like sharing a house with hormonal teenagers.'

Jay flicks a V at her.

'In any case, I'll be delighted when she sods off. I've never met a more arrogant bitch in my life. I felt like asking permission to sit in my own lounge when I dropped Serendipity off. That's when I managed to move all the empties out of the way so that I could get in, of course.'

'She's drinking?' Jay closes his eyes in despair.

'Like a fish with a very large drink problem,' confirms Sam. 'But what's new?'

'I just don't want to tip her over the edge again. She's pretty fragile.'

Sam snorts. 'Take my advice, stop being such a doormat and give her the elbow. Then you'll be happy, Ellie will be happy, you can have a big white do and Mrs Andrews will be delirious.'

'Sam!' I feel my face flame, but Jay is laughing.

'Talk about jumping light years ahead! Can't I take Ellie out for dinner first?' he says, catching my eye and winking.

'Yeah, give my dad a break, Sam,' I say. 'He's still paying for Annabelle's bash.'

'And from what I hear, that's on the rocks.' Sam sees the horrified look on my face. 'Sorry, but you may as well hear it from me. Mark hasn't been home since he dropped you at the station. Poppy must be like a huge gulp of fresh air after living with Annabelle.'

Annabelle and Mark on the rocks after only a couple of months of married bliss? And who introduced Mark to his new lover? Me, of course, the harbinger of disaster and doom to all in my acquaintance. I only hope Mum doesn't find out just yet. This is all she needs in her state.

'Anyway, who gives a toss about any of that?' Sam turns her attention back to the sombre scene. 'I'm staying here while you sort out Serendipity. Could you find my lucky crystal too while you're there? I'm going to need all the luck I can get right now.'

So Jay and I leave the site, barging through the reporters and cameras, and set off for number 43. As we drive the short distance we're both silent, wrapped in thoughts so bleak that neither of us can voice them.

For once Jay has his keys, and we're spared the indignity of having to climb over the wall. No reporters linger by the gate, and inside the house is cool and still. I follow Jay through the hall and into the lounge. The curtains are drawn and the air is stale. Lying on the floor by the side of the sofa are eight empty wine bottles and the remains of Jay's whisky. Roxy has obviously fallen off the wagon with a crash. Piles of magazines are strewn across every conceivable surface. Stockings and various refugees from a designer size six wardrobe are drying on radiators, tables and windowsills, and I'm relieved to see that even beautiful people can make a hideous mess. Somehow I've never imagined Lily Cole et al. surrounded by crap and mouldering coffee cups. It's all very heartening.

I yank open the curtains and light spills into the room, pooling on the carpet and showing up some very dodgy stains. Dust motes spin in the air. Twenty-seven is, I realise suddenly, too old to be living in a student hovel. It's time to move on in all areas of my life.

'This is it,' I tell Jay. 'No going back if you tell her about us.'

'I don't want to go back.' He stands behind me and rests his chin on the top of my head. 'I can't lie to her. It's crueller in the long run to keep somebody's hopes up if you've got no intention of fulfilling them. I owe it to her, and to us, to be totally honest.'

'Then can we go back to Sam? I can't bear to leave her there just waiting. There must be something we can do.'

He drops a kiss on to the top of my head. 'There's nothing we can do except wait. But of course we'll go back.'

The sudden patter of slender feet coming down the stairs makes us break apart guiltily. Roxy may have treated Jay badly, but she doesn't deserve to be humiliated. Sam has a firm belief in *what goes around comes around*, and I'm not tempting fate to dump on me again from a great height.

As Roxy poses in the door, all damp and shiny from the shower, she lets her towel slip a little to reveal her golden cleavage.

'Jay, honey,' she purrs, one lean brown foot curling around a shapely calf. 'I was wondering when you'd get back. I've been so lonesome here.'

Jay clears his throat. 'Roxy . . .'

'Yes, honey?' Her words drip with syrup, but the eyes holding mine are hard and cold. This girl means business.

Jay speaks more firmly. 'I've got something important to tell you.'

'Oh, honey, me too!' she coos, tossing her glossy curls back from that perfect flushed face. 'And I've been wanting to for ages but I was just scared that you'd be mad! I can't wait any longer, though. No, Jay, don't interrupt. Let me tell you my news first.'

Roxy flings herself into his arms, causing him to stagger backwards.

'It's just the best news. And I know it's going to make everything better. I've poured away every drop of alcohol in this house, which shows you just how serious I am.'

She has? Thanks a bundle, Roxy.

'Roxy, what's going on?' Jay asks impatiently as he tries to unpeel himself from her clutches.

'Oh, Jay! Can't you guess? Don't you know why I had to leave Rick and come back to find you? Honey, I'm pregnant! We're going to have a baby!'

Serendipity

Jay is rooted to the spot. His face turns the same colour as the peeling white walls.

'Is this some kind of sick joke?' he demands. 'Are you trying to mess with my mind again?'

'No, I swear!' Eyes wide, Roxy holds his gaze bravely, one hand fluttering down to her stomach. 'I swear on my father's life, I'm pregnant. I'm having your baby.'

His breathing is ragged. 'You have to be kidding.'

'I need you, Jay! *We* need you!' Roxy pleads, one exquisitely manicured hand on his broad chest, the nails blood red against the white fabric of his T-shirt. Her plump lower lip trembles and there's a catch in her voice. 'What will happen to our baby if you're not there to help me? I won't be able to cope!'

'What about Rick?' Jays says. 'You left me for him, remember? Sure it's not his? If it exists at all, of course.'

'It does and it's yours,' Roxy sobs. 'I swear. I'll show you the scans. Rick was a mistake. You know I wasn't thinking right back then. I'd only just got out of rehab. I was a mess. Jay, I need you. Please!'

Jay catches my eye from over the top of her glossy head. His look is blank with misery and his stubble seems shockingly dark against the sudden pallor of his skin.

'I'm so sorry,' he mouths. Then he folds Roxy into his

arms and she sobs prettily into his chest. No froggy eyes and snot for her. She looks like a weeping angel.

I feel like bashing my head against the sideboard. It's like being offered the most addictive drug on the planet, getting well and truly hooked and then being told that you'll never score again. I'm already going cold turkey.

'You guys need to talk,' I whisper. My eyes are prickling with tears, but I'd rather eat Mud's toenail clippings off the carpet than let them see me cry. Plenty of time for me to howl later.

Wandering miserably into the kitchen, I click the kettle on and perch on the work top. The accumulated debris from the last few days is starting to fester, and I wouldn't be surprised to find intelligent life developing in the fridge. Once Jay and Roxy have gone from number 43 and Mud is home safe and sound, I'll tidy up the kitchen and finally discover what the draining board looks like. It'll be cathartic, a kind of symbolic clearing away of the clutter in my life.

'Blimey! You've got a face longer than *War and Peace*.' The back door opens and, unannounced as usual, Poppy breezes into the kitchen and helps herself to a digestive. 'Oh goody, the kettle's on. Tell me all the goss!'

'Jay's ex is pregnant,' I say.

'Pregnant?' Poppy's mouth drops open, masticated biscuit displayed fetchingly for all to see.

'Yes, pregnant!' I almost yell. 'Up the duff. In the club. Bun in the oven. Pregnant.'

'Bloody hell!' Poppy breathes. Her tarot-reading skills must be slipping if she hasn't seen this one coming. 'But I thought you and he were getting together? That's what he said when I made him give me the car.'

There's a rugby ball in my throat.

'So, what happens next?' she continues, picking sequins from her sari and flicking them across the kitchen. 'Will it live with you or will you have the ankle-biter to stay in the holidays?'

I never fail to be amazed by Poppy. She operates on a totally different morality system that runs basically along the lines of doing whatever she wants whenever she wants. Actually, it seems to work pretty well. Adoring lovers, forgiving and tolerant friends, and an E-Type Jag.

'Jay's going to stand by her, of course. What else can he do?'

'Send her a cheque each month and stay with you?' It really is that simple to Poppy.

'She needs him,' I say dully, sloshing boiling water into mugs and sniffing the milk warily.

'Bollocks!' snorts Poppy, spraying me with bits of biscuit. 'Her dad's a millionaire! She's just determined that nobody else will have her man!'

'That's not the point.' I decide to risk the milk. What's food poisoning compared with a broken heart, anyway? 'Jay's got to follow his conscience, and you know as well as I do that he'd never let her face having a baby on her own.'

'I think you're both mad,' Poppy says. 'Go for what you want, that's what I say.'

'Like you have with Mark?' I can't help asking.

She puts her hands on her hips with a jingle of bangles. 'If you think I've stolen Mark from Annabelle, then you're wrong. He made all the moves on me.'

'Of course he did! He's low and unhappy!'

'Which says a lot about the state of his marriage!' shoots back Poppy. 'She gave him an ultimatum: it was either her or the cars, and guess what? He chose the cars! And if I was there to make the decision a little less painful, then so what? Why should people live miserable small lives just because it's the safe thing to do? Look at yourself. You and Jay are clearly mad about each other; everyone around here knew it for years except, apparently, your good selves, and here you are about to chuck it all away because some skinny cow decides that she's not going to let somebody else play with her toys!'

My head hurts. There's sense in what she says, but life just isn't like that. Responsibilities come along, and some of us actually have to embrace them. If Jay abandons Roxy, what sort of man would he be? The answer is simple: not one I could respect or want to be with.

I sigh. From beneath the table comes another equally woeful sigh and a rather noxious smell. I glance at Poppy.

'It's not me!' she protests.

Serendipity! The dog that hasn't been fed for twenty-four hours and which I promised Sam I'd sort out as soon as I got home. I feel awful. Serendipity lives for food like I live for chocolate.

Sure enough, lying beneath the table, head lolling sadly on her paws and looking about as miserable as I feel, is Mud's greyhound. Her ears are flat against her head in a pitiful portrait of canine despair.

'What on earth do they feed her on?' wonders Poppy, sounding very nasal as she holds her nose.

'Vegetarian dog food. Reconstituted beans and other pulses, Sam said.'

'No wonder she hums. I thought dogs were carnivorous?'

'They are.' I pat the dog on her bony head. 'Why do you think she looks so miserable?'

Poppy opens the fridge and plucks out a massive T-bone

steak that Jay must have bought on his last M&S run. 'Try this for size, you poor, underfed little doggy.'

She shoves the steak beneath the table and pushes it right under Serendipity's nose, but the dog doesn't bother to lick the juicy meat or even so much as sniff it. Instead she heaves another huge sigh and closes her eyes.

'Maybe Sam has reformed her. Perhaps Serendipity now thinks that meat is murder too? Where's that bean stuff?' asks Poppy.

'Cupboard by the sink.' I crouch beneath the table, feeling rather ill, and not just because of the smell. What a bloody awful day this is turning out to be. And now I seem to have a hunger-striking dog on my hands. 'If anything happens to Mud's dog, Sam will never forgive me.'

Suddenly Serendipity comes to life. Her head raises and her ears prick up as she peers hopefully from under the table. After a few moments of gazing longingly at the door, she slumps back down again, looking more miserable than ever.

'Did you see that?' I say, amazed. 'When I said 'Mud' she perked up!' And sure enough it happens again. 'She's pining for her master!'

'Blimey,' says Poppy.

'So,' I continue, 'if we want her to eat, we'll have to take her to where he is. Let's take Serendipity over to the site!'

I rummage in the kitchen drawer and find the manky bit of string that Mud uses as a lead. Outside, it's tipping down with rain. I tear down the path to the street, where, rather worryingly, Poppy is already sitting in the driver's seat of the Jag and revving the engine joyfully.

'You can't drive!' I holler, opening the passenger door and bundling the dog inside.

'I know!' Poppy shouts above the booming stereo. 'But

you can teach me. All I need is someone to sit there and tell me what to do.'

A nasty thought occurs. 'How did you drive over?'

'I copied what you always do in Esther. I hit a few kerbs and everything.'

'It's just as well I'm suicidal,' I tell her while I struggle to fit into the seat with half a ton of sodden dog sprawled next to me. 'And that I'm in a hurry, or I might have taken time to debate the logic of this with you.'

A sharp thud on my window makes us both jump. Blurred through the rain-patterned glass is Jay, his hair beaded with raindrops and his T-shirt sticking to his body. My insides turn to mush while my heart constricts with despair. I wind down the window and steel myself for more open-heart surgery.

'I'm so sorry,' he says, leaning into the car and touching my cheek tenderly. The rain makes his dark lashes clump together like spiky stars. 'I never meant to hurt you. If I'd had any idea that this was going to happen, I swear I'd never have got involved.'

'I don't regret a thing,' I whisper, unable to manage any volume. 'You made me happier in those few hours than anyone else ever has. I hope everything works out the way you want.'

He shakes his head, rivers of rain racing down his face.

'I doubt that I'll get what I want, but maybe I'll get what I deserve. And clearly I don't deserve to be with you. I might have made a mess of my own life, but I'm not going to ruin yours as well.'

By now the lump in my throat is so huge that I can't speak. Jay kisses me softly on the lips and I taste the salty tang of tears, though his or mine I can't tell. Then he's walking back to the house. His shoulders are hunched and his head is bowed; he looks like a study in total dejection.

Seeing my crumpled face, Poppy says, 'Oh, come on, chick. It's not that bad. At least he's not dead.'

Poppy once went on a course to become a counsellor. Funnily enough, she never qualified.

Gritting my teeth, I decide to concentrate on getting us safely to Ethy Woods.

'Brake!' I scream as Poppy ignores a Give Way sign. Clinging like a limpet to the dashboard, I make a swift decision. If I can't be with Jay, then at least I can do my best to sort out the awful mess I've unwittingly landed his sister in. And to do that I need to live for at least another twenty-four hours.

'Enough,' I tell Poppy firmly, as she sits smiling and tossing her hair at the infuriated drivers who have nearly crashed into her. 'I'm driving. There've been enough traumas for one day. I'm not as desperate as you are to go and chat up the doctors in A&E.'

Poppy is about to protest but suddenly notices she's stalled slap-bang in the middle of the dual carriageway. Some of the gestures from other drivers give me horrible reminders of gory news bulletins about road-rage killings. If I'm going to go, I want it to be in style. I don't want to be stabbed to death with the car keys of the driver of the Ford Cortina who is at this very moment making his menacing way towards us. Swapping seats with more speed than style, I turn the key, put my foot down and roar off with a wheel spin that would make the Stig envious.

'What on earth did you bring the dog for?' Sam eyes Serendipity with irritation. I can almost hear her thinking that here is yet another problem she'll have to deal with when all she wants to do is concentrate on hoping that Mud will soon be found.

'Dippy's lonely,' Poppy explains. 'She's pining.'

Sam sighs. Her braids are plastered against her head, the dye from the silks running and mingling in tracks down her pinched face.

'I know how she feels.' She bends down and pats the dog. 'Where's Mud, then, Dippy? Where is he?'

I glance across to where the rescue teams are still digging. They look exhausted. Apparently the rain has only made things worse. We met Sean on our way across the site, and he said that the fear is that the sudden influx of water will make the tunnels even more unstable. It seems that time is running out. Fast.

'Where's Jay?' Sam straightens up.

Now doesn't exactly seem the right time to tell her that the daughter of Satan is about to make Sam an aunt. Besides, my disappointment fades into insignificance in contrast to what she's going through.

'At home.' That, at least, isn't a lie.

'Oh.' She stares stonily ahead. Then, 'Did you find my lucky crystal?'

Bollocks. I totally forgot. Just as I'm searching for the words to tell her tactfully that it has slipped my mind, there's a short and sharp tug on my arm. Serendipity is pulling at the lead with more energy than I've ever known her to muster.

I tug back. 'Cut it out!'

There's a good reason why most dog owners don't keep their dogs on bits of string. String makes a rubbish lead. Mud's dog might be the most bone idle and greedy hound since Scooby Doo, but she's certainly strong. Serendipity pulls, and I pull back, until suddenly the string snaps and I fall backwards into the mud with an ungainly splat, while the dog shoots forwards like an Olympic athlete on steroids.

'Oh, great, thanks so much, Ellie,' Sam says, exasperated, while I sit on my sodden and aching backside and watch the dog streak across the site, past the diggers, round the press and under the cordoned-off area where the rescuers are toiling away. As she runs, she barks her sleek head off.

'Now she's right in the middle of it all.' Sam glares at me. 'I don't need this now, I really don't.'

'Sorry, sorry.' I clamber to my feet. 'I'll go and get her.'

'Yeah, because she really listens to you. I tell you what: I've got nothing better to do so I'll sort it out, shall I?'

Sam's mouth purses and my heart sinks. I know that look of old. When I lost her Latin homework, turned Rupert down, failed to pay the rent . . . the list goes on and on.

I scuttle after her, my ridiculous platform shoes sticking in the mud.

'I'm sorry,' I pant. 'I'm really sorry. I thought that she was pining and—'

'Shush!' hisses Sam, stopping so abruptly that I cannon into her thick knitted coat. 'Look! Over there!'

I follow the direction of her ring-covered index finger. About ten metres away from the rescue team, Serendipity is scrabbling frantically in the earth. Loose dirt and stones shower the area around her, and as she digs, she gives sharp little yelps of excitement and wags her stumpy tail like mad.

Sam and I look at each other in sudden wonder.

'You don't think . . . ?'

'Is she . . . ?'

We both look again. Serendipity is still digging furiously. The rain and the thick soil don't seem to bother her at all. Compared with the sad and forlorn picture that greeted me earlier, she's now a radiant portrait of joy. My heart starts to pound, and Sam's eyes glow with sudden and unexpected hope.

'That's where they are!' Sam starts to run towards the rescue team, still calling to me. 'He's in the half-finished tunnel, not the main one! Serendipity's found him! Thank God you brought her with you!'

Well, after this it all goes a bit bonkers. The rescue team doesn't take much persuading that Sam's right. In fact, one fireman tells me that they phoned earlier for a rescue dog and handler, and they swiftly turn their attention to the spot where Serendipity is yelping and digging with gusto. Somehow Sam and I manage to drag the dog out of the way, but she still strains against her collar and barks maniacally as the firemen take over and the excitement grows.

Across the site I notice another group of people gathering, only they don't have glowing and expectant faces; rather set expressions and an air of disinterest. Their expensive coats and Range Rovers immediately mark them out as the opposition. They must be the directors of Taply Construction, waiting for this irritating hold-up to finally be resolved.

One man stands apart, shielded beneath a vast umbrella and talking urgently into his mobile phone. The beautiful camel coat sits perfectly on his muscular frame. The shoes, unmarred by mud, have the soft glow of the most expensive

Italian leather. As if sensing my eyes upon him, he looks up and gives me a sad smile.

What on earth does Marcus have to feel so sad about? This is all his doing. He could have stopped the whole development. The fate of the woods and the surrounding lands was his to decide. And he screwed up.

No one's talking. All that can be heard is the slap of earth and the dull drumming of rain on leaves. Sam's grip on my hand is almost painful, and Poppy has started to rock backwards and forwards, which is always a bad sign.

'Hey! Over here!'

The unexpected shout scrapes the stillness. Sam's nails dig into my flesh.

'Yes!' Another yell, this one jubilant. 'We've got them!'

A huge cheer blasts through the site. As one, we surge forward as far as we dare, craning our necks for a better view. First of all, a short, stocky young man staggers into the daylight, heavily supported by two firemen, and following him is the lanky figure of Mud, lolling between two more rescue workers. One of the joys of life is having new and varied experiences and, at this minute, for the first time ever, I'm genuinely delighted to see Mud. He can park his bum on our sofa until the next millennium as far as I'm concerned.

Sam flies to his side, her steel-toecapped DMs barely touching the ground, while Serendipity bounds around and around the small group of smiling people, barking joyously. The cameras are whirling and clicking as the news teams catch the excitement, and suddenly microphones are everywhere as reporters seek sound bites.

Ignoring the press, Poppy and I squelch through the quagmire towards the ambulance where Mud and Animal are taken. Sam climbs into the ambulance to go to hospital with Mud. There's no way she's going to let him out of her sight now.

'He's fine and it's all thanks to you, Ellie!' she calls to me, just as the paramedics start to shut the ambulance doors. 'If you hadn't brought Serendipity, we'd never have found him! You saved Mud's life!'

I gape at the retreating ambulance as it bumps and jolts towards the gates. The woods might be lost and Jay out of my reach for ever, but at least Mud is safe.

Poppy is patting Serendipity and pulling at her now pricked ears. 'Who saved her master's life, then? Who's a clever girl?' She grins at me. 'You do know what 'serendipity' means, don't you, El?'

Poppy reads Dostoevsky for pleasure and I read chick lit. That's one of the many differences between us.

'Go on,' I say.

'It means, and think how appropriate this is, "happy accident"!'

And as if to confirm this and solder it into my mind for ever, the greyhound sighs contentedly and lets rip the most noisy and noxious fart of all time.

'I might owe you one, Dippy,' I say sternly, 'but I do not have to like you.'

And as the dog coolly returns my gaze, I get the impression that she feels exactly the same way.

'Excuse me!' A microphone is being dangled above my head. 'Ellie Andrews? Can we have your comments? I'm Ben Brown from *Bucks Today*.'

'Of course!' I chirrup, too happy to care what I'll look like on TV.

Ben gives a thumbs-up to his crew, who surge forward with light monitors and clapperboards. 'OK, Ellie, look at me, not the camera. This is live! Here goes!'

He turns to face the camera, instantly becoming terribly serious and RP.

'This afternoon in Ethy Woods, near the historic town of Taply-on-Thames, the final two protesters from the Taply bypass demonstration were rescued, alive and well. This was partly down to the hard work of the Taply Fire Brigade, and Ellie Andrews, the girlfriend of local MP Marcus Lacey.'

'Ex-girlfriend,' I say loudly, looking straight at the camera. 'Very ex, actually. In fact, if Marcus and I were the only two people left on earth, I'd be asking earthworms how I could become a hermaphrodite.'

'Right.' Ben now has a nervous smile on his lips. 'But you were part of the protest, weren't you, Ellie?'

'Only by accident,' I tell him. 'I was delivering food and I was winched up into a tree by mistake. I don't like heights much and I was sick. There were no toilets either. It was horrible.'

'So tell us, Ellie,' continues Ben, through gritted teeth, 'even though you were only there by accident, what was it like being part of the drama?'

I pause. 'It was quite scary.'

This is putting it mildly, but I don't think *fucking awful* is a phrase for the delicate ears of the *Bucks Today* viewers, and besides, my mother watches that show.

'The worst bit was when this hideous black and blue-spotted spider jumped on to me and—'

'Say that again!' A small man with straggly grey hair and wire-framed glasses pushes through the TV crew and barges right in front of the camera. 'Did you say a black and blue-*spotted* spider?'

'Excuse me, *sir*,' hisses Ben Brown, two pink spots

appearing on his cheeks, 'but you are interrupting a live television broadcast!'

'Never mind that! Was it black with blue spots?' the stranger demands, so close to my face that our eyeballs are almost touching. 'Was it?'

I rack my brains. 'Well . . .'

'Think, girl!' he snaps, shaking off the members of the film crew now attempting to drag him from the scene. 'This is very important! Tell me what that spider looked like!'

I think. I remember. I shudder. What's that in Latin?

'Definitely black with blue spots. And horrible hairy little legs. I know exactly where you can find one. The spider that crawled down my neck is on the bedroom carpet at my friend's house. It's dead, though, thank God!'

'Yes! Yes! Yes!' The insane stranger punches the air and grins jubilantly at the cameras. Ben Brown looks like he's on the edge of a nervous breakdown, no doubt seeing his broadcasting career flash before his eyes. 'They're here! I knew it!'

Mad spider man turns towards me, and his face is all lit up and shiny with joy. He looks like a religious fanatic who's just seen a vision, and I half expect to see the Virgin Mary and Baby Jesus peeking over my shoulder and waving at him.

'Can we stop talking about spiders for one moment and get back to the real news?' pleads Ben.

'This *is* the real news!' The stranger grins a great gappy grin and plants a soggy kiss on my cheek. 'You, young lady, have just saved this ancient woodland from certain destruction.'

Ben, myself and the viewers of *Bucks Today* goggle at him.

'What?' I whisper.

'That spider is the Lesser Spotted British Blue, one of the rarest arthropods in the British Isles; so rare, in fact, that it's only been found in two other locations and is in serious danger of becoming extinct. Which makes it,' he beams triumphantly, 'an endangered species. And as an endangered species, its habitat must be left intact.'

Ben Brown is excited now. Here is real news in the raw. He thrusts the microphone right under spider man's nose.

'Ben Brown, from *Bucks Today*. You are?'

'Professor Peacock, from Oxford University. I run the world-famous Ecology and Entomology Department.' The professor is rummaging deep in the pocket of his shabby coat and pulls out a piece of paper. Camera crew, Ben and I all crowd round for a good look. Closer inspection shows this to be an illustration ripped from a textbook depicting a small but distinctly black-and-blue spotty spider.

That's the bugger that crawled down my bra all right.

'Yes, that's it,' I agree, with a shudder.

'This means that these woods are now officially a conservation area!' Professor Peacock throws his arms around me and I'm enveloped in a sweaty hug. 'I've long suspected that Lesser Spotted Blues exist in the Thames Valley, and Ethy Woods was the next place on my list of sites to investigate. You can imagine how horrified I was when I turned the news on two days ago to hear that the woods were about to be dug up. If it hadn't been for this young lady and her sharp eyesight, the species, and the woods, would have been lost for ever.'

A cheer breaks out from the protesters who have gathered around us. I have mixed feelings, because I really do hate spiders and personally can't help but think that to kill a few of them can only be a good thing. On the other hand, I'm elated that the woods will be safe after all and that I, however unintentionally, have played a part in helping to save them. It's pretty heady stuff to go from being an unwitting mole and destroyer of the protest to being the saviour of it in just a couple of days. I stand in amazed silence until a member of the film crew whispers in my ear that my mouth is still hanging wide open.

As Ben moves away to interview the professor further and to watch him scrabble in the leaf litter for his precious little spiders, the crowd of protesters and general onlookers break into laughter and clapping. Somebody somewhere starts to play a merry little tune on the flute, and I see Sean gleefully giving the finger to Marcus. But Marcus doesn't notice. His eyes are trained on me, and are full of such pain that I feel uneasy.

The site, which was cordoned off and eerily silent, is now full of people rushing around and talking excitedly. I see Swampy talking to ITN; Chris Packham has appeared and is discussing spiders; while near the gate, Poppy and Serendipity are posing prettily for the *Taply Gazette*. The air of gloom and despondency of only minutes before has lifted like an evil cloud. Even the rain has ceased. I send a little prayer of thanks heavenwards and promise that in return I'll try to be a better person and not moan too much about losing Jay.

I delve in the pocket of my coat until my fingers close around my car keys. With any luck Esther won't be too cheesed off about being abandoned for days and, if I'm really lucky, will start first time. Then I can slot my *Abba Gold* cassette in, crank the volume up and transport my cocktail of emotions home. Hopefully with Jay and Roxy gone, life can return to normal. Or at least what somehow managed to pass for normal before I turned Rupert down, started seeing Marcus and Jay moved in.

I swear I'll sort my life out and get a proper job, just as I've promised my mother. After my bath, and a howl and a good blast of crap TV, I'll go and buy the papers and have a trawl through the job vacancies. Maybe I'll even break the habit of a lifetime and ask Dad if I can come and work in the family company. After all, in my chick lit novels the heroines always have high-flying jobs in finance and journalism. Somehow, working in a hippie shop doesn't have quite the right dash of romance and excitement, which must be where I'm going wrong. Handsome men called Darcy don't tend to frequent Blue Moon as a rule. We cater more for dred-heads who want a new bong or another pair of ethnic-print trousers. No wonder my life isn't going according to plan.

I'm so wrapped up in my fantasies of a fabulous new career like something out of a sex and shopping bonkbuster that I almost have heart failure when I realise that the slim figure leaning against a battered Land Rover and flicking through a magazine is my sister Charlotte. Blood is extracted from stones with more ease than Charlotte is prised away from her beloved horses, and I feel cold to the marrow.

Something's wrong. It has to be Mum.

10.47 a.m.

The happiest day of my life and downstairs all my nearest and dearest should be gathered to celebrate my union to the man of my dreams.

Instead, judging by the yelling and a rather dubious crash, World War Three has broken out in the kitchen.

The hairdresser is trying really hard to be professional and ignore all the screaming, but when there's a second huge crash, she jolts from her seat and nearly gives me a first-degree burn in the process. The smell of singeing hair fills the room.

'Get that bitch out of here!' Another crash. 'I'm going to kill her!'

A fresh battle must have broken out in the war between Annabelle and Poppy. Oh God. How could I ever have been so stupid as to imagine they could cease fire for one day? It's like asking Bush and bin Laden to be mates for the afternoon.

My heart is sinking faster than Katie Price's last single. I *knew* getting married was a bad idea. What on earth was I thinking when I agreed to have a big white do with everyone coming along for free booze and a roast dinner? Nobody I know can agree on anything or bear to be in the same vicinity for a minute, let alone an entire day. It's going to be carnage. We'll probably appear on one of those wedding disaster video shows, and for once it won't be because of me.

Why didn't I insist we ran away and just got married on our own? Never mind that our nearest and dearest might be outraged. At least they'd all still be in one piece.

This is my mother's fault. It was her that wanted a big wedding, not me!

'Get that bitch out!' shrieks Annabelle again, channelling her inner fishwife.

'That's my sister, the matron of honour,' I explain brightly to the hairdresser. 'You're doing her hair next, I think?'

The hairdresser looks rather faint. 'Could I possibly have a glass of water?'

She looks as though she could do with a brandy, but who am I to argue? I go to the bathroom to fetch her a drink, pausing only to glug some Rescue Remedy, and am only away for three minutes, tops. Yet on my return she's vanished, only the smell of hairspray and singed hair evidence that she was ever here at all.

I glance out of the bedroom window, and sure enough the pink minivan bearing the legend 'Tracey's Mobile Hair and Make-Up' has vanished. Bollocks. She really has done a runner and now I have half a curly head and half a straight head, which isn't really the look I was aiming for.

'Blimey!' Poppy bursts into the room brushing shards of glass from her clothes. 'I could be wrong here, but I don't think your sister likes me very much.'

The Capulets probably liked the Montagues more than my sister likes Poppy.

'That's because you're a husband-stealing bitch!' Annabelle screeches, hot on her adversary's heels as she launches herself into my room. She makes a lunge for Poppy, who ducks behind me, and wallop! Annabelle's bunched fist, complete with knuckleduster engagement ring, hits me full in the face.

Never mind seeing stars. There's an entire universe here. I'll just close my eyes for a minute . . .

'Ellie! Ellie!' I'm being yanked upright and somebody is slapping my face, which more than smarts seeing as my sister has just punched me.

'Don't let her close her eyes,' someone says. 'She can't pass out.'

'That eye's coming up a treat,' brays Charlotte. 'Get some steak to put on it. Chop, chop!'

'We don't have steak in this house,' I hear Sam say, a familiar sanctimonious note creeping into her voice. Any minute now she'll start berating Charlotte about fox hunting/shooting/fishing and then I won't be the only one with a black eye. 'Meat is murder.'

My big sister is snorting rudely. 'We're designed to eat it, you silly girl. Why do you think God gave you incisors? To nibble lettuce?'

'Never mind all that,' interrupts Poppy before Sam can retaliate. 'We need to bring the swelling down. We can't have Ellie walking down the aisle looking like she should have an ASBO.' I feel her long, cool fingers prod my poor eye. 'What a shiner. I'm glad I ducked.'

Annabelle mutters something that sounds suspiciously like *next time, bitch*, before she's dispatched to root some peas out from the freezer. Minutes later she's back again, triumphantly waving a soggy green mass.

'Will this do?'

I open an eye nervously. 'That looks like tripe!'

'I've told Mud a thousand times! Dippy is a vegan,' says Sam furiously.

'Sit still, Ellie,' barks Charlotte, backing me into the corner and forcing me to flop on to the bed.

'But it's tripe!' I wail. Forgive me for being picky about the parts of dead cow I want on my face, but a stomach?

'A cow died to give you that tripe,' retorts Sam. 'Don't be so ungrateful.'

So here I am, on my wedding day, lying on my bed in my bum bra and vest with cow innards on my bruised face, hair like something out of *Star Trek* and surrounded by bickering bridesmaids. All it'd take is for Tracey Emin to join us and we'd win the Turner Prize for certain. *My Wedding Bed*, a postmodern take on the fusion of patriarchal Western traditions with the murder of the ideals of feminism. Or something.

Oh dear. I *am* concussed.

'It's still early,' Poppy is saying soothingly to the others. 'Why don't we leave Ellie to recover for a bit? I can come back in a while and do her make-up.'

Since Poppy's idea of make-up is pale foundation, heavy black eyeliner and blood-red lips, I'm not jumping for joy at this offer, and neither does it gladden my already heavy heart when Sam offers to do my hair. With dreadlocks, Goth make-up, smelling of tripe and wearing a too-tight wedding dress, I'll be like an extra from the Hammer House of Horror.

'Besides,' I hear Poppy say cheerily as they head downstairs, 'I need to get the mud and roots off those gerberas. They were a bugger to pick. Hope I got enough. I had to leg it when the parkie saw me. Honestly, Charlotte, the things I've done to get your mum's favourite flowers.'

Broken glasses, doubts, stolen flowers, an escapee hairdresser and now a black eye. God couldn't say *don't get married* any clearer if he came down from Heaven and bellowed in my ear. Peeling the tripe from my eye and feeling pretty close to turning veggie myself, I retrieve my mobile from my bag, scroll down to his name and press dial.

It's time to call this disaster off.

Sisterly Love

'About bloody time too,' says Charlotte brusquely when she catches sight of me tramping through the mud. 'Thought you'd never leave. Haven't even been able to get to the bookies to put a bet on for the three-fifteen.'

'Sorry,' I say. How come I'm twenty-seven and still being bossed around by my older sister?

'Never mind, you're here now.' Charlotte puts her copy of *Horse and Hound* on the filthy bonnet and crushes me in a hug that smells of Barbour wax, horses and lavender. 'Now we need to get going. Chop chop!'

Charlotte is my oldest, and secretly my favourite, sister. Being fourteen years younger, I didn't see that much of her, as she was away at boarding school and then married her society portrait painter husband, Barnaby Ketton, at the tender age of twenty-one. That probably explains why I like her more than the others, who have enjoyed far more opportunities to torment me and make my life a misery.

'What are you doing in Taply?' Untangling myself from her embrace, I feel uneasy. Crocodile Dundee is more at home in New York than Charlotte is in a town.

'I knew they couldn't have got the message to you. I left about five with that American girl. Typical foreigner.'

'Roxy,' I say sadly. But Charlotte has long lost interest in that conversational cul-de-sac. Now she's opening the car door, yelling, 'Down, Lear! Down, Cordelia!' as two big Labradors throw themselves at her in a frenzy of joy. I step back hastily.

'Hop in!' barks Charlotte. 'Don't look so horrified. They've only rolled in fox poo, it won't kill you.'

My sister sweeps a head collar, a bag of Bonios and a jute rug on to the floor and I sit down. Lear's heard rests on my shoulder, and when I finally breathe, the stench nearly makes me gag. And I thought Mud stank. Compared to my sister's dogs, he's fragrant.

Charlotte rolls her eyes. 'Buck up, Ellie. Stop being such a townie. I need you to listen and keep your chin up. Mum's operation has been brought forward, which is why I came here to find you.'

'Brought forward? Why?'

Charlotte takes my hand in her rough, weathered one and squeezes it. 'She went for a pre-op check yesterday and they found another lump. The oncologist doesn't want to risk things by making her wait another week, so he took her in last night. She went into theatre this morning and should be out any time now.'

I think I'm going to throw up. Lucky Charlotte came in her battered Land Rover rather than Emily in her flash BMW. If I puked in Emily's car, there'd be another Andrews family member in hospital.

'Don't look so scared,' says Charlotte briskly. 'It's a fairly routine procedure, apparently. Bloody horrible for her, of course, but there you are. Must look on the bright side. She'll be able to show-jump without her breasts getting in the way. Or trampoline, come to that.'

I look at my sister in total amazement. When I don't see her for a while, I forget how totally barking she is.

'Mum doesn't show-jump or go trampolining.'

'Well, no,' agrees Charlotte. 'But she could now, if she wanted to.'

How do you argue with logic like that?

'So what's the plan?' I ask. 'Are we going straight to the hospital?'

Charlotte shakes her head whilst tying on a Hermès headscarf. That must be something they teach you to do at Sloane school.

'She can't have visitors yet. Granny Stevens is there, but Daddy thought it might be nice to have all the family around over the next few days, which is why I'm here too. Lucy and Henry are on their way and Emily has promised to take the day off. Time to put our differences aside, Daddy says.'

Is my father insane? The Andrews family don't even get on when we're dotted all across the globe.

'Mum'll need a bit of looking after,' booms Charlotte above the thrashing of gears. 'So that's what we'll do. Good show on the telly earlier. Loved it when you landed that pompous little prick a punch on the nose. Wish I'd done it myself. Can't abide people who want to ruin the countryside; they need shooting.'

Charlotte is known for her strong opinions. She'd pull us all out of Europe, ban football, make fox hunting the national sport and pass a law that made everyone eat British beef at least once a week. And for God's sake don't mention vegetarians. I don't like to point out that she's probably got more in common with Marcus than with the eco warriors.

In the gloom of my day I clutch at my one faint hope as a drowning man clutches straws.

'So Mum went in yesterday?'

'That's right. Do listen, Ellie. It's such a bore to have to repeat oneself. That's what I always say to Barnaby.'

'So she wouldn't have seen the news?'

'I doubt it. That would just about finish her off,' guffaws Charlotte. 'She was incandescent with fury when you were arrested. She told Daddy you'd never find a decent husband now that you were associated with the criminal underworld.'

I roll my eyes. 'Sam and Mud are hardly Taply's answer to the Krays.'

'They do say that cancer is caused by stress, so maybe it's time to calm down a bit, Ellie. Find a decent chap? Maybe Barnaby's brother?'

'Oh please, not Barnaby's brother again,' I cry, exasperated. Think David Cameron crossed with Barry from *EastEnders* and there you have it: Charlie Ketton. He's got to be more interbred than Charlotte's Labradors.

'And that's a horrible thing to say about stress causing cancer,' I add, feeling my guts twist with guilt. 'That's like saying it's my fault that Mum's sick.'

'I'm not saying it's your fault. I'm just saying that it's time to stop having all these flings with ridiculously unsuitable men.'

I can almost feel Jay's hands on me again; his lips tracing hot kisses along my collarbone and gradually lower. My face grows hot. I must think of horrible things like John McCririck naked.

'Spare me the lecture,' I say wearily. 'There's nothing you can say that could possibly make me feel worse than I do already. Don't you think I know I keep screwing up?'

'I'm not trying to make you feel bad, I'm only looking out for you. It's high time you settled down. Isn't there anyone you can think of who might be worth taking a punt on?'

To my total amazement – after all, how can I possibly have any tears left? – I begin to cry.

'Oh Christ!' Charlotte swings the car abruptly into a lay-by and violently yanks up the handbrake. 'There, there,' she says, patting me awkwardly on the shoulder. 'Let it all out and have a big blow.'

I blow dutifully into the large horse-scented hanky thrust under my nose.

'That's better.' Charlotte digs into the pocket of her Barbour and draws out a hip flask. 'Here, have a swig of this.'

I swig and nearly choke. Neat brandy, hot as fire, courses down my throat.

'My cure-all.' Smiling, my sister replaces the lid. 'That's how I cope with the twins when they're bloody awful. Now tell me all about it.'

So I do. And it's such a relief, because I feel like all my emotions have been poured into a food processor and switched to high speed.

'You poor cow.' At least Charlotte is sympathetic in her own way. 'What a disaster. But you can't sit about blubbing for ever. You've got to get a grip and put all this sordid mess behind you.'

Yet that magical time with Jay doesn't feel like a sordid mess. In fact, it feels like the only part of my life that's made any sense. And now it's over before it even began.

'I'm sorry for you,' continues Charlotte, helping herself to a swig of brandy, 'but there's only so much sitting around and weeping a girl can do before the rest of us run out of tea and sympathy. You've got to buck up before we all get bored with you having a face like a wet weekend.'

My sister: the master of tough love.

'Which is why once Mum is feeling stronger, you are to come down to Hampshire to stay with Barney and me. You can have a little holiday.'

I feel myself pale. I'd rather cut my hair with a Flymo. Staying with Charlotte would be the antithesis of a restorative break. I'll be dragged out of bed at some ungodly hour and forced to muck out the horses, coerced into 'enjoying' bracing gallops, and, what's worse, roped into the role of nanny/entertainer/slave for Charlotte's fiend-like twins, Tristan and Isolde. On my last visit they *accidentally* locked me in the tack room. For six hours. I still shudder when I remember how I was forced to pee in a bucket.

'That's kind, Lottie, but—'

'Nonsense!' she shouts as the car roars back into life. 'What else are sisters for, eh? Anyway, I always need help at the yard. I know!' Charlotte thumps the steering wheel with excitement as an idea occurs. 'I'll bung you some cash in return, like a proper job. You can have a complete break from Taply, some fresh air, and some work. Everybody's happy!'

Everyone except me. But since when has my opinion counted?

'We're having a house party in two weeks' time,' adds my big sister, turning to me and nearly taking out a pedestrian. 'Whoops! Anyway, yes, a house party with dozens of eligible men. There's bound to be one to take your mind off Jay.'

'Great.' I say weakly. There's no point arguing with Charlotte. She's a force of nature and not to be resisted, so instead I look out of the window and watch the green Buckinghamshire lanes roll by. I don't have any choice but to forget about Jay; perhaps I ought to take my sister's advice?

★

Over the course of the next week, I start to notice that something very odd is happening to me. By odd I actually mean totally bloody unprecedented. A mystery of such vast, enigmatic proportions that even Mulder and Scully would be stumped.

I'm losing weight.

Without trying.

At first I put it down to imagination and wishful thinking, but as my waistbands get steadily looser and my spare tyres look less like part of a monster truck, I can no longer deny the evidence. For once in my life, misery is making me thin. I'm so sad and exhausted that even the thought of raising food to my lips makes me feel knackered.

'Do you notice anything different about me?' I ask my mother while she reclines in bed puzzling over the hospital's dinner menu. 'Have I changed in any way, do you think?'

Mum drags her attention away from the dubious delights of roast beef versus chicken korma and eyes me thoughtfully.

'You've lost weight,' she says at last, pushing herself up slowly on to the pillows in order to have a better look. 'Those jeans were always too tight on you before and now they look like they might just about fit.'

'They've always fitted!' I'm offended. These jeans, genuine 1970s flares picked up from a retro shop in Tooting Bec, are my favourites.

'Yes, you've definitely lost some weight,' Mum continues. 'That's wonderful, Ellie, especially if you're going to be able to borrow anything of Lucy's to wear to

Charlotte's house party. Keep on with the diet. You'll look lovely.'

I perch my significantly smaller rear end on the bed.

'Actually, I haven't been on a diet,' I say. 'This has just happened.'

'Well, I'm delighted either way,' my mother says, ticking roast beef with a flourish. 'Both Lucy and Charlotte were married by your age. It's time to stop messing around and find yourself a decent man. I won't know a minute's peace until you do. I have to be sure my baby's properly taken care of. Then I can concentrate on all this silly cancer nonsense and start getting better.'

Ouch. There's that stab of guilt again.

'But never mind all that for now,' she continues, peering up at the drip that looms above her. 'What about this? The bag's empty and all the lovely fluids are gone. Honestly! The fortune your father pays for my treatment and they can't even manage to change my drip. Ellie, run over to the nurses' station and find somebody to sort this out, will you? And then pop down to the shop and fetch me some Evian and a sandwich. How I'm supposed to recover when nobody bothers with me, I really don't know.'

Much as I love my mum, and feel desperately sorry for her having to undergo such an ordeal, she is not, to put it mildly, an easy patient. I've barely left her bedside since she's come out of theatre and have quickly assumed the dual role of slave and whipping boy. Going to Charlotte's is starting to look like a restful option.

★

It's annoying that soon after our brief show of Andrews solidarity, my sisters all vanish off again to various pressing family commitments. This leaves me, of course, as the sole single sister, to look after my helpless, bewildered father and keep my increasingly impatient mother company. As we sit in the hospital canteen, only hours after Mum's operation, I listen in disbelief as each of my sisters makes her excuses.

Emily hasn't even lasted twenty-four hours. Apparently Goldman Sachs just can't manage without her. No wonder the entire planet has gone into financial meltdown: Emily Andrews had to take a day off work.

'I couldn't possibly expect you to understand,' Emily says condescendingly, when I selfishly suggest that she takes a week's leave and spends some quality time with her mother. 'Unlike you, Ellie, I have a proper job where people depend on me. I'm needed on the trading floor. I am central to the success of my team.'

'There's no i in team,' I mutter darkly, but Emily is ignoring me. She spent most of our childhood doing this, so I shouldn't be surprised. She only ever spoke to me if I needed to borrow an advance on my pocket money, sitting me down at her pink desk to explain the exorbitant rate of interest she was intending to charge, before fleecing me for the next six weeks. She made Shylock look like Robin Hood.

'You can easily give up working in that grotty shop,' Emily continues, shrugging on her latest Stella McCartney jacket and running a hand through her immaculate razor-sharp bob, 'but I can't afford to have time off. It's just as well you never took Daddy up on his offer of a position in the company. At least you don't have a career to worry about.'

'I like working in Blue Moon,' I protest. 'And anyway, I have to work to pay my rent. I don't live at Sam's for free, you know.'

'Why you live there at all is a mystery.' Lucy shudders. 'You could be living in the family flat. I loved living in the family flat. There are some amazing shops in Primrose Hill, and Sadie and Kate are practically our neighbours.'

'I don't want to live in the family flat,' I say through gritted teeth. 'I like living in Taply and being independent.'

But my sisters don't get independence. Until each of them was married, they lived in family properties, cushioned by the family dosh and meeting the suitable sons of family friends. The fact that I never wanted to follow suit is still inexplicable to them.

'I'll have to shoot off too, darling,' Charlotte sighs. 'Blue Smoke's been kicked in the field and Barney says he's in a pretty bad way, poor old man. Legs like glass, that horse. Still, don't worry, Ellie, the others will help out.'

'Actually, I'll have to go home too, and I can't possibly come back until next week,' Lucy chips in. She checks her perfect reflection in the back of a teaspoon and pouts prettily at herself. 'Consuela phoned to say that Imogen's come out in a ghastly rash and she needs me, poor baby. And George has a wobbly tooth. I'm a mother, Ellie, and my children have to come first. You'll understand that one day.'

I stare at her. If George and Imogen see their mother once a week they're doing well. How Lucy fits them in at all between Pilates/manicures/blowdries is a total mystery.

'You and Annabelle will have to sort things out between you,' Lucy finishes, with a toss of her glossy blonde head.

Well, of course Annabelle isn't having this. If the others are off, then she doesn't see why she should be stuck in the hospital.

'I'm going home too,' she chimes in, 'Some of us have

husbands and responsibilities, Ellie. It must be lovely to spend all day swanning around and being interviewed for the television, but I have Mark to think about.'

I feel like telling her that actually it's a little late to start thinking about what Mark might want. From what I can gather, Poppy is doing a great job of sorting out his needs. Then I remind myself that scoring points this way isn't only cruel but probably incendiary. After all, who introduced Mark and Poppy in the first place but yours truly?

'Besides,' Annabelle carries on, whilst picking disdainfully at the lurid dish masquerading as chicken tikka, 'you're single and have tons of time to spare. You ought to be glad that our parents want you, since nobody else seems to.'

I enjoy the spontaneous and very satisfying sensation of tipping my curry all over her beautiful blonde head. Somehow seeing Annabelle dripping in crimson sauce makes me feel so much better. I would defy the Priory Clinic to devise a better form of therapy. So what if my life is still crap, I've lost the man I love and my sisters are more bovine than a herd of Friesians? At least Annabelle looks as awful as I feel. As I leave the table I can almost hear the final thud of nails being driven into the coffin of our sisterly relationship, but by this point I'm past caring.

So now I'm the only remaining Andrews daughter in the hospital and therefore get to do all the running around. I'm not saying I'm not willing to do it – I do love my mother – but it annoys me that she sings their praises all the time yet always finds fault with me. Why can't anyone except my good self see that my glorious, beautiful, talented sisters are totally and utterly selfish?

At least being this busy keeps my mind off Jay and Marcus, and has the added bonus of burning off some flab. Although Marcus is continually texting and sending flowers, I'm ignoring him, and the last I heard, Jay and Roxy had flown back to the States. Even when Marcus calls to say that something amazing has happened, he's a changed man and he wants nothing more than to prove it to me, I ignore him. It seems I do have some willpower after all.

★

'Your sisters are the absolute limit,' says Sam, when I manage to snatch a few minutes away from the hospital and dash into Taply. 'I've never met such selfish cows in my life. And as for Annabelle, that one's got more front than Brighton.'

'But not, apparently, nearly as nice a front as me!' chips in Poppy from where she's squatting on the floor of Blue Moon sorting out joss sticks.

Sam rolls her eyes. 'Drag your brain out of your groin and do some work, will you?'

Poppy grins. Something about the sparkle in those wicked brown eyes tells me more than I actually want to know. In spite of everything, I feel a twinge of pity for Annabelle.

'Here.' Sam places a bowl of apple and parsnip soup in front of me. 'Get this down your neck. You look awful.'

'I'm not hungry.' I push the bowl away. It smells good but I just can't summon the enthusiasm to attack it. Lifting a spoon feels like too much effort.

Poppy tucks in for me.

'This is a good one,' she says thickly, through a giant mouthful. 'Mud dreamed it up last night. He's really getting into cooking.'

'Are you sure you're not upset about him having your job?' worries Sam, looking concerned.

I shake my head. Although I didn't want to leave, I know they'll make a great team in the shop.

'Mud says that the production team really want you to appear on *This Morning* with him,' Sam tells me. 'Apparently Phil and Holly love the whole spider story. Mud reckons this could be a whole new career for both of you.'

'Talking about spiders?' I shudder. 'No thanks.'

I was hoping to forget the past few weeks, not that there seems to be much hope of this. The fickle public is proving not to be quite as fickle as I would have liked. Weeks on and I'm still attracting stares and comments. I take my hat off to Jordan. How she lives with this every day I really can't imagine. Anyway, the whole sorry affair is superimposed with the image of Jay's bleak face awash with summer rain as he said goodbye. No wonder I can't eat.

'Jay asked after you,' Sam adds, as though reading my mind.

'He did? When? What did he say?'

'That he's sorry and hopes you guys can be friends.'

I close my eyes. 'Maybe one day.'

'He doesn't love Roxy,' Sam says. 'He's only with her now because he's got such an old-fashioned sense of duty. He feels that he owes it to her to be there.' She snorts. 'My brother the hero. That girl's such a slapper. I've got as much chance of fathering that baby as he has! But Jay won't be told, of course. He says he's got to face his responsibilities and that he's got no intention of wrecking your life as well.'

Bit late for that, I think.

'It's ridiculous!' cries Poppy, springing up from the floor and sending joss sticks flying. 'You want to be with him, he

216

wants to be with you, so what's the problem? Roxy's old man is loaded; it's not as though she'll be a penniless single mum. Jay can still bung her some cash once a month, and bingo! Everybody's happy.'

'Jay wouldn't be Jay if he abandoned her,' I say.

'And Ellie wouldn't be Ellie if she pressured him to leave,' adds Sam.

'Men are from Mars and women are from Venus,' declares Poppy helpfully. She was glued to that book for weeks. In the end, Mars and Venus went on a date to the bin, courtesy of Sam.

I give her a weak smile. 'If men are from Mars then I wish they'd bloody well stay there and save me all this hassle. Life would be a lot easier.'

'True,' agrees Sam. 'But wouldn't we be bored! And Ann Summers would soon run out of vibrators!' She picks up the soup bowl and carries it into the tiny kitchen. 'I'm gutted that Roxy has pulled a stunt like this. I really wanted you and Jay to finally get it together. After all, I never did shag Mark Owen, and it only seems right that one of us should fulfil a teenage fantasy.'

'Maybe a crush is exactly what it should have remained,' I say wearily. Then I glance at my watch and groan. Time to get back to the hospital with the latest edition of *The Lady*. 'I'd better go, girls. I'm picking Dad up and taking him to visit Mum.'

Poppy's lighting joss sticks, and the scent of lavender fills the shop.

Sam thrusts a handful at me. 'These are great for relaxation, and you look like you could do with some of that.'

I stuff them into my tatty old rucksack. 'Thanks. I'm not sure I'll get the chance to use them, though. I'm being bundled off to Charlotte's after the weekend to meet eligible men without chins as part of my mother's wedding project.'

'And that's supposed to cheer you up?' Sam asks incredulously.

'Take my mind off things was how Charlotte put it.'

'Come back soon, won't you?' Sam kisses me on the cheek. 'It isn't the same when you're away. I won't let your room out this time, I promise.'

As I walk away down Taply High Street, I wonder how I can tell Sam that things are never going to be the same again. In her clumsy and domineering way Charlotte is right; maybe it is time for a change.

Once sitting in Esther, I reach across to the back seat and pull Jay's thick fisherman's sweater into my arms. Like a child with a comfort blanket, I bury my face in the prickly wool and drink in the soft tang of his scent. Then I place the jumper on the passenger seat and blink back my tears. I'm moving on. I have to.

Double Trouble

'Is that you, Ellie?' my father calls the moment I put my key in the door. 'Come into the study for a moment, will you?'

I toss my keys on to the polished table by the stairs, narrowly missing an antique bowl that swims with pink roses, and then from habit perch on the bottom stair to pull off my boots. Mum might be in hospital but I can't bring myself to break the rules she's instilled in me over the past two and a half decades.

Padding across the chequered hall tiles, I push the study door open with my socked foot. A warm fug envelops me. It might only be September, but Dad still insists on laying a roaring fire, and inside the study the scent of applewood mingles with the heavy tang of pipe smoke.

'You OK, Dad?' I drop a kiss on to the crown of his head. The hair is thin, the scalp pink and vulnerable. Seated in his favourite armchair, one that Mum has long banished from the sitting room, he looks tired and smaller somehow. 'Have you had lunch?'

'Yes, yes.' He swats the air impatiently with his hand. 'Never mind that. Something's happened.'

My mouth dries.

'Mum?'

'Oh darling, no, don't panic. Not Mum. It's Charlotte.

Barney just rang in a terrible state. Apparently Lottie was out exercising one of her horses and has taken a really nasty fall. She's in Basingstoke Hospital with a broken leg and possible internal injuries. Barney said she's in agony.'

'Poor Lottie,' I say, trying to look sympathetic, even though I secretly think that people bonkers enough to tear around the countryside on huge wild beasts deserve all they get.

'You know what Barney's like,' continues my father, distractedly ironing out the creases in his *Financial Times* with a forefinger. 'He's gone to pieces without her.'

I certainly do know what Barney's like. He's temperamental, to say the least. Charlotte keeps him on an even keel and makes the excuse that he's an artist, which he most certainly is: a piss artist.

'Mum will panic,' says my father. 'She really doesn't need news like this right now. You know her. She'll be trying to shoot down to Hampshire to sort out Charlotte when what she really needs to do is rest and get her strength up for the chemotherapy.'

'Why do I get the feeling I'm not going to like what's coming next?' I ask.

My father sighs. 'You know Mum, darling. We can't have her fretting. She'll be insisting that somebody has to be there to sort out the twins.'

I agree. How about borrowing Supernanny? Or a week in boot camp? That's the kind of sorting out those little darlings need.

'What about Barney?' He might be crap, but surely even Tristan and Isolde can't destroy the place if their dad's there?

'Charlotte said he's got to go away tomorrow; he's painting some footballer and his wife. The kind of money they're offering isn't to be turned down.' My father reaches into his desk and plucks out his pipe, another relic long banned to his study by my mother. He begins to pack it with Golden Virginia, which is his well-established and very successful avoidance tactic. Lectures over my school reports, debates about the length of my skirts; you name it, they all started with Dad excavating his pipe.

'You want me to go now rather than next week?' My heart doesn't so much sink as plummet. Living in the presence of Tristan and Isolde makes Broadmoor look like a sane option. After twenty-four hours with those monsters, a padded cell will be exactly what I'll need.

'I'd certainly appreciate it,' admits my father, drawing upon his pipe as a drowning man would gasp at air. 'We can't have your mother upset at a time like this. Besides, Barney promises to be back in two days, and there's always the au pair to help out.'

I don't hold out a lot of hope there, since Charlotte's children are to au pairs what Rentokil is to insects. Ingrid is the latest in a long line of Ulrika Jonsson lookalikes, and judging by the nervous twitch she'd developed when I last saw her, at Annabelle's wedding, I can't see her coping with children, horses, pets and a mountain of unpaid bills. On the other hand, I can't see myself coping either, and I don't even have a nice language barrier to cower behind.

But how can I possibly refuse to do as my father asks? I'm still feeling hideously guilty about all the embarrassment I caused my poor parents by wrecking Annabelle's wedding and then winding up on the news more often than Trevor McDonald. This is penance, and I will do it without moaning.

Well, without too much moaning.

Before long, Esther and I are chugging round the M25 to the strains of Abba, inching our way ever closer to Hampshire. I drive slowly in a futile attempt to delay the inevitable, and lose count of how many times I'm given the bird. But I'm made of sterner stuff, and besides, I'm trying to paint my nails at the Fleet junction and don't have any fingers free, so I save all my pent-up aggression for my nephew and niece.

It's gone six by the time I finally swing on to the meandering drive that leads to Ketton Place.

'Last night I dreamt I went to Manderley again,' I mutter through teeth that rattle as my poor car lumbers over the ruts. Dark swathes of rhododendrons crouch alongside the drive, blocking out the light and scraping against the sides of the car, while thick tufts of wild grass grow down the centre like small islands between the deep puddles. The air of neglect and isolation makes me shiver. Whatever Charlotte and Barney spend their money on, it certainly isn't the upkeep of their drive. *No wonder Charlotte drives a four by four*, I think, as I cling on to the steering wheel and wince as my boobs bounce around with more energy than the Andrex puppy.

Rounding a bend in the drive, I'm relieved to break out of the gloom and see the crumbling façade of Ketton Place itself. Although historians rave about Ketton, with its genuine thirteenth-century hall and pre-Reformation chapel, it still looks like the scary house all the bats fly out of at the start of *Scooby Doo*. Charlotte and Barney only inhabit one wing of the house, because the rest is falling down around their ears. I don't think anybody has given it so much as a lick of paint since the Middle Ages.

I'm still getting over the horror of my last visit here. Besides being locked in the tack room, I was also subjected to an evening of ghost-story telling. All very well and good in the cosy lamplight of the kitchen, but not quite so funny an hour later when I was tucked up in my antique four-poster bed, icy cold and flinching at every unfamiliar sound. When a shrouded figure glided through the door to stand menacingly at the foot of my bed, I almost died from fear. And so did bloody Tristan when he threw back the hood to reveal his evil freckled face. The joke didn't seem quite so funny when Auntie Ellie had her hands around his throat.

'Ellie! At last!'

A wild figure flies out from the front door, matted grey hair streaming behind him and glasses clinging perilously to his nose. Barney Ketton, brother-in-law, trendy society painter and all-round loony, is practically yanking Esther's door off in his eagerness to pull me out. Things must be dire.

'I'm so pleased to see you!' Barney scoops me out of the Fiesta and crushes me in a bear hug.

'How's Lottie?' I ask when he finally releases me. Paint is now daubed across my chest. It looks like my FCUK fleece is the first casualty of my stay. Mum will be delighted.

'Charlotte?' Barney regards me with wild eyes whilst raking a hand through his grey mane. 'Charlotte's fine. *She's* in hospital and *I'm* here! You have no idea what it's been like!' His voice rises to a plaintive wail. 'The au pair's locked herself in her bedroom with my mobile and is refusing to come out. Christ knows how much the bill will be, because she'll have been ringing Sweden all day. She hasn't cooked so we haven't eaten yet. The stable girl's got flu so I've had to see to Lottie's horses, and you know I'm allergic to them.'

I'm beginning to feel pretty allergic myself.

'Tristan and Isolde turned the taps on in the guest bathroom and put the plug in, so we've had a flood on our hands. Don't be surprised if the electrics go tonight. I've bodged them up as best as I can but I can't afford to get anyone in. And as if that isn't enough, the bloody twins have run off with my Polaroid camera and haven't come back all day. Do you think I should call the police?'

'That's a bit drastic, Barney,' I say, surprised at this unusual display of paternal concern for his offspring. 'They've always had the run of the place. I'm sure they'll be back.'

Unfortunately.

'Not to find the twins. To rescue my camera and teach those little bastards a lesson,' hisses my brother-in-law. 'And hopefully lock them up until Lottie gets home. I can't cope.'

'Shall we go in?' I ask pointedly, when Barney shows no sign of budging. 'I could do with a hand with my bags.'

'Of course. Go in. Help yourself. I'm sure there's everything you need. Ingrid should be able to help you, if she ever comes out of her room, that is.'

'You're off already?' The speed at which Barney wants to leave is almost indecent.

'Afraid so.' Barney's practically sprinting across the weed-strewn cobbles towards his car. Taking a second look, I notice that the Volvo is packed with enough suitcases to last him a month, never mind a few days. Alarm bells start to ring.

'It's a long drive to Manchester,' he calls over his shoulder while diving into the driving seat. 'I'd better get going. I promised Steven and Alex I'd be ready to start tomorrow.'

Clutching my car keys so tightly that they dig into my hands, I watch in despair as Barney's car splutters into life, backfires and then screeches out of the courtyard.

Heaving the kitchen door open, I'm immediately knocked flying by Charlotte's huge dogs, barking and growling in outrage that a stranger has invaded their kitchen.

'Bugger off!' I yell as I go flying and land with a thud on the cold stone floor. 'Down, Lear! Down, Cordelia! Who do you think is going to feed you for the next heaven knows how long?'

Maybe the dogs are more intelligent than I believe, or maybe it's my tone of voice, but they stop barking and slink back to their baskets, eyeing me with something like respect. Watch out, Cesar Millan! If I can just do the same with the twins, I'll be sorted. But first things first. I need a huge glass of wine for Dutch courage.

Charlotte's vast kitchen is more like a living room where food sporadically appears when anyone can be bothered to cook. There's a massive oak table that stands in the middle, completely submerged in clutter, a big saggy sofa housing half a dozen cats and, over by the door, a huge Welsh dresser where unpaid bills, rosettes and rotting fruit jostle for pole position. Herbs, saucepans and various bits of bridle hang from the ceiling and there's an enormous Aga on the far side. No wonder Ingrid's in her room and refusing to come out if she's expected to cook on that. Where the hell is the microwave?

'He has gone, yes?'

The light, accented voice comes from the shadowy corner over by the door, and I jump so violently that my

225

feet leave the ground. That's what you get for watching *Most Haunted*. Ingrid is hovering nervously in the doorway. Her left hand is clutching a Nokia and I notice that all her nails have been gnawed off. Oh dear. I've already nibbled mine away. What else can I chew? Lear and Cordelia's bone?

'Mr Ketton has gone,' I sigh. 'Couldn't see him for dust, actually.'

'I was waiting for Mr Ketton to leave before I call a taxi,' says Ingrid. 'I am not wanting a scene as I go.'

'You're not leaving as well?'

'I am sorry.' Ingrid plops down on to the sofa, sending cats flying. 'I am at the end of my rope.'

Hmm. Quite a good description. Too long here and I'll probably be putting a noose around my own neck.

'Tristan and Isolde are out of control,' she continues. 'They are rude to me. They put frogs in my bed. They swear very loudly. I have enough. I am sick of Mr Ketton doing nothing and I am sick of ghosts and noises. But most of all I am sick of the mucking out the horses! None of my friends are having to do this.'

You know that bit in *Titanic* when Jack and Rose are clinging to the top of the ship and then even that starts to sink? Well that's exactly how I feel at this moment. No Charlotte, no Barney and now no Ingrid. Just good old Auntie Ellie and the twins from hell.

'I need a drink,' I say weakly.

'Wait till this time tomorrow,' warns Ingrid with a tight smile. 'I am thinking it is more than one drink you'll be needing.'

'I'll want an intravenous drip administering hemlock. That or a gun to finish the twins off.'

Ingrid jumps up from the sofa and starts burrowing in

the bread bin. With a triumphant cry she pulls a bottle of 1972 Merlot from the mouldy depths.

'Mr Ketton is not leaving his wine for me to drink so he hides it. But I am knowing that nobody keeps bread in the bread pot here!'

She rummages in a cupboard and unearths a corkscrew.

'You will need to be firm,' she instructs, slopping wine into two mugs of dubious cleanliness. 'Or those children are not respecting you.'

'Too late for that,' I say gloomily.

Before leaving, Ingrid shows me where Charlotte keeps the food. Basically, imagine the most unlikely places for things to be and that's exactly where you'll find them. Dog food under the sink, fridge hidden beneath a pile of New Zealand rugs, toaster actually in the fridge. You'd need a seriously disturbed mind to figure out how to survive in this household. Even Bear Grylls would be stumped. The only ray of light is that hopefully I too can find an equally peculiar hiding place and stay there until either I starve or the twins find me. I'm not sure which fate is worse, but judging by the way Ingrid is chewing on her long blonde plait and peering hopefully out of the grimy window, it's probably the latter.

'They can't be that bad,' I say, desperate to stop her from getting on the train and leaving me. 'After all, they're only kids.'

Ingrid's blue eyes shoot me a look of incredulity.

'They must be all right when Charlotte's at home, surely?' I continue, clutching at straws. If all else fails, I can always threaten the little gits with their mother. Surely the NHS will be delighted to save cash by kicking her out of bed very, very soon?

'Mrs Ketton is busy with her horses,' says Ingrid, who clearly has a promising new career beckoning as a diplomat. 'She does not have the time for the twins. And as for Mr Ketton?' Her shrug speaks volumes. 'He is very seldom at home.'

I'm starting to get the picture. When they're not packed off to boarding school, Tristan and Isolde can pretty much do whatever they want so long as they keep out of their parents' way. They'll eat me for breakfast and chew on my bones for lunch.

Sitting in Charlotte's kitchen, swigging wine like there's about to be a world shortage, I remember why I wasn't tempted to do a teaching training course during my post-degree panic. Suddenly temping for Rupert and working in Blue Moon seem like heaven. In fact, Rupert seems like heaven too. So what if he actually enjoys watching *News 24* and listening to opera? These aren't exactly dumpable offences, unlike being a two-faced spying git or being engaged to a beautiful and very pregnant model. If I'd only said yes when I'd had the chance, none of this mess would ever have happened. No dating Marcus and sabotaging the protest, no falling in love with Jay, no losing my cushy job. Right now, I'd probably be at some cosy little drinks party in Kensington, discussing my choice of seating plan and worrying about the flowers. Mum would be happy, and best of all I wouldn't be anywhere near Ketton Place.

Do I still have Rupert's number? Would he take me back if I really grovelled?

'The taxi is late.' Ingrid checks her watch. 'My train is at eight. I am not wanting to be missing it.'

I'm praying hard that the taxi won't turn up at all, but only moments later a car draws up outside and honks its horn cheerfully. Nelson Mandela being freed from Robben Island must have had a similar look on his face to Ingrid as she flies out of the house. Crossing to the window, I watch miserably as she flings herself into the car. Gulping another mouthful of wine, I resolve to hunt around Ketton for any other potential alcohol hiding places. Maybe my nephew and niece won't seem so bad if I'm pissed.

'Good luck!' Ingrid calls from the cab. The words *you'll need it* hang heavy and unsaid in the air. Then the car pulls away and she's gone, leaving me bereft and clutching my glass like a security blanket.

Just as I'm sussing out the possibilities of the Aga as a potential hiding place for very expensive wine, the back door flies open and smashes against the wall with such a crash that the ancient and weary walls of Ketton shake. I shake too, because the mini whirlwinds that fly past me, dive under the New Zealand rugs and begin strewing the contents of the fridge across the floor are my nephew and niece.

'I'm starving!' shrieks Tristan, from inside the fridge.

'Try this,' shrills Isolde, stumbling from the pantry, her face buried in a bowl of dubious-looking meat. 'Is it stew, Trist? Or has Mum put cat food in the larder?'

I feel the start of a migraine in my right temple.

'Hello, guys,' I say, feeling just like Daniel when Nebuchadnezzar asked him to go and play with the lions. Give me the lions any day.

Tristan withdraws his head from the fridge long enough to give me a look that clearly says I'm slightly more distasteful than something nasty on the bottom of his shoe.

'Hello, Ellie,' Isolde says, before attacking the cat food/bolognese with a spoon.

'Should you eat that?' I ask, alarmed at how fast she's shovelling the meat away. I have awful visions of clearing up vomit, and worse, all night long.

She looks at me pityingly. 'What else is there?'

'Eff all,' groans Tristan, slamming the fridge shut and throwing himself on to the sofa, scattering dogs and cats across the kitchen. 'I hate this place. Where's Ingrid?'

'Hello, Auntie Ellie, how are you?' I say with maximum sarcasm. I top up my glass and Tristan sighs.

'You're pissed,' he says, with the pitying look of one beholding a sad and terminally embarrassing old relative, the sort of look I normally give my parents or Auntie Ethel. Having it shot at me is kind of disconcerting. I'm young and trendy, aren't I?

'You're always pissed, Ellie. You were pissed at Laura's christening and at Auntie Annabelle's reception. No wonder nobody can do anything with us,' declares Isolde theatrically, putting down the bowl with a clatter and wiping her mouth with the back of her hand. 'It's our bad blood. That's what our head of year, Miss Congdon, said.'

'I'm not pissed!' I say indignantly, and then, more gently, 'I'm afraid I've got some bad news. Ingrid's had to leave suddenly and I don't think she's coming back.'

'Yes!' Tristan yells, punching the air. 'Let's celebrate! Mum's in hospital, Dad's in Manchester, Ingrid's gone and we can do what we like!'

'Cool!' Isolde grins like a Jack-o'-lantern.

'Err, no you can't. I'm in charge, so it's my rules now,' I say, with what I desperately hope is some kind of authority.

The twins shoot a pitying look at me.

'Yeah, whatever,' yawns Tristan.

'I mean it,' I tell them, doing my best to be firm but knowing that it's going to be impossible to earn their respect because a) they've seen my exploits splashed all over the papers and b) they don't respect anybody. 'I'm here until your mum gets better and I'm in charge. So that means doing what I tell you.'

'We're so scared!' Tristan sneers. 'Hasn't Ingrid told you all about us? About how we shaved her eyebrows off that time?'

Actually, I just assumed that was high fashion, along with Brazilian bikini waxes and wheat allergies.

'Or the time we swapped her shampoo with hair remover,' pipes up Isolde. 'Or when we sewed up all her trousers? Or when—'

'All right! All right!' No wonder she couldn't leave quick enough. 'But I'm family and that makes a difference.'

'How?' asks Isolde.

I'm thinking rapidly now in a desperate attempt to save myself from days of deeply unamusing practical jokes. 'We're related, so we ought to like each other a bit more.'

'That's crap,' sneers Tristan. 'We're related to the olds and we hate them. They're totally sad.'

'I've got the money so I'm in charge of food,' I say quickly. 'If you two don't behave, then I won't feed you. Simple as that.'

For a split second Tristan looks worried, before he remembers that looking worried isn't cool. 'Yeah? Well if you starve us, then I'll tell social services and *you'll* go to prison.'

I've had enough. I stick my face right up against his and hiss, 'Listen to me, you little monster. Right now a spell in prison seems like a bloody good idea compared to being stuck here with you. If you want to live on Whiskas for the foreseeable future, be my guest! Otherwise, we are going to do things my way. Got it?'

Tristan is recoiling from my breath. Suddenly I'm glad I stopped at the services and had garlic bread.

'You're well tight,' he sulks, pulling his hat even lower over his face.

'You'd better bloody believe it,' I agree. 'I'm so tight I make Tom Jones's trousers look baggy.'

'Who's Tom Jones?' asks Isolde, watching this exchange with fascination.

'Never mind, sweetie.' I switch from Queen Bitch back into Auntie Ellie. Round one to me, I rather feel. 'Now, where does your mum keep the food?'

Beneath her mop of carrot hair Isolde's round freckly face falls. 'There's never any. That's why I ate the cats' supper. Mum only uses the freshest livers; she never feeds the animals anything unhealthy. It'll be all right, won't it?'

'Of course it will,' I say cheerfully, trying to ignore the fact that Isolde is looking rather green. 'Everyone knows how good liver is for you.'

'I'm starving,' moans Tristan, now beeping away on an Xbox. 'Sometimes we get chips if Mum's been in to Salisbury.'

'Will this help?' Isolde pulls a credit card out of a cornflakes packet. 'We can always order some pizzas.'

'That's not mine!' I'm aghast. 'And it's certainly not yours! Where'd you get it?'

'I nicked it off Dad before he went out this morning!' She looks totally delighted. 'It's a gold one and everything. That will buy a few pizzas, won't it?'

'Isolde, most eleven-year-olds are reading *Harry Potter*, not stealing credit cards and Polaroids.'

Tristan looks up from the Xbox. 'Harry Potter's gay.'

He is? I must have missed that bit, and me an English graduate too.

'Most eleven-year-olds don't have to eat cat food,' my niece points out with impeccable logic. 'It's easy, Ellie, all you have to do is phone up and pretend to be B. Ketton. I'd do it but I think they're more likely to believe a grown-up. They were a bit suss last time, weren't they, Tris?'

Oh Lord. I've just joined Fagin's gang. While I debate what to do, my stomach lets out an almighty rumble, and suddenly just the thought of a Meat Feast is enough to drive me to crime. Something tells me that *if you can't beat 'em, join 'em* is going to be my motto for the foreseeable future.

Well, either that or live on cat food.

'Get the number,' I order Isolde, who explodes into an enormous cheer. 'I'll do it this once, but tomorrow we are going to the supermarket. Is that clear?'

'Cool!' she replies, fishing the Yellow Pages out from inside the Aga.

'We can't go to Asda,' Tristan tells me. 'They've banned us.'

In my hand, the phone grows slick with sweat. Is it illegal to lock children up? Surely the entire world would be a safer place with Tristan and Isolde out of harm's way?

Taking a deep breath, I dial the number of Domino's Pizza and embark on my new life of crime.

'You'll never guess who's bought the house down the lane from us.' Isolde, speaking thickly through a huge mouthful of Hawaiian pizza, is busting at the seams to tell me.

'No, you'll never guess!' echoes Tristan.

The three of us are sitting squashed up together on the kitchen sofa, sharing pizzas straight from the box. From the way the twins are gobbling up the slices, you'd think they hadn't been fed for days, which is quite possibly the case. All around us sit assorted dogs and cats, staring up in drooling anticipation of the bits of crust that might come their way. I've bribed the twins with the promise of half a glass of wine each if they can unearth Barney's secret stash, and lo and behold, several bottles of very good claret have appeared from the most unlikely places. Now I'm tucking in with gusto, feeling a guilty little glow of pride that I've just committed a crime and got away with it. Still, I decide as I reach for my fourth slice, Barney and Charlotte should at least feed us, and I can always justify myself in court by saying that my starving niece and nephew had been forced to eat pet food. Surely nobody could put me away if I've saved innocent little children from such a fate?

'Well?' demands Isolde. 'Go on! Guess!'

I pause in my chewing. 'Somebody cool? Is it Justin Bieber?'

'Gross!' shrieks Tristan, spraying me with pizza. 'He's not cool! Guess again!'

I search the dim recesses of my brain to dredge up the little knowledge I have of teen culture. I knew I should have got up earlier on Saturdays. Who knows, by now I might even have learned to distinguish Ant from Dec. 'Eminem?'

'I wish,' sighs Tristan. 'That would be sick!'

'You'll never guess,' Isolde says smugly.

I'm starting to feel intrigued in spite of myself. 'Madonna? Sting?'

'No!' shouts Tristan. 'It's Xander Thorne!'

'Oh, she doesn't know who he is.' Isolde looks crestfallen when I don't go wild.

'She's too old,' adds her brother disparagingly. 'Xander Thorne, *you know*, the lead singer in Dark Angel. They are so sound, man!'

'Well sound!' agrees Isolde.

The penny drops. Of course, you'd have to have been living in one of Mud's tunnels for a year not to have heard of this band. Their latest hit has been at number one for weeks. Every billboard in town is plastered with advertisements for their album, and it's hard to switch on the telly without seeing Xander giving an interview. With slanting cat-like eyes, a wild mane of golden hair and a lean, rangy body, he looks every inch a dissolute and fallen angel tumbled from heaven. Personally I think his music sounds like a load of banshees in pain, but I'll keep this opinion to myself. Clearly the twins are big fans.

'Sound!' I parrot. 'Which house has he bought, then?'

'He wanted this one. But Daddy wouldn't sell, because Kettons have always lived here,' says Isolde sadly. 'We could have had a lovely new house with central heating and Sky TV. But it didn't really matter, because he's so rich he just bought Sutton Court instead, so that makes him our next-door neighbour.'

I'm impressed. Sutton Court is a Victorian monstrosity that sprawls for acres, complete with tennis courts, paddocks, swimming pool and helipad. I went there years ago with Charlotte for a hunt ball. My memory of the place is a little cloudy, however, probably thanks to the enormous quantities of booze on offer that night. But it seems that

Xander Thorne is loaded, even if his music is a pile of pants. Suddenly my own tone-deafness doesn't seem such a hindrance after all.

'What does your mum make of it all?' I can't exactly imagine my prim and proper sister being too keen on living next door to a rock star.

'Mum's cool.' Tristan lets out a huge belch to make room for his eighth slice of pizza. 'Xander's just bought one of her horses and he wants to hunt next season so she loves him. He's given us tons of Dark Angel stuff.'

'We're going to sell it at school and make a packet,' says Isolde excitedly. 'He says we can have loads more.'

'And when we sell the pictures, we'll be even more loaded,' adds Tristan smugly.

Immediately, my responsible-aunt antennae are fully pricked. A missing Polaroid, a rock star next door and the twins' materialistic instincts are an explosive combination. What exactly have they been up to all day long with their father's very expensive camera?

I fix my nephew with a steely glare. 'What pictures?'

Ever seen a Venus fly trap snap shut? That's exactly what Tristan's mouth looks like.

'What pictures?' I repeat.

Total silence. A very bad sign. I look around the kitchen for some means of threatening them. Jumping from the sofa, I pick up the kitchen scissors.

'If you don't tell me,' I threaten, 'I'm going to cut the plug off your television set, and then your Xbox and then every single thing you own that goes bleep, whizz or ping.'

'You wouldn't dare,' says Tristan confidently.

'Oh, wouldn't I?' I stand over the plug socket, scissors poised. 'What photos?'

The twins scowl at me. My interest grows; these are

obviously some pictures. My imagination breaks into a gallop. They haven't been taking photos of Xander Thorne in flagrante, have they? Looking at those two glowering faces, I wouldn't put it past them.

'Right,' I say briskly. 'I warned you.'

With a snip I sever the cable. The telly goes dark and emits a loud pop.

The twins stare at me in shocked silence.

I glance thoughtfully around the messy kitchen. 'What's next, I wonder? The stereo or the Xbox? Or are you,' I fix them with a beady stare, 'going to give me the photos?'

The twins look at each other. Then Isolde shrugs. 'You're well tight.'

'Yeah,' sniffs Tristan. 'No one *ever* tells us what to do.'

I feel rather chuffed at the note of awe in his voice. Maybe I ought to rethink my views on a career in teaching?

Tristan puts his hand down his baggy jeans and pulls out a handful of Polaroid snaps, which he then holds out to me. I look at them dubiously. I don't exactly fancy the idea of touching anything that has been down Tristan's pants.

'Take them, Ellie, but please don't cut the plug off my Xbox.'

'It's a deal.' I swap the photos for the scissors. Then I steel myself for what I'm about to see. Naked rock stars in various sexual positions, I presume, happily unaware that they are being spied upon by two amateur paparazzi.

My eyes widen like saucers and my face grows hotter than the chillis on the pizza.

The pictures show Xander Thorne, all right. In all his naked glory, fast asleep by his pool.

'Told you they were good,' says Tristan proudly. 'He was flat out; probably all that booze.'

'He shouldn't sunbathe, though. Miss Congdon says it's

very dangerous and you can get skin cancer,' his sister says sanctimoniously. 'And boozing by the swimming pool is really silly. He could drown.'

Good old Miss Condom. Seems she's full of good advice. Shame she hasn't taught the twins that stalking is against the law, though.

I look again; I just can't help it. I know I'm sworn off men, but there's something about the way he's sprawled across the sunbed. Although his eyes are closed, a smile still plays on his wide, generous mouth. I'd be smiling too if I were that rich and gorgeous.

Hang on, if I look closer, isn't that his—

'If you're looking for his willy, we didn't take a picture of that,' Tristan says sternly. 'We do have some morals, you know.'

My face turns the same colour as the pepperoni.

'I wasn't looking for his willy! I'm not interested in this person at all! Not his face, not his body and most certainly not his willy!'

'Why ever not?' says an amused voice.

I practically jump out of my skin. In all the excitement of plug cutting and picture grabbing, a total stranger has managed to let himself into the kitchen. Looking up, I find myself staring into the very same sculpted face that stars in the Polaroids in my hand.

'Now if you don't mind,' says Xander Thorne pleasantly, 'could I please have those pictures?'

Rocking My World

'Hello, Xander,' pipes up Isolde, the picture of wide-eyed innocence. 'Would you like a cup of tea?'

'I'd rather have some of Barney's Bordeaux,' says Xander, patting Cordelia/Lear and plonking himself on the sofa. 'Grab us a glass, Trist, before I start to get annoyed about being spied on.'

While Tristan scrabbles to attention, knowing he's in serious trouble, I just about manage to drag my chin off the slate floor and gather my wits. Oh my God. There is a bona fide rock star sitting in my sister's kitchen. Can life get any more surreal?

Xander smiles at me across the cluttered table. 'I don't think we've met? I'm Xander.'

I open my mouth to say something witty, but find I can't speak.

Xander's sleepy eyes twinkle and his mouth curves up in a cheeky grin. 'Don't you recognise me with my clothes on?'

Three thoughts run through my mind at this point. The first is, please could I drop through the floor now; the second is, why did he have to arrive when I've got pizza all over my top and my hair needs washing?; and the third is, why do these things always happen to me?

'That's our Aunt Ellie,' Isolde explains to Xander while

I just do a goldfish impression. 'She's in shock because you're famous.'

Xander sloshes some wine into a chipped Peppa Pig mug. 'I'm still a bit shocked about that myself. Relax, Ellie. I don't bite.'

'Not even the heads off bats?' Tristan says hopefully, but Xander shakes his head.

'Especially not the heads off bats. They're an endangered species. Besides, I'm a vegetarian.'

'You're a vegetarian?' I squeak finally. 'But I thought you were going hunting with Charlotte?'

Xander winks. 'Drag hunting.'

'Drag hunting's for girls,' Tristan says witheringly.

'Fine by me,' Xander says, and his merry amber eyes meet mine teasingly. 'I'm more than happy to hang out with the girls. Now, much as I'm sure you enjoyed looking at those pictures, Auntie Ellie, please could I have them now? I'm supposed to be taking drugs and smashing up hotel rooms, not snoozing by the pool. You could wreck my entire image there.'

I realise to my total and utter mortification that I'm still clutching the pictures in my hand.

'Oh! Sorry! Yes, of course.' In my haste to hand them back, I trip over a cat and go flying. Seconds later, I find myself sprawled across Xander Thorne, whose drink splashes all over his shirt.

'Steady there, Auntie,' he says, and his arms close around me. For a second his big, laughing mouth is only inches from mine and I'm squashed up against his chest. His toned, muscular, rock star chest.

Oh God. I think I'm going to faint.

'Ellie's been drinking all day,' sneaks Isolde. 'She's

always drunk. She's got to look after us, too. How's she going to manage that?'

'I'd start by having another drink,' Xander says to me, with a wink. Then, before I can even reply, he's set me on my feet and is pulling off his ruined shirt. In the flesh, he's even more toned and golden, like Michelangelo's *David* carved out of butterscotch.

I. Must. Not. Lick. Him.

'Trist, dude, go and get me one of your dad's smocks,' Xander orders, and off trots Tristan without so much as a squeak. Gorgeous and with twin-controlling superpowers? Is this man for real?

Once he is wearing one of Barney's paint-covered smocks, rather incongruous with Armani jeans and designer boots, Xander pours more wine for himself, tops up my mug and then manages to locate the milk and whip up some hot chocolate for the twins.

'You seem very at home,' I remark.

'I am.' He nods. 'Lottie and Barney have been really welcoming. Sutton Court is all very well, but I rattle round there like a pea in a drum. Much more fun over here.'

'Fun?' I ask incredulously. In my experience, having a swim in a piranha tank would be more fun than hanging out with the twins. Probably safer too.

'Yes, fun.' Helping himself to a cold slice of pizza and picking off the meat, Xander removes a cat and sinks back on to the sofa. 'It's never dull over here, and the twins are great, aren't they?'

I catch Tristan and Isolde exchanging a smirk.

'Absolutely,' I fib.

'How did you know we'd taken the pictures?' Isolde asks.

Xander narrows his eyes. 'Ever heard of CCTV?'

The twins nod gravely.

'My manager caught you on it. Just like he caught you pinching apples from the orchard and sneaking into the studio. Not to mention the cake you stole. And my boxer shorts. How much did they go for on eBay in the end?'

The twins turn so white their freckles look like bruises.

'Are we in trouble?' whispers Tristan.

'Any more photos and yes, big trouble,' Xander says, nodding his golden head sternly. 'And no more breaking and entering or there won't be any more Dark Angel stuff either. You get it?'

The twins nod like the Churchill dog. They get it all right.

'And there's one more condition for me not taking this any further,' he finishes. 'You guys are to do *everything* your auntie says. No messing, no tricks and no arguments. OK?'

Tristan and Isolde know when they are beaten. They badly want to flog that stuff at school. 'OK,' they mutter.

'Fantastic,' says Xander. Then he glances at his watch. 'Right, it's almost nine o'clock. Bedtime for you guys, I think. Off you go, and don't forget to do your teeth!'

Like magic, the twins slink out of the kitchen. I stare at Xander in awe. Never mind rock god. In my eyes, this man *is* God!

'Are you Mrs Doubtfire in disguise? How on earth did you do that?'

Xander shrugs his broad shoulders. 'I spend a lot of time on my own watching telly. *Supernanny*'s always on.'

'Well, I'm impressed,' I say, scooping up pizza boxes and stuffing them into the bin. 'You ought to give lessons. Or maybe get a show. *The Teen Tamer*?'

He laughs. 'If I change career, it won't be for reality

TV. I'd like to cook, maybe open a restaurant. That's my passion. Do you like cooking?'

He's talking to a girl whose culinary skills just about stretch to toast and Marmite.

'Love it!' I cross my fingers behind my back. Well, I love eating cooked stuff, which sort of counts.

And as though this is a cue to start chatting, Xander is up and running, telling me all about his favourite dishes, how he likes nothing more than cooking for his friends and family and how his biggest ambition is to have a Michelin star.

'It's not very rock and roll, though,' he finishes, tipping the last of the wine into our glasses. 'I've probably just blown my image.'

'Actually, I was so busy listening to your ideas, I totally forgot that you're *the* Xander Thorne. And your descriptions of food have made my mouth water!'

'Thanks.' Xander smiles. 'That means a lot. Normally the people I'm out with are more interested in clubbing and coke than the merits of a perfect coulis. And as for the women, most of them seem to exist on air. No wonder they're so bloody skinny.'

I glance down at my less than skinny body.

'And boring, too,' Xander says, pulling a face. 'I mean, what's the point of being able to afford the best restaurants if nobody wants to eat there with you?'

'It's a waste,' I say. Oh dear. I think I'm slurring.

'As you can tell, food is my passion. But I already know yours, don't I?'

He does? Who told him about my thing for carrot cake and Captain Kirk?

'The environment!' Xander says. 'I knew you looked

243

familiar. You're the girl in the tree, aren't you? The girl who found the spider?'

'Yep, that's me,' I say wearily. 'Spider woman.'

'Don't be bashful, that was an amazing thing you did.' In his excitement, Xander grabs my hands and holds them. 'I totally respect people who stand up for their beliefs like you did. I think it's awesome. You risked everything to save that wood.'

I smile modestly. Come on, I'm only human. Would *you* tell the truth if a beautiful man like Xander Thorne was singing your praises?

'You're an amazing woman,' Xander insists. 'You're funny, you have principles and you're gorgeous. I am so glad the twins chose today to play up.'

We're the best part of our way through a third bottle of wine now, and his eyes are practically crossing with drink. He probably hasn't a clue what he's saying. I am covered in pizza, my hair is a tangled, frizzy mess and I smell of dog. He must be very pissed. In fact, the kitchen's revolving like a fairground ride and the lights are shimmering.

The next thing I know, he's folding me into his arms, brushing the pizza sauce from my cheek with his thumb and kissing me. And although I miss Jay and wish so desperately that things could have been different, I'm soon kissing Xander back, loving the way his mouth still seems to laugh as he kisses and the way that his long hair tickles my nose. By the time the old grandfather clock strikes midnight, we're giddy with snogging.

Blimey. I feel like a teenager. Nobody will ever believe I've pulled Xander Thorne. Where are the twins and their Polaroids when you need them?

'Christ, look at the time,' Xander says. 'I'm supposed to be recording tomorrow.'

'And I'm dealing with the twins,' I say gloomily. What a thought. Talk about sobering up fast.

'They'll be fine,' Xander promises, ruffling my hair. 'Don't worry, I can blackmail them indefinitely. It'll cost you, though.'

'I'm skint,' I say with a sigh. 'I'm sure the bank manager crossed the road to avoid me last week.'

'Then I'll have to think of another way for you to pay,' Xander says slowly, and my heart goes into freefall. Surely not? I mean, I've heard all about rock stars and their wicked ways . . .

'Don't look so alarmed.' He laughs. 'I was thinking of dinner, not dragging you to some wild orgy.'

Xander stacks the dishwasher and blows me a kiss before letting himself out. As the room dips and spins, I drag myself up the stairs, where I collapse on to the ancient four-poster bed and am practically asleep before my eyes even close. At least I'm too drunk to worry about ghosts. Although if drinking three bottles of wine and snogging a rock star is the only way to get a good night's sleep at Ketton Place, my liver and my sanity could be seriously at risk.

It might be fun, though.

★

'Wake up, Ellie! Wake up!'

There's a pneumatic drill going off in my head and I'm blinded by light when the curtains are ripped open. My stomach is churning, and it's not helped by Isolde bouncing up and down on the bed.

'I think I've got meningitis,' I groan, burying my face in the pillow. 'Call the doctor.'

'Crap,' says Isolde cheerfully. 'You're just hung-over.

Daddy's always like this in the morning. A cooked breakfast is what you need.'

Cooked breakfast? In Charlotte's kitchen? What's on the menu? Cat food and eggs? Pizza crust?

'There's no food,' I croak.

'Xander's brought loads over from Sutton Court,' Isolde tells me. 'He's busy cooking right now. And he's mucked out the horses so you won't have to worry about that either. Then he's going to take us to Waitrose and maybe Thorpe Park. How cool is that?'

'Very cool,' I agree weakly.

I make the mistake of trying to sit up. Blimey, I don't need to go to Thorpe Park for a head rush, that's for sure. The whole room is whirling and dipping. Maybe Isolde's right and I need some food. And water, and Nurofen . . .

Oh dear Lord. Did I really snog Xander Thorne last night, or was that just a very pleasant dream?

Gingerly shrugging on some jeans, a clean hoody and my Uggs, pausing just long enough to sweep mascara on to my lashes, I shuffle down into the kitchen, where sure enough, Xander is at the Aga stirring a pan. The smells of toast and hash browns fill the air, and in spite of feeling like something the cat threw up, my mouth waters and my stomach rumbles. Tristan and Isolde are already sitting at the table shovelling down huge amounts of grub, while the kettle whistles merrily on the hob.

'Morning.' Xander turns round and beams at me. I have a vivid flashback to last night and can hardly meet his eye. I can't believe I'm nearly thirty and still getting pissed and snogging strangers. I *have* to stop drinking.

'How are you today?' he asks, while expertly flipping an egg in the pan. In spite of the fact that he drank at least as much as I did, has had less sleep and has already mucked out five horses, he looks amazing. The faded blue jeans sculpt his body perfectly, clinging to his long, lean legs and sexy bum, while the tight black shirt moulds every muscle of his toned chest. Even his hair is bouncy, pulled back into a ponytail with a strip of leather. It's sickening. I look like somebody even Gok Wan would reject.

'How on earth are you so perky?' I groan, placing my throbbing head in my hands. 'I feel like death warmed up.'

'I'm a rock star, remember? Surviving monster hang-overs is all part of it.'

And that, I suppose, is why I'm not a rock star but an unemployed English graduate. Well, that and the fact I can't sing.

'Tuck in,' says Xander, whacking a massive plate of food in front of me. 'We've got a busy day ahead.'

I spear a mushroom thoughtfully. 'Aren't you supposed to be recording?'

He shrugs. 'I'll do that another day. Today seems like a day for fun. What do you think, guys?'

The twins cheer and my head thuds. In my opinion, today's a day for hibernating in bed, but there's no hope of that. Not with the male equivalent of Mary Poppins here to chivvy us all along.

'Haven't you booked the studio?' I ask hopefully, be-cause then he'll push off, and I can plug the kids into the Xbox and crawl back to bed.

'Xander's got his own studio,' Tristan brags. 'He can do what he likes.'

'And what I'd like is some fun,' Xander tells us, sitting down at the table with his own food. Tossing a piece of toast to the dogs, he adds, catching my eye, 'I had lots of fun yesterday.'

I think my face could double for one of the tomatoes on

my plate. I avoid his gaze and pretend to be fascinated by my enormous breakfast. I'm not sure I can cope with any more fun today, but the twins are already bouncing with excitement and planning what rides to go on. Who am I to spoil their fun? At least while they're strapped into a roller coaster they won't be tormenting me.

★

Once breakfast is over and the kitchen cleaner than I've ever seen it, we all pile into Xander's huge four by four and zoom off to Waitrose. We do the shopping and Xander wears the most enormous baseball cap and shades imaginable, which couldn't make it more obvious that he's someone famous. As we pile the trolley high with just about everything the twins could ever want (sod the E numbers; I've got blackmail on my side now), shoppers take pictures of Xander on their camera phones and he huddles miserably into his leather jacket.

'I hate this,' he sighs as we meander along the frozen aisle, me riding on the trolley as Tristan pushes. 'I wish I could give it all up and be anonymous.'

'Can't you?' I ask.

'I guess so, but then I'd be letting down the others and the fans. Still, there comes a time when a guy just wants a quiet life. Maybe settle down and have a family. What's the point of having big houses and money if there's nobody to share it with?'

Blimey. He still wants a family after hanging out with Satan's sprogs all morning? Personally I'm tempted to get my tubes tied, but then I'm related to these monsters and genetically could produce some just like them, so every precaution must be taken. I owe the world that much.

'If you retired from music, you could open your restaurant,' I suggest.

Xander nods. 'Yes, I could. I guess I could do anything if I really put my mind to it. That's what life's about, isn't it? Taking opportunities.'

'It's about paying the bills for most of us,' I point out. 'Then we fit the fun bits in round that.'

'So let's have fun today,' says Xander, and grabbing the trolley from Tristan, he races me so fast down the aisle that my eyes water and we lose half our shopping.

★

Four hours and six rides on the roller coaster later, Xander's not looking quite so enthusiastic. The twins stuff their faces with candy floss and hot dogs and then whoop delightedly as they are tipped upside down to scream and vomit. Actually, it's quite good fun seeing them looking terrified, especially from my vantage point on the ground, but not so much fun for poor Xander, who gets splattered. Yet again he is the centre of attention wherever he goes and patiently has his photo taken with all his fans, but I notice lines of strain appearing around his mouth, and his merry eyes are no longer so sparkly.

By the time we get back to Ketton Place, we're all exhausted. The twins go to bring the horses in while I collapse on the sofa and Xander makes tea. For a second, I think of Jay, who always drank his treacle dark and with so much sugar your teeth practically rotted as soon as you took a sip, and my throat grows tight.

'Hey, are you OK?' Xander places my tea before me, his handsome face concerned. 'You look sad.'

'I'm fine,' I tell him. 'I'm just tired.'

'Have an early night,' he suggests. 'I'll take the twins

over to my home cinema and they can watch a movie. They'll love that. I'll get my housekeeper to rustle up some popcorn.'

Is this man for real? I can almost hear my mother yelling at me to snap him up now.

'My manager can drop them back,' Xander continues. 'Or if you like, come too and have a bath. There isn't a great deal of hot water here, is there?'

Now he's talking. I'd like nothing more than to wallow in hot water. Ketton's ancient pipes produce a lukewarm trickle the colour of Earl Grey, and you'd have to wait a week to fill one of the enormous claw-footed baths. No wonder Charlotte always smells of horses.

'No funny business, I promise,' he adds, with a slow smile. 'Just a bath and a movie. Lottie's told me that you've been nursing your mum. It's about time you had a break.'

Jay is gone for ever, but Xander, kind and gorgeous Xander, is here right now, and when he pulls me into his arms and kisses me, I don't protest.

Jay has moved on. Maybe it's time I did too. Besides, didn't Poppy predict that I'd meet my soulmate, the love of my life?

What if it was never Jay at all, but somebody totally different?

Somebody just like Xander?

11.15 a.m.

I can't believe he's turned his phone off! Of all the stupid things to do on our wedding day! How can I call the wedding off if he won't answer the phone? I suppose I could leave a voicemail or even text, but that's a bit harsh. If I'm going to jilt my fiancé, then the least I can do is tell him to his face. Unless he's changed his mind too and is ignoring me. Maybe he doesn't love me at all? Maybe he too has realised that this is a big mistake?

To be honest, it has always seemed a bit too good to be true that he'd ever want to be with me in the first place. If I call the wedding off, then I won't have to go through all the pain and trauma of a divorce when he realises that short, curvy girls with frizzy hair aren't all they're cracked up to be. We haven't even lived together properly yet – what will he think when he sees me without my make-up on? That'll probably be grounds for divorce in itself.

Right, change of plan. If I can't leave a message, I'll have to drive over to his and speak to him. He'll understand if I explain about all these bad omens.

And if he doesn't, he'll just think I'm nuts and he won't want to marry me anyway. Besides, one look at me in this tripe get-up will be enough to send him running to the hills. I look like a budget Lady Gaga.

'What are you up to?' Sam barges into my room with a face like thunder. 'I've just had Marcus banging on the door demanding to see you. You're getting married in less than three hours! I don't care what he says or how amazing he is. You can't see him yet!'

I can't? Bang goes that plan, then.

'And don't go thinking you can sneak out the window, either,' Sam adds, seeing me glance towards the street. 'Apart from the fact that the drainpipe is plastic and will never take your weight, there's already a load of paps gathering.'

'What?' I fly to the window, and sure enough, three guys in leather jackets with cameras slung around their necks are perched on the wall chatting to Poppy as she unloads her flowers.

'Surely you're not surprised?' Sam says as she whips the cover from my wedding dress. 'Anyone involved with Xander Thorne is going to be tabloid fodder. They'll all be gagging for a shot of you in your dress.'

'But I'm not the celebrity. Xander is!'

She shrugs. 'And you're the girl he gave it all up for. They're fascinated by you. They all want the big-money shot.'

My blood feels as though it's turned to Slush Puppie. Pictures of me in my dress are big money? I *knew* I should have used that exercise bike rather than hanging my clothes on it.

'I told you to sell the pictures to *OK!*,' Annabelle snaps, barging in with an enormous wheelie bag brimming with make-up. Her perfectly manicured hand brandishes an aerosol can of Fake Bake, which nearly takes my eye out.

'Ellie is not selling the most important day of her life,' flares Sam. 'This wedding is about love, not commercial transactions. And besides, this is all about what your mum wanted, remember? The big family do? The best wedding of all?'

Annabelle has the grace to look a bit shamefaced. 'Yes, yes, whatever. Anyway, I've come to give you a quick spray tan, Ellie. You'll look far too pasty otherwise.'

If I wasn't already thinking about jumping out of my bedroom window, I would be now. This is the girl who cut off all my hair when I was six and drew on my face with an indelible pen. And she thinks I'm going to let her spray me orange? I'll look like a baked bean in a wedding dress.

'You are not spraying an aerosol in here!' Sam grabs the bottle. 'Don't you know what that does to the environment?'

'But she'll look so much better brown!' Annabelle

insists. Snatching a framed picture from my bedside table, she waves it under Sam's nose. 'She was brown then.'

'She was in Hawaii!' Sam rolls her eyes. 'Of course she was tanned.'

Actually, I'd been for a St Tropez the day before that picture was taken, but best not tell Sammy this.

I study the picture of me and Sam sitting on a sun-drenched terrace. I look relaxed and happy, which is proof that the camera really can lie. That had to be one of the worst weeks of my life. How could I ever have thought that things would work out?

One huge mistake was made that week. I really can't make another one.

'Can I have a few minutes alone?' I plead, curling my fingers around my mobile.

Annabelle sighs. 'I don't want to be cruel, but it's going to take me a really long time to do your face. I'll need all the time I can get.'

That's my sister, right at the back of the queue when charm was given out.

If Sam wasn't a pacifist, I think she'd probably wallop Annabelle. Instead, she shows great control by merely propelling my sister from the bedroom and saying over her shoulder, 'Five minutes, Ellie, and then that's it. We're getting this wedding on the road. Five minutes!'

'Fine,' I agree. 'Five minutes is all I need.'

Five minutes to compose two texts that will change my life for ever.

Paradise Lost

'I can't believe this place!' Sam shakes her head in awe as she steps on to the terrace and gazes out at the sparkling Pacific Ocean. 'I feel like I've landed on another planet.'

She's not the only one. The Picasso-blue skies and shimmering turquoise waters of Waikiki are a world away from the pewter rooftops and wet pavements of Taply, as is the warm sunshine that pours on to the golden sandy beach. As Sam and I sit on the terrace of the Royal Hawaiian Hotel and stare across the bay to the acid-green heights of Diamond Head, so fringed with skyscrapers that the volcano looks like it's wearing its very own hula skirt, we enjoy the novelty of wearing bikini tops and shorts rather than woolly tights and jumpers.

'Remind me why people live in England again?' I say, raising my face to the sun. Who cares if I turn into a giant freckle? I'm in Honolulu, baby! Yeah!

'No idea,' Sam says. 'Jay had the right idea moving out here, that's for sure. I'm starting to understand what he sees in Roxy after all.'

Hmm. I'm not going that far. It's going to take more than palm trees, turtles and pounding surf to get me joining Roxy's fan club, although this huge breakfast of waffles, pancakes and crispy bacon might help to sway it. No wonder they have an obesity problem in the States, with food this yummy and Maccy Ds on every corner. I only arrived last night and I've probably put a stone on already. Whether or not I'll be brave enough to stroll along Waikiki in my bikini is wholly dependent on whether or not I can resist having seconds. Or even thirds.

'I'm still surprised you came,' Sam says, regarding me thoughtfully through narrowed eyes. 'Jay's wedding can't be easy for you. I wasn't sure you would.'

That makes two of us. When the invitation plopped on to the doormat last month, my first instinct was to toss it on the fire and go and get very drunk. Why on earth would I want to fly to Hawaii just to see Roxy finally get her claws into Jay for good? And why would he even want me there? It was hardly tactful.

'Because you're old friends,' Sam explained, when she found me snivelling into my toast and with the butter-smeared invite propped up against the Marmite jar. 'Jay wants to see some friendly faces before he signs his life away to Satan's daughter.'

The trouble was, though, that before he'd vanished off to the States, Jay and I had been rather more than friends. The dynamics of our relationship had shifted and I wasn't sure they could ever go back to where they'd been before, wedding or no wedding.

'Anyway,' Sam added, 'it would do you good to see him tie the knot. It would give you closure.'

'You,' I said sternly, 'have got to stop watching all those dreadful talk shows. I knew it was a mistake to let Mud put a telly in Blue Moon.'

'Sorry,' said Sam. 'Psychobabble gets in your head when you hear it all day! But you know what I mean. It would be like the end of a chapter, wouldn't it? And it's not as if you're still in love with Jay. You're with lovely Xander now.'

Sam's right. I am with Xander, and he is indeed lovely. Apart from the fact that he has the body of a god (so do I after eating all his delicious food, except I'm Buddha to his Adonis), he's funny and kind and for some reason absolutely mad about me. Since we met at Charlotte's, we've spent lots of time together, Xander normally in a baseball cap and dark glasses combo to hide from the press, and me feeling generally bemused. I've been papped a few times, but they thought I was the cleaner lady and so far I've got away with it. I've pinched myself so many times in disbelief that Sam is starting to stress about self-harming.

'Stop stereotyping me,' Xander said when, for the millionth time, I pointed out that he ought to be dating a model and zooming about in a sports car instead of pottering around Taply in a Fiesta with the very un-model-like me. 'I've told you, I've done all that stuff and it's bollocks. You make me laugh, you're dead sexy, and best of all, you eat!'

Xander's idea of fun is trawling the supermarket for ingredients that, even when hampered by my kitchen, end up being transformed into some amazing veggie dish. Sometimes I go over to Sutton Court, but the house is so big and echoey that we tend to head for the noise and bustle of Ketton Place. The majority of our time, though, is spent at number 43, and when he isn't away recording and performing, Xander is usually to be found watching telly with Mud or pottering in the kitchen. Somehow he's managed to become a part of daily life, once we all got over the shock of having a rock god in the kitchen. Xander isn't vain and is just as happy in scuffed trainers and a hoody as he is in designer gear. He fits into life so easily that after only two months, I feel as though he's been around for ever. He's also pretty good at shooing the persistent Marcus away.

Marcus. I shake my head at the thought of him. Talk about a transformation. Last month he shocked the nation by resigning from his seat, and then made a press statement in which he apologised for his role in the Taply protest. I was a bit cynical, suspecting another PR initiative, and continued to delete his texts and voicemails without even opening them. As far as I was concerned, he was a chapter in my life I'd rather not revisit, and on the few occasions he turned up at number 43, Xander was only too happy to send him on his way.

Then, a few weeks ago, I was standing in for Poppy in Blue Moon when the door harps jangled and in strode Marcus sporting dark glasses and a black suit like something out of *The Matrix*. I froze. Had he come to sort me out? Was this what all the messages were about?

For a second I thought about leaping the counter and running – bearing in mind that the last time I saw him I was mashing his face to a pulp – but I was wearing a tight denim miniskirt and likely to do myself serious damage. As Marcus advanced, I found myself wishing Sam had installed a panic button rather than a bubble machine. I supposed I could lob some soapy liquid at him and make a break for it, but I didn't really fancy my chances.

'What do you want?' I asked nervously. I might be stereotyping, but he wasn't really the type to require tie-dye flares and angel cards. If Marcus was here to thump me for wrecking his glittering political career, I hoped it would be over with fast and preferably not hurt too much.

'I want to talk to you,' he said quietly. 'Which is proving

rather difficult, seeing as you never reply to my messages and seem to have employed a bouncer.'

'Xander's my boyfriend, actually,' I told him. 'And the reason I haven't called you back is because we have absolutely nothing to say to one another. You made your opinion of me very clear.'

Marcus sighed wearily. 'Ellie, I know I've let you down, and believe me, not a day goes by when I don't regret the things I did and the choices I made, but I was a different person then. I've changed. Thinking I could be responsible for the deaths of two young men . . .' His voice tailed off and he hung his head. 'I'd never felt so bad in my life.'

'Mud and Animal didn't feel so great either,' I said coldly. 'And neither did I when I realised it was my fault for shooting my mouth off. I trusted you, Marcus! I had no idea you were using me. I was starting to think we might have had something.'

'We did!' cried Marcus. 'And we still could if you'd just give me another chance. I'm different now, Ellie. Just let me prove it!'

I shook my head. The Last Chance Saloon was well and truly closed. Although the papers were still writing endlessly about Marcus's regret over the Taply protest, and David Cameron was apparently keen to include him in the coalition cabinet, as far as I was concerned, Marcus Lacey was bad news.

'Just forget it,' I said wearily.

'I can't!' Marcus cried. 'I can't live with this on my conscience! I have to make things right.'

With this heartfelt cry, he tore out of the shop at full speed, dreamcatchers spinning and wind chimes jangling in his wake, while I gaped after him, totally taken aback. I'd heard all the rumours of a religious conversion and change of heart, but being confronted with the evidence was another thing entirely.

Just *how* hard had I hit Marcus that day?

I pondered this for the next few hours, and had just reached the conclusion that Marcus was having some strange kind of breakdown when the door harps jangled and in he came again like a scene from *Groundhog Day*.

'It's all right, I'm not going to keep on trying to convince you,' he said as he strode to the counter and laid his briefcase on it with a thud. 'Why should you believe a word I say? I haven't exactly got the best track record in the truth department.'

I said nothing. I was far too busy eyeing the briefcase as he unclipped it. What was in there? A gun?

'So maybe this will convince you.' He plucked out a thick sheaf of documents and thrust them into my hands.

'What's all this?' I asked suspiciously. Was he suing me for the smack on the nose? 'A writ?'

Marcus grimaced. 'Of course it's not a writ! Just read it and then you'll see. Perhaps this will prove to you that I really am sorry.'

He picked up the briefcase, and minutes later the door jangled shut behind him while I stared down at the papers. I was paralysed with mingled shock and disbelief.

In my hands were the deeds to Ethy Woods and all the surrounding land.

And these deeds were made out in my name.

I ran after Marcus to protest, but he insisted the land was mine, and although I argued that I couldn't possibly accept, he flatly refused to take it back. No matter what I said, it seemed I now owned millions of pounds' worth of prime Buckinghamshire land covered in rare spotty blue spiders. The huge responsibility of all this nearly made me fall down in a heap on the pavement. Luckily, once they'd recovered from the shock of Marcus's generosity, Sam and Mud hit on the ideal solution – why not donate the land to a wildlife conservation charity and ask Professor Peacock to help? Within a month, the Ethy Woodland Trust was born, and funky blue spider T-shirts were being worn all over the county. In spite of everything, Marcus Lacey had played a vital part in protecting Ethy Woods for future generations.

Maybe he really had changed after all.

'Ellie? Ellie?' Sam snaps her fingers under my nose. 'Hey! You're miles away!'

'Sorry! I was thinking about Marcus and the woods. I still can't get my head around it all.'

'St Marcus of Lacey,' muses Sam. 'Well, the Lord works in mysterious ways, I suppose. People can change.' Her green eyes narrow thoughtfully. 'You're not thinking of trying again with *him*, are you?'

'Hardly!' I laugh and wave at Xander, whose furious front crawl is slicing through the bright blue infinity pool.

Sam looks relieved. 'Good. I'm glad Marcus has seen the light, but even so, I'm much happier that you're with Xander. I'm so glad he persuaded you to come to Hawaii.'

'I nearly didn't come,' I confess. 'But Xan thought it would be a good idea. The pressure's getting to him and he says he wants a break.'

What I don't tell my friend is that I think Xander also wants to see that I'm really over Jay. He knows the bare bones of the story, but I suspect Charlotte's given him all the juicy details, and as much as I protest that things are over between me and Jay, I don't think his mind will be at ease until he knows my ex is safely married. He's been so generous, paying for us to fly out first class and stay in one of Honolulu's top hotels. Sam was in agonies over flying, but eventually her desire to support her brother outweighed her horror of consuming fossil fuels, and besides, to travel by boat would have taken months.

'Hey, I've got more money than sense,' Xander teased when we tried to protest at the cost. 'If I can't spend it on my friends, what's the point? Besides, I've got some huge decisions to make and some time out in the sun is exactly what I need. You're doing me a favour by giving me the excuse to go.'

So here we are, courtesy of Xander, in Honolulu's glittering golden mile, exclaiming excitedly as giant turtles swim past and people-watching sunburned honeymooners strolling across the beach, surfers waiting for a wave and thin Japanese matrons with Dior handbags heading off to the designer stores. I feel like I've stepped into somebody else's life.

'Will he quit Dark Angel?' wonders Sam as Xander pulls himself out of the pool, his strong golden body glittering with diamonds of water.

I shrug. 'He says so, but it's a big decision. He was looking at restaurants in Henley last week, so maybe.'

'He's seriously good at cooking. I'm sure an upmarket vegetarian restaurant would do really well. It's not like we don't have enough celebs living in the Thames Valley, with all their whacky food fads.'

I prod my squidgy midriff ruefully. 'He's a feeder! I'll have to make sure I don't let him get carried away trying out all the yummy grub Hawaii has to offer, or the plane home will never take off.'

'Watch out,' Sam whispers as Xander strolls towards us,

shaking his blond mane dry. 'I think he's a man ready to settle down. Maybe he's *the one* Poppy saw?'

I'm starting to wonder the same myself. So far, so very good.

'Hey, girls,' Xander says, joining us at the table and helping himself to a slice of mango. 'Beautiful morning, huh?'

With his tall body, six pack and twinkling eyes, Xander is pretty beautiful too, and I constantly remind myself how lucky I am that he's with me. There's no logic to it; we must look like Beauty and the Beast when we hang out.

'Shall we go sightseeing today?' he asks. 'Pearl Harbor has to be a must, or if you're feeling energetic, we could hike up Diamond Head. Or how about snorkelling at Hanauma Bay? Apparently there's a natural rock pool called the Toilet Bowl that fills and empties with the tide. Sounds like fun.'

Sam gives him an arch look. 'Sitting in a toilet? Is that a weird rock star fetish?'

Xander raises his hands. 'You have me there. I was going to chuck a telly in too, and maybe arrange an orgy.'

I laugh. 'He was reading the guidebook for most of the way over. He's got this whole trip planned.'

'Before we get too carried away, it's Jay's wedding to-morrow. I thought Ellie and I should sort outfits and maybe go over to visit,' Sam says, and even though I'm sitting in paradise with the world's most beautiful man holding my hand, the words *Jay's wedding* still feel like broken glass being dragged across my heart.

'Cool.' Xander nods, easy-going as always. 'Why don't you two check out the designer stores in Waikiki? Plenty of time for sightseeing later. Put whatever you want on to my card and we can sort it out later.'

So off Sam and I go to spend a happy few hours trawling the glossy stores where Louis Vuitton, Armani and Chanel jostle for pole position. Skinny women like insects with huge sunglasses and mahogany tans elbow past one another in their haste to reach the designer clothes, while the wives of wealthy Arabs sit in private suites and let their personal shoppers do the legwork. Although we're armed with Xander's Amex, neither Sam nor I find anything we really want (or in my case that might fit a size twelve) so, after a caffeine overdose at Starbucks, we hit the international marketplace, where we find exactly what we're looking for – rows and rows of pretty flowery prom dresses in every colour imaginable and only forty dollars apiece. Versace is probably spinning in his grave, but we're happy. Then it's on to buy glittery sandals and beads before heading back to the hotel to have pedicures and facials. By the time Xander meets us for lunch, we're both relaxed and definitely in the holiday mood. A glass of Hawaiian punch and some hula dancing later and I know I'm in Polynesia. All I need is a lei around my neck and Elvis to turn up and I'll have enjoyed every cliché this amazing island has to offer.

In the end, I wimp out of visiting Jay and Roxy's house high up in the lush green hills of Manoa Falls. Sam takes a cab over while Xander and I whiz around to the north coast, where we eat violently coloured shave ice and walk for miles along deserted icing sugar beaches. I'm even brave enough to strip off into my bikini and run into the bath-warm ocean, where Xander and I float on the gentle waves, chatting about everything and anything while watching cotton-wool clouds scudding past a gold-sovereign sun.

'Paradise,' I say happily.

Or it would be if I didn't have Jay's wedding to deal with.

Xander pulls me into his arms and kisses me; a slow, sexy kiss that makes my legs melt and my heart race.

'Let's stay for a while,' he says, his breath warm against my cheek. 'Get this wedding over with and then do some island hopping. Maui's supposed to be amazing.' His hands slip lower and the waves bob us together in such a way that there's no mistaking what's on his mind. Goodness, that's impressive.

'Sorry,' he grins, looking anything but. 'What do you say? Shall we make a holiday of it? It'll be easier here, away from the paps.' Gently smoothing strands of soggy hair back from my face, he whispers, 'I really want to get to know you better, Ellie. I think we've got something very special.'

And as he kisses me again I close my eyes and savour every delicious second. He's right; there *is* something special here. It's not the heart-pounding longing that I had when I was with Jay, but we all know how that ended. Violent delights have violent ends and all that. This thing with Xander is sweet and tender, and above all it feels safe. What could possibly make more sense than getting to know somebody as lovely as him in a tropical paradise?

'What about my mum?' I ask. When I left, she was back in hospital for more treatments, and it was terrifying seeing her so pale and wired up to all the monitors. I nearly backed out of coming to Hawaii, but Mum loves Xander and was adamant I went. I think *she's* hoping he might be the one too.

'You never know,' she whispered, taking my hand in her papery blue-veined one, 'maybe you'll have some good news for me soon. I'd love to see you settled. It worries me to think of leaving you on your own, Ellie. I'm not sure how long I've got left, but one thing I do know is that he's a good, kind man and he'll look after you. Don't mess this one up.'

So, no pressure there, then.

Xander drops a kiss on the tip of my nose. 'We'll only stay a few weeks. If there's any problem, I promise I'll get us back as soon as possible. I can always charter a jet.'

Charter a jet? Get him. I'm lucky to afford a bus ticket.

'So what do you say?' he asks softly, those melting eyes holding mine. 'Shall we stay?'

Paradise or rainy England? I smile and kiss him back.

'Let's stay.'

★

Here's a word of advice. If anyone ever suggests it's a good idea to go to the wedding of the guy you once thought was the love of your life, ignore them. In fact, don't just ignore them, punch them on the nose, hard, and tell them exactly where they can stick their bright ideas. Then, if you really want pain, go and do something fun like walking over hot coals or sticking pins in your eyes. But do not, I repeat, do not watch the man you loved marry someone else.

Jay and Roxy are getting married at Lanikai Beach, one of the most beautiful spots on the island. The powdery white sands stretch for about a mile and are overlooked by the beachfront mansions of the seriously loaded. One of these belongs to Roxy's father, and as Xander guides the BMW along the winding ribbon road, there's no mistaking which house is hosting the wedding. Not only is it the biggest, most sprawling mansion of the lot, practically dipping its toes in the perfect turquoise waters, but a huge pergola has been built on the beach with a shocking-pink carpet leading up to it. Although we're early, guests are already gathering on the bowling-green-smooth lawn, clutching glasses of champagne and chatting in the sunshine.

'I thought this was supposed to be a small wedding?' Xander looks worried. Automatically he reaches for his shades.

'Jay said it was a small wedding,' Sam says, a frown creasing her brow.

'Jay was wrong,' says Xander. 'This is huge.'

There must be at least four hundred people here, all beautiful and all wearing the kind of clothes I've only seen in magazines. My green-and-pink prom dress, which I thought looked so fresh and pretty when I put it on, suddenly looks very dull, and the silky pink flowers Sam pinned up in my hair seem cheap and tacky.

I *knew* that coming to this wedding was a bad idea. Why did I listen to Sam?

A valet parks the car and our invitations are checked at the gate, my Marmite-smeared one greeted with a look of disdain by the well-dressed flunky. Then we're ushered to our seats out in the lush garden, shaded by huge potted palms and lulled by the waves and the strains of a string quartet.

'That's Roxy's dad,' hisses Sam, pointing to a fat man poured into a white suit and with the world's worst comb-over. Every time the breeze lifts his hair, his head looks like a giant exclamation mark. How he ever fathered somebody like Roxy is a total mystery.

We sit and wait for twenty minutes, by which time I'm really starting to regret the enormous frappuccino I guzzled on the journey over. I cross and recross my legs, but it's no use, I have to use the loo, bathroom, john or whatever they call it here.

'You are hopeless,' sighs Sam. 'Be quick. The celebrant's just arrived.'

I tear into the house and locate the loo in record time. Then I play a little with the Molton Brown hand cream, shove a few more pins into my collapsing up-do and squirt myself with some of the free perfume before tearing back out into the corridor.

And cannoning straight into Jay.

I feel like I've stepped off a window ledge and into thin air.

'Ellie?' He grabs my shoulders to steady me (not a great idea, because I'm not convinced the St Tropez has dried) and couldn't look more shocked. 'My God, you came!'

He isn't the only one who's taken aback. I haven't seen Jay for a few months, but I'm horrified by how tired and drawn he looks. His face is tanned, but violet shadows bruise his eyes and his cheekbones are ski-jump sharp beneath his skin. His hair is still as black and glossy as a raven's wing but longer than I remember and curling over the collar of his gold shirt. I have to clench my fists in an effort not to touch it.

'Of course I came,' I say, while my heart plays squash against my ribs. 'You can't get married without your friends around you.'

His hands tighten on my shoulders. 'I can't tell you how good it is to see you. You look fantastic.'

I've just looked in the mirror, and with my hair frizzing in the heat, make-up sliding off my face and the bright-green dress, I look like a cabbage wearing a pot plant as a hat.

'You need contacts,' I say.

Jay stops my words by placing his finger on my lips before sliding his hand to the back of my head and gazing into my eyes. He's so close that I can see myself in the inky depths of his pupils and feel the warmth of his breath mingling with mine. His mouth curves shyly and then his eyes crinkle into that familiar heart-stopping smile.

'*You* are a sight for sore eyes,' he murmurs. 'Oh, Ellie, if you had any idea how much—'

'Hey, there you are! We were starting to think you'd got lost— Oh! Sorry, I didn't mean to interrupt.' Xander joins us, his open, honest face all smiles, and guiltily we step apart. If Xander notices this, he's too polite to say anything. Instead, holding out his hand to Jay, he says, 'Hello, I'm Xander. Ellie's plus one.'

Jay shakes his hand, looking perplexed as he tries to place Xander. It'll come to him, probably in the dead of night like it did Mud. Although hopefully Jay won't run around the house naked yelling *Xander Fucking Thorne was in my kitchen, man!*

'Nice to meet you,' he says as he looks from Xander to me. 'I'm Jay.'

'Ah! The groom.' Xander slides his arm around my waist and gives me a comforting squeeze. 'Best of luck, mate. I guess it comes to us all.'

'I guess it does,' replies Jay. His green eyes hold mine, the expression in them so bleak that my stomach twists and my mouth feels like someone's tipped half the beach into it.

Oh, bollocks. I still love him.

Not good, Ellie. Not good at all.

★

After this untimely realisation, the wedding passes in a blur of misery. Although it feels like someone's pouring battery acid on to my heart, I somehow manage to slap a smile on my face and hold Xander's hand without scoring it with nail marks. Roxy is radiant in little more than a white lacy petticoat, which strains across her burgeoning stomach. Six-inch Gina sandals make her slender legs even more coltish and her sunshine hair tumbles down her back in a riot of curls. Pregnancy makes her glow. Or maybe that's triumph.

The vows are exchanged, the rings slipped on and the bride is duly kissed to a flutter of applause. And that's it. Jay and Roxy are married. Game over and time for me to do what I do best at weddings: get bladdered on the free booze.

'Oh God,' Sam says, as we traipse away from the pergola. 'I can't believe he's actually gone and married her. I really need a drink now.'

'Me too,' I echo. Actually, I'd like to have so many drinks that I pass out. And then a few more just to make sure I don't wake up for several weeks. This is far, far worse than the school prom.

We wander on to the beach, where suited waiters are popping so many champagne corks it sounds like we're standing in a giant bowl of Rice Krispies. Roxy and Jay are hand in hand talking to her father, and Sam joins then, rising on tiptoes to kiss her brother's cheek.

As I try to pretend I can't see Jay tenderly tucking a frangipani bloom behind Roxy's ear, Xander is busy retrieving the millions of messages clogging up his mobile. He only turned it off for the twenty minutes the wedding ceremony took, but when you're a rock star, everyone wants a piece of you.

'Bloody hell,' groans Xander, deleting his tenth message. 'What bit of the word *holiday* don't they understand?

Here, have a look at this missed call log; it looks like the telephone directory!'

He shoves his BlackBerry under my nose and scrolls through names.

'Wow,' I say. 'Was that really Mick Jagger?'

Xander reddens. 'Err, probably. And my mum, again. I expect she's worried I'm not wearing enough sunscreen.'

'And Charlotte,' I point out. 'Does she normally call you?'

He frowns. 'No, not unless the twins have gone AWOL. Huh, she's called six times *and* sent a text saying to call her as soon as I can. I hope everything's OK. The twins have probably burnt my house down.'

Unlike my crappy pay-as-you-go phone, Xander's is all set up for roaming, and he's probably the only person I know who can afford to phone across the world on a mobile. As he dials, I accept a glass of champagne from a waiter while my treacherous eyes slip again to the happy couple. Don't look, Ellie. It's self-harm for the soul.

Xander's speaking now, and, although I can't hear a word, his tone is low and urgent. When he turns to face me, his face is pale and his amber eyes brim with concern. What have the twins done now? Robbed a bank? Nothing would surprise me.

'Do you want to speak to her?' Xander is asking. 'No, no, I totally understand you can't. Of course I'll tell her. I'm so sorry, Charlotte. What a hideous shock for you all.'

In spite of the burning sun, I suddenly feel as though I've been hurled into a freezer. When Xander takes my hand and leads me away from the party and into the cool of the house, my heart is pounding so hard I think I'm going to pass out. What can be so bad that Charlotte can't face telling me herself?

There's only one thing it can possibly be, one unthinkable, terrible thing, and when Xander starts to speak, I know before he's even finished what is to come; understand that my world is about to dip on its axis, never again to be the same.

'I'm so sorry, Ellie,' he whispers, pulling me into his arms and pressing his lips fiercely against the top of my head. 'I'm so, so sorry.'

He doesn't need to continue.

I know without being told that my mum has died.

Letting Go

When you think about it, funerals are actually a lot like weddings. The same collection of friends and family arrive en masse at the same pretty village church to sing hymns in their best clothes and then stuff their faces afterwards. If I close my eyes and try very hard not to think about the solid-oak coffin at the front of the church and pretend that the cloying scent of lilies comes from a bouquet, I can almost kid myself that I'm back at Annabelle's wedding and none of the past hideous months ever happened. Auntie Ethel is behind me, *sans* teeth this time because she's lost them, Imogen is kicking the back of my pew, and next to me are my sisters, all as golden and as beautiful as ever. Even Daddy in his smart suit could just be waiting to give one of the girls away.

It all feels like a bad dream.

The past ten days have certainly taken on a nightmarish quality. From the agonisingly long journey back to England to the stark reality of having to steer my bewildered father through the mechanics of death and funeral arranging, it's just been one horrible hurdle after another. Unsurprisingly, my sisters have been useless: Annabelle has gone to pieces, Charlotte's still on crutches, Emily is too busy to do much at all apart from shop for black velvet and diamonds, while Lucy as usual pleads her duties as a parent. I've gone from all I know about funeral arranging fitting on a postage stamp to being an expert. When I fall into bed at night, caskets in various types of wood drift before my vision and the choices of handles and satin linings whirl round and round like a morbid merry-go-round. Dad's too devastated to do anything, and because my mother never expressed a preference, it's suddenly left to me to decide. This is where the education system lets me down. I may be able to put condoms on bananas and quote great chunks of Shakespeare, but I know sod all about arranging a funeral, which is a far more useful life skill.

In the end, I plump for a solid-oak casket lined with white satin and trimmed with curly silver handles. I think Mum would have approved. I may never have managed to give her that last dream wedding she longed for, but at least I can get her funeral right. I'll feel guilty for the rest of my life that I went away and never said goodbye properly. Add to that knowing that she died without seeing me settled as she'd so longed, and I want to hurl myself into a six-foot hole in the ground. No matter how many times my father reassures me that she died peacefully in her sleep, I still can't ignore the churning sensation in the pit of my stomach.

I have been a bad daughter. A failure. How can I ever make it up now?

'You OK?' whispers Xander, squeezing my hand, and I nod, because what else am I supposed to do? This funeral, where we all dress in black and crank up our stiff upper lips, is going to be as proper and as English as they come. I might feel like howling, but I owe it to Mum to do this properly.

Thank heavens for Xander. I don't know how I'd have got through the last week without him. If I hadn't already been aware of what a good man he is, I certainly am now. He's patient, kind and has done everything he can to help. And not just financially either, although of course flying us back must have cost a fortune. He's been great at the small things, like making sure Dad eats properly, posting an obituary in the *Telegraph* and buying me endless boxes of Kleenex Balsam tissues. He even came with me to the chapel of rest and waited while I said goodbye to Mum. I nearly flooded his Range Rover on the drive back to Taply, but he just gave me a hanky and held me until my tears subsided. I just wish I didn't feel so numb and could appreciate him a bit more.

We're crammed into the family pew, but as we rise to sing 'The Lord's My Shepherd', I notice Annabelle and Mark sitting with a great gap between them and my heart sinks. He's still seeing Poppy and it's only a matter of time now before Annabelle finds out. I hope Dad's bought a family plot in the cemetery . . .

I glance up at the big stained-glass window and watch as splashes of jewel-bright light dance across the floor and blush the coffin with soft rosy light. Outside it's a glorious winter's day. A dazzling sun sits on the horizon, making the grass sparkle like spun sugar and glittering on the tangle of iced spider's webs that lace the hedgerows. Where are the leaden skies and the drizzle? That's what I wanted today. A stop-all-the-clocks moment. The world is supposed to be in mourning, not looking like a glittery advert for John Lewis.

Somehow I survive the service. Xander's hand holds mine all the way through and he doesn't let go even when we wander outside for the committal. The beautiful flowers are at odds with the gaping wound of the graveside, and as we wait silently for the pallbearers – my sisters' husbands, my father and a serious-faced Tristan – I read the cards and draw comfort from them. One wreath in particular catches my eye, a small circle of pink and orange gerberas, which were Mum's favourite flowers. Slipping my hand from Xan's, I kneel down to have a closer look and read the simple message,

Thinking of you, love always, Jay.

A lump is in my throat. How thoughtful of him. My bad news must have thrown a cloud over his wedding, even though Xander and I tried to leave as unobtrusively as we could, and the fact that he made the effort to send flowers while on his honeymoon means so much. Even when I join my family at the graveside I still feel comforted. I know that later I'm going to howl and cry till I look like a hobgoblin, but even as the casket is lowered and handfuls of earth are scattered on to the coffin, I feel better just knowing that somewhere out there, Jay is thinking of me.

And Xander too, obviously. He really is the sweetest, kindest man on the planet. I just need time, that's all.

Time is something I have a lot of over the next few months. I move in with Dad, and slowly but surely we begin the bleak task of packing away my mother's things; a few items a week at first until we both feel able to bring ourselves to fill bags with dresses and shoes, which we take to the clothing exchange. Sometimes a few hours go by when the aching loss grows dull and I'll find myself lost in a book or laughing at something Xander says, but later I'll spot Mum's sewing box up on a shelf or her monthly subscription copy of *The Lady* will plop through the door and I'll find myself sobbing again. One awful time I went into the study only to find my father slumped in his favourite chair weeping silently and hopelessly into one of Mum's cardigans. I backed out of the room with tears running down my face and tore upstairs to the bathroom, where I opened her last bottle of Floris and inhaled the comforting, familiar scent until my pulse slowed and my tears dried. Will it ever get easier?

★

'I've got a surprise for you,' Xander says one December morning, turning up unannounced at my father's house. Is it me, or is he looking a bit on edge today? 'Come on, get dressed. I'm taking you out.'

I'm less inclined to leave the house than Miss Havisham. In fact, she probably looked better dressed in her ragged bridal gown than I do in Jay's old sweater, baggy trackies and my Uggs. My hair is scraped back into a ponytail and my face has forgotten what make-up is. But Xander's in an uncharacteristically forceful mood, and before long I'm being frogmarched along the drive and into his Range Rover. Although it's mid-morning, it's a dark December version, and as we drive in to Taply, Christmas lights shimmer in shop windows and people are wrapped up against the cold in scarves and coats.

'It's snowing in Hampshire,' Xander remarks. 'Maybe it'll snow here too? Then we'll have a white Christmas.'

'Great,' I reply dully. The way I feel about Christmas this year makes Ebenezer Scrooge look festive. Actually, I wish I could sleep through the entire festive season. The sooner this year's written off, the better.

Xander sighs. 'I know it's not going to be easy, Ellie, but you're going to get through this, I promise. Your dad will be fine having Christmas with his brother. Something different is exactly what he needs.'

I nod. I'm not sure Christmas with Charlotte, Barney and the twins is what *I* need, though. I've asked Santa for therapy.

We drive in comfortable silence, Xander's hand on my knee as he guides the car through the busy traffic. We pass Taply Square, where the Christmas tree towers above busy shoppers, before turning left over the ancient stone bridge. Although it's cold and gloomy, the pewter-ribbon river is busy with rowers and small boats, while chilly ducks huddle in the reeds. A few minutes later, Xander slows down outside a beautiful house built of blush-pink stone and topped with a mop of thatch. A stretch of lawn rolls down to the Thames, and facing this is an elegant wrought-iron conservatory with stunning views of the river and the weeping willows.

'Do you like it?' Xander asks, crunching the car across the gravel drive and pulling up.

'It's beautiful,' I tell him.

'That's a relief.' He smiles nervously into my eyes, then reaches out to cup my face in his hands. 'I hoped you'd like it, because I've bought it.'

'But you've already got a house. What about Sutton Court?'

'That was just a stupid status symbol. I'm putting it straight on the market. What do I need twelve bedrooms for? Or a helipad? I haven't even got a helicopter!'

I glance out of the window. 'This place is hardly small, Xan! You could fit number 43 in it ten times over!'

Xander's amber eyes crinkle. 'When I say I've bought it, I guess what I really mean is that I've bought it for us.' He takes my hands in his. 'Ellie. I was going to tell you all about how I've quit the band—'

'You've left Dark Angel?'

'As of sending my manager a text just before I picked you up.' He grins. 'I feel like I've been set free from jail! Isn't this place just perfect for that restaurant I've been talking about?'

'You're really going to do it? Good for you.' One thing I've learned this year is that life really isn't a dress rehearsal. 'It's still huge, though!'

'Yes, it is,' Xander agrees happily. 'But there's a reason for that. I was kind of hoping that maybe I won't be living here by myself. It could be a perfect family home.'

My eyes turn into dinner plates and I feel as though I'm perched on the edge of a very high diving board. Is he saying what I *think* he's saying?

His fingers squeeze mine tightly and I feel like I'm descending in a lift very, very fast.

Xander takes a deep breath.

'I love you with all my heart, Ellie. Will you marry me?'

He's handsome. He's generous. He's kind. He loves me.

And Jay's married to Roxy.

Well, what would you say?

Wedding Daze

I've never been to a pagan hand-fasting before. The bit when Sam and Mud leapt over the fire was a bit worrying, especially when a beribboned Serendipity tried to follow them. It'll probably be weeks before the smell of singeing greyhound fur leaves my nostrils. But now, according to the Druid-type person who officiated, Sam and Mud are *hand-fasted*, which to us uninitiated types means married. They even have matching wooden rings and nose studs.

Who says romance is dead?

'Well, that was different,' Xander remarks as we all traipse from the freezing depths of Ethy Woods towards our cars. 'I enjoyed it, but I don't think I want our wedding to be held in a wood. And call me old-fashioned, but I'd quite like to wear a suit!'

I laugh and kiss his cheek. 'Don't panic. It's all going to be as traditional as possible. That's what Mum would have wanted.'

'Phew!' Xander mimes mopping his brow. 'I don't think my mum would be very happy otherwise. She's so excited about buying her mother of the groom outfit, it'd break her heart if I told her the dress code was yak skin!'

This isn't as crazy as it sounds. The bride and groom, and in fact the majority of the guests, are wearing thick Peruvian jumpers, rainbow-coloured flares, Afghan coats and multiple face piercings. Even Sam's dad sports an eyebrow bar.

I totally understand why Sam and Mud wanted a quick and quiet affair; in fact, I'm quite jealous. Weddings are stressful. I've only been planning mine for six weeks and I'm shattered already. I'm trying to diet (which probably explains why I'm now obsessed with food), I've booked the church, I've even started buying *Bride* magazine. If she were still with us, Mum would be proud.

At least I hope she would be. When I start obsessing over colour schemes and favours, I'll know I'm in trouble. I'm looking forward to marrying Xander – of course I am because, like everyone says, he's perfect – but I wish it didn't have to be so traumatic. Still, this is what Mum wanted and I'm going to fulfil her last wish even if it kills me, which it might do if I have to stick to this diet for much longer. I'm so hungry I'm almost tempted to eat those vegan rissoles Mud made for the reception.

'I never thought Sam would get married,' I say to Poppy and Mark, who are hand in hand beside us. 'I thought she believed it was an outmoded expression of patriarchal power.'

Poppy, buried beneath a huge fake fur hat, laughs. 'She did until she fell in love. And after nearly losing Mud, it probably seemed like the best way to celebrate.'

'I totally agree,' Xander says. 'And hopefully you'll all come and celebrate our engagement next weekend.'

'We were planning to throw the engagement party this weekend but had to cancel when Sam and Mud sprang their wedding on us, which is a relief. I mean, which is fine,' I amend hastily when Xander throws me a quizzical look. 'I'm looking forward to it.'

'You don't sound as though you are,' Xander says, a worried frown crinkling his brow.

'It's just everything's happened so fast and I'm struggling to get my head around it. You must feel the same?'

My fiancé stares at me. 'Actually, I can't wait to get married. The sooner the better as far as I'm concerned. I thought you felt the same?'

I take his hand. 'Of course I do, but see things from my point of view. One minute I'm a single girl, the next I have a massive rock on my finger, a devoted fiancé and most of the press are going mad. I'm still in shock from losing Mum, too.'

'Grief can affect you in many ways, according to Oprah. And Oprah knows everything,' chips in Poppy, not very helpfully. I give her a steely glare and, taking the hint, she heads to the buffet.

Xander doesn't look convinced. 'Are you sure that's the problem, Ellie? You're not changing your mind, are you?'

He sounds so sad as he says this and I feel terrible. What on earth is up with me? This kind and generous man is offering me everything a girl could possibly dream of. I have to get my act together.

I squeeze his hand. 'Of course not. I'm just a bit nervous about the whole engagement party thing, that's all.'

'Leave all that to me,' says Xander cheerfully. 'I've already got an idea in mind that I just know you'll love. You won't have to do a thing except turn up looking gorgeous.'

As we join the others at the buffet, I feel too worried to eat. Shouldn't I be dying to marry Xander? What's wrong with me? To keep up appearances, I pile my plate with nut loaf, but inside my stomach's turning cartwheels.

'I thought Jay might have come over for the wedding,' I say to Poppy. Mark and Xander are deep in discussion about some old banger so it's safe to talk about my ex. Xander's far too thoughtful and tactful to say anything, but I can tell he's a bit sensitive where Jay's concerned. Not that he needs to be. Married and about to be a dad, Jay's no longer a part of my life.

'A bit short notice for him,' Poppy points out. 'And the sprog must be due any minute. You haven't still got a soft spot for him, have you?'

'Don't be silly,' I protest. 'I'm with Xander now, aren't I?'

'Hmm,' says Poppy, sounding unconvinced. If an engagement ring and a fiancé don't convince her, then I don't know what will. I'd better make sure the engagement party's a huge success. That will surely get me in the wedding mood.

'Anyone up for dancing?' Mark asks, jigging to Clannad.

'Not unless they play some decent music,' says Xander. 'I wonder if the DJ has any Dark Angel?'

'Weren't they that band who split?' Poppy widens her big chocolate-button eyes. 'Didn't the lead singer walk out because he fell in love?'

'Yup, just blame Yoko Ono here,' he laughs, ruffling my hair while I pull a face. OK, so some fans were put out and the press were a pain for a few days, but after that it all went quiet. A replacement lead singer was duly appointed, the new line-up rocketed to number one and now Xan spends all his time renovating his restaurant and experimenting in the kitchen. It's a shame. I quite miss his tight black trousers.

'You boring old farts! Come on, boys! Just one dance!'

Poppy sashays on to the dance floor, towing Xander and Mark in her wake.

'Watch her!' The new Mrs Malcolm Evans (yes, Mud really does have a normal name!) plonks herself next to me and fans her face furiously with a beer mat. 'I thought she was about to settle down, but now she's got her mitts on your gorgeous fiancé, I'm starting to wonder.'

'Somehow I can't imagine Poppy settling down,' I say. 'That would totally upset my view of the world. It would be like hearing the Queen burp.'

Sam sloshes organic wine into a glass. 'Sorry if our wedding's stolen your thunder.'

I laugh. 'Don't be silly. We'll have an engagement party another time. So what's it like, then?'

'What's what like?'

'Being married; sorry, *hand-fasted*. Does it feel any different?'

Sam looks thoughtful. 'I don't know. It's too early to say. But I tell you one thing.' She grins wickedly.

'What?'

'I still want sex!'

'Too much information!' I cry, and we shriek with laughter. When Mud and Xan can't bear listening to us cackle any more and drag us up for a dance, I glance across at Sam and see how her face glows when she smiles up at her new husband. I wind my arms round Xander's neck and hope I'm looking at him the same way.

In the end, we have to put our engagement party off for a couple of weeks because Sam and Mud are off to Somerset on a yoga retreat courtesy of her father and there's no way I can celebrate without my best friend by my side.

Apparently we're going to hold the party in Water's Edge, Xander's new restaurant and my future home.

Well, when I say *we,* I actually mean Xander, because he's organising the whole shebang. If it was left to me, I'd be happy just going for a curry with Sam and Poppy in the local Indian, but when I suggested this, Xander was horrified.

'It's our engagement, Ellie!' he cried, shock written all over his handsome face. 'We can't just celebrate with a chicken tikka masala and a naan bread, can we?'

'Why not? I *love* chicken tikka masala and naan bread!'

'This is a really special occasion. It's a chance to show everyone how we feel,' Xander insisted, taking my hands and gazing intently at me. 'Don't you want to do that?'

'Isn't it enough that we're together? That's what the wedding's all about. Why do we need to shout it from the rooftops?'

'I know you're still grieving and probably don't feel that it's right to celebrate,' Xander said gently, raising my hand to his lips to kiss the palm. 'But you deserve some fun and you can't punish yourself for ever for being away when your mum died. Besides, from what I knew of your mother, she'd have been overjoyed you're having an engagement party.'

I couldn't argue with that. She'd have walloped me over the head with her designer handbag if she'd heard me trying to decline a big bash.

'I know!' Xander cried suddenly, looking excited. 'We'll combine the party with a fund-raiser for breast cancer research. That way you won't have to feel guilty at all. Leave it to me, hon, I'll sort everything.'

I didn't have the heart to tell him that my reluctance to throw the mother of all engagement parties had nothing to do with being grief-stricken or shy. I just felt as though somebody had amputated my emotions. I knew I ought to be really excited, but instead I was numb. Maybe Xander was right and I was still floored by grief?

In the face of such enthusiasm, what else could I do except agree to let Xander take care of everything? All I needed to do was buy a new dress and turn up.

★

'I wish you'd tell me where we're going!'

Xander chuckles. 'We're nearly there. And no peeking. It's a surprise.'

I grimace. Whizzing along in the car with a blindfold on isn't my idea of fun, even though my fiancé has told me at least twenty times that I'm in for a wonderful surprise. I hate surprises. In my experience they're more commonly called shocks.

The car stops, Xander's door opens and shuts, then I feel the cool night air on my face as he scoops me out of my seat and sets me on my feet. My new green velvet dress whispers to the ground and I shiver. Maybe bare shoulders in December wasn't such a smart idea. If my mother were still alive, she'd tell me I need a vest.

Suddenly there's a lump in my throat the size of Xander's Range Rover. If Mum were alive, she'd be so excited to be attending my engagement party. Does it still count as fulfilling my promise, even though she's not here to see it?

Xander takes my hand and leads me, still blindfolded, across soft grass into which my new heels sink and skid. Then I'm tapping across wooden planks and hands are reaching out and lifting me up and over what feels like a

285

fence before Xander steadies me and, plucking off the blindfold, cries; 'Surprise!'

That's one way of putting it. I'm on the deck of a river cruiser.

I *hate* boats.

Shit! Xander doesn't know I'm rubbish on water. How could he? This is what happens when you have a whirlwind romance.

I'm a landlubber. Get me out of here!

'It's a boat,' I squeak. Why on earth haven't Sam and Poppy told him I hate boats?

'Keeping this venue a secret nearly killed me, but I managed it!' Xander says proudly. 'I had the devil of a job getting everyone to a surprise location without giving away what we were up to, but I've pulled it off! Well, what do you think?'

His sweet face is so hopeful and excited, I don't have the heart to tell him that what I'm actually thinking is *where are the life belts?* and *has anyone got some Kwells?* Besides, this boat is beautiful, and in the darkness the reflections of the white fairy lights strung across the decks dance in the inky river like diamonds. A jazz band is playing on the top deck, delicious cooking smells drift from the lamplit interior, and all my nearest and dearest are standing on the deck cheering and shouting *surprise*.

I have never longed more for the gaudy interior of the Taply Curry House in all my life.

'It's great,' I tell him faintly.

'I knew you'd love it!' He beams.

And suddenly I feel like I've stepped off a cliff. My fiancé, the man I've agreed to stay with till death us do part, doesn't really know me at all. Which is probably why he wants to marry me.

'Come on, sweetheart,' Xan says, squeezing my hand. 'Everyone's here for us. Come and have some champagne.'

The boat is bursting with friends, family and even the odd celeb who's popped in to see Xander. It's a fantastic party and he's thought of absolutely everything. The food is delicious – all prepared and cooked by him – the drink flows like the river, and after a few glasses I almost forget that we're sailing along the Thames. Everyone wants to see my beautiful emerald and diamond ring and tell me how lucky I am, which of course is true. This churning sensation in my stomach is because of the swell and the dip of the boat, that's all. I know how lucky I am and I am not, repeat not, going to balls this up.

Slipping my hand from Xander's as he chats to my father, I wander to the far end of the boat and lean against the railings as we chug gently towards Henley. The night is dark and the sky bright with glittery stars. Mum would have been so happy and I am going to get this right for her. This year has been a disaster, but at least the engagement has ended it on a positive note. Things can only get better from here on.

'Happy?' Poppy asks as she appears at my shoulder. She's been rather elusive this evening, probably because Annabelle is here too and on the warpath after hearing on the grapevine that her estranged husband has been spending far too much time in Blue Moon. Wearing huge sunglasses and a long black dress is going a bit far though, even for Poppy.

'Ecstatic, apart from the boat thing,' I tell her.

'Yeah, sorry about that,' Poppy says. 'None of us had a clue where we were going until it was too late. I'd have bought you some Kwells if I'd known. Still, boats aside, you're happy, aren't you?'

'Of course I am. But you know that anyway, seeing as you predicted this all those months ago.'

Poppy's smooth white brow crinkles. 'You what?'

'The union of a lifetime, of course!' I remind her. 'You said I was going to meet the one!'

'And you think that's Xander?'

She's at my engagement party, so go figure. Maybe I need to spell this out.

'Of course I think it's Xander! I'm marrying him, aren't I?'

'Blimey.' Poppy looks stunned. 'I thought you were marrying him because it's what your mother would have wanted. I never thought he was the love of your life.'

'I thought you liked him?' I ask. I'm rather put out she isn't more enthusiastic, seeing as she's been hoovering up his nut loaf for months.

'I do! I do! He's lovely,' says Poppy quickly. 'And I'm happy if you're happy. I guess I always thought Jay was the love of your life and I hoped you two would end up together.'

'I'm over Jay, well and truly,' I tell her. Which is true. I hardly think about him at all. I reckon I'm down to once or twice a day now.

'Really?' Poppy looks doubtful. 'Cross your heart and hope to die?'

Are we still at school?

'Yes, yes,' I say impatiently.

'Phew! That's a relief,' Poppy says. 'Sam was really worried you still had a thing for him. That was why she said I mustn't—'

'Mustn't what?' I demand, instantly alarmed when she clams up like a bad mussel. 'What's Sam been keeping from me?'

288

Poppy gulps. 'I wasn't supposed to say anything, not with the party today. Sam will kill me.'

'Kill you for what?' All this riddling is starting to make my head spin.

'Everything's working out for the best, Sam says, and the last thing she wants is to upset you.'

'Pops, you're starting to worry me now. What on earth could Sam say that would upset me tonight of all nights? It's my engagement party!'

Poppy exhales, looking relieved. 'Yeah, of course. She's just being overcautious. Why on earth would you be bothered whether Jay's come back or not?'

I stare at her. There's a weird roaring in my ears and the gentle river suddenly seems to be rushing past like the Severn Bore.

'He can't be back,' I insist, and my voice sounds tinny and distant. 'He lives in Honolulu with Roxy. They're having a baby. They're married.'

'Not any more, apparently,' Poppy says airily. 'He arrived out of the blue this morning in a right state. She's had the baby and it isn't his. The whole thing was nothing but lies.'

Now my head's really spinning. 'How can they know that already? DNA tests take ages, don't they? On *Jeremy Kyle* they always have to wait.'

'They didn't need a DNA test. Rick Elliott, the guy Roxy left Jay for, is the father. You do know who Rick Elliott is, don't you?'

My mouth swings open. Of course I know who Rick Elliott is. I live in Taply-on-Thames, not the moon. Rick Elliott is the USA's answer to Alan Sugar.

He's also an African American.

'So, Roxy and Jay are no more,' Poppy finishes. 'She's

fled to Rick, and Jay's come back to his family. He says their relationship is over, and judging by how relieved he looks, I'd say he means it. He's already filed for divorce. But like you say, you're over him now, so that doesn't matter to you any more. You're marrying Xander.'

I can't speak. My vocal cords have fallen down in a dead faint. Glancing across the party, at the crowds of happy people dancing and sipping champagne, I catch Xander's eye and he raises his glass, giving me a smile of such sweetness that I can hardly breathe.

Jay is back.

11.46 a.m.

There's got to be something wrong with this phone. I sent my two messages over half an hour ago, and so far so silent.

Why haven't they texted back? Calling a wedding off is supposed to be a pretty big deal, so why does nobody but me seem bothered? You'd think the groom would at least call, even if only to give me a mouthful of abuse or demand he keep the dinner service. I've been on tenterhooks for ages, and every time I hear a car door slam or voices downstairs, I practically jump out of my bum bra. I'm so full of nervous energy I could power the National Grid.

'Will you stop twitching?' Annabelle narrowly avoids poking my eye out with a mascara wand. 'How am I supposed to stick your false eyelashes on?'

I rip my attention away from my phone and nearly cry out when I catch sight of the massive spider-like false eyelash waggling at me from the tip of my sister's finger. For a second I fear I'm having an Ethy Woods flashback.

'You're not putting that on me! I've no desire to go down the aisle looking like a drag queen!'

Not that I'm going down the aisle, but even so I feel I have to put my foot down. I know I'm the girl who let her sister slap tripe on her face, but even I have my standards, and Katie Price eyelashes are a step too far.

'Your loss,' huffs Annabelle, stuffing the eyelashes back into her bag. Then she steps back, crosses her arms and regards me through narrowed blue eyes. 'Right. My work here is done. If I do say so myself, I've done a bloody good job. You actually look quite pretty.'

'Ellie always looks pretty,' Sam says sharply. Annabelle snorts but doesn't argue. Although Sam is now sporting a green velvet bridesmaid's dress, her small hands are still smothered in silver rings, including one massive skull confection, which, if pushed, could double as a knuckle-duster. Annabelle has no desire to be the second Andrews sister with a black eye.

Wait a minute, my eye! I can't go down the aisle with a black eye. Imagine the photos. I'll have to call it off.

'I'm not sure about my eye,' I say loudly. 'It must look awful. I don't think I can get married with a black eye.'

'Time to look in the mirror,' Annabelle declares, propelling me across the room to my dressing table. 'I've done a great job with that concealer. It hardly shows. And I've rescued your hair, too.'

I stare in the mirror and, not for the first time in my twenty-nine years, feel like howling. Apart from a rather pinky tinge, my eye looks fine, and even my hair has been coaxed into smooth ringlets.

'The bridesmaids are all dressed,' Sam says, leaning forward and tweaking a curl into place. 'Even Isolde's been pinned down and forced into a frock.'

'She screamed a bit and shouted that it was gay,' Annabelle adds. 'But Charlotte just sat on her until she gave in. And Tristan's locked himself in the bathroom because he's too embarrassed to be seen. Did you really say you'd post their pictures on Facebook if they put a foot wrong?'

In spite of my growing panic, I relish the warm glow of revenge. I hope that Tristan's enjoying wearing the knickerbocker and floppy hat combo as much as I enjoyed picking it out for him.

Sam is busy unzipping my dress from its clear case. As the acres of lace and frills burst forth like a bridal version of *Alien*, my heart starts to pogo in my chest.

Oh. My. God. This really is it. Once that frock's on, I've had it. There's no way I can shin down a drainpipe in that.

Why hasn't anyone responded to my texts? Normally my phone beeps more than a pre-watershed Gordon Ramsay show, but not today. I'm trying to call off my wedding here. You'd at least think the groom might have an opinion on the matter. And as for the other text recipient . . . well, I thought he'd care that I was cancelling my wedding. After all, he's spent months telling me that marriage is about more than a frilly frock and a hot holiday.

I'm going to have to take matters into my own hands.

Flying Away

'We actually scrub up all right,' Sam declares as she scrutinises her reflection in my dressing table mirror. 'I would have thought a green bridesmaid dress would look minging, but I was wrong. I might even get a nose stud to match it.'

'Don't do that, hon, it'll look like snot,' Poppy points out. 'Think of the photos. They'll be on Xan and Ellie's wall for the next sixty years.'

Sixty years? In the mirror, I turn the exact shade of my wedding dress. Sixty years is a long time. I'll be . . . I'll be . . . well, quite old by then. Nearly ninety. I'm going to be with Xander until I'm nearly ninety?

It's two months after the engagement party, and in spite of what Poppy might have thought when she dropped her bombshell, my wedding is still very much on. I've been shopping in the West End and spent a fortune on dresses, shoes and glittery slides for Poppy and Sam. My dress is simple; I'm wearing the cream silk sheath and lacy over-tunic that Mum wore when she married Dad back in 1970. Mum was a bit slimmer – well, actually a lot slimmer – than me, so I can't do the back up yet, and as I twirl, my red-and-white polka-dot knickers stick out like a kinky bustle. I'm going to lose at least a stone for the wedding, once I've eaten the deep-pan pizza Sam has just ordered and the cheesy garlic bread.

It's getting closer, though. Maybe I'll just buy some Spanx.

I was really shaken when Poppy told me that Jay and Roxy were no longer together, but I've made my decisions and I'm going to stick with them, and it's not as though Jay has beaten a path to my door, begging me to change my mind. I'm nearly thirty and it's time I accepted that fluttering hearts and twisting stomachs have more to do with tummy bugs than they do with love.

OK, so if my life were a Mills & Boon novel, Jay would come charging over to my father's house, declare his love for me, challenge Xander to a duel, then sweep me away into the sunset. However, I live in the boring real world, and although he's been back weeks, I've hardly seen anything of him. Which is probably just as well. Things would never have worked out between us. It was a silly crush that got out of hand.

Anyway, I love Xander, the church is booked, the invitations have gone out and the cake is ordered. There's no way I can call it off now, even if I wanted to.

Which I don't.

My resolution is further strengthened when I think how hard Xander is working to get his restaurant up and running, and all the lovely food he's been trying out on me. He doesn't even complain when I fill the bed with toast crumbs. So what if he hates Marmite and refuses to come near me until I've cleaned my teeth? The guy has to have some faults. At least he doesn't have any fiancées secreted away, or imminent love children.

No, I'm doing everything properly this time. Xander has moved in to Water's Edge, but I'm still at number 43. We think it's more romantic and old-fashioned to stay living apart until the wedding. After all, we have the rest of our lives to be together, so what's the rush?

'Are you sure you still want to go ahead with this wedding?' Sam asks, catching me frowning at my reflection.

'Of course I'm sure,' I say, tweaking the straps of my dress and sucking my stomach in. 'I'm completely over Jay. I know he's your brother, Sam, but things really did work out for the best.'

Sam chews one of her braids thoughtfully. 'So Xander is the one? You're absolutely sure?'

Why do all my friends keep asking me this?

'Of course I am,' I tell her firmly. 'I'm not a kid any more, Sammy. This time I'm going to do the right thing. I'm going to marry a decent man who will take care of me and be a good husband. I'm not about to turn my back on him and run away.'

I mean it, too. It's time I grew up a bit. Yes, it's been hard knowing that Jay is back and staying up the road with his dad, but I'm an engaged woman now. I've avoided seeing him, deleted his number from my phone and refused his one offer to have a drink. It's a pity Xander's been flat out with the restaurant, otherwise I might have been able to persuade him to take me on holiday somewhere far, far away. Instead I've been driven to skulking around Taply for the past two months, frantically calling Poppy or Sam to check Jay isn't going to be around and going out when he's due to visit. Serendipity has never had so many walks, and if this was a just world, I would be a size zero. Hiding from the ex love of your life is exhausting.

No matter how doubtful Poppy and Sam look, I'm determined I'm going to do things properly. I'm throwing myself into the wedding planning, I'm buying endless amounts of stuff to turn Water's Edge into a family home and we've even started discussing babies. I'm finally thinking and acting like a grown-up.

I'm going to spend the rest of my life with Xander, in sickness and health and till death do us part.

Oh God, I feel faint. I can't breathe!

'Ellie?' Poppy looks worried. 'Are you all right? You've gone a funny colour.'

'Grab her, Pops,' I hear Sam say, and her voice sounds like it's coming from miles away. 'I think she's going to faint.'

I gasp and clutch my chest where my heart is busy tap-dancing on my liver as I struggle to draw breath. I'm dying!

'Hold on, Ellie, I think you're having a panic attack,' says Sam. She tears from the room and returns with a carrier bag. 'Here, put this over your mouth and breathe into it.'

My eyes are bulging now, and, although I'm pretty certain this technique involves a paper bag, not a plastic one, I practically nose-dive into the carrier and puff away with all my might. Gradually my heart stops pounding, my lungs decide to work again and my blood stops zooming round my veins like something out of Formula One.

'Breathe slowly,' Sam soothes, stroking my back. 'In and out, in and out.'

'What the hell just happened?' I croak.

'A panic attack,' Sam explains. 'This engagement stuff has really stressed you out.'

'I can't be stressed about getting married. Xander's perfect,' I gasp, reaching again for the carrier. 'He's kind, and loving, and . . .' I puff into the bag a few more times, 'he's crazy about me.'

'But are you crazy about him?' Sam asks. 'Are you in

love with him and marrying him because you can't live without him? Or is this all because of losing your mum and feeling that you need to make it up in some way?'

Poppy nods. 'You feel that if you marry Xander you'll be giving your mum her final wish.'

'I'm fine, just a bit nervous,' I say.

Poppy's eyes widen. 'You just had a full-blown panic attack. I think you're more than a bit nervous.'

She has a point. I've been waking up in the middle of the night after awful dreams with my heart racing. The one that plays on repeat is where I'm halfway down the aisle to marry Jay, who turns round to reveal Xander's face while I run screaming from the church. I don't need to be Freud to figure this one out.

'Things have moved really fast,' Sam says gently. 'Maybe you should put the brakes on? Call it off until you're certain?'

'Call it off?' This thought makes me feel like having another panic attack. 'I can't do that! It's all booked. There's a reception at Cliveden, a honeymoon in the Maldives and all the invites have already gone out! Besides, it'll break Xander's heart. I can't do it to him. Everyone will hate me.'

No matter which way I turn, there's no way out. I feel totally and utterly trapped. 'How can I *not* marry Xander?'

'You can't marry somebody out of pity,' Sam points out. 'The only reason to marry someone is if you can't live without them for the rest of your life. Like I know I can't live without Mud. I wanted to die when I thought I'd lost him. Is that the way you feel about Xander?'

I gulp. To be honest, I quite enjoy the nights when I don't see my fiancé. He's wonderful, of course, but he can be quite intense, and I'm starting to be a little weary of hearing my praises sung non-stop. But then he hasn't lived with me yet. He's in for a real shock when he discovers that I'll happily stay in my PJs all day watching *Jeremy Kyle* reruns and eating ice cream out the tub. The Ellie Andrews he loves is a *Stepford Wives* version of me, and living up to her is flipping hard work. The thought of doing it for the rest of my life makes me want to collapse with exhaustion.

'Is it?' Sam presses.

I close my eyes wearily. If I never saw Xander again, I'd be sad but I'd probably get over it. But that's far healthier than the all-consuming feelings I have for Jay. Who can live the rest of their life on the emotional edge? Surely calm and steady is preferable?

'I don't know,' I whisper.

'If it isn't, you know what you have to do. And if you're not sure, then maybe this will help to make up your mind: Jay is flying back to the States tonight. And this time he's not coming back.'

My eyes snap open. 'But I thought things were over for good between him and Roxy!'

'They are,' Sam agrees. 'But there's nothing for him here, or so he thinks. He's well known out there and he has a great career. He says he's through with England.'

'Beats me why he came back in the first place,' I say.

Poppy rolls her eyes. 'He came back because he loves *you*, you muppet! And we all think you love him too, but you're too stubborn to admit it! Stop using poor Xander as a smokescreen.'

Sam nods. 'Jay loves you, Ellie, but he wouldn't dream of screwing things up for you because he thinks you're happy. Believe me, he's way more upset about you being engaged than he is about Roxy taking him for a ride.'

I gape at them. Jay loves me? Even after everything that's happened?

'Why didn't he say anything?' I whisper.

'Because you made it clear that you love Xander,' Sam explains. 'And good for you, *if that's the case*. Let Jay go back to the States and stay there, eh? After all, you *are* over him.'

Over him or not, I know that I can't let Jay leave on bad terms. I've been avoiding him because I still have feelings for him, but he's not good for me. Xander is my love-life equivalent of Bran Flakes, whereas Jay is a huge bar of Dairy Milk that I just want to rip the wrapper off, sink my teeth into and—

'Do you still love my brother?' Sam interrupts my thoughts. 'If you do, Ellie, please do something about it. I can't bear to see either of you hurting any more.'

Our eyes meet in the mirror. I nod. Of course I do. I've loved him every day since I was fifteen.

'Then you need to tell him,' Sam says firmly. 'Never mind all the other stuff. You need to get this dealt with, or neither of you will ever move on.'

She's right. I can't face a lifetime of what ifs. How can I marry Xander until I've dealt with my feelings for Jay? But can I marry Xander at all if I feel like this about another man? My head is whirling and I reach for the carrier bag again.

'He's flying from Heathrow at eight.' Already Sam is taking charge. 'That's in just under three hours. He needs to check in to Terminal 3 in an hour. If you leave now, you might be able to catch him.'

'How?' I shake my head. Esther finally conked out last week on the M40. Sam doesn't have a car, and there's no way I can afford a cab to Heathrow.

'I'll take you!' Poppy declares. She leaps up and grabs my hand. 'Let's go!'

'Dressed like this?' I glance down at my wedding dress.

'You don't have time to change! If I put my foot down, we can just about make it by the time check-in opens. Let's go!'

Before I can so much as open my mouth to protest, I'm dragged down the stairs, Sam's shoving a smelly woolly coat round my shoulders and Uggs on my feet, while Poppy rams her deerstalker on her head. Then it's out the door, into the chilly February dusk and Poppy's Jag. She's only just passed her test and has been gagging for weeks to go for a blast around the M25, so I'm not fooled that this is all for my benefit. I'm just a crash-test dummy in a wedding dress.

'Good luck,' says Sam, kissing me on the cheek. 'Just follow your heart. And no matter what, Mud and I are always here to help sort things out.'

The door slams and Poppy screeches away, whooping like something from the *Dukes of Hazzard*, and then we're on our way to London at a speed that would make Lewis Hamilton blanch. I'm gripping the seat so tightly, the leather will probably bear my nail imprints for years to come.

'Blimey!' Poppy exclaims for about the twentieth time as she turns on to the A40. 'You finally realised you love Jay!'

I nod, my throat tight with terror, as Poppy overtakes a Porsche. The speedometer reads well over 110 miles per hour, and the dark fields speed by, other cars little more than blurs. Soon huge road signs claim that we're approaching the M25 and Heathrow. My mouth dries. Whatever can I say that will convince Jay I love him and show him how sorry I am for all the mistakes and for ignoring him since he came home?

'Heathrow!' With a squeal of excitement, Poppy swings

the car across a multitude of white chevrons on to the M25. I close my eyes and pray while she plays dodgems with the traffic.

'Oh bugger,' says Poppy. 'That's torn it.'

Eyes still tightly closed, I ask, 'What?'

She puts her foot down and the car surges forward. 'It looks like we're being followed.'

I flip down the passenger's sun visor. Sure enough, in the mirror I see flashing blue lights.

'Pull over, Poppy.' I start to sweat. Exactly *how* fast has she been driving?

'Pull over?' Poppy echoes. 'Are you mad? We can easily go faster than they can.'

'Pull over!' I shriek, all but grabbing the wheel. 'We've had it now. We'll be done for speeding. We don't want to be done for resisting arrest.'

Muttering mutinously, Poppy obeys. The car shudders to a halt and we wait on the hard shoulder, me in terror and Poppy in a strop. Memories of my night in Taply police station flood back. But who will rescue me this time?

There's a smart rap of knuckles on the window. Poppy presses one of the numerous buttons on the dashboard and the glass hisses down.

'Can I help you, Officer?' she says sweetly.

This policeman is so young, he looks like a baby Brad Pitt in uniform.

'Do you know what speed you were doing, madam?'

Mournfully Poppy raises her large brown eyes. In the dim interior lighting, the glitter on her eyelashes shimmers like tears.

'No, Officer.' The eyes are lowered. 'I'm so ashamed.'

'You were doing one hundred miles per hour, madam. That's thirty miles over the speed limit.'

'I'm so ashamed, Officer, because,' Poppy exhales dramatically, 'I'm horribly dyslexic with numbers. I just can't work them out at all. I was so sure that I was looking at the right point on the speedometer.'

I've seen Poppy play her 'helpless little me' routine a million times. Tonight I don't hold out much hope.

'Would you mind stepping out of the car, madam?'

'I most certainly would.' Poppy sounds outraged. 'How do I know that you're a real policeman? Besides, I can't leave my sister. She isn't safe to be left on her own.'

He looks confused. 'I assure you, madam, that I am a real policeman. Please accompany me to my car.'

In all the years I've known Poppy, I have never ceased to be amazed by her ability to charm and manipulate men, and now she's turning her considerable powers on this poor policeman, who seriously looks like he shouldn't be out this late without his mum. He doesn't stand a chance if Poppy's really determined.

'It's my sister, you see,' Poppy peers at his badge, 'Police Constable Luke Hunter – can I call you Luke? She's seriously depressed. Suicidal, in fact. Forget racing to hospital to have a baby, I expect you've heard that one a thousand times; I've got to get her to the airport. Luke, this is a matter of life and death.'

'The airport?'

What *is* Poppy drivelling on about now? I begin to chew my thumbnail. Time's trickling away and my hopes of seeing Jay are vanishing fast.

'Yes, the airport! If she doesn't get there in time to see her boyfriend leave for the States, I dread to think what she'll do to herself. I mean, just look at the state of her already! She's even put her wedding dress on!'

I pause mid-chew. I'd prefer it if she said less about

what a state I look. From under my tangled fringe I glower at my friend.

'Does she look right in the head to you?' Poppy insists, her slim brown fingers plucking at the policeman's sleeve and her huge eyes trained imploringly on his.

PC Luke looks at me pityingly. The wedding dress and the smelly coat are not a good look. Thank goodness he can't see the polka-dot pants.

'I know I shouldn't have taken her out of hospital. I know it's wrong to interrupt the electric-shock treatment,' continues Poppy, warming to her theme. 'I swear I'll bring her back just as soon as she's said her goodbyes. And I'll make her take her tablets. But if she doesn't get to see him . . .' her voice cracks with emotion, 'I'm afraid it will be too much for her. It wouldn't be the first time that she's tried to . . .' Her words tail off, and a big tear rolls down her cheek and plops on to her frilly top. 'What will I tell our mother? How will I live with myself if she does something terrible?'

Policeman Luke is unflatteringly convinced that I look like an extra from *One Flew Over the Cuckoo's Nest*. Through the window he pats Poppy's arm comfortingly and, pro that she is, Poppy presses home her advantage.

'Her ex-boyfriend's plane is due to leave soon. And if she doesn't see him and if she kills herself it will be all my fault!' Her voice rises into a wail. 'It's all my fault for being dyslexic and reading the speedometer wrong. All my fault for not getting her there in time . . .' Poppy starts to weep, her face buried in her hands and her dark mane of hair spilling over her shoulders. In spite of my outrage at being so swiftly cast as a nutcase, I can't help but be awed by such a performance.

'Madam, please don't cry.' PC Hunter is young enough

to still be moved by tears, and suddenly I see a little glimmer of light. Surely he isn't going to fall for this ridiculous story?

'Is this the first time you've been stopped for speeding?' he asks sternly.

Poppy draws a long, shaking, brave breath.

'Oh yes, of course,' she says. What a fibber! I know for a fact that the E-Type is now the most pulled-over vehicle in Buckinghamshire even though Poppy hasn't long passed her test.

'In that case, and bearing in mind the exceptional circumstances, I'll let you go with a warning,' PC Luke tells her. 'Drive more slowly in future, please.'

'Oh yes, Officer, I will,' says Poppy so breathlessly that she makes Marilyn Monroe sound robust. 'Thank you.'

She starts the car, and the sexy roar of the Jag coming to life fills my ears.

'Wait!' Luke's angelic face appears back at the window. 'If you need anything, any help I mean,' he adds, turning crimson, 'I'm at the Uxbridge police station.'

'Thank you,' breathes Poppy. 'I'll remember that. I'll pop by and tell you how it went.'

And then we're away, this time at a sedate sixty miles per hour, both waving cheerfully at Luke as he zooms past us and off the motorway towards Uxbridge.

'You are awful.' I hope I radiate disapproval. 'There ought to be a law against you doing that.'

'Doing what?'

'That thing you do with men.'

'Oh, *that*.' She shrugs. 'That's what women have done for centuries.'

'Well I can't do it.'

'That's because you look like shit,' says Poppy bluntly. 'Use that mirror and sort yourself out, will you? Otherwise you'll scare Jay all the way back to Boston. Have a rummage in the glove box. I think I left some stuff there.'

Sure enough, the glove box contains a Chanel bag full of very purple make-up. I experiment a little but decide the Alice Cooper look is best left to Alice. By the time I've finished spitting on a hanky and scrubbing off the make-up, we've entered the weird tangle of roads that make up Heathrow Terminals One, Two and Three.

Once Poppy has parked, slightly scarily going the wrong way around the multistorey and driving up a down slope, she kills the engine.

'Blimey,' she says, sliding her hands from the wheel and flexing her fingers. 'We made it. I didn't think we would.'

I fling open the door and hop out. 'We're not done yet. We've got to find Jay.'

As I scuttle across the concourse of Terminal Three, towards the departures board, I start to doubt the wisdom of this entire venture. What if Jay doesn't want to see me? What if he thinks I ought to be with Xander after all? What if Sam got it wrong and he doesn't still love me?

Poppy halts abruptly under a television screen covered in lurid green text. 'I can't read any of that without my glasses. Can you see anything about Boston?'

I squint upwards. The bright fluorescent lights of the concourse makes my eyes water.

'Honolulu. Detroit. San Francisco,' I read. 'LA. Boston!'

'Well?'

'Due to board.'

'We're in time!' Poppy crows. 'That's a first for me!'

But I hardly hear her. My insides are turning into baked Alaska as I spot a body that I know only too well weaving its way through the crowds towards the check-in desk. Dressed in Levis and a cherry-red fleece, with a rucksack slung on one shoulder and his hands pushed deep into his pockets, he stands head and shoulders above all others and is totally oblivious to the admiring glances thrown his way by trolley-towing females.

'Houston, we have lift-off,' Poppy says, nudging me with her bony elbow. 'Go on then! What are you waiting for?'

But now that he's so near, Jay suddenly feels further away than ever. I'm terrified, rooted to the spot. How can I bear it if he doesn't want to know?

'Ellie!' Poppy gives me a shove. 'That's Jay, the man you love. The man we've just driven miles to find, remember? Go and sort it out, will you! Then we can all go home.'

'Maybe this is a bad idea,' I whisper, watching Jay's head bobbing steadily nearer to the departures gate.

'Bollocks it is!' roars Poppy. 'Don't you dare wimp out on me, Eleanor Andrews! Move your arse! If you don't get to him now, that's it, you've lost him.'

And suddenly I find that I'm running across the polished floor. I cannon into people, trip over luggage and bash my shin on a trolley, but none of this matters. I'm beyond pain now; even the stitch in my side is irrelevant. I just have to get to Jay. I want to yell, but I don't have enough breath left.

I'm almost there; one more push of energy and I can reach him, touch him, tell him how much I love him and make him see how sorry I am for all the stupid things I've said and done. His broad, strong back is only feet away, and nothing stands between us now except for a couple of suitcases and months of misunderstanding. All I have to do is jump over this luggage and I'm there.

Hoicking up my skirt, I prepare myself for a leap that would amaze the athletics teacher at St Hildas. But the tight wedding dress isn't quite as giving as I hope; after all, it's been designed with gentle dancing in mind rather than strenuous physical exercise. I try to jump, but catch my foot in the flowing fabric, falling to the floor like a silken version of Humpty Dumpty and bashing my head on a suitcase as I sprawl on my stomach. I don't see stars so much as an entire galaxy whizzing past.

'Jay!' I call, and even to my own ears it's more of a pathetic bleat. 'Jay! Stop!'

I have a worm's-eye view of the concourse, and in between the Nikes and DMs and Jimmy Choos, I see a pair of scuffed desert boots stand still for a moment.

'Jay!' I croak.

The boots stay put for a few seconds more, then began to stride towards the departures gate.

I sit up, and the world dips and rolls.

Clambering unsteadily to my feet, I make for the gate. There he is; I can see the back of his dark head bobbing above the milling crowds. I'm going to make it! I can catch him!

'Passport, miss?' An airport security guard jumps in front of me, all six feet of him blocking my view of Jay.

'I'm not going anywhere!' I pant, desperately craning my neck to peer around him. 'I just want to stop that man!'

The security guard looks at me suspiciously, probably thinking that I have some lethal weapon concealed under my dress. I'm very glad he doesn't know how very little I actually do have on underneath the layers of silk and lace. 'You can't go into Departures without a ticket and your passport.'

I look up at him imploringly. 'My friend Jay's leaving for America and he thinks I don't love him. I have to see him. Please let me through. I'm not going anywhere, I promise!'

'I'm sorry, miss, you can't go through,' repeats the guard. 'It's a security risk.'

Do I look like a terrorist? I want to shriek. But then I guess that's the point. Who knows what a terrorist looks like? They could have frizzy hair and be wearing a wedding dress.

Dashing away tears with the back of my hand, I admit defeat.

It's too late. I've lost him

12.46 p.m.

This is getting ridiculous. It's been over an hour and still no reply from either of them. I may be laced into my wedding dress and about as mobile as Tutankhamun's mummy, but it looks like I'm going out the window, weak drainpipe or not. I've checked the front of the house and there are even more paps milling around, so there's no way I can just waltz out the front door. Not that I'd get away with this anyway, with Sam on guard. She doesn't trust me an inch. She knows I'm likely to do a runner.

I've tried explaining to her that I've changed my mind, but she won't hear a word of it. She says I'll thank her later, which is highly unlikely.

This is all my mother's fault. And my overzealous guilt complex.

OK. Back window and over the wall it is. How on earth I'm going to get to his house when I'm dressed like a giant loo roll cover and wearing five-inch heels will take some sussing out, but I'm sure I'll think of something.

I'm just levering myself out of the window – which is trickier that I thought when you're wearing a hoop under your dress – when my phone decides that now is the perfect time to beep. If this is a text from Orange telling me my bill is available online, I think I'll hurl the phone out of the window and myself after it.

I tumble back into the room and grab my phone.

Can we meet? Taply Bridge? Asap?

Meet now? What can he want? Has one of the others spoken to him?

The phone buzzes again with his next message.

Where are you? Shall I come to yours?

Not a good idea with half of Britain's paps camped in the front garden. The last thing I need right now is him storming through like a paratrooper to get to the woman for whom Xander Thorne gave up fame and fortune. The press will go bonkers, and that will go down like cold sick with Xan. The last thing he wants is any more press about me. In fact they're all shouting and yelling already and I can hear the pop of flash bulbs, which reminds me of the awful time when . . .

No. I am *not* going to think about that now.

I text back a firm instruction to wait at the bridge and say that I will come to him just as soon as I can figure out how to get out of this window. Broken neck or not, I am going down that drainpipe. Now. It doesn't matter if I'm wearing an antique dress that's delicate and accustomed to resting in acid-free tissue paper, or that I've got flowers in my hair. I don't care. I am escaping.

I'm halfway out the window and clutching the drainpipe with both hands when there's a bellow of horror followed by the thud of footsteps across my bedroom floor, and suddenly I'm being pulled back inside and strong arms are wrapping themselves around me.

'Ellie, darling! Please don't jump! I'm here now!'

Am I having a weird trip from inhaling all the hairspray? Or maybe a bad reaction to hanging upside down out of my window? Either way, I could swear this is Marcus Lacey speaking, he of the never-ending bouquets and annoying apology texts peppered with Bible verses. I actually preferred him when he was just a git.

'Get off her!' yells Poppy. 'How dare you come charging in here demanding to see her? This is Ellie's wedding day and she doesn't want you anywhere near her!'

'You're wrong,' says Marcus smugly. Releasing me, he plucks his BlackBerry from his bespoke suit pocket and waves it triumphantly. 'Ellie sent me a text to say that she can't go through with the wedding and that she needs to see me! Read it if you don't believe me!'

Ever had that feeling of descending in a lift very, very fast?

I have sent my texts to the wrong people.

I am such a plank.

'Oh, Ellie,' Marcus is saying, clutching my hands and staring into my eyes. 'I knew you'd come around in the end! I knew you felt the same way I do! I'm not the same man, I promise! I've changed.'

I can't get a word in, because Marcus is up and running, telling me how after the protest he suddenly realised what he'd lost, how he no longer cared about making money and how he's now found Jesus too.

Which is kind of apt, seeing as he's received the text I thought I sent the vicar.

I slide my hands out of his grasp. 'Marcus, that text wasn't meant for you. Much as I'm flattered' – and more than a little freaked out – 'that you still have feelings for me, I don't want to be with you.'

Marcus stares at me. 'Of course you do! Besides, I promised the Lord I would make everything better by taking care of you.'

How on earth do you argue with that? I couldn't feel more stuck for words if somebody had bunged my tongue in a pot of Super Glue. Luckily Annabelle chooses this moment to charge into the room.

'What have you done to your hair?' she screeches. 'You've wrecked it!' Her big blue eyes fill. 'Why doesn't anyone appreciate what I try to do for them? Dad, you, Mark . . .' My sister slumps on to my bed and weeps prettily, tendrils of golden hair curling around her damp cheeks. As she gazes up at Marcus from beneath tear-dewed lashes, I am suddenly blessed by inspiration so heavenly that I'm amazed a few angels don't swoop down and start singing. All that time hanging out at my grandpa's church wasn't wasted after all.

'Are you sure God means *me*?' I whisper, nudging Marcus and nodding my head so hard in my sister's direction that a few flowers fall off. 'I'm about to get married. A sacred, godly union between a man and a woman. You don't want to get in the way of something as important as that. Maybe you've misinterpreted Him? The Lord does work in mysterious ways.'

I'm crossing everything here that isn't trussed up or sucked in, because, let's face it, only a man with God on his side stands a hope of surviving my sister. When Marcus offers Annabelle his perfect white hanky and she turns to thank him, I know I'm home and dry.

All I need is for them to leave me in peace and I'll be out that window, down the drainpipe and over the wall before you can say *runaway bride*.

Quite what I'll say to my fiancé is another matter entirely . . .

'If you want to top yourself, why don't you just jump in the Thames?' Poppy says cheerfully as she catches hold of my legs and somehow manages to stop me falling into the water butt.

Much as I'm annoyed to have been caught in the act of escaping, I'm quite glad she's here, because the idea of breaking my neck doesn't really appeal. Climbing out of the window is a lot harder than it seems, and not only did I nearly hang myself when my dress snagged on the drainpipe, but I've also now got a lovely green slime stain on it. If Mum could see me now, she'd be horrified.

'I don't want to top myself,' I say impatiently, brushing brick dust from my dress. 'But I can't stay here! I'm going to call this whole thing off. I don't know what I've been thinking. It's not as if my mum's here, is it?'

'This is still about your mum?' Poppy asks, looking taken aback. 'Don't you love him?'

'Of course I do! That's never been in question. It's just . . . just . . . all this stuff.'

While Poppy looks ever more incredulous, I explain how I've decided to call the wedding off and am meeting my fiancé on Taply Bridge to break the news. To be fair to Poppy, what makes perfect sense in my head does sound a little deranged when spoken aloud. And just a few hours before the actual wedding. I realise that my timing sucks.

'But you guys are great together,' she says.

Until recently I thought so too, but I've made so many mistakes in the last eighteen months, and this might be about to be my biggest one yet. I do love him, but what if I'm getting married for all the wrong reasons? This huge do, the wedding planner, the church, the cake that would feed a small nation for a month – this isn't my dream. It's my way of making things up to my mother. I've hardly seen him properly for weeks, as we've both been so busy planning the wedding. What if we're not right together any more? What if the time apart has put a barrier between us?

'Rubbish,' Poppy says when I tell her how I feel. 'Just marry the poor bastard and be happy.'

The problem is, I've made too many mistakes to have any faith in my own judgement. Most of them I've been mulling over all morning, but there's still one I haven't even dared to dwell on because it's too painful and too un-pleasant.

'I don't deserve to be happy. Not when I've betrayed Xander.'

Poppy rolls her eyes. 'We are not going through this again! That's ancient history, and if Xander can get over it then so can you. You are getting married, and that's that. I'll drive you to Taply Bridge myself and you can sort it out once and for all with *him*, and then we're off to the church. Got it?'

I nod miserably. After all, this is my mess. My mistakes and my lorryload of guilt to deal with. Besides, Poppy's right. I do have to sort this out for once and for all.

But one thing I do know for certain is this: I cannot go through with this big white wedding. I can't face fighting through the paps, walking up the aisle and saying my vows in front of everyone. Marriage is about more than the flowers and the frocks, and just lately I think I've for-gotten this. Marriage is about wanting to spend the rest of your life with the person you love. It isn't about guilt or obligation.

Now it's time to face the music.

Not Plane Sailing

I stand miserably by the departure gate, trying desperately not to cry.

'I'm so sorry, Ellie.' Poppy hugs me tightly. 'At least you tried.'

'I was too slow,' I say, pressing my face against her shoulder. 'Oh Poppy, I've really screwed up this time. I've lost Jay for ever.'

'No you haven't,' says a slow, deep voice from somewhere just behind me. 'Not if you really *do* want him.'

I freeze, too scared to turn round.

'Ellie, look at me.' Two hands grasp my shoulders, and although I still have my face buried against Poppy's shoulder, I can tell she's smiling.

'I don't think you need me any more,' she says, giving me a little shove.

I open my eyes. An inch away from my nose is a red fleece, encasing that familiar broad chest and those strong arms. I breathe his wonderful lemony scent, and raise my eyes to see that Jay is smiling down at me.

'Hello, you,' he says softly.

I open my mouth to pour out my endless stream of regrets and to plead with him for understanding. To tell him I thought I'd lost him for ever, how I only dated Marcus because I wanted to show I didn't need him, and how although I do adore Xander, my feelings for him are totally eclipsed by how I feel when I'm with Jay. The teenage crush that never went away.

I love him. It's that simple and that difficult, and all the words I'm so desperate to say rise up like a spring tide.

'Shh,' Jay murmurs, placing his finger on my lips and pulling me against him with his free arm. 'Don't say a word. You don't need to.'

'This thing with Xander,' I try again. 'He was kind, you were married, I thought . . .'

He shakes his head as he tenderly strokes the hair back from my cheeks. 'I know, I know and I'm so sorry. Why do you think I came back? You must know that I love you?'

'I love you too,' I say wonderingly. 'I always have. It's just that so much stuff kept getting in the way.'

'No more stuff,' says Jay.

'Deal,' I agree, and he kisses me then, so long and so deeply that I forget all about everything else. I love Jay and he loves me. As he kisses my mouth, my neck and my tear-stained cheeks, nothing else in the world matters and I have the feeling nothing else ever will. All I have to do is kiss him right back and listen to the fireworks going off.

'Ellie!' Poppy's voice plucks me back to earth, and I realise that these aren't fireworks after all, but rather the popping and flashing of cameras. Stars dancing before our eyes, Jay and I suddenly find ourselves surrounded by the press, all delighted to have photographic images of Xander Thorne's fiancée kissing another man.

'We need to go,' Jay says quietly, taking my hand and weaving through the queues of stunned passengers. I stumble behind him, unable to see thanks to Poppy throwing her coat over my head.

Somehow I manage to flee from the concourse with

cries of 'Ellie! Who's your mystery man?' and 'Is it over with Xander?' ringing in my ears.

My heart's trying to escape through my mouth. In my joy at seeing Jay, I totally forgot sweet, kind Xander, and now pictures of me kissing another man will be posted on the net before you can say *cheating harpy*. Horrified at myself, I pull away from Jay in distress. The last thing I want is to give them any more ammo.

By the time we reach the car park, the majority of the press have given up – they have their pictures after all – and I am panting like a woman in labour. I vow to start exercising. No more excuses. I need to grow up. I'm nearly thirty and I cannot be the baby of the family any more. This is the last thing poor Xander deserves. I have to talk to him. For once in my life I am going to do the decent thing and face up to the mess I've made. No more hiding like I did with Rupert, or pretending that everything's great when inside my warning bells have been sounding for months. It's time to step up.

Jay slips away to the Tube, leaving me and Poppy to screech away in a fug of burning rubber before crawling painfully around the M25. I stare out of the window, lost in my miserable thoughts, while Poppy surfs the radio channels until finally Capital FM plays ball and announces the story to the whole of London.

'Bollocks,' we say in unison.

Minutes later, my mobile rings. It's Xander.

'I love you,' he says sadly after I tell him how sorry I am. 'Just bear that in mind, please. I know you two have history and that maybe it's something you need to work through, but I really do love you and I know I can make you happy. You know we're good together.'

I bite my lip. We *are* good together, and most of the time he does make me happy. But Xander isn't Jay. And I know beyond all doubt that I love Jay. Loving Jay is tricky, painful and terrifying. Life with Xander will be none of these things, and my mother would be yelling at me to use my head. But only my heart will do. As Xander waits on the phone, telling me over and over again that he loves me and wants to marry me still, I know I have to make a choice.

Heart or head? Mum's dreams or mine?

The guilt of my unfulfilled promise is millstone heavy, and the misery in Xander's voice only adds to its weight. How can I do this to him? He doesn't deserve it. And can I trust Jay to be as good as his word? His track record hasn't been great.

A husband is for life, I remind myself.

Taking a deep and shaking breath, I give Xander his answer. And it's the hardest thing I'll probably ever have to do.

1.14 p.m.

The definition of conspicuous has to be dashing through Taply dressed as Wedding Day Barbie. It isn't up there with my brightest ever ideas, but the traffic is busy on such a sunny August Saturday, so I have no choice but to jump out of the E-Type at the traffic lights and run.

Get me. I'm like Forrest Gump in a frock.

For a second, I stand panting on the bridge while the Thames swirls beneath and pleasure cruisers chug downstream to Henley and Cliveden. The sun is warm and it's a perfect day to get married; everything I could have wanted my special day to be if only I'd had the guts to go through with it. But no matter how hard I try, all I can think is *am I making another mistake?*

I spot him instantly. There's no mistaking the figure walking towards me with his hands buried deep in the pockets of his suit. His face is set in a serious expression and I know from the way a muscle dances in his cheek that he's trying hard to keep his emotions in check. Our eyes lock.

He stops just a few feet away. 'I got your message.'

'It wasn't meant for you,' I say. 'I sent you the wrong text. I'm an idiot.'

His beautiful face is bleak. 'Ellie, what's going on with us? What's happening?'

'I can't do it,' I say. 'I can't do the whole church thing. What if we're making a mistake?'

He steps forward and takes my hands in his. 'Ellie, we've been through this a thousand times. It's going to be fine. This is what you wanted.'

I swallow. 'It's what my mother wanted. I was always thinking of what she wanted.'

'And you wanted to do this for her,' he reminds me softly. 'It means the world to you. It's why we agreed to get married this way, remember? Even after everything that has happened, we still felt it was the right thing to do. We've moved mountains to get this wedding sorted. I think your dad had to bribe the vicar to marry me in a church! It hardly goes with the image.'

I hang my head. 'I know. I know.'

'I'd marry you anywhere.' He raises my hand to his lips. 'None of this matters to me. All I want is to be with you.

Married, unmarried, engaged, unengaged, it's not important. I want you to be happy, and preferably with me. I don't care about the stuff with the other guys. I just want you.'

Tears fill my eyes. I don't deserve him. I know that none of this wedding stuff matters to him – he did it just for me, and it got in the way of everything. We've concentrated on that and not on each other, and now my thoughts feel like Spaghetti Junction. This is a good man, an honest man. What's the matter with me? Why am I so scared?

'We can call it off,' he says softly. 'If that's what you want. We can forget the whole thing. No wedding, no pressure. I can cancel it all right now and you'll be free to walk away. If it's really so awful, don't marry me. Only marry me because you love me. Not because you're afraid not to.'

The three hundred guests will already be on their way. All hell will break loose. Dad will freak at the waste of money. On the other hand . . .

'But I don't think calling it off will make you happy,' he continues, staring into my teary eyes. 'Getting married like this is important to you because of your mum, but I know it means a lot to you too. It shows everyone how we feel about each other. Ellie, listen to your heart. You know there's more at stake here today than just you and me.'

I nod.

'I'll always love you, but this has to be your choice now. No more chopping and changing, Ellie. Time to make a decision.'

I close my eyes. He's right. He's always right. The only one who has ever truly understood me. Friend, lover and maybe husband?

If I'm brave enough.

'I'm going to head to the church,' he says, dropping a soft kiss on my open mouth. 'I'll be waiting for you there – if you still want to marry me, that is.'

And then he's gone, a tall, lean figure walking away from me maybe for an hour. Maybe for ever.

Time has run out. No more thinking, no more trying to figure out what Mum would have wanted. I have to make *my* decision.

2.10 p.m.

This is it. The Bentley has driven the short distance from number 43 to St Jude's and circled the block several times while I grip my father's arm and chew all my lipstick off. The bridesmaids, all looking lovely in their green dresses and stolen gerberas, have already set off, and Poppy has done a sterling job of rescuing my hair and make-up. OK, so I look a little more gothic than I may have intended, and my wedding dress is like a before advert for Daz, but these are the least of my worries. I'm going to get married.

Goodbye toast in bed and old life at number 43. I am about to take the plunge.

The chauffeur pulls up outside St Jude's. The ancient stone is mellow in the honeyed light, and pink dog roses drowse above the porch. It's perfect, and everything Mum would have wanted. For a second I think I catch sweet notes of Floris in the air and a rush of warm air across my cheek . . .

My father leans across and smiles at me. 'Mum would have been so proud of you, my darling.'

'Just for getting married?' I shrug. 'Enough people seem to do it.'

'Ah, yes,' says my father thoughtfully. 'But the trick is to find the right person, isn't it? Not the one who looks good on paper but,' he raises his hand to touch his heart, 'the one who's right here. I found your mother in the end, didn't I? And I loved her every day from that second onwards. I love her still.'

My eyes widen. Never in twenty-nine years has my father spoken to me about emotions.

'This is about you making choices,' he says, squeezing my hand. 'You've had a tough year and you've had some even tougher decisions, but you've made the right ones. I'm proud of you.'

I would cry now, but Poppy has covered my lashes in really thick mascara and I am not going into the church looking like the lost member of Kiss.

'He's a good man,' he says. 'Mum would be pleased. He's honest and true and he'll look after you. I know you'll be very happy.'

As the organ starts to belt out 'Ave Maria', Mum's favourite, I feel faint. This really is it. The most important decision of my life. No more mistakes.

Annabelle is straightening my veil while Emily smoothes my skirt. Isolde and Tristan look miserable in their outfits, which is exactly as it should be, and the little ones look cute even though I know they are Satan's imps. I'm wearing my mother's beautiful dress and holding the flowers she loved, and all her nearest and dearest are gathered here just as she would have wanted. As I wait for the vicar to give us the signal, I tell her that I love her and miss her, and that this big white wedding is dedicated to her. I really hope that wherever she is, Mum knows she's mother of the bride for this one last time.

Just as the heavy door swings open, a ray of light streams

in through the stained-glass window, warm, dancing with jewel-like hues, and I know this is my answer.

But as I walk up the aisle and the man at the altar turns to smile at me with such love that my heart almost breaks, suddenly I also know, with total and utter certainty, that this day isn't just because of Mum.

This wedding, this marriage, is for *us*. I love him and I never want us to be apart again.

How could I ever have doubted it? I've *always* loved him. There's never been anyone else for me. Not since the age of fifteen and not ever. Even when I thought there might have been and that all hope was lost, he was always there, waiting for me. As I walk towards him, all my worries vanish like sea mist in the sun. There are no more second thoughts.

He's the one that Poppy saw. There's no doubt about it. All my anxieties slip away. Nothing could ever be so right as being with him.

My friend.

My lover.

And very soon my husband.

'Hello, Jay,' I say with a smile.

The Beginning